RECKONING

RECKONING

AN FBI THRILLER

CATHERINE COULTER

WILLIAM MORROW

An Imprint of HarperCollinsPublishers

HarperCollins books may be purchased for educational, business, or sales promotional use. For information, please email the Special Markets Department at SPsales@harpercollins.com.

FIRST EDITION

Library of Congress Cataloging-in-Publication Data

Names: Coulter, Catherine, author.
Title: Reckoning : an FBI thriller / Catherine Coulter.
Description: First edition. I New York : William Morrow, [2022] I Series: FBI
    thriller; volume 26
Identifiers: LCCN 2022007100 (print) I LCCN 2022007101 (ebook) I ISBN
    9780063004139 (hardcover) I ISBN 9780063004146 (trade paperback) I ISBN
    9780063019966 I ISBN 9780063242029 I ISBN 9780063004153 (ebook)
Classification: LCC PS3553.O843 R43 2022 (print) I LCC PS3553.O843
    (ebook) I DDC 813/.54—dc23
LC record available at https://lccn.loc.gov/2022007100
LC ebook record available at https://lccn.loc.gov/2022007101

ISBN 978-0-06-300413-9

22 23 24 25 26 LSC 10 9 8 7 6 5 4 3 2 1

TO ANTON, AS
ALWAYS YOUR EDITORIAL EXCELLENCE
SHINES THROUGH.

ACKNOWLEDGMENTS

To Karen Evans—You're the trainer in my corner and the fixer of my technology stuff. You're always kind, and best of all, you're always there for me.

To Angela Bell, FBI—How I will miss you. You've helped me so much over the years, but now the world awaits. Enjoy every minute of your travels around our magnificent earth.

RECKONING

RECKONING

1

Porte Franklyn, Virginia

Porte Franklyn, Virginia

Allison slid back under a single sheet after a middle-of-the-night trek to the bathroom. She lay still, breathing in the sweet deep-summer air, listening to the night sounds outside her open window—the symphony of crickets, the hoot of a barn owl, the wind rustling the oak leaves near her window. The air was heavy, and it was humid, so she soon kicked off the sheet. Even in her sleep shorts and sleeveless tank top, it wasn't enough. She rolled out of bed and walked to the wall switch beside her bedroom door to turn on the overhead fan. Her finger was on the switch when she heard slow, light footsteps on the stairs, tiptoeing steps, and the familiar creak of the seventh stair. One of her parents was up? She opened her door, looked out into the dim hallway, started to call out, and froze. Two men were walking quietly toward her parents' bedroom at the end of the hall. In the hallway night-light she saw that each man carried a gun. At first she didn't understand, then she was afraid, paralyzed. Should she scream out to her parents, warn them? She pushed her door closed, grabbed her cell phone in its charger on her desk, and punched in 911. Instantly a deep man's voice said calmly, "What is your emergency?"

She whispered, "Two men are walking toward my parents' bedroom and they've got guns. Help, please, help."

She heard two popping sounds, knew they were gunshots. Allison's voice caught on a sob of terror. "Pl-please, hurry, I heard them shooting my parents!"

The man's voice was whip-sharp. "Can you get out of the house?"

"Yes, yes."

"Go now! Hide. Help is coming right now."

She needed to do something, wanted to help her parents, but what? The man on the phone was right, she had to hide or they'd kill her, too. Allison pushed out the bedroom window screen, climbed out on the ledge, and jumped on the thick oak branch nearly touching the house.

She was sobbing she was so afraid, and clumsy, but she'd done it so many times, she didn't fall. She shimmied down from branch to branch, sometimes swinging, sometimes crawling. She heard a low vicious voice shout from above her, "I see the little bitch! Let me do her!"

Allison heard a shot and felt a slap of pain just above her right ear. She saw white, the world tumbled and spun, and she nearly fell off the branch, but she flattened herself and hung on. She heard three more shots, all of them above her. She felt a shard of wood dig into her arm and a hit of pain. She was dizzy, the world spinning, but her fear brought her back. She knew she had to get down to the ground, she had to hide or they'd shoot her like they'd shot her parents. She'd climbed up and down this tree from her earliest years, and though her head pounded and her arm felt like it was on fire, she didn't hesitate. She stepped down onto the lowest branch, sucked in her breath and jumped the last six feet to the ground. She rolled up and ran toward the thick forest of oaks and maples bordering her house. She ran all out toward the mass of trees, dark shadows huddled together, sobbing, her breath hitching. They seemed a thousand miles away, but she kept running. Two more shots sounded and kicked up grass beside her feet. She changed direction, zigged and zagged, looked back over her shoulder at a man's shout, and nearly stumbled. She realized blood was snaking down her forehead and into her eye from the wound in her head. Allison staggered into the trees, breathing hard, fell to her knees behind a huge old oak, and swiped at the blood on her face. She looked at her hand, wet, sticky, the blood black in the moonlight. She felt a wave of nausea and the world tilted sideways. She fell onto her side, hugging herself. She keened with pain and fear, until she heard shouts and realized she couldn't stay there. The men were coming, running toward the woods, toward her. She had to move, had to hide or they'd see her, run her down, and shoot her dead.

Black, terrifying thoughts ricocheted through Allison's brain, of her parents dead in their bed, covered with blood, black like the blood on her hand and sliding down her face. Her parents. She could practically hear their voices, yelling at her to move, to get to safety. She pushed away the grief, staggered to her feet, and ran toward a familiar leaf-strewn trail through the forest that passed by the entrance to Williker's Cave, tucked beneath an overhang of thick-leaved oak branches. She'd spent hours there, her own private hideaway when she was younger, but rarely now because she was twelve, her first teenage birthday only six months away. She fell to her hands and knees when she reached the cave, lifted the brush covering it, crawled in through the narrow entrance, and pulled the brush back into place. It didn't matter that she couldn't see inside because she knew the cave well, knew the narrow, winding stone corridor widened as it wove back into the hill, where the cave ceiling soared above her head.

She mewled as she crawled onto the ancient threadbare

blanket still in a tangle on the sand against the cave wall. Jumbled images came to her of herself as a child hiding in her sanctuary, drinking forbidden Diet Coke and eating junk food, feeling cocky that she'd fooled her mother. The ancient grocery bag she'd kept next to the blanket was still there, filled with her childhood treasures. She grabbed a Lenny Stiles T-shirt from the bag that felt clean enough. She pulled off the tank top she'd worn to bed, wiped the blood off her face with it, and pressed it against the bloody wound on her head like they did on TV. Her arm wasn't bleeding much, but it throbbed like a nail trying to shove through her flesh. When the bleeding stopped, she pulled on the T-shirt and sank back against the cave wall. Her head was still spinning, she wanted to vomit, so she focused on the ancient grocery bag she'd kept here for years now, filled with childhood treasures. She felt frozen, so afraid her breath came out in gasps. She felt a new pain. She looked at her bare feet, scratched and a few cuts oozing blood. She hadn't felt a thing on her wild run, but now—wait—was that voices? Men's voices? She slapped her fist against her mouth to keep the sob quiet. They'd followed her, they were close. Would they see the cave opening through the leaves and the brush? She scooted backward into the cave, around a corner, and waited, unmoving. Then she heard sirens but knew it was too late to help her parents. She heard the men's voices, knew they were closer. They'd find her. She was crying as she pressed her back against the cave wall.

2

Kings Canyon
Northern Territory
Australia

"It's all right, sweetheart, you're all right. You're safe. Come on, wake up, you had a nightmare. You're okay. I've got you."

She heard his voice, a man's voice, and he was close, too close. Terror squeezed her throat, made her heart kettledrum. The men were near, coming to kill her like they'd killed her parents. She fought like a wild thing, hitting at his arms holding her.

He held her tightly against him and continued to whisper against her cheek, his voice low and calm. Slowly she came awake, hiccuping at the knot of fear in her throat. She saw a dim face above her, a face she knew, a face she trusted. He was holding her, stroking her back as he continued to speak in his low easy voice, saying nonsense, really, reassuring her. Finally, she knew who it was.

Another nightmare.

Allison whispered, "Uncle Leo?"

"Yes, baby, I'm here. It's all right. You're safe. I've got you."

"I'm sorry."

Leo continued to hold her, lightly rubbed his hands up and down her back, slow and easy, like she was a wounded and terrified kangaroo joey tangled in a barbed-wire fence. "Don't be daft. I'd have bloody nightmares, too, if I'd been through what you have. That's right, breathe deep, that's my girl." He kissed her forehead. Slowly, the images from her dream blurred and faded. It was odd but sometimes in her dreams she felt the pain from her bullet wound on the side of her head, and the gash in her arm from the wood shard. She sucked in another deep breath, locked her arms around his back, and pressed her face against his chest.

The paralyzing fear wasn't as hard to shake off this time. Even though it was pleasantly warm in the tent, she shivered. She burrowed closer, felt Uncle Leo's steady strong heartbeat against her cheek, the warmth of his large hands stroking up and down her back. The world, her new world, wove itself together again.

The nightmares came less often now, but still, when they were on walkabout with one of their small tour groups, Uncle Leo slept in her tent, his sleeping bag close. "Do you think any of the jocks heard me scream?"

She always asked. His voice was low and gentle, his warm breath feathering the cool night air against her cheek. "No, you didn't scream this time. Do you realize this is the first nightmare you've had in a week? That's very good."

"Then how did you know?"

He didn't tell her whenever she tossed even once, he was wide awake. "You were moaning and thrashing around in your sleeping bag. Take some more deep breaths now, sweetheart. Here, drink some water."

Leo handed her bottled water, watched her chug, water dripping off her chin. He remembered the first night he'd been with her, sleeping on a cot in her hospital room. He'd jerked awake when she'd screamed, grabbed for his gun that wasn't, of course, anywhere near. He remembered how helpless he'd felt, but he'd pulled her against him then, too, hugged her and spoke nonsense until she quieted, nodding to the nurse who came silently to the doorway. Even after six months, it still ripped his heart out when she had that nightmare.

He rocked her now, feeling her finally ease. He remembered the phone call he'd gotten from the police in Porte Franklyn, Virginia, informing him his sister and her husband had been murdered, and his niece was in the hospital with a head wound. It had taken him a full day in a single-engine prop plane and a series of flights across the Pacific to reach her. He was grief-stricken, furious, demanded to know who had done such a thing, but the police had no answers. Maybe a home invasion, a robbery gone wrong, they'd said. He'd called Detective Jeter Thorpe every week at first, but after every phone call, he'd had to tell Allison there was nothing new. At least she was safe with him now, her only living family, in her new home in Australia. At first he'd been terrified he had sole responsibility for a twelve-year-old girl, but that hadn't lasted. Now she was his.

Leo was single, loved what he called "safe" danger. He was thirty-one years old, viewed by many as a throwback to swash-buckler days. He'd become a celebrity, something that always amused and amazed him. Because he wrestled crocs? He didn't. Because he knew how to survive in the outback? He did.

This weekend, he and Allison were leading a group of four jocks from Alabama on a challenging trek in the Northern Territory, along with his good friend Jawli, an Aborigine. He'd established his company with Jawli six years before—Extreme Australian Adventures. They'd both survived just about everything the outback could throw at them, and Leo loved the life, loved owing nothing to anyone except his partner. But now there was his sister's twelve-year-old daughter, who'd survived her parents' murder, survived being shot herself. Just before he'd arrived in Porte Franklyn there'd been a second attempt on her life in the hospital, thwarted by a nurse who'd screamed until the man had raced away down the stairs. He hadn't been found, either. It curdled Leo's blood to think she might have been killed in her hospital bed. The police had welcomed him as a savior when he arrived. Not only was he Allison Rendahl's uncle, he'd take her to Australia, on the other side of the planet.

Leo had brought her home to his sprawling glass house outside of Port Douglas atop a cliff overlooking the Great Barrier Reef. His niece was a silent, skinny kid, lost and grieving at first, afraid of every sound and wary of him, though she knew he was her uncle, her mother's younger brother. He'd taken her to a place as strange to her as an alien planet. Thankfully she'd slept most of the way on the flights from Washington to Sydney and Sydney to Cairns, and when she was awake, he'd kept it simple. The seasons in Australia were opposite of those in the US; winter was summer and summer was winter. He told her kangaroos hopped around his front yard, and she had to be careful of the crocodiles. He'd cupped her face and told her Australia was so beautiful it would make her heart race. She'd whispered to him, "I read all about Botany Bay, how the English sent their prisoners there."

Six months ago, he thought, *and now it's already January*; such a short time in the scheme of things, yet she'd taken to her life with him more easily than he'd dared hope, woven her way into his life and into his heart. For the first time in his life, he felt fiercely protective of another person. Allison was no longer the silent little ghost with blank eyes any longer who'd held his hand so tightly his bones hurt when there was an unexpected sound. She was wary of everyone at first, even at his house near Port Douglas. Not knowing what else to do, he'd taken her on a four-hour dawn hike around the Uluru Base Walk in the Northern Territory with a family from Norway. She was a fit, athletic kid, so he wasn't too worried it would lay her flat, though he took more breaks than usual for her. To his great relief, she'd taken to being out there with him like a koala to eucalyptus leaves. She was enthralled to hear all about the story of the rock's significance to the local Anangu people and how many Aussies had fought to ban climbing the rock, to preserve it and to respect the Anangu. He'd seen Allison smile then, her mother's smile.

From that day on, she'd thrived, and he did everything in his power to see her smile again. He said quietly now, "We need to get some sleep or those college jocks might even show us up tomorrow."

Leo kissed her forehead again, rubbed her back. He'd learned that soothed her like nothing else. She whispered against his shoulder, "I won't let you down, Uncle Leo. I've looked them over, sooks the lot of them." She'd learned quickly that Aussies said sook, not wimp. He felt her mouth curve into a grin. "We'll leave them moaning in the dust. Did you see those dark sunnies they were wearing even after the sun went down? They look like wankers."

She settled against his side, breathed in his familiar scent. She trusted this man she'd met only three times in her life before he'd come to her at the hospital. Her mother had chuckled about him, called him the family "wild hair." Her father had rolled his eyes when he showed her a postcard he'd sent of the Blue Mountains near Sydney that called that place a bushwalker's spiritual pilgrimage. Allison had loved that word *bushwalker*, it called up visions of adventure. And now she'd actually hiked there, on a four-hour trail with two intrepid older couples from Maine. The first time out, she'd been exhausted, but now, after six months, that Blue Mountains hike was easy for her—a piece of piss in Aussie talk. She loved the smell of the eucalyptus trees that stretched as far as she could see, the cockatoos screeching across the valley. She couldn't wait for another group to book a tour to the Blue Mountains.

Uncle Leo took her to other landscapes so strange, so incredibly beautiful—he'd been right to tell her they could make you cry—and so profoundly hot they'd quickly kill you if you had no shelter and water. This strange and awesome world was her world now. She thought every day of her parents, but less and less of her structured life in Porte Franklyn, with its sleepovers with girlfriends talking about makeup and boys, the volleyball and basketball teams. All of that was a world away.

Tonight, she and Uncle Leo were in Watarrka National Park with four extreme adventurers—actually, four college guys who'd bragged they could hike anything, in any conditions. She knew Uncle Leo would test them to their limits. In three hours, well before dawn, she and Uncle Leo and Jawli would lead them on the demanding six-kilometer Kings Canyon Rim Walk. If that didn't knacker the jocks, if they proved themselves up to it, Uncle Leo would add on another hike he'd mapped out himself along the starkly beautiful Larapinta Trail in the Northern Territory. When they returned to Port Douglas where they planned to scuba dive the Great Barrier Reef, Uncle Leo would take them to the Down and Out Pub and buy them some cold ones as the Aussies called beer, and the lot of them would probably drink their brains out, get legless, another Aussie saying. And they'd salute Leo and maybe Allison, too, if she stayed long enough to drink a glass of lemonade.

She enjoyed young men, always eager to show how tough they were. She remembered the fourteen-day trek in the outback leading six English soccer players from Manchester United, their demand, made with a smirk, to see what this outback was all about. And they'd looked at the skinny now-thirteen-year-old girl and joked among themselves who would end up carrying her. She'd nearly killed herself, but she'd made it. So many adventures, a few unpleasant if the clients were jerks, but usually they'd get into it and their excitement would crackle in the air. And now she was an accepted part of Uncle Leo's team. If not for the nightmares, her life would be perfect.

She'd eased herself back down to sleep, but Leo knew she was still awake. It was a good time as any, he thought, and he said, his voice matter-of-fact, "Jawli agrees with me it's time to give you a new name. Tell me what you think—Kirra. It's an Aborigine name Jawli picked for you. It means 'to live' in the Murri dialect of southern Queensland. In part it's for your protection, sure, but I think it suits you."

Allison focused on the name—Kirra. Yes, she liked that, it was fitting. After all, that's what she'd done, she'd lived, and now she had a new life, so why not a new name? "Kirra—I like it, Uncle Leo. But Rendahl—that's still from my other life." *My other world, ----- my other planet.*

"I'm pleased you like it." Now for the tough part. Leo said slowly, feeling his way, "If you agree, I'd like to adopt you. You'd be Kirra Mandarian." It was yet another way to keep her safe if the men who'd killed her parents decided to come after her. He didn't think there was any more danger, but he didn't want to take any chances. He didn't mention that to her or that it was for his peace of mind. She'd know that, too.

Kirra Mandarian. She leaned against his well-worn T-shirt and breathed in his familiar scent, man and sweat, not at all unpleasant. She felt his strong heartbeat against her cheek and knew she was safe. She whispered, "Does that mean I'll never have to leave you?"

"That's exactly what it means. We're a team, you and I."

On her eighteenth birthday, Kirra Mandarian opened her acceptance letter from ANU, Australian National University, in Canberra, Australia's capital. She and Uncle Leo had visited the campus six months before, met professors, monitored several classes, and she'd told him she loved the place as they sat in an air-conditioned café, out of the ferocious February heat. Uncle Leo had helped her application because he was even more famous now than he'd been when she'd first come to Australia, a fact she'd slowly realized when she was fifteen. The prime minister had asked Leo to lead a private tour for him and a half dozen of his friends and top politicos to Fraser Island in Queensland, the planet's largest sand island, with its incredible rain forest, white sand beaches, and the vivid blue waters of Lake McKenzie. Even though there was no swimming because of riptides and sharks, it was one of Kirra's favorite junkets. Uncle Leo had planned an undemanding walk for some of the older members of the group. Unlike the adventures Uncle Leo usually led, this one was relaxing and lazy, the company convivial. The PM liked Kirra, which didn't hurt with ANU admissions because he and the other pols she'd met wrote glowing letters about her accomplishments, despite the fact she hadn't stepped into a classroom since she was twelve years old. Uncle Leo had arranged for her to be homeschooled, along with the half-dozen other children of the Extreme Australian Adventures team. Kirra had learned even more from the team themselves, each with their own expertise. Jawli had taught her how to throw a boomerang and how to feed a baby kangaroo separated from its mother. And she'd learned from their clients, athletes and sportsmen mostly, who'd come to learn skills to survive in the outback from Uncle Leo. She'd learned about their cultures, learned how to read people and put them at their ease. She'd described her education to the admissions office as eclectic—she probably knew less about fusion than some, but a whole lot more about the habits of wombats.

She was proud she'd been accepted as part of the team, jubilant because she'd actually added to the company's bottom line. She'd come up with the EAA's motto—*Learn how to survive the worst, appreciate the best.* She designed T-shirts and sweatshirts with some of the incredible scenery she'd seen on the hikes Uncle Leo had mapped out, but her favorites were ink drawings of Uncle Leo in profile. Most of the team thought Uncle Leo was wasting his money, but it turned out the shirts were so popular, they couldn't keep them in stock so Uncle Leo gave Kirra permission to hire some locals to make the shirts for them. By the time she left Australia to attend law school, they had a line of EAA clothes so popular they had orders from Kuala Lumpur and Paris.

Leaving Uncle Leo and the EAA team was difficult for Kirra. She knew she wouldn't be like any of the other students at ANU—an American with an accent who spoke fluent Australian that was even on the edgy side, like most of the other members of the EAA, except for Jawli's wife, Mala, an Aborigine guide and chef, who'd taught her how to cook, use a bullwhip, and fly a drone. In her martial arts classes at ANU, the instructors weren't surprised at her skill and toughness; after all, she'd been raised by Leo Mandarian with the outback her backyard. Kirra was as fit as any of the major athletes. No one crossed her. She briefly fell in love with an Aussie whose dream was to race at Daytona Beach and Le Mans. He taught her how to drive, really drive. Unfortunately, he was doing drugs, so she dumped him.

Kirra imagined if she was popular at all, it was because she was Leo Mandarian's adopted daughter. But she'd known for many years that she'd attend university, study law, then move back to her childhood home in Porte Franklyn, Virginia, larger now than when she'd left, not quite the size of Richmond, but close. Her goal was to be a prosecutor in the Porte Franklyn Commonwealth Attorney's Office. It still hurt to leave Australia and Uncle Leo, but she knew she had to find out who killed her parents and tried to kill a twelve-year-old girl. It was her most important goal. Uncle Leo understood even though he didn't want her to do it. *You know how to escape a pissed-off crocodile, but a cold-blooded murderer? Different animal and more dangerous.*

Even now she had the occasional nightmare about the night the men broke into her home and murdered her family. Maybe those men were still in Virginia, and still free.

3

EMMA

San Francisco

PRESENT

Emma Hunt always wore three layers, enough for a Tahoe snowstorm, her dad would say, and she'd laugh, because San Francisco could freeze your bones just as fast. Sometimes, in March, there was brilliant sunshine and a warm breeze, but today, her bones creaked and groaned in the damp chill and her face burned from the sting of the whipping wind. She tugged her Giants ball cap down tighter. The sun occasionally broke through and gave some hope again, but they both soon disappeared somewhere on the far side of the San Francisco fog.

Her cell rang. It was her mom calling, telling her she was caught up in the insane Van Ness traffic, made worse than usual by the endless construction. Emma heard the concern in her mom's voice, urging her to wait inside Davies Hall where it was warm. *And safe.* Her mom didn't have to say it out loud, Emma knew she was thinking it. Her mom and dad always worried when she was out by herself, and she understood, but didn't they realize she wasn't a little kid anymore?

Shivering, Emma stepped back toward Davies Hall and saw Mrs. Mayhew, her piano teacher, as she came out a side door. She gave Emma a wave and called out, "Kennedy Center won't know what hit them when you play that Chopin prelude, Emma!" Emma grinned and waved back. Mrs. Mayhew wrapped her awesome, purple-knitted scarf three times around her neck and made her way through the wind to her grandson's souped-up red Chevy.

Davies Hall was quiet inside, most everyone gone for the day. The doors would be locked soon, but not before her mom got there, she hoped. Emma hummed the Chopin Prelude in D Flat Major Mrs. Mayhew loved so much, one of the pieces Emma would be playing at the Chopin Retrospective at the Kennedy Center in Washington, D.C. She'd been allowed to select it, since it was her favorite, too, romantic and heartrending. It touched her deeply and always made her mother tear up. Her dad would say her mother could cry if she wanted to, but Emma couldn't or she'd get the keys wet and her fingers would slip and slide.

Her mom called again. She was closer. Emma was to stay inside. She walked to sit down on a bench facing the glass doors. She was rehearsing in her head, her fingers playing a glissando on the bench when she heard a man whistling, probably one of the maintenance crew. She turned automatically and saw a man walking toward her. He wasn't maintenance; he was wearing dark glasses and a ball cap pulled down over his forehead. His dark coat was open, showing a black turtleneck and dark slacks. Except for the ball cap, she'd have pegged him as one of the city attorneys from the nearby Civic Center. Emma rose, took a step toward the doors.

He held up his hand. "Wait! Please. I need directions."

Her parents' voices drummed in her head. *Walk away if*

something doesn't feel right. Get help. All he wanted was directions? But deep inside she wasn't sure. It wasn't six years ago. She wasn't a helpless little kid now. But what was he?

The man kept coming, striding easy as if he didn't have a care in the world. But there was something about him, something off about the way he walked, steady as a metronome, focused on her. Gooseflesh skittered over her arm. That long-ago fear welled up from the deepest part of her where it had always been. Who was he? He was staring at her, only her, and she felt again the terror of the six-year-old child when another man called Father Sonny had taken her, only a little girl then, out of a park not twenty feet from where her mother was shooting photos. Emma gasped for breath, headed fast toward the doors. He broke into a run after her.

She wasn't going to make it through the doors before he caught her. She didn't scream for help, there was no one to hear her. She folded into herself, heard a small moan that came from her own throat. It angered her, that helpless sound, snapped her back. She wasn't that helpless little girl now. Her dad had taken her to his dojo on Lake Street for years where she'd learned Tae Quan Do from Master Liu himself, and still worked with him twice a week.

Emma dug down deep. She wouldn't run, she wouldn't fold. She whipped around to face him and yelled, "What do you want?"

He paused, surprised, and held out a gloved hand. "Come on, Emma, don't be afraid. I'm not going to hurt you. I just want you to come with me." His voice was low, cajoling. He nearly whispered the words. *He knows your name. He knows who you are.* The terror disappeared and in its place came anger, clean sharp anger. She wanted to hurt him, it was that simple. She drew a deep steadying breath, focused on her assailant, as Master Liu had taught her. She let out a yell, ran right at him, kicked her right leg high and straight out. Her booted foot slammed into his throat. He stumbled back, grabbed his throat, gagged, and fell. He tried to yell, but his words came out as a croak. "You little bitch! You're going to pay for that!" He staggered to his feet, still rubbing his throat, reached into his coat pocket, and pulled out a gun. Emma didn't hesitate, she tasered him. The electric shock wave put him down and this time he didn't move. She knew he was in bad pain, but it wouldn't last long. She wanted to grab his gun, get his wallet, but she did what she'd been told to do countless times by her parents. She ran. She made it out the door and across the street to the Civic Center where there were people and safety.

She looked back across the traffic and caught her breath, her heart pounding in her throat. But of course he wasn't following her. She, Emma Hunt, had made the monster run away. She remembered Dr. Loo, her psychologist, was always telling her how important it was to face her fears about what had happened to her. She had and she'd won. Dr. Loo would be proud of her. *You're strong, confident, you can do anything.* Emma pulled out her cell to call 911 when her mother pulled up in Charlotte, her prized SUV. Emma jerked the door open and jumped in. She was almost sorry she had to tell her mother because she knew how upset she'd be. She'd call her father right away, and he'd rush home if he wasn't in court, and they'd fret and worry about her even more, maybe even demand she never leave the house alone. She couldn't imagine one of her parents tagging along with her and her girlfriends. But the man had come after her. He'd known her name and that was the scariest part.

Molly said, "Em, sorry I'm late. What's wrong? What happened?"

Her mom was instantly afraid, even before she told her. She

touched her palm to her mother's cheek and said, "Mom, please don't be scared. I put him down with a kick and then when he got up again, I tasered him. I was about to call 911."

"W-what? Emma, who did you run off? 911?"

"I was waiting inside for you when I saw a man walking toward me, focused on me. He knew my name, and he wanted to take me. I couldn't outrun him, so I centered myself, like Master Liu taught me, and I kicked him in the throat. It didn't stop him so I tasered him. I left him on the floor. I put him there, Mom, I put him there."

Molly grabbed her and hugged her tight. "I was late. I'm so sorry, Emma. If I'd only been here on time—"

"Mom, listen to me. I'm okay. Before you call Captain Trolley, let me tell you the guy was wearing a dark coat and a ball cap and sunglasses, so I couldn't really see his face. By now he's probably gone, but maybe Captain Trolley's officers can find him."

But they both knew he wouldn't be close. He was long gone. Her mom was still pale and Emma knew she was reliving the terrible memories when Emma had been kidnapped half her lifetime ago. She hugged her mother. "I'm not a helpless kid now, Mom. I fought him, tasered him, and ran away. You know what? It felt good. I won and I know I could do it again if I have to."

Her mom managed a smile, swallowed her terror. "I'll call Virginia and then I'm calling your dad. He needs to know, Emma. We've got to figure out why that man wanted to take you." She couldn't help herself and hugged Emma close again. "There's no way that man is going to hurt you, Emma. We won't let him." She drew back, gave Emma a brilliant smile. "You won't let him. I'm so proud of you."

Emma saw love and worry in her eyes. What she'd been thinking came out of her mouth. "What makes these horrible men want to hurt me? Is it something about me? Is it my fault?"

4

KIRRA

67 Wendell Way
Outskirts of Porte Franklin

EARLY APRIL

For the first time since she'd come back to the States more
than five years before, Kirra drove her dark metallic blue turbocharged Audi A3 through the neighborhods, shopping cen-
ters, and parks of Porte Franklin to its outskirts, toward her
childhood home. The closer she got, the more anxious she felt.
She hated that her heart was already racing as she approached
the house and memories of that long-ago terror rose stark in
her mind. She saw the young girl listening to two men quietly
climbing the stairs on their way to murder her parents, saw
herself climbing down the old oak tree, wounded, in shock,
running, running, into the woods to her cave.

The closer she got to the end of the street where she'd find
the gutted remains of her family home, the more difficult it
became not to turn around and drive away. But she didn't, she
couldn't, and all because of a hunch.

She remembered telling Uncle Leo about her visit to a local

art gallery where she'd found one of her father's paintings. The manager told her the painting's owner had sold it to the gallery the month before. The price was astronomical, but of course Kirra had bought it. It was an oil painting of a small sailboat moving smoothly toward a dock, a white-whiskered old man on deck holding a rope ready to loop it around the stanchion. Her father had loved to paint the incredible array of boats he saw on the Potomac, from skiffs to fishing trawlers and mo- torboats, and the occasional yacht. It was sad his beloved sub- ject didn't sell well. It was his country scenes and portraitures that had kept the household afloat. She shook her head at the irony of that—her father had to die before his paintings be- came valuable. And then, just this morning, she'd remembered her father occasionally stored paintings in the shed. The killers hadn't burned it down. She knew the odds were against her, but she had to look.

Her cell phone buzzed and she looked down at a text from Uncle Leo. He always seemed to text her when she needed him to. She could put it off a while longer. She pulled over her Audi and read it.

HEY, KIDDO. JAWLI SAYS HI. HE MISSES THROWING YOU IN THE DIRT.

I MISS YOU, TOO. LOVE YOU, LEO.

She laughed. It was all too true. She'd landed in the dirt sparring with Jawli more times than she cared to remember. He'd taught her most of what she knew about how to fight, how to defend herself. She answered right away.

TELL JAWLI HE WON'T HAVE A CHANCE WHEN I SEE HIM IN JUNE.

ALL IS GOOD HERE AND YES, I'M FINE, I LOVE AND MISS YOU, TOO.

KIRRA.

She missed them all, missed Australia. It was still very early spring cold here on this side of the globe. In Australia she could be enjoying a glorious end-of-summer day at her uncle Leo's house overlooking the Pacific. She missed scuba diving the Great Barrier Reef, missed lazing in the fresh water of nearby Lake McKenzie, lying on the pure white sand slathered in sunscreen against the fierce Australia sun. She even missed the dingoes who sometimes dashed in and stole your sandwiches and fruit if you let them. They loved apples.

Even though Uncle Leo had understood Kirra's decision to make her career in law and return home, he wasn't happy about it. When she'd told him she'd taken a job as assistant commonwealth attorney less than an hour from where she'd spent the first twelve years of her life, he never mentioned what he knew to be true, that she'd become a prosecutor in her home town because she hoped to find her parents' killers.

She and Uncle Leo had kept up their correspondence through the years with Jeter Thorpe, the detective who'd found her that night and investigated her parents' murder in Porte Franklyn. The three of them had become friends, and when Jeter made lieutenant, they'd sent the new lieutenant, a pro basketball fanatic, season tickets to the Washington Wizards. Though Jeter had tried for years, he never found the killers, and her parents' case was in a cold file now.

Kirra had made a few other friends, of course, mostly at law school at UVA, including her best friend, Cila McCayne, who was in New York attending a seminar representing her law firm, Alden, Carruthers and Smith. She missed Cila, and her whacko adventures with so many boyfriends they'd both lost count. But Kirra missed Uncle Leo more.

She forced herself to pull back onto the flattop and continue driving slowly forward to the last property her parents owned, the property that was hers now as their only heir. She'd asked Uncle Leo to keep the property just as it was, frozen in time, not obliterated by some contractor, her parents forgotten. She'd turned down half a dozen offers for it over the years, but she didn't mind that because the land was only becoming more valuable because of the oak and maple forest it bordered that stretched undisturbed for half a mile.

She'd put it off long enough. Kirra's knuckles were white on her Audi's steering wheel when she pulled onto the weed-infested driveway. She saw the forest had steadily encroached over fourteen years. Weeds filled the concrete foundation where her home had stood, growing over the fallen beams and burned detritus. It hadn't been much of a house, she realized now, but it had been her home, her parents' home. She felt tears sheen her eyes, swallowed.

She couldn't seem to pull her hands off the steering wheel, simply stared at the foundation through the windshield. The huge oak tree outside her bedroom window had burned down with the house. She'd loved that old tree. She'd shimmied down it when she'd run into the woods to her hidden cave. Fourteen years ago. And Jeter had found her, saved her. Her parents had died but she'd lived, thanks to him.

Kirra slowly got out of her car, her legs stiff, her heart pounding. She remembered something had always needed repair in the house. She pictured her mom replacing a pipe underneath the sink, plunging out the toilet, and planting purple and white petunias in a simple wooden box her father had made, trying to make the modest house look warm and welcoming. Where had her mother gotten the money to buy flowers? How hard had it been for them to make ends meet from her father's sporadic sales? She remembered her mother had worked as an assistant manager in a grocery store, but later, she'd stayed at home. As a young child she hadn't wondered about that, realized only later when her mother got sicker she'd been too ill to work. But her parents had loved each other, and they'd loved her. Kirra closed her eyes. It was hard to keep from trembling, from crying over what had been destroyed.

As she stood there, another long-forgotten memory flooded back. She'd heard her father saying to her mother, *Don't worry, sweetheart, I know what I'm doing. When you're well again, you'll be dancing with me in Paris.* Was he only trying to cheer her mother up, or had he really thought he'd be bringing in a lot of money? Was that what had brought those two monsters into their home?

You didn't know monsters like that existed, did you, Dad? You meant no more to them than a pebble in their way and they kicked you aside, snuffed out your life.

She looked up again to where the huge old oak branch had nearly touched her bedroom window, heard a voice shouting again, *I see the little bitch! Let me do her!* She didn't hear rage in the voice, she heard excitement.

Kirra shook her head, forced herself to walk to where the front door had stood, and looked down at the concrete foundation, where the weeds had grown and tangled, and vines had speared upward and climbed over the concrete. She turned away. Her home was no longer there, and neither were her parents. There was nothing here for her.

She looked again toward the forest. The shed still stood near it—she had prayed it would still be there—weather-beaten and slowly rotting, weeds pushing against its sides and burrowing into the cracks.

Jeter and his team had wondered if the murderers had burned down the house because she'd escaped and they couldn't find whatever they were looking for, something her father might have had that was a threat to them. Maybe whatever it was got him killed?

Please, please, let me find something. She crossed her fingers as she walked through the weeds and tangled vines to the dilapidated shed. Let there be some of his paintings and not only her dad's ancient lawn mower.

A rusted old padlock hung on the door. Had her father put that padlock on fourteen years before for a specific reason? There was no key, but it didn't matter, the door was rotten. Kirra kicked the door hard once, twice, and it fell inward off its creaking hinges.

It was too dark to see inside. She pulled her cell phone from her pocket, switched on the flashlight. A rat was walking between spiderwebs that were everywhere, its eyes fixed on her until it scurried across the rotted wooden floor and out through a hole in the wall. The shed was small, maybe six by eight. There was the ancient lawn mower, rusted through now, and two sagging shelves with dust-covered gardening tools her mother had used. She remembered her father staring at those tools and looking bewildered and her mother laughed, took down one of the tools, and showed him how to use it.

Kirra's heart began to pound. She saw it—a thickly bubble-wrapped canvas leaning against the far wall. Rats had chewed on the plastic, but they hadn't eaten all the way through. All that thick impenetrable wrapping, it had to mean something. Would her hunch pay off?

She pulled out her Swiss army knife and went to work on the packing, so thick she imagined a truck could have run over it without damaging the canvas. Finally, she pulled away the last sheet of bubble wrap. Kirra slowly lifted out the large canvas and carried it outside. She set it against the side of the shed and took two steps back.

She looked at a large yacht, maybe eighty feet long, its name in big square letters on its starboard side—*Valadia*. Three men stood on the top deck in serious conversation, their faces well defined and clear. She easily recognized one of the men even though he was a young man in the painting, not more than in his midtwenties. It was Ryman Grissom. He looked muscled, ripped, like a young bodyguard. Next to him stood his father, Elson Grissom, a handsome man in his late forties when her father had painted him fourteen years before. It was obvious he was the undisputed man in charge. Both men wore polo shirts and chinos, and deck shoes on their feet, and neither father nor son wore a hat or sunglasses. The third man looked to be around thirty, dressed in a light blue sweater and jeans, black sneakers on his feet. He was slighter than the two Grissoms, black haired and dark-complexioned, perhaps South American? She studied his face. Who was he?

Kirra lifted the painting to lay it on the bubble wrap and stopped cold. A small envelope was taped to the back. Her heart began to race again when she remembered her father's longtime habit of taking photos of a scene before he began painting it to remind him of the details and the lighting in case he had to stop. She opened the envelope and pulled out a half-dozen photos, both panoramic and close-up shots of the yacht and the men. She saw in the close-ups her father's rendering of the men's features had been excellent.

She studied the third man again more closely. His sweater was pushed up on his forearms. There was something on his arm that had been indistinct in the painting. What was it? She held it up in the sunlight, looked more closely. It was a tattoo— two large letters: M and S. It struck her. MS—was he MS-13? She knew MS stood for Mara Salvatrucha, the international criminal gang known for human and drug trafficking, arms dealing, extortion, and vicious brutality. The gang had been born in Los Angeles, but their roots were in El Salvador. She remembered wondering what the 13 stood for. Her law professor had said the 13 was the position of M in the alphabet.

Obviously her father had seen man's tattoo, would have wondered about it. If he'd looked up what it meant, read about MS-13, he'd have realized he'd witnessed a meeting meant to be very private, hidden away on Grissom's yacht, a meeting Grissom couldn't allow to be made public. Grissom was already a prominent citizen in Porte Franklyn. She'd heard of him even then, seen him in the local papers. If it became known he was involved with a MS-13 gang member, it would have destroyed his reputation as a businessman and philanthropist. He would have been investigated and from what Kirra knew, MS-13 would have cut him out entirely if he came under suspicion, even killed him to make sure he kept his silence. She knew the detectives had determined one of the likely causes of her parents' murder had been an attempt at blackmail. She hadn't wanted to accept it, but finally, Jeter had convinced her there could be no other reason.

And here was the proof Jeter was right. She was staring at it. Her father must have seen his picture as a stroke of luck, the only way he could get the money he needed to pay for her mother's heart surgery. Had he sent a copy of the photos to Grissom, demanded money for them? Threatened to take the painting to the police? Of course he had, and Elson Grissom had easily found out who he was and arranged the murder of her dad and her mother both. Nothing else made sense. One thing she was fairly certain of—she didn't think the MS-13 gang member had murdered her parents. They were known for their cruelty when they killed someone, preferring torture, leaving mangled remains to send a message. Her parents had been shot, no muss, no fuss, and to Kirra, that meant Elson Grissom probably with his son, Ryman, had come to her house that night to eliminate the threat.

Heart pounding, Kirra pulled out her cell to call Jeter, stopped. She had only photos, no real proof on anything. Slowly, she slipped her cell back into her pocket. She rewrapped the canvas in the bubble wrap and carried it to her car.

She had a lot of thinking to do.

5

SAVICH

CAU—Criminal Apprehension Unit
Hoover Building
Washington, D.C.

TUESDAY MORNING

Denny Roper handed Savich a large envelope marked PERSONAL, Savich's name printed on it in large black block letters. Denny's eyes were alight, and he was grinning ear to ear. "It was left by the security station. No one saw who left it. No postmark, only your name. I checked personally. Nothing dangerous inside."

Savich dumped out the contents of the large envelope on his desk, looked up. "Sorry, Denny, no mysterious puzzle pieces this time."

"That's a bummer, would have been interesting," Denny said. He paused a moment, looked at the stacked papers, realized Savich wasn't going to tell him anything more. Savich thanked him, watched him stop at Shirley's desk to chat and filch one of her sugar cookies before he left the unit.

On top of the pile was a photo of an older man, his wrists zip-tied to a railing, his feet secured with duct tape. He'd been left at a side entrance of what was obviously a police station.

There was a pillowcase over his head and a legal-size envelope was fastened to the front of his coat with large black block letters across it—JUSTICE. He looked to be unconscious.

There were half a dozen other photos with the pages, two flash drives, and a folded letter.

He unfolded the letter and read:

Agent Savich,

I delivered this man, Elson Grissom, to the Porte Franklyn Central Police Station at 8:30 last night. Enclosed are copies of the evidence I've collected against him. There are two flash drives of conversations between Grissom and known felons involved in interstate drug distribution, as well as with Porte Franklyn city council member Judith Warder and two state legislators, Lester Graves and Lewis Hampstead. These conversations took place at Grissom's private vacation home at Lake Lawson in Bellison, Virginia. I used a parabolic mike and my phone to record them. Some of the conversations are with people I couldn't identify, but they prove Grissom's involvement in drug distribution. There are also business and bank records showing he uses several of his businesses for money laundering, including the local police and firefighters' pension funds Grissom has administered for the past fifteen years.

You may not be familiar with Grissom, but locally he's a mover and shaker, one of the most powerful men in the county. His primary residence is in Porte Franklyn. He calls himself an investment manager, a legitimate and lucrative cover for him. He also owns a chain of grocery stores throughout Virginia and North Carolina that provide him much of his opportunity for money laundering. He has bought or strong-armed his way to influence with local authorities.

His adult daughter, Melissa Kay Grissom, thirty-five, was arrested last year for driving drunk in Bellison. She sent a woman to the hospital, but was given only a five hundred dollar fine, no arrest, no suspension of her license. Who did Grissom bribe?

His son, Ryman Grissom, forty, is a criminal jack-of-all-trades, but he's primarily his father's enforcer. There are complaints against him for assault and arson, but he's never been arrested. He also does jobs for one of his father's criminal friends, Kahn Oliveras. None of them have ever been arrested.

I would have waited to gather more evidence before I acted, but I may already have waited too long. I believe Elson Grissom recently ordered the murder of Josh Atwood, thirteen, the only child of his widowed mother, Hildy Atwood. Josh was a bright, athletic, responsible boy, who delivered papers in Bellison, near Grissom's vacation house. His body was uncovered by scavengers and found by hikers two days after his murder in the woods on the outskirts of Bellison, his undelivered papers still beside him. His mother had reported him missing immediately, and Bellison Chief of Police Harlan Jacobs had officers tracing his newspaper delivery route. After Josh was found, Mrs. Atwood told Chief Jacobs Josh had seemed upset and anxious the day before he disappeared, but he'd only told her he'd seen something important and he was writing a letter addressed to you, Agent Savich. It's obvious Josh wrote to you because he believed you were a hero, believed you would help him. But the email was never sent—he was killed evidently before he was satisfied with what he'd written, or more likely, before he'd gained enough damning information to give to you.

Hildy Atwood had looked over Josh's shoulder at the

email he'd been writing, saw he believed he'd seen drug dealers speaking with Elson Grissom at his lakeside home. He heard them talking about cash deliveries and distribution routes, heard the words MS-13. She told him never to go back there, but he did and he was killed for it.

Mrs. Atwood didn't know the passwords Josh used on his computer, but Chief Jacobs said the police could deal with that, and so she gave it to him. Later he told Mrs. Atwood Josh must have deleted the email, because it wasn't on his laptop. Luckily, Mrs. Atwood remembered most of what Josh had written and told all of it to a friend. Three days after Josh's death, his mother's car went over a cliff and she was killed. Mrs. Atwood's friend told all the neighbors her suspicions before she spoke to Chief Jacobs. Jacobs listened, and he again insisted Josh must have deleted the email he was writing, if there was one, which he was beginning to doubt. He promised to look into everything thoroughly, but without Mrs. Atwood to testify, there wasn't any proof.

Two weeks after Josh was found, Chief of Police Harlan Jacobs announced a transient had probably killed the Atwood boy, a wrong place/wrong time scenario. Hildy Atwood's death was ruled an accident.

Enclosed are copies of two wires to the account of Chief Jacobs's wife, Sandra Jacobs. The sender was a holding company you will see I traced back to Grissom.

Agent Savich, let me emphasize these crimes are only an example of how far Grissom's tentacles reach. We're talking about a man who's guilty of at least fifteen years of state and federal crimes, including murder, and yet he's never been brought to justice. But with the evidence documented against him in this envelope, I can't imagine Grissom can escape being tried and sent to prison for the rest of his miserable life.

Since the bulk of the evidence involves state crimes, the commonwealth attorney in Porte Franklyn, Simon Hailstock, will be in charge of prosecuting those crimes for the state. Unfortunately I have questions about Hailstock's commitment to seeking justice if it might interfere with his long-term plan to run for a seat in the House. That would require large cash donations and support from people a lot like Grissom and Kahn Oliveras. That makes him an ideal candidate for their influence, but I have no proof he's actually compromised.

You may wonder why I'm sending all my collected evidence to you, personally. It is because Josh Atwood believed in you. And I've researched you myself. I've seen you on TV. You're smart and you seem tenacious. I trust you to seek justice for Josh and his mother and close Grissom down once and for all.

Please don't waste your time trying to identify me.
Sincerely,
Eliot Ness

Savich paused a moment. Eliot Ness. He smiled. A perfect name for a vigilante—the agent who'd brought down Al Capone in the thirties. Savich was on the point of sliding a flash drive into MAX when he looked up to see Sherlock in his doorway, a big smile on her face, her hand on her stomach. "How about some spaghetti pomodoro? Yes, yes, with garlic bread." She paused, wiggled her eyebrows. "You can also tell me about that envelope Danny gave you addressed to you personally."

Savich cocked his head at her. "But you weren't— I see, Denny told Ruth and she told you."

"No, Denny told everyone."

Savich rose, shrugged on his jacket. "Looks to me like we've got ourselves a vigilante with a lot of skills. Calls himself Eliot Ness."

Since it was lunchtime, the elevator was packed, so everyone was listening as Savich told her what he knew so far on the ride to the seventh-floor cafeteria. All cops, didn't matter if they were federal or local, were a curious lot. "He used a variety of ways to collect the evidence, from old-fashioned recorded conversations and long-range photos, to hacking into Grissom's email and computer files, company and bank records."

"Which means he's computer savvy."

Savich nodded. "I'll check out the Porte Franklyn common-wealth attorney, Simon Hailstock, and the state legislators he mentions by name, see if there's any evidence they're in Gris-som's control."

Sherlock cocked her head in a way he loved making her curly hair bounce and dance. "Ruth told me Commonwealth Attor-ney Simon Hailstock is known as Mr. Lowball, the big plea bargainer himself, basically it's criminals in and then out again. She said Dix has heard stories about how the PFPD morale has taken a nosedive since his becoming commonwealth attorney last year. Since you have your doubts and you'll undoubtedly be talking with Grissom and Hailstock, are you going to go take a federal prosecutor with you to Porte Franklyn?"

He nodded. "I think Pepper would jump into this extraordi-nary situation, don't you think?"

Pepper Jersik, tough as her country grandmammy's old hound Brutus, she'd say, had a rep for diving in the deep end and coming out dragging a shark. FBI agents loved her because she always had their backs.

"Oh yes, nothing revs her more than mixing it up with big-time crooks."

"I'm also taking Griffin. He doesn't miss much. I can have

him interview Hildy Atwood's neighbor for a start, see what she remembers what Josh's mom told her about his email to me."

Sherlock said, "I wonder if the vigilante Eliot Ness is a prosecuting attorney in Porte Franklyn. Or maybe a cop in the PFPD."

Savich said, "Maybe. Certainly someone with computer skills who understands legal procedures and knows the local players."

She grinned up at him. "You do realize, of course, since Griffin is so gorgeous, all the women you meet will fall over themselves to tell him everything they know, maybe even what they really don't know."

"Truer words were never spoken," said a female agent, and she sighed. One of the male agents said, "Get a grip, Agent Pam, or I'll tell your husband."

Sherlock grinned at them. "As for you and Pepper, the two of you have a mean vibe going that'll scare the crap out of anyone hiding anything."

They heard some laughter as they got out with the rest of the group and walked into the noisy cafeteria with all its amazing smells. They got in line at the always-popular Italian kiosk. Sherlock said, "I can't wait to hear how Eliot managed to be onsite at the police station when Grissom was delivered. I hope the garlic toast is nice and crispy."

When he was winding spaghetti around his fork, Savich leaned close, said, "It will be interesting to see when and if our vigilante strikes again."

Sherlock crunched down on some thankfully crispy garlic toast, chewed thoughtfully. "I guess it'll depend on whether his interest in Grissom is specific or if he's only the first in line."

"Who knows?" Savich felt his blood stir, felt his hunting

instincts fire. He couldn't wait to read all the evidence, give Pepper Jersik a call, and tell Special Agent Griffin Hammersmith he now had a new assignment. He added, "If Eliot Ness succeeds with Grissom, I doubt he'll stop with him." And he thought, *Well, Eliot Ness, you've stirred up a hornet's nest all because of the murder of a thirteen-year-old boy*. But he wondered if the boy's death was all his motivation.

6

TUESDAY MORNING

Though Alec Speers, assistant commonwealth attorney and chief of the Homicide Unit, was the sleep-deprived new father of twin girls, the contents of the envelope he'd found on his desk that morning had hit his bloodstream like a dozen espressos. He was hyped, jittering around in his chair. He nodded to his newest assistant attorney, Kirra Mandarian, hired just eight months ago and already assigned to the Homicide Unit. At first he'd been annoyed when she'd been foisted on him, though she'd graduated UVA law school near the top of her graduating class and clerked with Amos Fielding, a powerful federal district court judge in the Eastern District of Virginia with big-time clout. But Alec had to admit Judge Fielding's assessment of her had been right on. Mandarian was a hard worker, smart and likable, and best yet, she connected well with a jury, not that she'd had much opportunity so far. Alec knew she'd spent her teen years in Australia with her famous uncle, Leo Mandarian, after the murder of her parents when she was twelve. She had juice, but she never talked about the high-profile adventures she'd led with her uncle that included some influential politicos, including Virginia's senior senator and his son.

Kirra said to her boss, "How much longer before the twins sleep through the night, Alec?"

"The pediatrician says two more weeks. Then she grins and I think she knows something we don't know and isn't telling us." He yawned just as Commonwealth Attorney Simon Hailstock walked in.

"Here we go," Alec said under his breath.

Simon Hailstock strutted into his private conference room ten minutes late. Of course he was late on purpose, Hailstock's way of reminding his attorneys who the boss was. He looked fit for fifty-two and preferred his Italian suits and Ferragamo loafers. He relished wielding power and was a good-old buddy to a select few. To all others, like his chief of the Homicide Unit, Alec Speers, and new hires like Assistant Commonwealth Attorney Kirra Mandarian, he was short on civility and long on condescension. They both knew never to disagree with him outright or even joke with him because he had no sense of humor, except in front of a camera where he always seemed ready with pithy sound bites and one-liners everyone knew his secretary, Mrs. Quigley, prepared for him. She was known for them.

His attorneys thought little of him because he forced them to offer plea deals that were wildly unjust to victims. As for most cases deserving to go to trial, Hailstock was usually opposed, not because of how much it would cost in time and money; no, if a case was lost, it would make Hailstock look bad and hurt his chances to move forward in three or four years to higher things, like a congressional seat in Washington. He didn't want the slightest chance of a case losing and spoiling his conviction record. Needless to say that made him beloved by defense attorneys. If Hailstock decided to run again for commonwealth attorney, Alec would wager his favorite high-tops t every defense attorney in Porte Franklyn would turn out to vote for him.

Hailstock remained standing and gave Alec his habitual stingy smile before he turned to Kirra. The stingy smile gave way to his stingy voice, cold and precise. "The only reason you are here, Ms. Mandarian, is that you were at the police station when Mr. Grissom was hand delivered with that envelope pinned to his jacket. I'm told his ankles were duct-taped and he was zip-tied to the railing at the side entrance at the PF central station. Is that correct?"

"Yes, sir," Kirra said. "That's correct."

"I understand you were chatting with the desk sergeant at the time and took it upon yourself to act as affiant. You called Judge Bentley and asked him for an affidavit for a search warrant. May I ask why you were at the police station at that particular time? In the evening, I might add. May I also ask why you did not immediately call your chief?"

Kirra sat forward, her hands clasped in front of her on the table. "I wouldn't have been at the station, sir, but I'd forgotten to return some notes Lieutenant Thorpe had given me on a case we were working on together. I called him and I knew he was still at his desk. It was the Kevon Martin case, sir, the repeat offender who used a six-inch serrated knife to terrorize the driver of a Honda in a carjacking. As you know, the driver, Mr. Henry Philpot, later died of a heart attack, his death a direct result of the attack. So that's why I returned to the station."

Hailstock looked ready to spew, but reined himself in, and said to Alec, "Mr. Speers, I believe you are working with opposing counsel on the *Philpot v. Martin* case to reach a reasonable compromise? I believe the defense attorney is willing to compromise on a sentence of three years in prison and a year of community service for Mr. Martin because Mr. Philpot died of natural causes. It seems reasonable."

It depends on what the definition of what natural is. Alec nearly laughed when that old chestnut flew into his mind. He wasn't about to tell Hailstock his reasonable compromise wasn't going to fly. Alec was going to stand firm on a sentence of ten years, reminding the defense attorney a trial would likely end in Mr. Martin being sentenced to Red Onion Prison for twenty years. Because he didn't want to get fired out of hand, he only nodded. If Hailstock called him on it later, he'd deal with it then.

Hailstock gave him a long look filled with threat, then nodded back to Kirra. "Continue."

Kirra said, "When I saw the man with a pillowcase over his head and an envelope with JUSTICE written across the front attached to his jacket, I realized whatever was in it might be inadmissible in court if it was opened without a warrant in police custody. It needed to be seen to, so I decided to take advantage of being there and act as the affiant myself."

"Am I to assume you don't think either Mr. Speers or I understand the definition and importance of affiant, Ms. Mandarian?"

"Of course not, sir, I only wanted to relay exactly what Judge Fielding always preached to me. My apologies for being unnecessarily detailed."

Alec said, "Had she called me sooner, I would have told her to proceed. I have blessed the fates Kirra was at the PF Central Station. I'm not saying it would have happened, but it's possible the police who found Grissom might have compromised any evidence in the envelope by opening it without a go-ahead warrant."

Hailstock didn't look happy. "Yes, that is one way of looking at it. However, Ms. Mandarian, you delivered the envelope to

Lieutenant Thorpe rather than this office and to me. Why?"

Kirra said, "Sir, when I got the warrant, Lieutenant Thorpe was still on scene. I apologize, but I didn't think it was inappropriate to have him open the envelope and I had no desire to bother you at home. I'm very sorry if I erred, sir."

Hailstock looked down at the sheaf of papers on the table in front of him. "I am still displeased. I didn't get copies of the envelope contents until this morning. My secretary, Mrs. Quigley, told me all the attorneys in your unit were given copies of the evidence against Mr. Grissom as well. May I ask why you felt you had the need or the authority to do that?"

Kirra cleared her throat. "Mr. Hailstock, I'm the one who distributed the evidence. I'm not as experienced as my colleagues and was anxious to have their input, as well as Lieutenant Thorpe's. I did of course ask Mr. Speers afterward and he believed it was appropriate."

Alec looked at her beneath his lashes. It was well done, fluent, though not quite true. Hailstock had sole discretion over whether or not a defendant would be prosecuted and tried, but Kirra had now assured Hailstock couldn't sit on this evidence against Grissom, for whatever reason. The evidence was a gold mine, but Alec wasn't sure how Hailstock would react, what he would do, and he hated that. He thought again of the *Philpot v. Martin* case and knew in his gut Hailstock would find out what he planned. Would he stop him? Fire him? Let him proceed? Alec looked again at Kirra, knew she understood their superior very well, and had acted the only way she could to make Hailstock take the appropriate course of action. Maybe.

Alec thought of his unit of six men and four women, ranging from Kirra's age, twenty-six and right out of a year clerkship, to Willis Horton, sixty-two, a tough old hound who was looking forward to spending his time fishing off his ancient trawler when he retired. He'd seen Willis sitting on the edge of his desk that morning, swinging his leg, more excited than Alec seen him in a long time, maybe as excited as Alec was. All the attorneys were hyped. He heard endless speculation on the identity of the vigilante, who'd initialed each page E.N., obviously Eliot Ness.

Alec got his reasoning together, sat forward, and clasped his hands. "Sir, we're facing a unique and potentially explosive situation. The press will be all over this and Elson Grissom has powerful friends. Everyone in the press and our citizens will want to see justice done. Every attorney in the Homicide Unit is prepared to assist you in any way."

Hailstock said in his courtroom voice, deep and smooth and sincere as a priest's, his parents having paid top dollar for a voice coach when he'd been in law school, "Chief of Police Pershing, Lieutenant Thorpe, and I spoke with Mr. Grissom earlier this morning. He's in the hospital under observation, claiming he was still disoriented from what turned out to be a ketamine injection his assailant jabbed in his neck, and pain in his kidneys from the beating he was given. Needless to say, he had two attorneys hovering around his bed."

Alec raised his hand.

"What is it, Mr. Speers?"

"If Grissom is still disoriented, how was he able to call his attorneys?"

"Evidently Grissom's son, Ryman, called them. He and his sister, Melissa Kay, were there at their father's bedside. I asked them to leave the room, which they did with ill grace. As to his abduction, Mr. Grissom claims he'd just arrived home from a charity fundraiser and exited his car when his attacker came up behind him, pulled something over his head, and jabbed a needle into his neck. Grissom said he fought back but his attacker was strong and trained, kicked and hit him in his stomach and kidneys until he fell, hit his head, and passed out. His attacker never said a word."

Kirra said, "Sir, I was told by the attending physician at Concord General there was no indication Mr. Grissom had been struck in the stomach or kidneys, no sign he'd struck his head."

Hailstock said with the exaggerated patience you'd use speaking to a child, "I didn't say what Mr. Grissom said was true, Ms. Mandarian, only that it is what he claimed. May I continue?"

"Yes, sir, excuse me."

"Thank you. Chief of Police Pershing asked Grissom who might have beaten him and turned him over to the police in such a humiliating way. He said he didn't know, but probably someone he knew who wanted to destroy him and take over what he had. I asked him why he believed he hadn't been killed instead. Grissom said his assailant was probably too afraid to kill him because Grissom had friends, also his son and daughter, who would hunt him down. He said if Chief Pershing didn't find his attacker, Grissom and his son and daughter would.

"Of course his lawyers knew they weren't entitled to see the contents of the envelope yet because Grissom hasn't been charged. Regardless, I know they will claim the documents are forgeries, the recordings are fraudulent, manufactured, and that Grissom is a law-abiding victim, a pillar of the community, he and his wife both active in myriad charities."

Hailstock waved the sheaf of papers, said in an acid voice, "I don't doubt these pages will soon be online for the world to see since you, Mandarian, gave copies out like candy. Mr. Speers, you will reiterate to your attorneys they are not to comment to the press or share this information with anyone outside this office. I don't want this situation to explode in our faces.

"Now, any drug distribution charges would be federal, not our responsibility. The most serious of the potential state charges against Mr. Grissom are the allegations he was involved in a conspiracy to murder the thirteen-year-old paper delivery boy, Josh Atwood, the boy the local police said was unlucky to be in the wrong place at the wrong time six weeks ago, somewhere near Mr. Grissom's lake house."

Kirra raised her hand. Hailstock gave her the stink eye, but nodded.

"The cover letter says Josh Atwood wasn't there by chance. He'd been there before, he'd heard something, and he went back hoping to find out more. He was spotted and murdered. I think he was a brave boy trying to do the right thing and Grissom ordered him killed. The papers in the envelope show two payments of $5,000 to Bellison's Chief of Police Jacob's wife, Sandra Jacobs, which could clearly be seen as a bribe."

Hailstock frowned and continued. "Regardless of your theory and your feelings, Mr. Grissom wasn't even a person of interest at the time, and there was no reason for him to be. The two payments add weight, but still, the evidence is circumstantial, and there's no definite link to the murder of Josh Atwood, only an email reconstructed from memory supposedly written by the murdered boy to an FBI agent, Dillon Savich, at the Hoover. It appears this email was neither sent nor did it make it into the hands of Bellison's police chief, Jacobs, who denied it was on the boy's computer."

Kirra said, "Sir, the evidence linking Grissom to Josh Atwood's murder is preliminary, granted, especially with the boy's mother now dead. We could remove Josh's computer from Chief of Police Harlan Jacobs, have it examined forensically since it's obvious Jacobs didn't do it. You know it's impossible to delete emails."

"I agree," Alec said before Hailstock could blast her. "I believe the murder charge is worth pursuing. Conspiracy to commit murder would send Grissom away for life, no parole. Our attorneys discussed this and agree the best way to proceed would be to use the other evidence in the envelope as the foundation—the drugs, their distribution, which are federal, but still, there's the embezzlement of the retirement funds through Grissom's investment firm, the recorded conversations of Mr. Grissom and his associates, known criminals, discussing drug distribution routes. We could easily show Grissom had ample motivation to kill the boy if he overheard any of Grisson's conversations. And his financial records point directly to embezzlement and money laundering. We probably have enough to charge him for those crimes now."

Hailstock picked up his coffee mug that said CHIEF on the side, took a refined sip, set it down. Giving himself time to think, Kirra knew. Hailstock said finally, "The recordings relating to federal crimes are for the federal prosecutors to pursue. As for the boy's murder, we have a few bits of circumstantial evidence to look into, but not nearly enough to bring charges. As for any alleged financial crimes, we'll have to have these documents examined by the forensic accountants in Richmond."

Kirra could only stare at him. *Circumstantial?* This collection of solid evidence he considered *circumstantial?*

Alec said, "Chief of Police Harlan Jacobs of Bellison is on the hook here as well. He and his wife need to be questioned about those two five-thousand-dollar payments. Is he in Grissom's pocket? It seems very possible."

"Perhaps," Hailstock said as he gathered the papers in front of him, lined them up smoothly, and paper-clipped them together. He nodded to Alec, gave Kira a dismissive look. He wasn't pleased. He wanted his attorneys to do what he told them to do, not stray out on their own outside the box, like Mandarian. If she didn't fall into line, he'd get her out. She was always deferential, but he sensed she disapproved of him. Was it because he was careful to keep his cases moving through the court system? Well, her parents had been murdered, and the killers never caught, and he'd cut her some slack, but still, he was tired of it.

He walked out of the conference room without a backward glance.

7

Savich Home
Georgetown
Washington, D.C.

TUESDAY EVENING

Savich sat beside Sherlock on the sofa facing a sluggish fire in the fireplace. The warm air was scented with a gardenia pot-pourri in a bowl on a side table.

"Sean was out after only one verse of 'Hearts on Fire.' He was either very tired or thought my newest country-western song was too boring to listen to."

Sherlock grinned, moved closer, and laid her head on his shoulder. "Well, I really like 'Hearts on Fire'—but I'm kind of glad Sean didn't stay awake for the part when the gambler's woman throws the broke gambler his Zippo lighter on her way out and wishes he dies from all the cigarettes he smokes."

"In my head the gambler's name is Maury, but I still need to figure out where to put that in." He hugged her. "I saw you were checking out the evidence Eliot included on that boy's murder. What do you think of it?"

"It still needs some nailing down, but I'd say there's enough solid evidence in that envelope even apart from Josh's murder to justify strapping Grissom to a whale's back and sending him off to Japan."

Savich laughed, kissed her ear, leaned in so her hair tickled his face. "I'd prefer the Arctic, but Japan would be okay too."

Sherlock said, "Some of that evidence still may be determined to have been illegally obtained, but it would all be inadmissible for certain if the cops had collected it like that. Makes me wish we had a bit more latitude. Eliot Ness did a thorough job. He is really committed, Dillon; I mean, even though he committed a felony kidnapping Grissom and hauling him to the police station, he did it for the right reasons. And he's talented, Dillon, focused and smart. Really good with computers, I think, something of a hacker. And our vigilante's nom de plume—Eliot Ness. Do you think we're supposed to think of Grissom as Capone?"

"It's a stretch. Porte Franklyn isn't the wild and woolly Chicago of the twenties and thirties. But like Capone, Grissom is near the top of the local food chain."

"But if Ness's evidence is verified, Grissom is a murderer who deals in drugs and embezzles from pension funds. What did the federal prosecutor have to say?"

Savich said, "Last I saw her, Pepper was waving pages from the envelope above her head she was so hyped. She's convinced it will all be admissible because an assistant commonwealth attorney was there at the police station when Grissom was delivered and acted as the affiant, called a judge to get a search warrant before they opened the envelope. But Pepper's not sure the commonwealth attorney, Simon Hailstock, will agree with her. It's common knowledge in law enforcement he doesn't like surprises and takes as few risks as possible. She's eager to go with Griffin and me to Porte Franklyn tomorrow morning."

Sherlock yawned. "Let's go to bed, Dillon, and don't worry about Emma; Sean and I are picking up the Hunts at Dulles tomorrow."

"Does Sean know yet Emma's coming?"

"All he knows is he has a surprise flying in. Can you believe it's been six years since we met Ramsey and Emma and Molly, when I was still pregnant with Sean? And now they have the twins, Cal and Gage."

Savich grinned. "Ramsey was telling me he doesn't know what crime he committed to deserve those two hellions. He said they listen more to Emma than to him or Molly."

Sherlock said, "I wonder if Sean will take one look at twelve-year-old Emma and still expect her to marry him." She laughed, remembered clearly the Christmas concert the year before at Davies Hall in San Francisco, when eleven-year-old Emma Hunt played Gershwin's "Rhapsody in Blue" to a full house. The lovely memory ended with applause and rolling laughter when her four-year-old Sean yelled out to Emma, asking her to marry him as she bowed to the audience.

"When I think of everything they went through six years ago—Emma being kidnapped and abused by that horrific pedophile, Father Sonny—and now this. She's too old to be taken by a pedophile, Dillon, so why now? Why her? What's going on here?"

"Whatever it is, Ramsey and Molly believe she'll be safer here, with that man who tried to take her at Davies Hall thousands of miles away in San Francisco. He said the SFPD hasn't made much progress tracking the guy down, much less finding out why he tried to take Emma. But Virginia Trolley is working on it hard, says she'll keep in touch with them." But Savich had a premonition they wouldn't find answers in San Francisco.

Sherlock yawned, kissed his neck. "You can bet every cop in the San Francisco PD is looking out for the guy. None of them want their favorite Judge Dredd and his family threatened.

Molly told me Emma worked with a police artist, but the man's eyes and hair were covered, so it's impossible to identify him.

"Imagine, Dillon, that beautiful talented girl will be playing Chopin in Kennedy Center at the Chopin Retrospective. I'm so proud of her."

"Ramsey says she's excited about it, completely focused."

"They're staying at the Hay Adams, an early birthday present for Molly, Ramsey told me, a corner suite so when the twins play cowboys and Indians, He and Molly hope there'll be fewer guests to complain."

Savich's cell sounded a text.

He read aloud, HAILSTOCK A PROBLEM. YOU'LL NEED TO NAIL GRISSOM ON FEDERAL DRUG CHARGES. ELIOT NESS

Savich did a trace, but no luck. He said to Sherlock, "No surprise. Eliot Ness used a burner."

8

WEDNESDAY MORNING

After introductions, Lieutenant Jeter Thorpe escorted FBI agents Dillon Savich and Griffin Hammersmith and federal prosecutor Pepper Jersik to a small interrogation room. He offered coffee, said in the same breath he'd drink the station coffee only if he was dying of thirst, and then it'd be iffy.

All three accepted bottled water.

Jeter eyed the man who'd called him the previous day to introduce himself and tell him Eliot Ness had sent him the evidence. Savich was a big man, looked as tough as Jeter's bulldog, Bruce. He had a cop's smart eyes, looked like he'd seen most everything one human being could do to another. And there was something else in Savich's eyes as he looked Jeter over, something well-controlled and intimidating, something unexpected that made Jeter think Savich knew things other people didn't, saw things other people didn't. It was odd, but it was true.

He shook Savich's hand. "A pleasure to meet you in person, Agent Savich. Needless to say, I've heard of you. I don't know if you're aware the evidence in the envelope has already been distributed to the commonwealth attorney's prosecutors, as well as our own chief of police. Actually, my only direct role is that I happened to be there. You mentioned when you called me yesterday that Eliot Ness's letter to you mentioned me by name."

"He obviously knows you, trusts you, and wants you involved, which means you know him. Have you thought it might be possible your being there wasn't an accident, that Eliot Ness knew you'd be there?"

"But I can't imagine who or how—" Jeter shook his head. "I suppose it's possible." He turned to Pepper. "I don't believe we've ever had a federal prosecutor grace our police station, Ms. Jersik. I like your name, Pepper, takes me back to my mom's goulash."

"Wouldn't that be paprika?"

Jeter grinned at this awesome woman. "It's surely a pleasure, Ms. Jersik." He took her hand, realized he didn't want to let it go. He felt something strange stir down deep, something he hadn't felt in a very long time, not since Judy's death six years ago. Jersik was over six feet tall in her three-inch black boots, at his eye level, with amazing light hair that looked nearly silver in the interview room's high-beam fluorescents. Her eyes were light blue, crystal clear, and as smart as Savich's. Jeter thought of an Amazon, then decided she was more a Valkyrie. He looked down at her hand and saw no wedding ring, quickly let her hand go when he realized what he was doing.

He stared a moment at Agent Griffin Hammersmith. He knew to his boots this man was potent with women, was so good-looking even Jeter's sour stiff-necked secretary, Ms. Plimm, had eyed him like a chocolate bar. He was tall and fit, looked like he could handle himself. Like Savich, his eyes were all cop. It was odd but Jeter sensed the same unexpected and inexplicable something he'd felt when he looked at Savich, something they shared that he didn't understand. "Welcome, Agent Hammersmith." They shook hands. "Please, all of you sit down."

When they were all seated, Savich said, "I understand the evidence Eliot Ness delivered has already been widely distributed. No harm in that, except that Grissom is likely to get his hands on a copy that much sooner. I did get a text last night from Ness, from a burner phone I couldn't trace. He implied Hailstock would be in no hurry to prosecute Grissom. That's why Ms. Jersik is with us. And it brings up the interesting question of how Eliot Ness knew so quickly Hailstock was a problem, or do you already know why that is, Office Thorpe?"

Jeter smile. "Why not first names? It'll make things easier. No, I don't know how." He shrugged. "I've got to say at the very least it shows our vigilante has someone giving him inside information about the commonwealth attorney's office. And the evidence—it's very detailed, very lawyerly. What do you think of it, Ms. Jersik, ah, Pepper?"

Pepper, no idiot, knew Lieutenant Jeter Thorpe was interested in her, no missing that. She didn't mind. He was big, taller than she was, solid. He had kind ancient eyes, a soft hazel, and he couldn't seem to help himself. His dark brown hair was a little on the long side, with a few strings of silver at his temples. He had no beard, a refreshing change from a lot of men these days. It suited him. Jeter, she liked his name; it brought to mind chowing down pizza, maybe riding on the back of his motorcycle, laughing wildly into the wind. Yes, a lot of laughter. She pulled herself back, cleared her throat. "I've gone over the evidence Eliot Ness sent us. Of course I concentrated on the drugs charges, which will be federal. It's amazing work. Bad luck for Grissom he got in Eliot Ness's crosshairs."

Jeter leaned forward, clasped his hands on the desk. "Very glad to hear you say that."

Savich nodded. "Okay, why don't we begin with the star of the show, then, Jeter—Elson Grissom. Tell us about him."

"We've suspected Grissom is involved in drug distribution since before I joined the force. We haven't charged him because he's been too well insulated, with too many players between him and the streets where the drugs are sold. Before he was delivered here to us, we've never had anything solid enough. And we never would have been able to gather much of that evidence Eliot Ness gave us without getting warrants we didn't have the grounds to ask for." Jeter leaned back in his chair. "I find myself wondering why Eliot Ness chose Grissom. Because we have another half-dozen high-profile possibilities just as bad as Grissom."

Griffin said, "Maybe it was something personal, Jeter."

Jeter said, "That's possible, I hadn't thought about that."

Savich said, "Let's turn to Grissom's unorthodox appearance zip-tied to the railing downstairs. We understand prosecutor Kirra Mandarian was in-house and acted as the affiant. What did she think?"

"She was very professional about it, made sure we followed proper procedures. When she saw what was in the envelope, she was as excited as I was. She hadn't heard about Josh At-wood's murder before we read that cover letter, and neither had I. She thought all that evidence of Grissom's other crimes meant there would be justice for Josh's murder, whether Gris-som was successfully prosecuted for his murder or not."

Griffin said, "About bringing in Grissom being personal—did you wonder why the boy's murder seemed to hit Eliot Ness so close to home?"

Jeter went on alert. "What do you mean?"

Savich said, "Let's back up a minute. You said prosecutor Kirra Mandarian happened to already be here the night Grissom was zip-tied to the police station railing, correct?"

"That's right. She'd come over earlier to talk about a case we were working on together. She dropped back by my office later to bring back some files she'd borrowed, and we talked about the case some more. She was about to say good night when I got the call from the desk sergeant downstairs about a man tied to the railing downstairs. Both Kirra and I gathered around with the others downstairs. It was fortunate she was here since she's a lawyer and knew we shouldn't open the envelope without a warrant. What do you mean about the boy's murder hitting Eliot Ness close to home?"

Pepper said, "I'm thinking along the same lines as Griffin. Jeter, you know Kirra Mandarian's name was Allison Rendahl before her uncle adopted her in Australia and changed it."

Jeter waved an impatient hand. "Yes, of course. Her uncle, Leo Mandarian, and I discussed his adopting her before he spoke to her about it. To tell you the truth, I was all for it since I thought it might help keep her safe, because she was a witness when her parents were killed. What's your point?"

Pepper said, "It sounds to me like you know Kirra well."

"Yes, both she and her uncle Leo. We've been close since she left at age twelve. Emails, phone calls at first, closer after she moved back to the States for law school. I've come to know her so well she's almost like my own kid sister. Are you asking if Kirra was upset about Josh Atwood's murder because she'd almost been killed at the same age herself? And there'd been no justice for her parents and no justice yet for Josh Atwood? Wouldn't you expect that attitude? She was only a kid then, and, yes, Kirra is keenly aware of what crime victims go through. But wait, you're implying more than that, aren't you?"

Savich said, "Yes, I am, Jeter. Kirra Mandarian trusts you, wants you to be involved. She's a prosecutor here in Porte Franklyn, which means she knows all the players—you, Grissom, Hailstock the commonwealth attorney. You told us Kirra was here with you that evening and then she left, only to return again to be on the spot when you got the call about the man tied to the railing. Did it occur to you how perfect the timing was? A lawyer happening to be here to act as affiant? I think it's quite possible Kirra Mandarian is Eliot Ness, or at least working with him."

Jeter wanted to belt him, but he calmed himself. He drew a deep breath. "Kirra Mandarian the vigilante? No, it's simply not possible. We're good friends, why wouldn't she tell me she was investigating Grissom, ask for my help?"

Savich said, his voice gentle, "You're too close, Jeter. You care a lot about her. We don't know her, haven't even met her yet. We only see what actually happened that night, and it makes a great deal of sense."

Jeter said, his voice stiff, "All right, I'll go over it in my mind again, but I'll tell you, it's really hard to get my head around. I know she's strong, well-trained—street fighting, martial arts—because her uncle Leo never wanted her to be helpless again. Taking down Grissom wouldn't be hard for her. And yes, I've seen her staring off into space and I wonder if she's thinking about her parents and who murdered them and why she was lucky enough to escape, maybe thinking revenge and how to get it. Leo told me the same thing. He said he never disturbed her when she looked like that, let her work her way through her grief.

"But listen, since she's been back here, I haven't had any reason to worry about her. She's normal, no thoughtful lapses, no talking about vengeance for her parents' murder. If anything, she seems stronger than most. I was thinking maybe Eliot Ness is a disillusioned cop, maybe here in my own shop . . . but you're right, a cop wouldn't know that quickly how Hailstock responded—only a prosecutor or someone from the office passing him information. But Kirra? That scares me to death. If it is Kirra, she's taking a huge risk—kidnapping Grissom is a felony. If she were caught, her career would be over, and she could go to prison. And she knows that as well as we do." He cursed, swiped his hand through his hair. "You and Griffin, you're FBI, and you, Pepper, you're a federal prosecutor. What are you going to do?"

9

Pepper said, "Don't worry, Jeter, we aren't going to do anything for the moment. Kirra Mandarian isn't our focus. We just wanted you to see the picture we're seeing. We need you to think about what she's likely to do next."

Jeter sounded infinitely depressed. "I haven't a clue. I'm beginning to believe I don't know her as well as I thought."

Pepper said, "Don't worry about it. It's Grissom we're here for. I can't indict Grissom on the state charges—that's up to Hailstock. But the interstate drug charges are mine—and I'm going to fillet him. This isn't about penny-ante bags of marijuana or cocaine, it's about a massive distribution network working directly with a foreign cartel."

She saw Jeter was distracted, more than likely thinking about Kirra Mandarian, feeling blindsided, maybe blaming himself for not seeing what was in front of him. She gave Savich a small headshake and backed up. "Jeter, tell us about Kirra and her uncle, Leo Mandarian. He seems like a real stand-up guy. I picture this macho guy wrestling crocodiles and trekking through the outback, killing scorpions and snakes with his bare hands."

Jeter laughed and waved his hand. "Yep, pretty close. He's a celebrity now, particularly in Australia and Japan, of all places, a famous survivalist. He leads clients on expeditions in the outback, took Kirra out with him while she was there. He and his team—all of them hard-asses—taught her about all about survival and how to fight. I've seen her fight, and believe me, she's fearless." He paused, added, "Leo comes to the States twice a year to see Kirra and she travels to Australia twice a year if she can. I even traveled there with her once, stayed with them at Leo's house in Port Douglas. They took me on what they called a little camping trip to see some pretty scenery—at least that's what they told me." He shook his head. "There were times I thought I was going to die. Looking back on it now, though, it was great.

"I like Leo, he's down-to-earth, a person you know you can trust five minutes after you've met him. Actually, Leo was here two months ago. Let me add, he raised Kirra well. They're very close, there's a bedrock of love and trust between them."

Pepper gave him a wonderful smile. "It sounds like he was the perfect person to save her again, after you did. Will you tell us one of his adventures?"

He cocked his head at her, smiled. "My favorite is the hair-raising time Uncle Leo fell into a sinkhole with a dingo and Kirra had to cut off a sturdy tree branch with a knife to save him. Best part? He came out with the dingo tucked under his arm."

Pepper said, "Was the dingo grateful?"

"Nah, the dingo tried to bite Leo and took off, shaking himself." He sat forward, looked at each of them. "Thank you for the time-out. Here's the truth. I can't imagine Leo going along with Kirra planning anything like this. And it's hard to imagine she would have told him, either. Above all she'd want to protect him."

Griffin folded his hands on the scarred tabletop. "All right, Jeter, now help us understand her. We know you were one of the detectives who worked her parents' murder case."

Jeter took a drink of his water, settled back. "At the time, I worked under lead Detective Amos Judd, who trained me, now retired."

Pepper said, "Trained you? You must have been a new recruit. How did you get the case?"

Jeter said, "I'd been a beat cop for a couple of years when Detective Judd spotted me, evidently liked what he saw and encouraged me to take the detectives exam. As a new detective, I was all gung ho to take on my first murder case, especially after I saw what happened there that night. Judd let me run with it.

"Maybe because it was my first murder, it stuck with me. Sometimes I still dream about it and always, I wake up wishing with everything in me I'd solved it, but I didn't." He shrugged. "It wasn't just the casual brutality of it, but because of the little girl. The killers shot Mr. and Mrs. Rendahl in their bed. I've always hoped they were asleep. We knew they had a young girl, Allison, who'd been mature enough to call 911, but she wasn't in the house, dead or alive. I was the one who found her huddled and bloody in a small cave in the woods, wouldn't have found it except for the blood trail. She'd cut her arm running through the woods, and a bullet had grazed her head. She was in shock, fought me tooth and nail until I convinced her I was there to help her, then she didn't want to let me go.

"To this day Kirra can't remember much of anything from that night, other than waking up when she heard footsteps on the stairs, seeing two men, calling 911, and running."

Savich said, "I understand Judson Rendahl was an artist, spent a good deal of his time with his easel on the shores of the Potomac, painting boats of all kinds?"

"That's right. And he did portraits. He wasn't famous then, barely sold enough to keep food on the table for his family.

His wife worked only occasionally at a grocery store when her health permitted. She had a severe heart problem. The point is there was hardly anything worth taking in the house, and if it was a home invasion or a robbery gone bad, why kill a twelve-year-old girl who couldn't identify them? Why burn down the house? It didn't look like a random killing, it looked like murder for a reason.

"When Kirra was older, I finally spoke to her and Leo. I told them it was clear her father was desperate for money, with her mom as sick as she was. Though Kirra hated hearing it, it was clear the only thing that made any sense is her father must have crossed some people he shouldn't have. He saw something, overheard something, had proof of something they didn't want known, and he tried to extort them. I found out he had no insurance, so I can understand if blackmail was the only way Rendahl could get enough money for his wife's care. Kirra didn't want to believe it, but she and Leo finally came around because the house had been torched for a reason. The killers were probably at the house not only to kill the Rendahls, but to find whatever her father might have been using for blackmail. When Kirra ran, they didn't have time to search for it, decided to torch the house and everything in it, make sure whatever it was Rendahl had burned in the fire. Of course to this day Kirra doesn't have any idea what her father could have had to use for blackmail or known that it would lead to such a horrific consequence."

Savich said, "That makes a great deal of sense. Rendahl couldn't have even considered what could happen or he wouldn't have tried blackmail."

Griffin said, "And in the end there was no closure, no justice. Can you imagine how Kirra felt? How she's felt all these years?"

Jeter said, "Lousy and furious and committed to finding the bastards come to mind."

Pepper said, "What bothers me is why the killers wanted to kill a twelve-year-old kid? Talk about overkill."

Griffin said simply, "Either the killers were hired and it was simply a job to them to kill everyone in the house or they were psychopaths and killing was a great game, gave them pleasure. Either way, it must have burned them when Kirra escaped."

Jeter said, "One of them did go after her in the hospital. Her nurse came by and screamed loud enough to chase him off. We arranged for a guard for her after that, until Leo came and took her back with him to Australia. Now, you want to hear something ironic? In the fourteen years since the Rendahl's murder, his paintings have become quite valuable. Nothing like a dead artist killed in a gruesome way to draw the attention of collectors. Today, Kirra has a couple of million in a trust from sales. I believe Leo also added to her trust, so she's in good shape financially."

Savich said, "Do you think Kirra might have determined Elson Grissom ordered the murder of her parents fourteen years ago and that's why she went after him?"

Jeter shrugged. "How on earth she could find anything to implicate him after fourteen years, I can't imagine. Believe me, at the time I turned over every rock, talked to dozens of people. I got nowhere. And why wouldn't she tell me if she had? Nothing Eliot Ness gave us has anything to do with Kirra's parents."

Pepper said, "If she'd had actionable proof Grissom was involved, she wouldn't have had to send us that envelope. I'm with Griffin, I can't imagine how it would feel, never getting closure, or justice, for your own parents' murder. It could be she thought she didn't have another choice."

Griffin said, "Maybe what shoved her over the edge was her

belief Grissom ordered Josh Atwood murdered. I can't wait to meet her."

Savich said, "I can't either. Now, Jeter, do you agree Porte Franklyn's commonwealth attorney, Simon Hailstock, will be a problem?"

Jeter laughed. "Problem's an understatement, Savich. They call him Mr. Lowball at the station because he has his attorneys plea-bargain most every case that could lead to a trial. And the good Lord help any of his prosecutors who go to trial and lose. He's always saying, with great pride, I might add, that the justice system here in Porte Franklyn should be a blueprint for cities all over the US. Needless to say, our cops can't stand him. And if any attorneys refuse to live with his dictates, they're gone fast."

Pepper said, "I don't see how Hailstock can avoid taking Grissom to trial. He's got buckets of evidence, no way any competent prosecutor could screw it up. Well, I suppose he could try to find a way to wiggle out of trying Grissom if Hailstock's in his pocket." Pepper sat forward, her incredible blue eyes focused on him. "Has Kirra told you exactly what Hailstock plans to do with all the evidence against Grissom?"

"Not yet." Jeter wondered how he could get Pepper's cell number. Maybe he could ask for her card. "Kirra said she'd call me after she and her boss have another meeting with Hailstock this morning. She's not optimistic."

Savich said, "I'll tell you what, Jeter. We'll be meeting with Kirra later this morning. We have no reason to tell her we suspect she might be Eliot Ness. We want to hear what she has to say, what her plans are. Trust me on this: we have no wish to do her harm. I know you're worried about her, but I'm going to ask you to hold off talking with her about what she's doing or whether she's Eliot Ness until we think it's time. Are we agreed?"

Jeter streaked a hand through his hair, cursed low. "It doesn't make me happy, but as long as I don't see her risking her life, I'll hold off. It's still hard for me to believe she's out there doing this, being like fricking Wonder Woman, but yeah, I can see it."

10

WEDNESDAY MORNING

Elson Grissom was speaking on his cell, his voice Gestapo sharp, when Savich, Griffin, and Pepper walked into his hospital room. "Get it done. I'll be released from the hospital in two hours and I don't want to be dragged to the police station and questioned." He punched off his cell, looked up at the three of them.

"Who are you? The Three Musketeers?"

A tall dark-haired woman was standing beside his bed, her hand on his shoulder. She turned to see them, stiffened all over, and stepped forward, blocking them, her eyes hot. So this was Grissom's daughter, Melissa Kay. Savich saw the father-daughter resemblance—the strong jaw, the upward-slanted dark eyebrows over dark eyes. She looked to be in her midthirties. Even if Savich hadn't read she'd been married and divorced three times, he might have guessed it. Her eyes were a roiling brew of violence, barely leashed, and who could live with that all the time?

Grissom's hand stayed her. "It's okay, Mellie. Stand down."

Stand down? He gave his daughter military orders? But she did stand down, staying quiet and close to her father. Savich said easily, "We're federal musketeers, Mr. Grissom. I'm Special Agent Dillon Savich, and I have Federal Prosecutor Pepper Jersik with me."

Melissa Kay stuck out her hand and Savich handed her his creds, looked directly into her eyes. "You're Melissa Kay Grissom, correct?"

"Of course I am." She handed the creds to her father, and he studied them for a long time. Savich knew he was thinking about how best to deal with them. Grissom gave the creds back to his daughter, motioned for her to give them to Savich. When she finally handed them back, she got in his face, said in a cold voice, "Can't you see my father is still recovering from getting attacked by that madman? What do you three want?"

Savich gently took her arms in his hands and lifted her to the side. For a moment she was too stunned to respond, but in a flash she stepped back in his way. "Cop or no cop, you can't do that. How dare you touch me?"

"Mellie!" She stopped cold at her father's voice. "I don't want you arrested for trying to protect me. Go stand by the window. That's right. Everything will be fine."

When she stood stiff and tall by the narrow window, vibrating with rage, Grissom looked Savich in the eye, waved a hand at the others. "Why the crowd?" He looked from Savich to Griffin. "What do you want?" But he didn't wait for an answer, turned to Pepper. "So you're a federal prosecutor? I thought maybe you were his assistant or his secretary or something."

Pepper laughed down at him. "Such a disappointment—I'd expect something more original, even from a man flat on his back, not that old chestnut. As Agent Savich said, I'm Pepper Jersik, federal prosecutor." She walked to the bed, leaned down, and said quietly, "You've been a very bad man for far too long, Mr. Grissom. I'm the federal prosecutor who's going to nail your butt in federal court, send you to a fine federal prison for the rest of your unnatural life."

Grissom didn't even blink. He even gave her a dismissive look, shook his head. "Right, lady, in your dreams. Say what you have to say and get out. My lawyers are due any moment to escort me home."

Pepper said, "We're here to tell you you're under federal investigation concerning allegations you've been working with the Cantrera drug cartel, setting up distribution points, here and in Mexico, off-loading drugs for them, and laundering money, both for them and for yourself."

Melissa Kay took a fast step toward Pepper. "That's ridiculous!"

Grissom sent Melissa Kay a look, shook his head at her, but said nothing. She stepped back, but looked like if she'd had a gun she'd shoot them all on the spot. Grissom gave Pepper a sneer that turned into an ugly laugh. "That's a lie, but nothing new, I've heard it all. If you had any real proof, you'd be arresting me. What else? You're going to tell me there's more crap from the Lone Ranger?"

Pepper smiled. "The Long Ranger's not involved that I know of. All the evidence against you is from Eliot Ness, neatly collected in an envelope delivered with you to the Porte Franklyn police station last night. I've got to say, Ness did a good job of it. We're already at work verifying and expanding on the proof he gave us."

"Doesn't matter what the buffoon calls himself. It's all a frame, probably engineered by one of my competitors, or the cops. The top cop, Pershing, wants to be reelected. Word is he'll do about anything. Have you given your so-called evidence to my lawyers? They tell me they'll make sure you can't use any of it. And they want to see it. Wait, what does Eliot Ness have to do with anything?"

Pepper said, "Your lawyers know perfectly well we can use it. And they'll hear our evidence in discovery after your indictments are returned against you by a federal grand jury. As for Eliot Ness, maybe you recall he was the agent who brought down Al Capone, just as the current Eliot Ness is bringing you down nearly a hundred years later."

Grissom snorted. "Who cares what the idiot calls himself? Like I said, it's all a frame. It's laughable. Come on, even you feds don't believe all that crap, do you?"

"Sure, impossible not to—talk about all your activities laid out in black and white; it's impressive how bad you've been for so long before our informant came along and put an end to you. Still, you can be sure we're looking into all the particulars carefully ourselves."

Melissa Kay pushed away from the window, her face red. "You're calling that man who attacked my father an informant? He assaulted him, drugged him, and you think he's a hero? He's the criminal. You should be talking about arresting him, not my father."

Savich said easily, hoping she'd leap on him rather than Pepper, "Didn't you know the doctors found no sign of any beating, Miss Grissom?" He waited, wondering if whatever control she had of herself would snap. He rather hoped it would.

Melissa Kay pushed away from the window, fists up, face red. "Look at my father! He's in pain!"

Grissom raised his hand to stay her. "Mellie's right. It's not those idiot doctors' kidneys that hurt." He gave a credible wince.

Pepper said, "The evidence included with your delivery to the police station last night also clearly shows you've been methodically embezzling from the police and firefighters' pension funds for years. If the world were a fairer place, I could turn this over to all the people you've been stealing from and let them deal with you. Talk about sore kidneys."

Melissa Kay shouted, "Shut up, you bitch! That threat is as stupid as you look. If anyone embezzled anything, it's obviously the person who sent you that so-called evidence or it was someone with a grudge against my father." She took a step toward Pepper, her fists up, ready to pound flesh.

Pepper laughed, wiggled her fingers toward Melissa Kay. "That's federal bitch, lady. I'm more than you want to deal with. Why don't you tell me what you did to your second husband, you know, the one who just up and disappeared? You made him disappear for good, didn't you?"

Melissa hissed. "You think I murdered the cretin? The bastard cleaned out my bank account and ran. He's still hiding—" She took another step toward Pepper.

"Melissa Kay, stop!" Grissom's voice was sharp. "It doesn't matter what any of them say. Go away, all of you. You can speak to my lawyers."

The hospital room door opened and three men marched in; in the lead was a white-haired gentlemen wearing a bespoke gray wool suit and a matching dark blue tie, a man whose manicurist probably came to his office to tend to his fingernails once a week. The second man was a younger clone of the first. As for the third man, Savich knew immediately he wasn't a lawyer. He looked a bit like Grissom. So this must be Ryman Grissom, his son. Savich knew he was forty, married and divorced three times like his sister. He had three children, all living with their mothers, all out of state, and why was that? Had he been abusive? It seemed likely. He was bigger than his father and fit, looked like he tended his body religiously. He had thick dark hair with a dash of white at the temples, and a well-maintained mustache. Unlike his younger sister's eyes, his were opaque, impossible to read, his expression well-controlled. He said nothing, merely stared at Savich and frowned, then at Griffin, and finally at Pepper, where his eyes fell lower, assessing her body. Savich looked away from Ryman Grissom, introduced himself, Griffin, and Pepper to the two lawyers as he presented their creds. As the creds were duly examined, Savich said to Ryman, "You're Mr. Grissom's son?"

Ryman Grissom leaned toward Savich, wanting him to step back, wanting to intimidate. Savich merely smiled. "I understand you've served as your father's fist for well on two decades. Did you murder Josh Atwood?"

Ryman laughed, a hard dismissive laugh. "You clowns are pathetic. Leave my father alone. Get out."

The elder lawyer handed back their creds and said in a resonant voice, "You will not attempt to interview Mr. Grissom again without our being present. Is that understood?"

A pity, but the fun was over. Both Savich and Griffin had wanted to see what Pepper could get out of Grissom's daughter. But now, there was no point in trying for anything more, not with his top-of-the-food-chain lawyers there.

"Sure," Savich said, and he smiled at Ryman Grissom, who looked like he'd be a happy man if he could get Savich into an alley. He'd enjoyed baiting Ryman just to see what he'd do, see if he'd stay controlled.

They walked out through a gauntlet of cold, hard stares. As they walked to the hospital elevator, Pepper said, "Bummer they had to show up, but no point in staying. Ryman Grissom, he's one scary dude, Dillon. Looked like both he and Melissa Kay wanted to jump you." She sighed. "I wish we'd had more time. I'd have liked to provoke Melissa Kay some more, see what she'd do, see if she'd come after me despite her father's orders. I'll bet you she uses her fists. No particular finesse, just naked violence."

Savich said, "Still, we accomplished what we came for, Pepper. We put them on notice federal agents are involved, that they're under investigation. That should disrupt business as usual for Grissom. And he knows silencing Eliot Ness won't make his problems go away. We did Eliot a favor."

She sighed again. "Still, I really wish I could have riled Melissa Kay some more, see, what she'd say. Anger like she carries around makes you careless."

Griffin patted her arm. "Maybe next time. She's a time bomb. You read her file, lots of bad behavior. She nearly lost it when you brought up her second husband. She could well have asked her father to make him disappear."

"If not for Grissom holding her choke chain, I could have ended up arresting her for attacking a federal prosecutor. She's too used to having her powerful daddy buy her out of trouble." Pepper said, "I do wish he hadn't called her off, I really wanted her to attack me." Pepper cracked her knuckles, gave them a mad grin. "Test out my black belt. Federal bitch—I like it, makes me feel all powerful."

Savich said, "Sorry, Pepper, I'd rather she'd have jumped Griffin or me, not you."

"Nah. You guys would hold back. I bet any domestic disturbance calls the police got during Melissa Kay's three short-lived marriages were on her. She's an active volcano."

Griffin said, "I have no doubt you could pin her feet behind her ears." He paused a moment, looked regretful. "I'd like to see that."

Pepper was smiling when the elevator doors opened and they got on. One young man and young woman stood at the back of the elevator, stethoscopes around their necks, looking like the walking dead. Savich would have bet his next paycheck they were interns. He'd been told by a physician friend that the year of internship was a rite of passage. Savich should have asked him, a rite of passage to what, exactly?

Pepper said, fully aware of listening ears, "I sure would have liked to kick her butt."

The young woman yawned, said with a crooked smile as she exited the elevator on the second floor, "I don't think I could kick my own butt right now, but good luck with that."

The young man looked at Pepper, a sudden twinkle in his exhausted eyes. "My money would be on you."

11

Office of District Attorney
Justice Plaza
Porte Franklyn

WEDNESDAY

Jeter told Savich that Hailstock was in his office. He also told him Hailstock's secretary would go to war rather than let anyone in to see him without an appointment, might even bite him if she thought he didn't wish Hailstock well. Savich considered trying to make nice, but when she looked up at him from behind her large nameplate—Mrs. Quigley—front and center on her desk, distrust and challenge on her face, he realized he had to bite her first. He whispered to Pepper and Griffin, "Leave this to me," and held his creds out in front of her face. He leaned forward and gave her a hard look. "I am Special Agent Savich, FBI. You will inform Mr. Hailstock we want to see him. Now." He looked at his watch, crossed his arms over his chest, didn't tap his feet because she wouldn't see it.

Mrs. Quigley started, licked her lips, whispered, "But he's busy, Agent Savich. I . . . is he expecting you?"

Savich leaned down to within an inch of her face, placed his hands flat on her desk. "I said now."

She bobbed her head and quickly punched three numbers on

her phone. "Mr. Hailstock, FBI agents are here to see you." She hung up before he could say anything, rose quickly, knocked on his door, opened it, and backed away fast without a word.

Pepper said under her breath, "I love to watch you play Mr. Iron Fist."

Commonwealth Attorney Hailstock rose quickly, so surprised Quigley had even let them near his office his mouth fell open. Then he stilled, assessing them. He wasn't stupid. He knew danger when it walked into his office. Savich introduced himself, Griffin, and Pepper but didn't offer a handshake. Each of them slapped their creds down on Hailstock's desk and waited, dead silent. Savich saw Hailstock's left eye twitch. He glanced around the big man's office. The row of wide windows overlooking Justice Plaza were large, glazed to prevent glare. The office was starkly modern and seriously minimalist, no computer, no papers, no framed photos of beloved family members on his glass and chrome desk. The pictures on the walls were starkly abstract, splashes of black and red that had the look of gutted fish.

Hailstock handed back their creds, cleared his throat, and said in a beautifully modulated deep voice, "Why are you here?"

"To discuss the evidence you've received against Elson Grissom."

"Ah. I must say I'm surprised you came so soon."

"Everything you have in your possession was dropped off at the Hoover Building yesterday."

"So then you wish to discuss the federal crimes he allegedly committed?"

"Among other things."

Hailstock gave them a sharp nod, pointed to a pale-gray leather sofa fronted by a chrome and glass coffee table. He sat opposite them in what looked like a king's chair, with two ornate arms and a high back standing on carved legs that put him a good six inches higher than anyone sitting on the sofa. Hailstock sat back, laid his hands lightly on the arms of the chair, the king holding court.

"I know of you, Agent Savich. Both you and your famous wife appear to enjoy camera time."

It was a nice swipe. Savich, deadpan, said, "I've heard of you as well, Mr. Hailstock, the King of the Lowball. I understand you're quite popular with Porte Franklyn criminal defense attorneys and their clients."

Hailstock turned stiff, his face turned red, but then after a moment he managed to regain his composure. Up went his chin. He said precisely, "I ensure that under my aegis the Porte Franklyn justice system isn't weighted down with defendants waiting in jail for over a year for their turn to be heard in court."

Pepper said, a smooth dollop of Southern in her voice, "I imagine the police don't like seeing criminals back on the streets so quickly, committing more crimes. But to business, Mr. Hailstock. Agent Savich, Agent Hammersmith, and I are here to coordinate our efforts with you. Once you've tried and convicted Elson Grissom on a number of state charges, including embezzlement and money laundering, you will of course want to reopen the investigation of Grissom's involvement in the conspiracy to murder thirteen-year-old Josh Atwood and his mother, Hildy Atwood, not to mention the likelihood the Bellison police chief, Harlan Jacobs, accepted a bribe from Grissom to suppress evidence of those murders. After you've tried Grissom and he's found guilty, we will try him in federal court for interstate drug trafficking. I'd anticipate that if we work together, Elson Grissom will serve a life sentence in Red Onion State Prison, and if he's still breathing when he gets out, we'll be transferring him to one of our federal facilities."

Hailstock tapped his fingers on the arms on his power chair, *tap, tap, tap*, thinking hard. He said finally, his voice didactic, the college prof lecturing a roomful of students, "The authenticity of the evidence presented by the citizen vigilante is being evaluated, and it's premature to predict how we might respond. There are always the procedural questions, and the need for further investigation, as you say, that make moving forward as quickly as you suggest somewhat problematic. If you, on the other hand, find the evidence pertaining to the drug charges convincing, you're free to bring your own charges against Mr. Grissom whenever you wish. If you try him in federal court first, you'll give us time to determine how best to proceed with the purported evidence against him in the Commonwealth of Virginia."

Pepper arched an eyebrow at him, her look one of amazement. "Purported evidence? Mr. Hailstock, I have personally reviewed that evidence, including the audio and video, presented to you on a proverbial platter, and my colleagues and I found it overwhelming. I daresay an intern would have no problem securing a guilty verdict for his financial crimes. Granted, the murder of Josh Atwood and his mother will require more investigation. It's your job to carry the ball forward for those two murders."

"There is no evidence Josh Atwood's mother was murdered."

Griffin said, "We understand your Porte Franklyn chief of police, Dunn Pershing, is willing to reopen the case of Mrs. Atwood's death, one ruled an accident by Bellison's chief of police, Harlan Jacobs. As you know, there is evidence Jacobs may have been bribed by Mr. Grissom to rule her death accidental."

Hailstock shrugged. "You're referring to the two checks written to Harlan Jacobs's wife? Those could be for anything, but Chief Pershing can do as he sees fit." He sat forward, the portrait of a reasoned, serious man. "As I said, if you believe the drug trafficking charges against Mr. Grissom carry the most weight and have the greatest chance of success in court, let me assure you I will not interfere with you, my word on it."

It was well done. Savich said slowly, "In my long experience, Mr. Hailstock, you are the very first state prosecutor who's offered up a criminal to us before he's tried in state court."

Hailstock said in a bored voice, "As I've already said, Agent Savich, much of the evidence presented regarding Mr. Grissom's purported financial crimes are problematic, their prosecution complex and uncertain. I predict such an indictment would result in a lengthy and expensive trial with an uncertain outcome given a jury's caprice. And such a trial I would just as soon avoid. These are lesser charges, in any case, whereas the federal drug charges are the more compelling." He added after a brief pause, "Many of the attorneys in my office agree."

Pepper wished his nose would grow with that whopper lie. Many of his attorneys agreed? She wanted to kick him. Time to appeal to his ego. "Mr. Hailstock, I must say I'm surprised you're not singing hallelujahs. Surely you must realize you would garner national publicity if you bring Grissom, a longtime criminal kingpin, to trial and convict him not only for embezzlement but also for the cold-blooded murder of a thirteen-year-old boy."

It was clear Hailstock hadn't thought of this possibility. Pepper let him consider that golden image of himself for a moment, then added the hammer. "But if you sit on this, Mr. Hailstock, if you don't act, if you aren't seen as moving quickly forward on the gold-plated evidence presented to you, you can count on it getting out because I'll make sure it does. The media will start asking questions you may not want to answer. Actually, I predict you'll be crucified. It you continue not to act, it's very possible people will be inclined to believe you're in Grissom's pocket."

Griffin gave Pepper a wink. None of them said anything more, willing to let Hailstock stew. They watched him rise and take two turns around his office. When he faced them again, he was in full control of himself, and his voice was austere. "I didn't run for this office to garner fame, Ms. Jersik. I ran to keep my city safe, and I want to do it right. I will not rush to judgment to make myself look like some kind of hero in the media." He paused. "It would seem to me the FBI is in constant need of positive publicity. If you send Grissom to prison for life for drug trafficking, you will claim the spotlight for yourselves. I willingly cede it to you." He splayed his hands. "The Department of Justice will give you medals, the public will celebrate you, and justice will be served." He paused again, and when he spoke, his voice rang out, passionate as an evangelist's. "As I said, I didn't take this office for the glory. My goal has always been simply to keep my city safe, and I'll judge for myself how to do that."

Pepper wanted to applaud. He'd surprised her, actually sounded believable enough to fill the collection plates in church. She could see now how he'd been elected. "That was impressive, Mr. Hailstock," she said. "I strongly suggest you study the evidence again, and listen to all your attorneys, not just those you say agree with you. If you fail to proceed with dispatch, fail to meet your responsibilities, you will force us to intervene. I'll remind you the chief of police in Bellison is already implicated as being bribed by Grissom and you don't want to raise the suspicion you may be compromised yourself, or if not compromised, then ineffective." She paused, put her second boot hard on his neck. "I imagine inaction might make people wonder if you should finish your term. Perhaps a recall would be in order with all the accompanying humiliation. None of that would leave you comfortable in your Ferragamos."

She saw he'd felt that one. He flushed, but said nothing.

Savich said, "It seems you have a good deal to think about, Mr. Hailstock. Ms. Jersik pointed out the benefits to you and to Porte Franklyn if you proceed with dispatch. We'll be in touch. Have a good day."

On their way out, Savich gave Mrs. Quigley a warm smile. She gaped at him, opened her mouth, shut it. When they were on the elevator, Pepper rubbed her hands together. "That was fun. We scared the crap out of him. What do you think he'll do?"

Savich said, "That depends on whether he's playing with the devil or believes his own hype."

Griffin said, "At least now we know what he is. And maybe that's one of the things Eliot Ness hopes we'll find out."

12

KIRRA

Justice Plaza
Porte Franklyn

WEDNESDAY

Just before noon, an assistant in the commonwealth attorney's offices directed Savich, Pepper, and Griffin to Kirra Mandarian's small office on the third floor with its one stingy window overlooking the parking lot. Savich paused a moment in the doorway. She looked to be studying something on her computer, making notes on her iPad, utterly absorbed.

She looked very different from the young girl he'd seen in a photo on Leo Mandarian's official web page, Extreme Australian Adventures, smiling big into the camera, her teeth sparkling white against her tanned face, maybe sixteen. She was standing with her uncle atop a cliff, an awesome canyon behind them, wearing hiking shorts and stout boots. A backpack was slung over one shoulder and Leo's big muscled arm over the other, her hair in a ponytail sticking out the back of a ball cap. Leo Mandarian was tall, grinning as widely as she was, a strapping outdoorsman who looked like he could take on a bear.

Kirra Mandarian today looked the classic young professional in a suit and heels, her hair pulled back from her fine-boned face in a chignon. She had her uncle's vivid green eyes and dark brown hair with lighter highlights added by an expert hand. She wasn't tan now, her skin a smooth light cream.

Savich cleared his throat. "Ms. Mandarian, could you spare us a few minutes?"

Kirra looked up, nearly froze. She knew he'd be coming, but not yet, not right on the heels of his visit to Hailstock. She also knew it would be normal for him to suspect her since she'd been at the police station last night when Grissom was found. She had to make certain he wouldn't suspect her, ever. She started to rise when she realized she didn't have her shoes on and quickly slipped into them. She smiled. "Special Agent Savich! What an honor. I've seen you on TV." She added in her professional voice, "I see you're still unbowed after your visit with Mr. Hailstock."

A black brow went up.

She laughed. "This place is gossip central. Anything that happens here is common knowledge in less than two minutes. Isn't it the same in the Hoover Building?"

Savich said, "As a matter of fact it is."

"How can I help you?"

Savich introduced himself even though she already knew who he was, showed her his creds, and shook her hand.

Kirra actually studied his creds, smiled again at him. "It's a pleasure, Agent Savich. Believe me, and let me say it again, your fame precedes you."

She heard a snicker and saw the woman standing behind him. Savich turned to her. "This is Federal Prosecutor Pepper Jersik."

Kirra stared as the woman came around Agent Savich to

shake her hand—mid-to-late thirties and gloriously tall, the prosecutor looked like she could wrestle one of Uncle Leo's crocodiles and come out with a crocodile bag over her arm, not a hair out of place. Her hair was so blond it was nearly white, worn loose in soft waves around her face. Her blue eyes were bright with intelligence and something else—humor? Kirra admired her red suit and her matching red fingernails. She seemed to Kirra like a woman who faced life head-on and loved every minute of it.

Kirra said as she shook Ms. Jersik's hand, "Ms. Jersik, I have a feeling I'd always want to be on your side in court."

"What a nice thing to say." Pepper studied the serious young face. She had to admit to surprise. Could they be wrong? Could this lovely young woman really be Eliot Ness?

Savich introduced the other special agent, Griffin Hammersmith. This one was fair where Savich was dark, and as tall and well built. He looked dead serious. A fed with no sense of humor, a slave to his rules and procedures? Kirra said, "You've got a strange and wonderful last name, Agent Hammersmith."

"That's what my mom says." Griffin shook her hand. He found himself sketching her cheekbones in his mind, strong enough to laser glass. It was odd, but she reminded him of how his mother stuck her chin out when she was ready to go toe-to-toe about something, a sign Griffin's dad always respected. His mother was gorgeous, too, turned men's heads at fifty-five.

Ah, so Hammersmith does have a sense of humor. She wouldn't underestimate him, or any of them.

Like Savich, Pepper had seen how fit Kirra was in her photos in Australia. She'd felt the calluses on Kirra hand when she shook it. But was she strong enough to have carried Grissom to that railing by herself? She'd bet her son Grant's basketball on it. She said without preamble, "You look remarkably fit, Ms.

Mandarian. I read as a teenager you spent years trekking the outback with your uncle and extreme adventure groups. Do you still spend much time in the rough, hiking and camping? Or maybe attend a gym? Practice martial arts? Yes, I noticed the calluses."

Of course they know about Australia. If they looked on Uncle Leo's website, done research on her, they'd also know she broke her wrist when she was fourteen saving a blowhard college boy from falling into a sinkhole. No way to hide it was easy for her to deliver Grissom by herself. It didn't matter, it proved nothing.

Kirra shrugged. "Not as much time in the mountains as I'd like, except when my uncle Leo comes to visit. And yes, I practice martial arts, both Tae Kwon Do and karate. It was a necessity given where our team led groups. I even tried Krav Maga when I was in Australia, my uncle's favorite."

Griffin said, "I'll bet you were also taught plain old street fighting."

"Oh yes, one of our team members, Jacko is his name, taught me, beat me up endlessly. I'll never forget the time I managed to kick his feet out from under him. Just the one time, alas. Ms. Jersik, do you practice a martial art?"

Pepper nodded. "But you sound much better skilled. I know Agent Savich and Agent Hammersmith could wipe up the floor with me. With you? I wonder."

Kirra said, "I'll give you the name of my dojo, if you like."

Savich had looked about Kirra's small office, her one office chair, and said now, "Is there somewhere we can speak privately?"

"Of course. Follow me."

She led them across a large open space crisscrossed with work areas to a conference room with a battered wooden table and plain wooden chairs and closed the door. The noise from the assistants and clerks working outside, as loud as an old-fashioned newsroom, magically fell away. Kirra motioned for them to be seated, and said with a crooked smile and the absolute truth, "I wasn't expecting to see you so soon. I knew you'd want to meet with me, of course, since I was the affiant, but you caught me trying to justify a plea bargain to myself that barely hobbles over to the right side of justice. If you'd come a minute earlier, you'd have seen me throwing my shoe at the wall."

Pepper said, "We understand all too well since, as you already know, we met with Mr. Hailstock this morning."

Kirra arched an eyebrow. "We were all surprised you wanted to see him so soon. I'm guessing it was the highlight of your morning?"

Pepper said, straight-faced, "I have to say it ranked right up there. An interesting man, your Mr. Hailstock."

"Could you tell me what he had to say about the evidence against Grissom?"

Savich said, "Let's just say when we left, he was considering all the consequences we pointed out depending on whatever action he decides to take. It was fortunate you happened to be at the police station meeting with Lieutenant Thorpe last night when Mr. Grissom was hand delivered."

Exactly what had Jeter told them? Kirra hated that her heart was beating a mad tattoo. She cocked her head. "Oh, did Mr. Hailstock tell you that?"

"Lieutenant Thorpe did," Savich said easily. "As I said, it was fortunate you were there last night when Grissom was brought in."

"Yes, I was with Jeter in his office, not an uncommon occurrence. I was helping him with a case that just might have a chance of going to trial. And so, I was able to act as the affiant.

I guess you know Jeter and I have been friends for many years. Uncle Leo, too, of course."

Savich regarded her closely as he continued in a deep, smooth voice that invited confidences, "We received the same envelope of evidence yesterday, along with a letter to me personally signed with a pen name, I guess you'd call it, Eliot Ness. Clever name, all of us thought. Last night I got a text from him as well, warning us what to expect from Hailstock. I found myself wondering at his urgency." He paused then. "I would have thought Lieutenant Thorpe would have told you all that."

Griffin said, "Well, we were with Lieutenant Thorpe, and he was busy, it makes sense he wouldn't have had time to speak to Ms. Mandarian."

Was this some sort of routine the two agents played? The first tried to rattle her, then the second agent eased back? Cat and mouse. She could do this. "As you said, Agent Hammersmith, it makes sense I haven't seen him yet today. It's also been a madhouse around here. Almost everyone has a copy of the evidence against Grissom—I passed that out myself. Everyone's discussing it and trying to predict what Hailstock will do. As you can probably guess, no one is optimistic. Do you agree after your meeting with him?"

Griffin said, "So you gave out those copies to keep Hailstock from burying it? Make it impossible for him to sit on it for as long as it suits him? To force his hand if such a thing is possible?"

Kirra rolled her eyes. "Every attorney in this office knows he'll do whatever he wants regardless of what any of us say or think. If we recommend a case go to trial, he preaches about the taxpayer's money we'd have to spend, the long staff hours a lengthy trial would require, and, of course, the risk of losing. So I'm sure he is thinking about losing on Grissom; it would make

Hailstock look bad and he'll want to avoid that at all costs." She paused a moment, fiddled with her pen. "But if he holds off on Grissom, some of us would wonder if those would be his only reasons."

Griffin said, "Would you like to tell us what you believe the real reason would be, Ms. Mandarian?"

"Now that's a question that could cost me my job, Agent Hammersmith."

Pepper said, "Of course everyone wonders who Eliot Ness is, right?"

"Of course."

Savich said, "Do you think Ness is one of the lawyers here, Ms. Mandarian?"

"It seems like a real possibility. Or maybe it's a disillusioned cop who wants to put Grissom away and has dealt with Hailstock long enough to make sure evidence is bulletproof. But even then—"

Savich sat back in his chair, tapped his fingertips on the table, never looked away from her. "It strikes me what Ness did to Grissom was personal. He took a huge risk kidnapping him and hauling him to the police station. He could have simply mailed the evidence he collected." He shrugged. "All that accomplished was to humiliate him, but perhaps that was the point."

Griffin said, "A cop could have come out of the station when Ness was zip-tying Grissom to the railing. Yes, it has to be very personal."

Kirra kept her voice calm and professional. "I hadn't thought about it quite like that. Some of us thought it was revenge, maybe for someone Grissom was responsible for harming, maybe the murder of that paperboy, Josh Atwood. That might have made it personal, don't you think?"

Savich said, "Yes, I think it could. Jeter told us your own

parents were killed fourteen years ago. You were only twelve, I believe?"

"That's right."

"It must have been very difficult for you. There are some similarities, I suppose, with Josh Atwood's murder."

Kirra felt a jolt of alarm, quashed it. She had to be careful. She had to stay in control. She said easily, "Similarities? Not really. It was a very different time, very different circumstances. As I said, anyone would be angered by Josh's murder. Weren't you?"

Savich nodded. "Of course."

Kirra sat forward. She would bring it up before they did, get it out of the way. "Yes, my parents' murder was very hard. But I had Uncle Leo. He took me directly from the hospital back to Australia with him."

Griffin said, "And we understand Lieutenant Thorpe led the original investigative team."

Kirra forced her voice to remain calmand said in her no-nonsense prosecutor's voice, "That's right, but he was much more. If Jeter hadn't found me in the cave, I don't know what would have happened to me." Her chin went up. "And that makes both Jeter and my uncle my heroes. They're why I'm here.

"So tell me, how do you plan to proceed? As you know, my own hands are tied unless Mr. Hailstock personally instructs me to prepare for trial. Will you be looking into Josh Atwood's murder yourself? Our own police chief can only help informally since it's not in his jurisdiction."

"Yes, we will," Pepper said. "The possibility Bellison's chief of police actively suppressed evidence gives us that prerogative. I imagine Eliot Ness knew that quite well."

Kirra ignored that smooth bit of bait. "I'm relieved you're

going to be involved. All the attorneys in the Homicide Unit know who you are by now. Needless to say, all of them are rooting for the big bad feds to hold Mr. Hailstock's feet to the fire." She looked at her watch and rose, extended her hand to each of them. "I'm so sorry but I have a meeting with a defense attorney in five minutes. I hope I've been of help to you."

"Of course you have, Ms. Mandarian." Savich shook her hand. "Thank you."

Griffin looked down at the rough sketch he'd drawn of her on his notepad and back at her face again. Tough and smooth as silk. He thought she'd make a good special agent.

13

Home of Kahn Oliveras
Carnavan Heights
Porte Franklyn

WEDNESDAY NIGHT

Kirra whispered over and over, "Come on, Ryman, move under the light, just a step closer, so I can see you both together." She couldn't believe it when she saw Ryman pull into the Oliveras driveway. She quickly set up the parabolic mike she always carried in her turbocharged Audi and left her baby parked a half a block away. She'd set it up in a thick copse of oaks and maples set between the sprawling stately homes in Oliveras's wealthy neighborhood just outside of Porte Franklyn. She knew no one could see her, the properties were set too far apart. She'd been here listening two times before, hoping to overhear Kahn Oliveras's conversations, hoping another big crime lord who'd gone untouched for years would be careless. And tonight Ryman was here. What would this be about? Her heart pounding, Kirra aimed her mike carefully at the front door and turned on her recorder.

Oliveras opened the door, paused a moment to look out over his large front yard, and stepped onto out the porch. He looked back over his shoulder, probably checking to be sure his wife was nowhere close.

His deep accented voice came through clearly. "Well, is it done?"

"Misel is enjoying the flames of hell," Ryman said with a bark of laughter. "Let's go inside. I need a whiskey. Thirsty work."

Oliveras said, "Not this time, wife's in the kitchen. Believe me, she doesn't need to see you. You made it look like an accident?"

"Of course, everything went just as you wanted. The cops will determine Misel had too much to drink, lost control of his car, and went flying over Jaspar Cliff. Two hundred feet down."

Kirra was so shocked she jumped and almost dropped her cell phone. She checked to be sure the recorder was still running. Ryman Grissom had just murdered Misha Misel, Oliveras's accountant? She didn't know much about Misel, only that he must have been helping to doctor Oliveras's books for him. What had he done to have Oliveras want him killed? He'd probably wanted a bigger cut.

Ryman said, "I was hoping for an explosion but nothing like that happened."

"That's only in the movies. Did you go down and check?"

"No, no need, the car struck the cliffside at least three times before landing bottom-up on a pile of boulders, breaking apart, parts flying everywhere. Don't worry, no one could survive it. A pity, his mistress was with him, a pretty girl, dancer at Pillys."

"How long before they're found, I wonder?"

Ryman laughed. "Who knows? A hiker might spot the wreck in a month or two. Don't worry. Misel is done and gone."

"Good. The bastard deserved it, threatening me. I thought he was smarter than that. It's not like I didn't pay him very well, the fool. There's no one to report him missing, except

Ewing."

Ryman said, "Ewing will be a piece of cake. I'll take her up to Green Hills National Park, bury her deep enough no one will ever find her." She heard his fingers snap. "She'd be gone. Like she just picked up and left."

Oliveras reached into his pocket, pulled out a fat envelope, and handed it to Ryman, who tucked it in his jacket pocket. "No, don't kill her, not yet. I want you to go over to Ewing's house, tonight. Tell her she's my accountant now, she'll be doing all of it. She won't be seeing Misel anymore. She won't report him missing. Make my job offer to her. If she doesn't accept, then you can kill her, and we'll make other plans. You clear on that?"

"Not a problem. Consider it done. Accept or join her former boss."

"Good. Tell me how your father's handling this situation."

As the men spoke, Kirra texted Jeter, reported the murder of Misha Misel. She started to text about the girlfriend when Grissom whirled around and looked up. "What was that? I heard something. Over there, in the trees! Someone's watching us!"

Kirra grabbed the parabolic mike and ran all out, crashing through the thick trees, back to the road. She dropped her cell phone, heard it slam against a rock in the bushes. She felt around but couldn't find it. Frantic, she fell to her knees, swept her hands through the leaves and the undergrowth. She couldn't leave without the phone, everything was on it, all the proof she needed to send both Oliveras and Ryman to prison. She heard Ryman Grissom yelling as he ran toward the trees, toward her. He fired two shots from a distance, then two more, from closer this time. *No phone, no phone.* She had no choice, she ran. Kirra looked over her shoulder back to where she'd dropped her phone, memorizing its location. She ran to her Audi, threw the parabolic mike in the passenger seat, and jumped in. She heard another gunshot and floored it. She saw Ryman Grissom burst out of the trees in her rearview, his gun raised, but he didn't fire again, she was too far away. Even if he ran, it would take him time to get back to his own car. She was safe.

Kirra was nearly home before her heart stopped its wild tattoo. She took a deep breath when the garage door closed behind her and locked into place. She pressed her forehead against the steering wheel. Too close, it had been way too close. She couldn't get her head around what had almost happened. How had Grissom known she was there? What had he heard? Her texting Jeter on her burner phone? Not even a bat could have heard that. Had he seen light reflected off her parabolic mike? Maybe, maybe, there was a half-moon, clouds off and on. But Grissom had heard or seen something. Grissom had also seen her Audi when he'd come out of the trees. Had he caught her license plate? No, that was impossible, she was too far away.

But she'd failed. She'd known who and what Ryman Grissom was, but she hadn't known he worked for Oliveras as well as his own father. She'd been lucky enough to overhear him admitting he'd murdered two people. But without her cell with its recording, she had no proof. She knew Jeter would question both Ryman and Oliveras, but it wasn't enough, there wasn't proof.

She knew she had to go back and find her cell phone. No choice.

Kirra's garage connected to the kitchen, but she'd dead-bolted the kitchen lock. She was safe in her garage, but now she'd have to open the garage door again and go outside, enter through the front door. She laughed at herself. Idiot. She hated she was afraid, her heart still pounding. Bless Jacko, he'd taught her to fight, and she practiced at Master Su's dojo, practiced religiously three days a week. And here she was, sweating with the fear of going outside. Kirra banged her fist on the steering wheel, disgusted with herself.

She walked fast from the garage around to the front door, quickly slid the dead bolt into place when she got inside, and leaned against the door. She turned on the lights, walked to her kitchen and pulled a bottle of her favorite chardonnay out of the fridge. She walked back to her living room, sat down on her red velvet Victorian love seat, and slugged down half a glass. Kirra closed her eyes, tried to remember everything she'd heard them say. Okay, she could do this. She opened her laptop and got to work. She typed everything the two men had said to the best of her memory. Then she went online. It didn't take her long to find the name of Misel's girlfriend at *Pillys*. Lulu had a Facebook page. She was blond, very pretty, built, and only twenty-two years old, and now she was dead. Kirra looked at the half-dozen photos Lulu had posted together with Misha Misel. She discovered after only a bit more research Lulu's real name was Nancy Jance of Vandenville, Ohio. She then punched up Misel's accountancy firm's website, saw his assistant's name was Corinne Ewing.

Kirra pulled out another burner cell phone and texted Jeter again.

OLIVERAS PAID RYMAN GRISSOM TO KILL MISEL. GRISSOM RAN HIS CAR OVER THE JASPAR CLIFF. WITH MISEL WAS HIS YOUNG GIRLFRIEND, LULU, AKA NANCY JANCE. CORINNE EWING, MISEL'S ASSISTANT, MAY BE NEXT. RYMAN GRISSOM'S ON HIS WAY TO OFFER HER MISEL'S JOB. IF SHE REFUSES, OLIVERAS TOLD HIM TO KILL HER. HURRY. WILL TEXT FURTHER DETAILS. SORRY, NO DEFINITIVE PROOF. YOU'VE GOT TO MOVE FAST. ELIOT NESS.

She read over what she'd written then added what she'd remembered of the men's conversation, pressed send. She smashed the burner and tossed it in the trash. There was nothing more she could do tonight.

A least she might have saved Ewing's life. Jeter was good. She hoped he'd be able to finesse Ewing into rolling on Oliveras. She'd been complicit, so cutting a deal, handing the books she still had access to over to the police would be to her benefit. Maybe Jeter could swing witness protection for her. If anyone could make it happen, it was Jeter.

Kirra pulled on her flannel pajamas and a pair of thick socks, turned on her fireplace, and curled up on her love seat with a cup of black tea. What a night. One thing she now knew for certain, Ryman Grissom was as big a monster as his daddy.

Tomorrow she'd go back and find her cell phone. She knew there'd be no more conversations between the two men for her to record. Oliveras and Ryman would never be that careless again. The cell phone and everything on it might be her only chance to be sure they'd join Ryman's father in prison.

14

Savich House
Georgetown
Washington, D.C.

WEDNESDAY EVENING

Thanks to very vocal demands for pizza from Cal and Gage Hunt, age four, and Sean, age five and a half, with Emma smiling benevolently in agreement, three now-empty pizza boxes were stacked on the coffee table in the Savich living room.

Molly and Ramsey Hunt sat side by side on the sofa, leaning into each other. Molly Hunt yawned, slapped her hand over her mouth. "Oh dear, excuse me. It isn't even that late for us. I think that wonderful pizza brought it on."

Ramsey hugged his wife closer. "I'm close to the edge myself. Look at the little heathens, still hyper, loud and happy. I was hoping all that pizza in their bellies would have them stretched out on the floor sleeping by now, talk about unwarranted optimism." They looked over to see Emma trying to supervise a loud and vicious battle between Dr. Whimsy and the evil Major Killjoy in their Lego village, no less than world domination in the balance. They knew Emma had been torn about overseeing the children or sidling up to the grown-ups since she was twelve now, but when her little brothers yelled out for her, she succumbed and got down on the floor with the twins and Sean and organized their game, a longtime habit. Sean announced he would help her take care of the twins and show them what was what since he was, after all, more than a year and a half older, and he knew lots of stuff they didn't. Kindhearted Emma solemnly told him she appreciated his help, which made Sean beam at her.

Emma wondered if her parents and Uncle Dillon and Aunt Sherlock would be discussing the man who'd attacked her at Davies Hall three weeks ago. But maybe not tonight; everyone was too tired, except the twins, of course. She heard her mom telling them about the sea lion they called Louey, who came by and barked up from the base of the cliff below them off San Francisco Bay every evening, hoping for another bucket of left-overs from Chad's fish farm.

She imagined Uncle Dillon and Aunt Sherlock already knew everything that had happened at Davies Hall. Even thinking about that terrifying few minutes still made Emma shake in reaction, until she made herself stiffen up and focus, just like she'd managed to do that afternoon. She'd kicked him, she'd tasered him. She'd beat him, put him on the ground. She shouldn't ever forget that. Still, she wished she didn't some-times feel that fear rolling around like a peach pit in her belly.

"Time to get ourselves to bed," Ramsey said as he gave Molly his hand.

Molly called out, "Emma? Are you ready to call it a night? Don't forget, you have your first practice with the orchestra tomorrow."

Emma nodded, told the twins it was bedtime, time to go back to their amazing beds at the Hay Adams. She was met with loud protests, then, predictably, louder yawns.

Sherlock watched Emma herd the boys, Sean beside her, helping them fetch their jackets. Unlike her mom who wore her red hair clipped behind her ears, Emma wore her thick dark brown hair, nearly the same color as her father's, in a fat French braid. She had her mother's eyes, only a lighter blue, nearly the same shade as Sherlock's, and clear white skin, her mother's dimples on each side of her mouth. She was wearing jeans, sneakers, and a San Francisco 49ers sweatshirt. People would look at Emma Hunt and see an attractive preteen, and no one would guess she was a prodigy.

Sherlock said to Ramsey and Molly, "We haven't seen Emma for six months and she's at least two inches taller and even more beautiful. And her hands, those perfect long fingers. You guys must be bursting with pride. She's amazing, so patient with the twins and Sean."

"Nah," Ramsey said, grinning. "It's the same ole, same ole. We're used to it."

Savich said, "She'll be taller than you, Molly."

"She nearly is already. She's always demanding to stand next to me on Saturday mornings so Ramsey can measure us."

As Emma shrugged into her leather jacket, she looked toward Sherlock's piano. Sherlock said, "You'll have to tell me if you like playing their Steinway more than mine. I met the Kennedy Center's music director, Gianandrea Noseda, last year, a charming man and a tremendous talent. I bet my top hat he'll adore you. Do you know who'll be conducting the Chopin Retrospective?"

Emma's voice was reverent. "Leonard Slatkin. I couldn't believe it when Mr. Slatkin actually called me. He told me he was looking forward to working with me—me!" She swallowed. "I don't want to disappoint him but—"

Sherlock said matter-of-factly, "Are you well prepared?"

"Oh yes, but—"

"Do you love the music you'll be playing?"

"Yes, but it'll be a new piano and—"

"Do you like giving people a chance to hear that music you love?"

"Of course, but—"

"No more buts for you, Emma. No doubt in my mind you'll be splendid, you've checked all the boxes. You probably won't be able to hear me because of all the other loud clapping. I'm thinking two encores, maybe three. Now, I understand there'll be one other young musician, an Italian boy?"

Emma's eyes sparkled, no missing it. "His name is Vincenzo Rossi. He grew up in Corsico, a suburb of Milan. They call it a commune in Italy. He wanted me to call him Vinnie, he thinks that's really cool, makes him sound like an American gangster. I told him absolutely not, his full name is far more professional and it rolls off my tongue so he's got to stay Vincenzo." She shot her dad a look. "We traded selfies. He's taller than me, and dark like Uncle Dillon and Dad."

Ramsey tried to keep his expression impassive, but Savich saw a flash of alarm. A daughter on the verge of being a teenager. He said, calm as a judge, which he was, "Selfies are okay, but nothing more, Em, not for at least fifteen years."

Emma laughed. "Sure, Dad, at least fifteen years. I didn't tell you Vincenzo's studied with Madame Berlusconi since he was five years old. She's as amazing as Mrs. Mayhew; both of them knew all the greats and they could play everything."

Up went Emma's chin. "We've been texting each other for the past three months. Vincenzo's played several times at La Scala in Milan. He can't shut up about the La Scala orchestra conductor, Riccardo Chailly; he worships him, says he's the best in the world and of course I tell him that's not true, it's Esa-Pekka Salonen in San Francisco."

Ramsey said to Savich and Sherlock, "Vincenzo and his

parents got here a couple of days ago. They're sightseeing. Emma, you said Vincenzo's still hoping the president will come to our concert."

"I told him fat chance."

Molly said, "We're having dinner with the Rossis Friday night after Emma's and Vincenzo's performances. That way none of us will be gnawing off our fingernails. We'll all be relaxed."

Ramsey laughed. "We'll be giddy with pride and champagne."

Sherlock said, "Emma, how do you and Vincenzo communicate?"

"He speaks fairly good English and I have a translator app on my phone. He's taught me some Italian and laughs at my pronunciation. I laugh at his English. When he speaks English, it sounds like he's nearly singing, kind of like Andrea Bocelli." Emma raised her chin again, just like Ramsey. "I'm six months younger than Vincenzo."

Molly smiled at Ramsey, who looked pained.

Sean materialized at Emma's elbow. "Who is this Vincenzo, Emma? You don't want him for a special friend, do you? Instead of me?"

Emma didn't hesitate. "Oh no, Sean, Vincenzo's what you'd call a colleague. My heart belongs to you." And the sweet girl gave him a hug.

Sean hugged her back, gave her a happy smile.

Savich said quietly, his eyes on Sean, "Emma, you are one of the kindest people I've ever met."

Emma gave him a blazing smile. "Maybe Sean will grow up to be an FBI agent like you, Uncle Dillon, and he'll protect me his whole life from—" Her voice fell off a cliff.

"—from any jealous pianist," Savich finished.

The nameless man in San Francisco slithered right into the middle of the living room.

Molly gave her daughter a hug. "Imagine Sean an FBI agent, but he could also have some form of his father's talent." She turned a moment to look at the painting above the mantel. "I love that work. Your grandmother was amazing, Dillon. You whittle and your sister is a political cartoonist. Emma, it's always fun to think and wonder and make plans about the future even if it's always possible things never turn out the way you think they might."

Ramsey looked down at his watch. "Good grief, it's late. Come on, troops, time to cash out."

Sherlock kissed Emma on the forehead, studied her a moment. "Goodness, you're going to be as tall as your mama by June."

Emma grinned. "I'm shooting for May."

Cal and Gage were both leaning into their father's legs, barely on their feet. He reached down, picked them up, one in each arm. Cal said against his father's cheek, "What was Mommy saying to Emmie?"

Ramsey said, "I'll tell you next time you beat me at basketball."

Cal nodded, yawned. "Okay, Dad, but you've got to lift me closer to the net."

Sean, pressed against Savich's side, called out, "Papa and I play horse—he calls it pony, but that's okay. I beat him sometimes. Well, maybe."

Amid laughter and more yawns, and Cal and Gage's slurred kid protests, the Hunt family left to drive to the Hay Adams Hotel.

After the Hunts had departed, Savich gently pushed a thick curl back behind Sherlock's ear. He kissed the end of her nose, then picked up their son. ."I saw you helping Cal and Gage. Well done, Sean. You ready for bed?"

Astro raced over on stubby legs, barked up at Sherlock.

She hauled up the wriggling dog in her arms, hugged him, and got her face washed. "Don't worry, Sean, I'll bring mighty dog. You can listen to him snore."

When Sean and Astro were finally down and out after Savich sang "Amazing Grace" three times, he climbed into bed, pulled Sherlock into his arms, and said quietly, "When Ramsey and I were in the kitchen, he filled me in on the details about Emma's stalker or whatever he is."

"Molly told me stuff, too, when we were sure Emma wasn't listening. Tell me what Ramsey said."

"Most of it we already knew. Three weeks ago, Emma was alone in Davies Hall after a practice session with Dr. Reisner when the man came to take her." He told Sherlock about Emma's bravery and poise, how she kept it together. "She came out the winner. I thought Ramsey would lose it when he told me what Emma said that day, that maybe it was her own fault. He and Molly told her the only thing she'd ever done wrong was letting the twins eat ice cream with her at midnight. They called her psychologist, scheduled a session with her the following day. She's okay now, seems balanced again, and optimistic and very excited about playing at Kennedy Center. Do you know, I doubt it ever occurred to this man that his target—only a girl kid, after all—wouldn't just fold, maybe burst into tears and beg, certainly not she'd fight him and beat him up." He paused. "I'd say Ramsey nearly burst with pride. I wish I could have seen her in action."

Sherlock wanted to hit something every time she thought about it. "Molly was proud as punch too. She told me the psychologist said Emma was getting it all out, the fears and doubts, the child's self-blame. But Emma's also had several nightmares again about what Father Sonny did to her six years ago. Thankfully they've stopped." She brightened. "Emma's debut at Kennedy Center is just the thing for her . . . well, performing and Vincenzo." Sherlock wiggled her eyebrows. "I think he's her first crush."

"It's good timing, both the performance and Vincenzo. Did you see Ramsey's face when Emma talked about him?" Savich couldn't help it, he laughed.

"I wonder what you'd do if you had a teenage daughter?"

"Don't ask. It's too terrifying. The thought of Sean as a teenager is enough to make me stutter."

Sherlock settled in, laid her palm over his heart. "Virginia Trolley assigned a woman officer to follow Emma whenever she left the house without Molly and Ramsey with her up until they left San Francisco this morning."

He kissed her ear, breathed in the light rose scent of her hair. "They've had no luck finding the man in the brown coat again. Ramsey said if Virginia hasn't found him by the time they're scheduled to go back to San Francisco, they might take her to Molly's father in Chicago."

Sherlock sighed. "Well, Mason Lord would keep her safe, for sure. Molly thinks it's a good idea. She told me her father's changed quite a bit over the years toward her and the family. He gives the kids great Christmas and birthday presents. But of course she'll never forget Emma wouldn't have been abducted six years ago if she wasn't Mason Lord's granddaughter. Odd, but Molly really doesn't mind he's a criminal kingpin. It's amazing, he's flourishing. As for Ramsey, he only shakes his head."

She raised herself up on her elbow, looked down at Savich in the dim light of the half-moon shining in through the bedroom window. "I think it might be smart for me to take some time off, stay close to Emma while the Hunts are here, be an extra set of eyes for them. At least they'll be more at ease. You know as well as I do there's no guarantee the man didn't follow them here to D.C."

He liked it. "You'll be our ace in the hole."

15

SAVICH

Hoover Building

THURSDAY

Savich's cell rang at eight A.M. the following morning as he turned into his parking slot in the Hoover Building garage.

"Savich, Jeter Thorpe. I don't suppose you've heard what's happened here in Porte Franklyn?"

"No, I'm just arriving at the Hoover Building. My boy tried to sprain his ankle dashing down the stairs this morning. I wrapped him in an ACE bandage so he could show it off to the other kids. Don't tell me Eliot Ness has struck again? So soon?"

Jeter said, "I wish that was all of it. Yes, Eliot Ness is back to her surveillance, she texted me twice last night. Ryman Grissom murdered two people, ran them off the road and over a local cliff. There's more, much more. I'm emailing you her best recollections of Kahn Oliveras and Ryman Grissom's conversation."

A couple minutes later, Savich said, "I got the email and read it."

"She used a burner phone, of course. By the time I got to

the crash site at two A.M. I got another text from her. It says she dropped her cell phone when Ryman saw her and chased her, so we don't have a recording. I swear I could see Kirra cursing when she texted me." He paused, sighed. "I didn't want to believe Kirra was Eliot Ness, but now, even though I hate it, I have to accept it's true. I'll tell you, Savich, I'm scared for her. She could get herself killed. I know I promised not to confront her, to try to talk her out of this, but she hasn't stopped and that scares the crap out of me. You know what these people are capable of. She's putting herself in real danger."

"Protect her, Jeter. Have one of your people follow her, see where she goes, who she sees, jump in if she's in trouble. It's got to be someone you trust to keep his mouth shut. But she can't know that you know. It's not that I believe she'll confess what she's been doing to you, I don't think she will. Can you imagine if it came out what it would do to the validity of Grissom's case, given she's a prosecutor in Porte Franklyn?"

"Doesn't bear thinking about. Now, a protector, that's a good idea. I'll put Hendricks on her, he's very good and I trust him to keep it quiet. Of course, Kirra's good, too. She told me once she had a race car driver boyfriend in college and he taught her all the tricks. So if she spots Hendricks, she could probably ditch him without much difficulty. She also seems to be able to look in all directions at once, like the lizards do in the outback, the only way to survive, she told me. I still don't like it. I'd like to put her on a plane back to Australia."

Savich said slowly, "I have a feeling she'll close this down very soon now."

Jeter heaved out a sigh. "I know she'll go back after her cell phone next. Probably today. At least Oliveras doesn't know she dropped it."

Savich said, "Back to Misha Misel. It's got to all go back to

Oliveras's books Misel was in charge of. He probably knew exactly what Oliveras brings in on a weekly basis. Misel must have stolen from Oliveras or demanded more money. Whatever he did, Oliveras ordered Ryman to murder him for it. The poor girl with Misel was collateral damage."

"Yes, that's what we figure. There also was another murder last night, Corinne Ewing, Misel's assistant. It was the middle of the night when we recovered both bodies from the wreck at the bottom of Jaspar Cliff. I left as soon as I could and drove to Ewing's house. I didn't play nice. I told her Misel and his girlfriend had been murdered by Oliveras and she was in danger. She refused to talk to me, said she'd call her lawyer if I kept after her. But she acted nervous, on edge, didn't seem to care at all about her boss, Misel. I realized Ryman Grissom had already been there and intimidated her, doubtless made her think she'd be safe if she stayed on as his accountant and kept her mouth shut. I told her not to believe it, that she could be next. I was ready to talk to her about immunity and witness protection, but she again threatened me with her lawyer. I again stressed her vulnerability given the murder of her boss. Then, like a fool, I decided to wait a few hours, let her stew and think it over, then I'd have her brought to the station. It was the wrong decision, Savich. I should have hauled her off then and there, with or without her consent. I realized once Oliveras convinced himself Eliot Ness had been there, listening, recording, there was no way he could trust Ewing. He had to eliminate her. She was too much of a risk.

"The only smart decision I made was to assign Foxxe, my newest detective, to park across the street from her house to make sure she'd be safe until I had her brought in.

"I got a call from Foxxe about four in the morning. He hadn't seen anyone near her house, or her neighborhood, for that matter, when he made his rounds. He was in his car when he heard two gunshots. He ran to the front door of Ewing's house, but when he heard an engine start, he ran back out into the street, saw a Chevy Camaro roar away. Foxxe pulled out his cell and snapped photos of the car. Then he went inside."

"Someone managed to get into the back of the house?"

"Yeah, broke in through the kitchen door. The intruder didn't count on Ewing being awake, much less owning a gun. It looks like Ewing heard him, confronted him, and shot him before he shot her dead. There was blood splatter in two places, which means we've got the assailant's blood and DNA."

He paused, and said, "She shouldn't be dead, Savich. It was my fault."

"Did you ID the Camaro?"

"Foxxe's photos, after we cleaned them up, showed it was bright cherry red. We got the license plate."

Savich said as he walked to the stairs, "I shouldn't be surprised Ryman Grissom worked for Oliveras as well as his father."

"Word is Ryman's got what you'd call a large lifestyle, starting with his penthouse apartment in a swank downtown Porte Franklyn skyscraper. He's also got three ex-wives and his children, a boy by each wife. He's got them all in private school. He likes to club and be seen with beautiful women on his arm. Does his father mind his earning some money from Oliveras? Evidently not.

"I'm having both Oliveras and Ryman Grissom picked up right now for questioning. I'm sure they'll have a fleet of lawyers with them. I wondered if you, Griffin, and Pepper want to come out again to Porte Franklyn?"

Savich knew Sherlock didn't need him while she watched Emma, and there was nothing hot going on in the unit his people couldn't deal with. "Misel and Ewing were involved in a criminal conspiracy with Oliveras to conceal his crimes. I'd be willing to bet that includes federal crimes as well. I'll give Pepper a call, see if she wants to pay you another visit. And yes, Griffin will want in, I'm sure."

"Ah, did you know Pepper has a kid, a teenage boy?"

"Yes, his name is Grant and he's quite a basketball player. How did you know?"

A moment of silence, then Jeter said, "We've—Pepper and I—have spoken a couple of times since yesterday. She told me she's divorced and has sole custody of Grant. She said Grant's coach thinks he might be good enough to play professionally someday. She's fine with that. Her only proviso is he has to play for Kentucky first, get his four-year degree."

"You're a fast worker, Jeter."

He laughed. "Nah, she called me first."

Savich said, "Thanks for keeping me informed. I'll let you know when to expect us, and whether Pepper will be along," and he punched off.

16

SHERLOCK

Kennedy Center

THURSDAY MORNING

Emma sat straight and tall at the glossy black Steinway. The orchestra was arranged in a horseshoe around her on the stage, an overhead spotlight making her beautiful dark hair glisten. Today for rehearsals her mother had braided her long hair in a thick fishbone braid, intricate and perfect. Emma was wearing a blue sweater and black pants and the simple locket Ramsey had given her for her birthday, with his photo with the twins on one side and she and Molly on the other. She was leaning slightly forward, her attention not really on her fingers, but on the sound of the music, as if she felt each note pulse through her body. She looked fierce. The conductor Mr. Slatkin stood quietly as she played, never looking away from her.

Sherlock sat in the rear orchestra near the back of the huge Kennedy Center concert hall listening to Emma's fingers fly over the Steinway's keys. She was playing Chopin's Étude, No. 5, known as the black key étude, one of Sherlock's favorites. Sherlock wondered if she'd looked as fierce as Emma when she'd played that étude so many years ago. She remembered the immense energy she felt, remembered how her heart galloped when her own fingers flew over the keys. She wouldn't want to try it now and embarrass herself, not after so many years of too little practice.

The concert hall acoustics were amazing, whether you sat center front, in the boxes lining the vast hall, or in the last seat in the second tier. From where she was sitting, Sherlock saw the other young prodigy and Emma's new friend, Vincenzo Rossi, standing in the wings, his eyes on Emma, listening along with her. He was a handsome boy, with a mop of black hair and dark eyes, perfect for Emma's first crush. Like Emma, he'd dressed up a bit, probably forced to by his parents, in black chinos and a dark green sweater. Not sneakers, but polished boots on his feet. Sherlock couldn't wait to hear him play. She settled in, listening to Emma's music, playing along with her as she always did when listening to other musicians.

Sherlock heard a door behind her quietly open, saw a brief beam of light. She turned to see someone quietly close the door and slip into the dim-lit rear orchestra. She rose slowly and stepped into the aisle, her hand on her Glock clipped at her waist. She watched the figure shrug out of a jacket under a narrow beam of light and saw it was a woman, her eyes on Emma, someone who worked here and wanted to listen to Emma play.

Sherlock caught the woman's eye and nodded, turned her attention back to the stage. Emma finished the Chopin Étude, paused a moment as many musicians did, her hands quiet over the keys, getting centered and calm again. She rose and looked at Slatkin. Both he and the orchestra applauded loudly, with a lone whistle from a viola player.

Emma gave them a beautiful kid smile and a little bow. She turned to give Vincenzo a wave as he walked onto the stage. He was tall for his age, gangly, on the verge of growing into manhood, already handsome as sin.

Slatkin called out, "Thank you, Emma. You gave us Chopin's heart. Now we will hear Vincenzo playing Chopin's Étude in C Major." He smiled at Vincenzo, nodded. Vincenzo seated himself, moved the bench back because he was taller than Emma. He settled. He looked up at Emma, who stood in the wings where he'd stood and grinned. He looked back down at his hands and let his fingers fly. Neither he nor Emma were dramatic like some pianists, weaving back and forth on the piano bench, hands going up and down, distracting from the music, Sherlock had always believed.

When Vincenzo finished, he flashed Emma a big grin and rose. He bowed to the orchestra as they applauded. Mr. Slatkin thanked him, looked down at his Piaget watch. "We'll take a ten-minute break." He smiled at Emma. "Then, Emma, you and the orchestra will play the Piano Concerto no. 2."

Vincenzo and Emma walked down into the front orchestra section where their parents sat together, looking thrilled.

After a moment, Emma led Vincenzo to the back of the rear orchestra to where Sherlock sat. She was grinning madly. "Vincenzo, this is Special Agent Sherlock, she's FBI and she could have gone to Juilliard but she decided she'd rather catch bad guys. Now, tell the truth, did we play well, Aunt Sherlock?"

Sherlock cocked her head to one side, looking from one prodigy to the other, gave them a slow smile. "Forgive me. I'm still catching my breath, calming my racing heart. I never did play those études as beautifully as you two did. I was so pleased to listen to both of you." Both young people cocked their heads back at her, wondering if she meant it all.. Sherlock crossed her heart. "Listen, you two, I'm not your parents. I don't have to lie to you. Remember, I'm FBI. You were phenomenal."

Emma beamed and Vincenzo said in the lilting accent Emma liked so much, "*Grazie*, thank you, Special Agent. Forgive my English, it is not very good."

A few minutes later, Emma was back at the Steinway, ready to play Chopin's Piano Concerto no. 2 with the orchestra. It was a long piece, demanding and romantic, a test of courage and endurance. Sherlock knew Emma would do fine with it, had already played this concerto with the San Francisco Symphony Orchestra, just as Vincenzo had already played his Piano Concerto in F at La Scala the previous year.

The two talented youngsters took Sherlock back to her youth, to the endless hours of practice when she was their age, and the joy she'd felt when she'd executed a piece perfectly. She wondered for the first time in a very long time what her life would have been like if her sister hadn't been killed when Sherlock was still a teenager. The tragedy had changed her life and set her on a different path. And that different path had led her to Dillon. There was no contest.

Midway through the concerto, Sherlock snapped to attention when the back door cracked open again, sending a narrow shaft of light into the hall. She turned and saw a figure peering around the door, not coming into the hall, but standing silent, listening and watching. Another employee? Why didn't he or she come in? She stood and walked down the aisle, toward the door. As Emma's music filled the hall, the orchestra drums and trumpets sounding, Sherlock said quietly, "Come inside, why don't you?"

A face peered through the door. She saw opaque sunglasses, a head covered with a ball cap.

Sherlock raised her Glock, said only loud enough for the man to hear, "FBI. Come in through the door. Now."

He raised something to his mouth. A tube? Or was it a flute?

Was he part of the orchestra? She heard a hissing sound, felt a sharp stab in her neck. It was the last thing Sherlock saw or thought. She crumpled, struck the arm of a seat and fell onto her side in the aisle.

17

KIRRA

THURSDAY, LATE MORNING

Before Kirra left Justice Plaza, she called Oliveras's office in midtown Porte Franklyn and was told Mr. Oliveras wasn't available. Kirra grinned, punched off her burner cell. Mr. Oliveras wasn't available because he'd left for the police station to get grilled about the violent death of his accountant, Misha Misel, and Misel's girlfriend, Nancy Jance, and the murder of Misel's assistant, Corinne Ewing. Everyone in Justice Plaza knew about it. She wondered how Jeter would handle Oliveras and Ryman Grissom since they'd be flanked by their top-drawer lawyers. But she knew regardless of how Jeter went at them, he wouldn't get far because he didn't have any proof, except a tip from an overheard conversation by someone who wouldn't come forward. That was all on her, her fault because she'd dropped her blasted cell phone. When she'd heard Corinne Ewing had also been shot dead in the middle of the night, she'd finally made up her mind. She called her shared assistant, Julie, told her she'd be at home seeing to a personal matter, and left.

She had to find her cell phone. She reviewed her plan for

the umpteenth time. When she drove her Audi past Oliveras's property she saw a silver Miata in the driveway of the big house. Mrs. Oliveras's car? Probably. She drove a couple of hundred yards past the house and pulled over, close to where she'd parked before. She saw no one. The next huge home was a hundred yards farther up Thornton Road. She tucked her hair under a ball cap, pulled on the sneakers she kept in the back seat, and stepped out. The air was chilly, the sun making a valiant effort to be seen through building rain clouds. Kirra followed the trail of crushed leaves and broken twigs she'd left on her mad run through the thick oak and maple forest the night before. She stopped every few steps and listened, but she heard no human sounds, only birds, the trees rustling in the light breeze, a squirrel scurrying through the underbrush. When she knew she was close to where she'd dropped her cell, she slowed, careful to stay on the path she'd run last night. It had to be somewhere close. She'd never forget the sound of it crashing against a rock.

She'd thought finding it would be easy, but now she saw rocks everywhere, many of them hidden beneath leaves and vegetation. Her next cell phone wouldn't have a black casing, nope, it would be red, the brighter the better. She thought of calling her number, but she couldn't take the chance someone would hear. There, finally she spotted it, half hidden under the edge of a rock, its screen broken. As she leaned down to pick it up she heard heavy footsteps coming toward her and froze. A man called out, "Billy said there's a dark blue Audi parked up the road. It was a dark car last night, so maybe it's the same one." Another man said, "But why would he come back? Doesn't make any sense."

They were maybe thirty yards away from Kirra. She grabbed her cell, stepped away as quietly as she could, then ran all out back the way she came. When she burst out of the woods onto Thornton Road, she heard their footsteps behind her, coming fast. She dug in, ran as fast as she could to her Audi, fobbed the door open from ten feet away, and jumped inside. She screeched away so fast her head fell back against the headrest. *Thank you, turbocharger.*

Kirra looked back and saw the two men burst out of the woods, guns raised, close enough they'd see she was driving an Audi. They ran after her, stopped when they realized they weren't close enough to shoot at her. Her heart was pounding, she couldn't get spit in her mouth, but she was safe. They'd be able to describe the Audi to Oliveras, and they'd know it was the same car Ryman saw last night. At least she'd had the foresight to muddy up the license plate. At least she'd tucked her hair under the ball cap, and she knew she didn't run like a woman, Uncle Leo had seen to that. They might report they'd seen a man. Thank you, Uncle Leo.

She wondered why Oliveras had set guards. He couldn't have known she'd dropped her cell phone, or that she'd come back. Maybe they'd been there last night and she'd been lucky she missed them. Or more likely he was taking extra care now— smart of him—and had them patrolling the grounds. At least she had her cell phone, resting snuggly in her jeans pocket. She prayed the broken screen didn't mean the recordings were compromised. They had to still be playable. They had to.

Kirra let out a breath when she pulled into her garage. She said a prayer, pulled her cell phone out of her jeans pocket, and punched open the recorder. She heard static, then Oliveras's jumbled voice, "Is it done?," then only a high-pitched hum until she heard Ryman Grissom saying clearly, "Jaspar Cliff." There was no video that she could find.

For a moment, Kirra sat back in her car seat. She wanted to

scream and pound her fists on the steering wheel. At least she had their voices, and some of their words. Was it enough? It was a start, enough to raise questions, maybe enough for voice recognition. Eliot Ness could transfer the file to a burner phone and text it to Savich and Jeter. They'd tell her soon enough what they could do with it. But she couldn't drive her Audi anywhere for a while. She ordered an Uber to take her to a nearby car rental. Thirty minutes later she drove back home in a rented black RAV.

When she neared her condo, she saw a big honking black Ford F150 in her driveway, Jeter leaning negligently against the door, reading something on his cell. She pulled in behind him, wishing at that moment he was a thousand miles away. She climbed out, called, "What are you doing here? I hope you haven't been waiting long."

Jeter tried to calm himself. When Hendricks called him, told him Kirra was on the move, headed to Oliveras's house, he'd been scared to his boots, knew she'd gone after her cell phone. Hendricks had followed, called him to assure him she was safe. Jeter knew he wouldn't be convinced until he actually saw her in one piece. And here she was, smiling at him. He wanted to shout at her, shake her once or twice, tell her she'd been lucky today, but he couldn't, not after he'd promised Savich he'd keep his mouth shut.

He said, ignoring her question, "I tried to reach you at your office, but Julie said you were at home, she didn't know exactly why. So you've been dealing with getting a rental car?"

For a moment, her brain went perfectly blank. Her uncle Leo had taught her many things, but he hadn't taught her how to lie clean. "Yeah, my poor Audi, I had to take her to the garage. Pretty cool rental, don't you think?"

He said slowly, the way he started interviews with a suspect.

"I hope it isn't a big problem. Your Audi is still under warranty?"

"Yes. I think it's an alignment problem. Come in, Jeter, I'll get you a beer. It's past noon, right?"

He looked down at his watch. "I'm on duty, but maybe something else? I have some news for you."

Jeter looked again at the RAV SUV. She was afraid the men at Oliveras's property had seen the Audi and so she'd hidden it away fast. He remembered when he'd pinned down Hendricks, demanding every detail, he admitted she'd come running out of the woods like a bat out of hell, two men with guns after her, jumped back into her Audi, and hightailed it out of there faster than he could follow her. He'd asked Hendricks again, and for a third time, to keep it all under his hat. He wondered if she'd found her cell phone, if Eliot Ness would be texting him the recording that was on it.

Kirra unlocked the front door, waved him in, pointed to the living room through an arched doorway. "Have a seat, Jeter. I've got some iced tea." In her small kitchen, Kirra drew in a deep breath. Jeter knew her too well. He'd know something was off. Uncle Leo had always laughed at her when she'd tried to lie to him, though she'd practiced in the mirror. Of course, he knew her better than anyone in the world, even better than Jeter did. She'd thought about confiding in each of them, getting their advice, but she knew if she told Uncle Leo, he'd drop everything and fly over, make her stop. And if she involved Jeter, he'd be putting his career at risk if he helped her. So it was a no go. She had no one else. She was on her own.

Kirra popped the tabs on the cans of tea, handed Jeter his, and sat down opposite him on a lovely fake Chippendale chair she'd found at a flea market.

He watched her take a sip, wipe her mouth with the back

of her hand. "I still see you sometimes as a twelve-year-old kid, you know, skinny as a parking meter—you were so brave."

It nearly broke her. "T-thank you, Jeter. I remember holding on to you that night." She got herself together, set her can on a newspaper, and changed the subject. "I heard all about Misel and the poor girl with him before I left work. Everyone's talking about it. But not much about Corinne Ewing, the other woman who was killed. Have I got her name right?"

He nodded. "We got to the wreckage very quickly. Eliot Ness"—he looked up at her—"texted me Ewing might be next." He dropped his head, clinched his fist between his thighs. "It frosts me, Kirra. If only I'd brought her right in last night, kicking and screaming if necessary, it would have saved her life."

Kirra said, "Maybe in the short term, but before any trial Oliveras would have had her killed. You know that, Jeter."

"I would have protected her."

She stared at Jeter until he said, "Okay, even with the best people, it's tough to guarantee complete protection, but, Kirra, her murder is still my fault, it's squarely on my shoulders. The only smart thing I did was to assign Clint Foxxe to sit across the street from her house. Still, the killer got in the house and shot her. Foxxe was fast on his feet, he pulled out his cell, and snapped photos of the fleeing car. It was a cherry-red Camaro. Our techs sharpened them up enough we could make out the Virginia license plate. The car belongs to the mother of an ex-con named Aldo Springer."

Kirra let him brood a moment. "Tell me about Aldo Springer."

"He's a bad dude, recently released from Red Onion after spending a dime for attempted armed B&E. The owner dropped him with his gun and called 911. Now all we have to do is find him. I didn't tell you, but Ewing also had a gun. They shot each other, but his bullet found her heart. How badly is he hurt? I don't know but I don't want him dying. I want him to tell us Oliveras hired him."

"If he's still alive and driving that Camaro you should pick him up in short order."

"Nah, he's dumped the Camaro."

She desperately wanted him to leave, but Jeter took another sip of his tea, sat back. He said, "It seems to me Eliot Ness has more guts than brains. Did I tell you he dropped his cell phone at Oliveras's property last night? I hope he has enough sense not to go back for it."

Does he know? How? He can't know. "Yeah, that would be dangerous. But what if Eliot Ness did manage to get the cell phone? If what he says is true, the recordings on it could help convict Oliveras and Ryman of murder and conspiracy. We'd all love to see that." *Please leave, Jeter, come on, you've got places to go, right? Visit Aldo's mama, maybe?*

"I'd like to tell Eliot Ness he needs to stop all this before he gets himself killed. I think he's done enough, don't you?"

"Sure. Right. He's given us a lot."

"Actually, I came here to tell you something else, something big." He rubbed his big hands together.

"Come on, then, Jeter, you look like you're bursting at your seams. Tell me."

"Even with everything that's gone down in the last twelve hours, I had to smile. You won't believe what Hailstock's done."

Whatever Kirra wondered Jeter would say, that wasn't even close. She stared at him. "Hailstock? I'm expecting the worst, but I see you're grinning so it must be good. Lay it on me."

"Your boss, Alec Speers, said Hailstock swaggered into the Homicide Unit and announced to everyone present he'd contacted the Commonwealth of Virginia's attorney general, Susan Standish. Of course she'd heard all about Eliot Ness and

Grissom. Hailstock asked if she would like to take over the Grissom case directly because he, Hailstock, doesn't have the staff to handle such a complicated case. That's right. He threw your unit under the bus. The attorney general agreed, probably jumped at the chance for a shot at the lead in such a high-profile case and all that media coverage. So the prosecution is out of our hands, but the best thing about it is that it's now out of Hailstock's hands as well. Then Alec said Hailstock raised his fist in victory, expecting applause, and so Alec gave everyone the stink eye until hands were clapping."

Kirra said slowly, "I've got to admit Hailstock's surprised me. That was well played, very well played indeed. Now Hailstock's off the hook, tickled he's saved his office and Porte Franklyn's courts the cost of a complicated trial, and hoping the voters thank him for it. From what I've heard, Susan Standish and the commonwealth attorney general's office is good. I bet they'll cheer when they realize they won't have to work their butts off for a conviction. Nope, they've got a slam dunk." She shook her head, sighed. "Like you said, Hailstock threw the Homicide Unit under the bus, made us sound like a bunch of incompetent boobs, and that isn't so, but I'm philosophical. Standish will get the max sentence for Grissom and I know he'll die in prison." Another sigh. "Still I've got to admit, Jeter, I'd had loved to be second chair to Alec at Grissom's trial, it would have made my year. On the bright side, Hailstock won't have any further involvement with what happens to Grissom."

Jeter said, "I hope the bastard lives for decades."

Kirra said, "I hope, too, Standish can find the necessary proof to tie him to Hildy Atwood's and Josh Atwood's murders and make it part of their case. I'd sure like to see the Atwoods get some justice."

Jeter looked at his watch. "Gotta go. I want to oversee the

search for Aldo Springer. Hey, when we get him and he rolls over on Oliveras, you might get to prosecute him."

"Or maybe Hailstock will ship it off to Standish and she'll be having dreams of being elected governor." Kirra thought of her parents, of her father's painting that put Grissom junior and senior in her sights. They'd prosecute Grissom, and maybe Aldo Springer would give up Oliveras and they'd get a guilty verdict on him, too. But it wasn't enough. There was Ryman, and they had nothing on him except a garbled recording. It wasn't time yet for Elliot Ness to stop.

Jeter looked down at his watch. "Gotta go." He gave her a long look, laid his hand on her shoulder. "You be careful, Kirra, you hear me?"

She patted his arm. . "Of course. I'm always careful."

Jeter said, "I'm having dinner with Pepper Jersik tonight."

"What? Dinner with a federal prosecutor?"

He nodded. "I'm driving to Alexandria to her place. She lives with her son, Grant. She's making Cajun, jambalaya, her mother's recipe, she told me. Hey, I just might fall in love."

"You're moving fast here, Jeter. Hey, you want my advice on how to deal with a teenage boy?" *Why won't he just leave?* .

"Nah, got that wired. You know I've got half a dozen nephews, all of them hell-raisers. Even if Grant is taller than me, I'm more wily."

"Good luck. You've got lots of good miles in you yet. You look good, Jeter, you're still at your fighting weight, you've got a flat stomach, and you're useful. Go for it." She saluted him with her empty lemonade can.

All the while Jeter talked, he was watching her. She had the cell phone. She wanted him gone.

The instant Jeter left, Kirra leaned against the front door and closed her eyes. *Did Jeter suspect? No, he couldn't know, he couldn't.*

Kirra walked into her bedroom, her eyes going to her father's painting above her bed. "Thank you for the painting, Dad. Even though I haven't yet got the proof Grissom had you and Mom killed, he's still going to jail forever. Now fingers crossed I can find something more on my cell phone before I ship it off to Agent Savich for his FBI techs to work their magic."

She prayed hard as she punched up the video again, but there was still nothing, not at all. Even the FBI techs wouldn't find anything when there was nothing at all.

18

SHERLOCK

Washington Memorial Hospital

THURSDAY, LATE MORNING

When Sherlock opened her eyes, she didn't know where she was. She was lying flat on her back, but where? And where was Emma? Was she all right? She felt a spurt of panic, started to jerk up, but hands were holding her down. She blinked and stared up at Dillon. He leaned close. "No, hold still, sweetheart. You're in Washington Memorial, in a cubicle, lying on a gurney. You're okay, I promise. The doctor will agree with me, you'll see." He cupped her cheek with his warm hand. "I'm so happy to see your beautiful blue eyes looking up at me."

Her brain began to knit itself together. She'd seen the man raising a flute, no, not a flute—a tube—and she whispered, "I was too slow, Dillon. He shot me with a blowgun in the neck, didn't he? Oh no, is Emma all right?"

"Yes, she's fine. Don't worry. He didn't try for her, he ducked out after you went down."

"But how can you be here? You, Griffin, and Pepper were going to Porte Franklyn."

"Jeter will have things covered."

"How long have I been out?"

"Nearly an hour." During which time he'd held her hand and promised a world of good deeds if only she'd wake up and smile at him.

Once she felt more clearheaded, Sherlock looked around the small curtained-off cubicle. "I hate hospitals, Dillon, all the nasty smells and needles coming at you, looking for the slightest excuse to jab you. At least you're here with me, not some guy with a scalpel standing over me. When can we leave?"

"The doctor should be back soon. They don't even know you're awake yet. Be patient a while longer."

Sherlock closed her eyes a moment, said slowly, "The dart was obviously meant for Emma's neck. He didn't expect me to be there at the back of the hall. He didn't think anyone would be there with her except her family. I must have caught him when he'd just arrived, looking to see where he might find Emma unprotected. Maybe his plan was to catch her in the wings, maybe backstage in a dressing room. If he managed to put her down, how would he have gotten her out of Kennedy Center?"

"He had a plan, but what it was I haven't figured out yet."

"I just don't understand this. He can't be a child molester, Emma's too old. Could he be an obsessed fan? No, I can't buy that. We've got to find out what's going on here. At least now he knows Emma's being protected so maybe he'll take himself back to San Francisco."

He helped her sit up on the gurney, leaned down, and kissed her pale mouth. "Can you describe him to me?"

Her head was clearer now. She saw the man looking around the edge of the door, his eyes on the stage, on Emma. "I'd say he was in his forties, maybe fifties. He was wearing a heavy coat, dark, probably black, a ball cap without a logo on it, and opaque sunglasses. I couldn't see his hair below the cap, so maybe he didn't have any, or shaved his head, or tucked it all under the ball cap. It isn't much, Dillon, but it sounds like the same guy who stalked her at Davies Hall in San Francisco. He was fast with the blowgun, Dillon, and he was good." She sighed. "Who knows if it was even the same guy?"

"You stopped this one in any case. Well done."

"He was left handed."

"What?"

"He held the dart tube in his left hand. It's not much, but maybe it'll help." She felt a wave of dizziness and leaned back against his arm.

A man in a white coat walked into the cubicle some minutes later. Sherlock thought he looked young enough to still go to the junior prom. He smiled, pleased Sherlock was awake and sitting up. He introduced himself as Dr. Zugoni, gently probed her neck where the dart had punctured her skin, and asked her questions to be sure she was fully alert. He did a quick neurologic exam, whistling as he did so, a catchy tune Savich didn't recognize. Was it to keep himself awake?

Sherlock said, "Do you know what he shot me with?"

"Your tox screen is pending, but those darts usually have ketamine in them, a drug that's used for general anesthesia and in dart guns as an animal tranquilizer. Now that you're awake, Agent Savich, you can expect to be a bit unsteady on your feet for a while, but there shouldn't be any lasting effects."

Sherlock said, "We need to leave, Dr. Zugoni, find the man who did this and keep him from hurting anyone else. Please discharge me now, so I don't have to leave against medical advice."

He nodded, smiled. . "None of us would want that, Agent

Sherlock. Love your name. Your exam is normal. I'd prefer to keep you a few more hours, but the truth is you should be safe enough so long as you have the big guy around to catch you if you stumble. So if you promise not to sue me, I'll write your discharge order and we can all stay friends." He paused a moment, frowned at the tiny puncture mark in her neck. "You FBI agents sure lead interesting lives." He gave Sherlock a singularly sweet smile and a wave over his shoulder as he left the cubicle, his white coat flapping.

Thirty minutes later Savich helped Sherlock into the Porsche, fastened her seat belt, and looked into her eyes, now perfectly clear. "Welcome back," he said, and kissed her. He wasn't going to tell her he'd been so scared he'd nearly wrecked the Porsche getting to the Kennedy Center.

He slid into the driver's side, pressed the start button, and his baby roared to life. As he turned out of the hospital parking lot into traffic, Sherlock said, "Please tell me Emma doesn't know."

"Sorry, but yes, she knows. The Italian boy she's sharing the spotlight with—Vincenzo Rossi—told her when she finished the Chopin concerto with the orchestra. It's thanks to Ramsey I got here so quickly. He told me he turned around every couple of minutes to check the doors into the concert hall, just to check, couldn't help himself, even though he knew you were there. He saw the man, saw you go down. He kept it together, excused himself. He made sure you were breathing normally and called 911, then me. I asked him to keep everything as quiet as he could including the EMTs' arrival and departure with you on a gurney."

Savich grinned at her. "Ramsey told me Emma said, and I

quote 'He must have surprised Sherlock or she'd have wiped up the floor with him.' Ramsey and Molly were scared spitless for you. All in all, we were lucky. I called Ramsey from the hospital. He told me no one at Kennedy Center knows exactly what happened to you, except Molly and Emma and Vincenzo's family, only that Ramsey called an ambulance for a family friend."

"Good. If they keep it quiet, maybe there won't be any press. I wonder how Vincenzo and his family are dealing with it? The stories they'll tell about the United States when they get back to Italy."

."As in the capital of America as the wild, wild West? Could be. Ramsey and Molly can tell us what the Rossis had to say when we see them tonight. Ramsey and his family will be coming to our house tonight to talk things over, if you're up for it. And yes, we'll be talking with Emma, too."

"Dillon, this guy, whoever he is, he's motivated. Like I said, no way he's a child molester, this is way beyond that. It's like he's obsessed, but why? With what?"

"No way to know, but we'll find out."

Sherlock leaned her head against the neck rest. "I keep going back to Father Sonny and his kidnapping of Emma when she was just a little kid, and his psycho mom, Charlene. But Dillon, they're both dead, and Emma had nothing to do with either Father Sonny's or Charlene's deaths. If it's someone after revenge for them, why not come after me? I was the one who shot Charlene."

"You know people don't need logic to hate and to act on hate. We could be dealing with a very disturbed person here, Sherlock, whether it's obsession or revenge." He paused. "I think we're dealing with an entirely different motive."

"Like kidnapping Emma for ransom? But Ramsey isn't rich."

"No, but Mason Lord is."

She huffed out a breath. Of course, Molly's father again, Emma's grandfather. "Anyone who thinks they can blackmail him to get Emma back is either stupid or has a death wish. When Mason Lord finds out what's just happened, I don't doubt we'll be dealing with him, too."

"The man who shot me with the dart, Dillon, I described him to you. I just remembered there were little sparkles on the rims of his opaque sunglasses, right next to the lenses, probably CZ's or just fakes. Why would a man have sparkles on his sunglasses?"

"Okay, two more pieces for Ramsey to pass along to Virginia. If we're lucky, he's worn them before."

"Dillon, don't take me home. My head's on straight now. Drop me off at Kennedy Center. I want to check the video footage. He can't have missed all the cameras. My car's there, too. I'll get back to the Hoover, and check the street cams in the area from there. I'll call Ben Raven at Metro to make sure we're not overlapping."

He gave her a long look, saw she was determined. He slowly nodded. "Okay, but only if you promise to get yourself home if you feel dizzy, okay?"

"Of course."

When she unfastened her seat belt in front of Kennedy Center, Savich gave Sherlock a kiss, saw her eyes were clear, and slowly nodded. "Don't forget, no overdoing. Let me know if you get a good look at him on the video. And Ben, of course. I'll ask Shirley to keep an eye on you when you get back to the unit. That means she'll be checking on you every five minutes."

She sighed. "Yes, I know. Okay."

Sherlock stood a moment watching the Porsche glide through the parking lot and merge with traffic. She rubbed her neck, felt only a bit of tenderness. Getting shot with a dart was a first, and an experience she didn't want to repeat. At least they knew now for certain the man after Emma didn't want to kill her, only take her.

Sherlock went inside to security. She imagined they'd already reviewed the videos, but she wanted to look at them herself, wanted to speak to everyone who'd worked here that morning. Maybe someone else had seen him.

19

Wipperwill Motel
Oldenburg, Virginia

THURSDAY

Aldo wanted a beer and oblivion. His shoulder throbbed and burned. He hugged his slinged arm tight against himself, paced and cursed and wondered if the pills the doctor at the clinic had given him were really for pain or for a rash or something. Even with the pain, he knew he'd been lucky. He'd taken his mother to that Urgent Care on Pine Street when she'd sliced her thumb, so he knew the layout, knew it was open 24/7. So at four A.M., he'd put on sunglasses, pulled a ball cap low on his forehead, and slipped in through the back. It was eerily quiet, very little business yet. In the first small office he came to, a young doctor was sitting alone next to his computer, munching on a predawn sandwich and reading a book. He'd stuck the gun in the guy's ear, told him to take care of the bullet wound, and keep his trap shut or he'd shoot his brains out and try someplace else. Then Aldo had tucked a hundred-dollar bill into his shirt pocket, to give him hope.

He'd held a gun on the skinny little white-coated dude the whole time he'd treated the wound in his shoulder. He'd refused any kind of pain med while the doctor cleaned it up, though he'd never felt pain that bad, even when a baseball bat slammed into his gut in the Red Onion Prison yard. He'd wanted to scream, but Aldo didn't; he held it in, because he had to seem to be in control, had to keep the doctor cowed enough he wouldn't try to run. He'd been tough, just like his father was, before a guard shot him dead during a bank robbery.

The doc had assured him in a nervous voice the bullet had gone through the outside of his shoulder, luckily not striking bone, only muscle. When the doc finally finished wrapping a bandage around his arm and shoulder and helped him into a sling, Aldo had thanked him, accepted a bottle of pain pills and antibiotics, knocked him unconscious, gagged him and tied him up, and stuffed him into a small closet that held medical supplies. On his way out the back door, he'd heard voices and turned to see a woman wearing a white coat leading a guy holding a bloody hand. She obviously didn't see him because she didn't call out. He didn't see anyone else.

Aldo threw the bottle of pills the doc had given him on the bed and swallowed three aspirin. He moaned now as he paced his motel room, cursing that bitch Ewing for shooting him. The job was going to be so easy, he'd been sure of it when he cut the two wires in her cheap alarm system and quietly broke the window of her kitchen door. He reached in and slid the chain off the hook, flipped the lock. He moved quiet as a cat in his ancient sneakers, through the kitchen and small dining room to the small front hallway. Before he could start up the stairs, there she was already coming down, looking like a ghost in her long white nightgown, a gun in her hand. She'd shot him the same moment he shot her. At least he was the better shot. The bitch was dead and he wasn't. That thought cheered him up for a couple of minutes before the pain in his arm got him to cursing a blue streak again.

How the bitch had heard him was the question Aldo couldn't stop asking himself. He'd barely heard himself. Had she been awake, too afraid to sleep after hearing her boss was killed? It didn't matter now. Ewing wouldn't be telling anybody anything.

He turned on the TV and was surprised to see a sharp color picture on the flat-screen. They'd changed out the grainy crap TV he'd had to watch the last time he was here. He watched Barbara shout at Penny that if she didn't stop sleeping with Barbara's husband, Lance, she'd be very sorry. He grunted, flipped the channel to the local news, and a few minutes later, there it was—a report on Ewing's murder. But the good-looking broad who delivered the news only reported an accountant, Corinne Ewing, was found dead at her home early that morning, the victim of a shooting. No other details. The cops must have put a lid on it really fast. Aldo thought of the young cop sitting in his mud-colored Kia in front of Ewing's house and smiled. He'd embarrassed that little craphead. He'd stayed out of sight in the neighbor's bushes, watched him get out of the car and stretch, and make his rounds around Ewing's house. Aldo had ducked down and he'd shined his flashlight right over Aldo's head. Aldo waited until he was back in his car, probably drinking cold coffee to keep awake.

But Aldo hadn't counted on having to use his gun on Ewing; he'd wanted to strangle her in her bed. He'd had the gun out because he was always careful. The shots sounded like two cannons going off. He'd raced out of the side yard and run all out to his mama's Chevy, hugging his arm hard against his side, feeling his blood snake down sticky and hot, hoping no blood soaked through his leather jacket and dripped to the ground because he knew all about DNA. And there was the chance his blood had fallen to the floor in the house for the crime-scene techs to find. He turned once to see the cop run into the house, his gun drawn. Given the distance and the sliver of a moon, there was no chance the cop could identify him or his mama's car. At least he hadn't botched the job. In a couple of days, when he felt better, he'd collect the rest of his money and head out of the country, maybe to Aruba, where he'd heard the white sand stretched forever. He'd lie on the beach under one of those striped umbrellas and think about the fine life that was his now. And he'd check out all those turtles he'd heard about. He'd loved turtles as a kid, always wondered if they ever got where they were going.

Why weren't the freaking pain meds kicking in? He swallowed two more, snarled at the gorgeous broad on TV who was talking about a stupid dog who'd saved his old lady owner who'd tripped and broken her hip. Maybe they should have put her out of her misery and helped out the dog.

Aldo eased down on the bed, slid a skinny pillow under his arm. He looked at his watch—nearly seven o'clock in the evening. He closed his eyes and started counting to a hundred. When he whispered ninety-seven, he paused. Yes, at last the pain wasn't so bad. Thankfully, he had lots of aspirin. He just had to hang on. In a couple of days, he'd pick us his fifty thousand dollars and rock 'n' roll to the Caribbean.

He was on the edge of blessed sleep when the motel room door burst open. Aldo lurched up to see a load of SWAT cops in their body armor and headgear pour in through the door, every gun trained on him. For an instant he froze, then nearly screamed with pain when he tried to lurch for his Beretta on the table beside the bed. How? There was no way they could have found him. He'd been careful. He was always careful after a job.

One SWAT cop shoved him back down, stuck his gun in his face. "Lieutenant, here's your guy, exactly where his mother told you he'd be."

Aldo's breath caught. He didn't understand. His mama had told the police?

"Hello, Aldo," a man said, looking down at him. "I'm Lieutenant Jeter Thorpe and I'd like to congratulate you on having such a law-abiding mother who loves her cherry-red Chevy Camaro so much. When I paid her a visit, she told us you hadn't visited her in weeks and her car was in the garage. Guess what, Aldo, that gorgeous Camaro was in the garage all right. You did try to clean up the blood on the front seat, but since it was dark, I guess you didn't see the smears you left. You hoped your mother wouldn't notice? She was very unhappy with you, called you a few names, said you were worse than her now-dead sleaze of a husband. She was happy enough to tell us that whenever she kicked you out of the house before you were finally shipped off to Red Onion, you usually came here to the Wipperwill Motel in Oldenburg."

His mama had told them? Because he'd borrowed her freaking Camaro and smeared a little blood on the front seat? He thought he'd cleaned it all off, but he was in so much pain he could barely see. He whispered, "No, you made her tell you, you threatened her. She's my mother."

"Life is hard, Aldo. When we told her what you'd done, that you'd probably left your own piece of crap car down the street and snuck in to take the Camaro and involve her in killing someone, she gave you up without a whimper. Really cool car, by the way."

His own flesh turning on him, betraying him. What else could a man bear? Aldo looked up numbly at the plainclothes cop. The look in his eyes was as mean as Jessup the Bull's at Red

Onion. The cop's voice turned flat and hard. "I'm sure you remember the police officer at Corinne Ewing's house last night, Aldo. He took a picture of your car as you drove away from Corinne Ewing's house. Amazing how well those cameras do now in low light. When we magnified the photos, we even got your license plate. The icing on the cake? You left some of your blood in Ewing's hallway and on the road, too. I'm sure we'll get a match." Jeter smiled down at him, crossed his arms. "Here's what's going to happen, Aldo. You'll go back to Red Onion without the chance of parole this time unless"—Jeter paused, stretched it out waiting for Aldo to meet his eyes—"unless you tell us who hired you to kill Corinne Ewing."

Jeter was looking down at him as if he was bored, as if he'd just as soon kick him under a car and run over him. Tough bastard. Aldo pictured putting a red dot in the middle of his forehead, but the SWAT cops already had his Beretta. But maybe he still held some of the cards. Aldo looked up at Jeter, a sneer on his mouth, and said easily, "I don't know what you're talking about."

Jeter leaned close. "As I said, my name's Lieutenant Jeter Thorpe of the Porte Franklyn PD, so you can believe me when I tell you I can persuade the commonwealth attorney to offer you a possibility of parole if you tell the court who paid you to kill Corinne Ewing."

Aldo's sneer grew bigger. He kept his mouth shut. Did this Thorpe think he's just fold without a written guarantee?

Jeter said easily to this idiot who thought he could outfox a fox, "If you refuse to cooperate, Aldo, if you think staying silent will keep you safe in prison, you've got it exactly wrong. Once you're back at Red Onion, you'll be a threat to Oliveras. You won't last longer than the first spitting contest. Another inmate will shove a bar of soap down your throat in the shower or maybe stick a shiv in your gut in the yard, and everyone will stand around and watch you bleed out. They'll set up a pool to bet how long you'll stay breathing. Maybe they'll use days, maybe weeks. Then it'll happen that fast, Aldo." Jeter snapped his fingers in Aldo's face.

For a second Aldo's rage took his pain away. He remembered his ranger knife, but it was snug in his boot, at the foot of his bed. A second later his shoulder was on fire again. It made him want to scream, but he didn't, not with all the cops standing over him, watching him. He said, his voice firm, as hard as the cop's eyes staring down at him, "You gotta make me a real sweet deal."

Jeter's eyebrow went up and he smiled, a vicious smile, one promising endless mean. "You think? Well, I'll see what I can do. Just to whet my appetite, Aldo, to show good faith, tell me how much Oliveras paid you to kill Ewing."

"You get nothing until I see an offer, signatures on the dotted line."

Jeter thought of Hailstock. He knew he'd make whatever deal with Aldo Springer he had to. Jeter didn't doubt it for a moment. At least they'd get Oliveras. But knowing how Hailstock would fold for a man who'd committed murder for hire burned him. Aldo must have seen him thinking that because his sneer was back in full bloom. Jeter couldn't help himself, he leaned down and whispered in Aldo's ear, "Then again, maybe Oliveras will have you killed in city lockup before I can get a deal for you." Jeter slipped, pressed his palm against his wounded shoulder to regain his balance. Aldo screamed.

"Sorry about that, Aldo. Shoulder hurting you? Okay, let's get your carcass to the hospital, get you fixed up while I speak to the DA, see what they say your future holds."

Aldo thought of Oliveras, a man with a blacker soul than

even this cop imagined. "I want a guard!"

Jeter laughed at him. "And I want the money Oliveras was going to pay you."

Aldo cursed, stared the cop in the eye. "I wish I could put out your lights."

Jeter gave him a full-on smile. "Yeah, Aldo, if that thought gives you pleasure, you go with it." Jeter stepped aside as two of the SWAT team hauled Aldo Springer to his feet.

Aldo shouted when they got him to the door. "Get me a deal!"

20

Savich House
Georgetown

THURSDAY EVENING

Savich watched Sherlock dab on a touch of pale coral lipstick, his favorite. She looked fit and healthy, but still, he couldn't let go of the fear that had nearly knocked him flat when he'd first seen her lying unconscious on a gurney. It wouldn't let go of him. He wished they could be alone this evening so he could hold her and feed her popcorn while they watched a *SpongeBob SquarePants* episode with Sean. But it was not to be.

Sherlock cocked her head toward the open door and smiled. "Sean's video-gaming with his favorite Italian plumber, Mario. He's been smashing mysterious boxes and cross-eyed turtles and mooning over Princess Peach. Sean's on the moon right now in samurai armor, and he's going nuts over it. Then I told him the Hunts were coming. He forgot Princess Peach for the moment he was so excited Cal and Gage were coming over, and his goddess, Emma, of course." She turned from the mirror and Savich saw the diamond studs he'd gotten her for Christmas dancing and sparkling through her curly hair. She looked bright-eyed and energetic, herself again. It was a huge relief, but still— He looked at his Mickey Mouse watch. The Hunts were due soon.

He said, "I like the black turtleneck and the black slacks. You look just about perfect."

Sherlock frowned at him. "Excuse me. *Just* about?"

"I had to factor in worrying about you."

She poked him in the shoulder. "Please, no more worrying." She rubbed her fingers over his sinfully soft dark blue cashmere sweater. "Very sexy and soft."

Savich grinned up at her. "I like the sound of some of that."

She gave him a quick kiss. "Perv. I need to see if Sean's put away his game, so I should hurry."

When they were downstairs, waiting, Sean told them in great detail about his samurai armor and the beautiful Princess Peach. "Papa, do you think Cal and Gage are old enough to play?"

"Give them another year or two. I think they're going to be bringing their own games, Sean. Do you mind playing theirs? Give them some pointers?"

Sean beamed. "Don't worry, Papa, I can show them what's what."

Two hours later, four pizzas were a memory. Sean and the Hunt twins were huddled together by the front window playing a game that appeared to call for a lot of shouting and fist waving. The adults settled in with tea and coffee.

Ramsey said, "Let me be honest here, Sherlock. When I saw you go down, I was scared spitless."

"But no worries now, Ramsey, please. All I'm left with is this Band-Aid on my neck for a day or two, that's all."

Sherlock noticed Emma was standing quietly against the

back of the sofa where her parents sat, listening in. She knew Emma was smart enough to know what they were about to talk about, and mature enough to hear it and so she was pleased when Ramsey called to her. "Come sit between us, Em. You should be a part of this. You should know as much as we do about what happened today."

Emma eased down between her parents, and they each took one of her hands. Emma said, clear-eyed and calm, "I know that man followed us here and shot a dart in Aunt Sherlock's neck. I know he meant to shoot me with it and take me." She drew a deep breath. "Like Father Sonny took me when I was six." Molly jerked and Emma squeezed her hand. "It's okay, Mom. It was really scary when I was six, but I know now he was sick. It's different now, I'm different. I'm almost thirteen." She looked over at Sherlock and Savich, then at her parents. "Don't try to take me out of it, I'm going to stay for my concert. With all you guys watching, no one will get near me. I'll be fine, really, I want to perform. I told Vincenzo how important it is to me and he agrees I should regardless of any stalker, or whatever he is."

Savich looked at Emma's defiant, hopeful face. She'd had to grow up too fast, survive looking at every stranger around her as a potential threat even as young child. But she'd not only survived, she'd thrived. He wouldn't have been surprised to see her tense and frightened, but instead she was composed and adamant about performing.

Ramsey said, "Your mother and I have discussed this, Em, and we agree. You will perform. You'll knock everyone's socks off and you won't worry about any of this, at least for tonight."

Emma kissed each of them on the cheek and beamed.

Sherlock said, "We'll do our part, Emma. Our friend Lieutenant Ben Raven at the Metropolitan Police Department, will be assigning officers to you at Kennedy Center, one at each exit, and a woman officer, Joy Trader, to stay close when I'm unable." She looked at Molly. "Of course your parents will be there for you as well."

Molly drew a deep breath. "That's right. Anyone even looks at you funny and I'll kick his butt. Now, I called your grand-father, Emma. He's very concerned. He wants us to come to the compound in Oak Park after you finish your performance at Kennedy Center if Uncle Dillon and Aunt Sherlock haven't caught this man yet."

Sherlock wasn't surprised Molly had called Mason Lord. They'd be safe settled in his compound in the wealthy Oak Park suburb of Chicago for the duration. Talk about a fortress replete with a couple of guards. If they did go there, Mason Lord would undoubtedly quadruple the guards. But how long would the duration be? Sherlock knew this couldn't go on; they had to shut it down, whatever it was, and fast. She said, "Four different security cameras at Kennedy Center caught Mr. Dart Gun. But with the sunglasses and ball cap, it wasn't very help-ful. I spoke to two employees who believed they saw him, but they couldn't provide any more information about him. I asked the security people to send over stills of all the cars in or near the parking lots that were within camera range. There weren't that many people there, mostly the orchestra and some theater employees because there weren't any rehearsals going on in the other two Kennedy Center theaters. Ben Raven said he'd have his people look through them as well as nearby traffic cams for any rentals or stolen vehicles. He's going to call me."

It all sounded good, but still Ramsey worried. "So a ball cap and sunglasses again, and we're not any closer to knowing who he is, or who they are."

Savich said, "That's right, we don't even know it was the same man. If it was, he used a different MO than he tried on

Emma in San Francisco." He sat forward in his chair, his elbows on his knees. "Like all of you, I've given this a lot of thought and I don't think he wants Emma for himself. He's hired to kidnap her. I think it's someone else who wants her, for a specific reason."

"That's what I think, too," Emma said. "I remember my grandfather had Father Sonny killed in the hospital after he tried to take me that last time on the wharf in Monterey. Don't look surprised, Mom, I overheard you and Dad talking about it. I remember thinking finally I was safe since he was finally gone. And then last year Father Sonny's crazy mother came back and tried to kill you, Dad, and Aunt Sherlock shot him. The thing is, they're both dead, so how can this man have anything to do with Father Sonny and what happened to me when I was six?"

Savich said, "Emma's right, I checked. There's no one close to Father Sonny or his mother left that I could find, and no close friends, certainly no one close enough to want revenge on you or your family, Emma, for what happened to Father Sonny. That would take commitment and money and planning. One of my agents, Jack Crowne, spoke with Warden Clapp of the Billings State Prison where Father Sonny was incarcerated for many years. Warden Clapp hooked him up with two long-term guards who were there the same time as Father Sonny. One of guards told Jack about an old geezer, a lifer who claimed Father Sonny bragged about a cousin on his mother's side who was planning on helping him when he got out, a meth head. Jack searched out this cousin's name, Mennen Lowe, but he couldn't find him, he's been off the grid for years." Savich paused. "Could the man in the ball cap be Mennen Lowe? I personally doubt it. Again, money, planning, commitment. Sherlock?"

Sherlock was shaking her head. "It can't be Mennen Lowe himself. He'd be at least sixty. The man with the blowgun moved much younger. Emma, you said the man who tried to take you at Davies Hall was younger, too, yes?"

"He was big and he moved fast and his voice wasn't old."

Molly sighed. "So that's a dead end. There's no reason to worry about Father Sonny or anyone he knew." She squeezed Emma's hand again.

Savich said, "Emma, would you mind giving us a minute and overseeing Sean and your brothers for a while? There's a couple of questions I'd like to ask your parents privately."

Emma gave her parents a long look and rose. She said, "I don't mind. I know I'll have you, Aunt Sherlock, and that Office Trader, looking after me. And I know this man may try to take me again, so I'll be extra careful." A smile bloomed on her beautiful face. "If he does, I'll take him down again."

Sherlock said, "If you weren't about to dazzle the world with your musical talent, Emma, I'd be telling you how great you'd be as a special agent."

Emma smiled, turned, and walked toward the kid mayhem.

Savich said, "I thought you should be the ones to decide what Emma should hear about her grandfather. You said you called him, Molly. I'm sure it's occurred to you Mason Lord could easily be the real target, whether it's someone out for a ransom, or for revenge, or for leverage against him. Don't forget, he was at the center of it when Emma was taken six years ago when his former partner, Rule Shaker, and his daughter tried to use Emma to destroy Mason and ended up having him shot and nearly killed. You were the one who put a stop to all that, Molly, when you threatened to expose them all. Do you think he could be involved again?"

"I've thought about that, it's one of the reasons I called my father and told him," Molly said. "So far as I know there's been no contact between my father and Rule Shaker for six years.

Shaker and his daughter, Eve"—Molly gave a mad grin—"my father's viper ex-wife, are still running their casinos in Las Vegas, living the high life. My father told me Eve remarried last year, Doulos is his name. Word is, Dad told me, this guy's a player, runs an elite gambling club for local movers and shakers called Exotica. Other than that, my father has never even mentioned either Eve or Rule Shaker. But I'm sure they still hate each other."

"People rarely stop hating," Ramsey said, "especially people like them. It's embedded in their DNA. I think they might have killed each other, Molly, if not for your threat to close them both down."

Ramsey drew in a deep breath. "As I'm sure you have, Savich, I took a look online at what Rule Shaker and Eve have been up to; I didn't see anything I didn't expect. As you said, they both seem to be enjoying the fruits of their labor. Evidently she travels back and forth to Palm Beach or her husband flies to Las Vegas, a strange marriage, but who knows?

"On the other hand, maybe it's as straightforward as Shaker not being able to let go of his hatred for Mason Lord and sticking with the peace with him Molly forced upon him six years ago."

Molly said, "And then there's Eve. I've always pictured her as a ticking bomb covered with a luscious candy coating, and relentless when it's something she wants."

Ramsey said, "Molly, do you think Shaker would take the chance of ignoring everything he knows you put in the hands of your lawyers six years ago?"

Molly said slowly, "I can't imagine what it would take to make that risk worth it for him unless his hatred for my father festered until he simply couldn't control it. Or maybe if my father went after Shaker, triggered him, pulled off something that hurt Shaker's bottom line or his reputation. My father would know if he did that. He didn't tell me."

Sherlock looked over at Cal, Gage, and Sean, Emma kneeling beside them, thankfully oblivious now of the adults. She looked at Molly and Ramsey. "That sounds logical, Molly, and seems like the best place to start. Is everyone agreed it's time we spoke to Mason Lord?"

21

Kirra's Condo

THURSDAY EVENING

The six thousand five hundred dollars Kirra had paid to Booger Watts to identify the young tattooed gang member standing with Elson and Ryman Grissom on the deck of the *Valadia* in her father's painting had finally produced results. Booger had warned her he might have to break into facial recognition databases she didn't want to know about, and even so, after all these years he'd have to get lucky. "Took me forever to hack in," he said to her. "I could have ended up in a Siberian gulag for the rest of my life if I wasn't so good. I should have charged you more, Kirra, but hey, you're a friend, so you got a discount."

She'd met Booger at Clancy's Bar in Washington's Foggy Bottom the previous year, and asked him where he got the name Booger, which earned her a toothy smile and no answer. He was nervy and funny and could outdrink her. They'd kept in touch and she'd called him, struck a deal. Even after he'd taken her money, he bitched and moaned on video calls complaining the frigging photographs she'd given him didn't have enough detail, and if he got caught and sent away for the rest of his unnatural life, what would his mother do? Then he laughed and tugged on his thick red beard, pushed up his aviator glasses again, always in danger of falling off his nose into his pocket protector. He always called her from his castle in his mom's basement, with piles of luggage and boxes sandwiching him in and a washer and dryer in the background.

She said, "You're the best, Booger, and even with my friend's discount, you're a lot richer. Tell you what. I'll take you to Clancy's Bar in a couple of weeks, buy you beers until you pass out."

"That shows gratitude, excellent. Now, Kirra, this guy is bad news, but you already knew he isn't a saint. You stay away from him."

Kirra looked down at a recent photo of the man that Booger had sent her as she walked into her living room and sat down with a glass of her favorite chardonnay. His name was Alexey Perez, and wasn't that a lovely name for a drug-running killer? He was in his forties now, swarthy with black eyes and glossy black hair without a single strand of gray. He was slim and well dressed in tan slacks, a white shirt, and a cashmere sports coat that looked to be handmade, and dark loafers, definitely Italian. She easily recognized him even fourteen years older, the intense young man she'd seen in her father's photos and the painting of the *Valadia*. Kirra pictured her father standing at his favorite spot on the shore of the Potomac, taking photos of boats as they passed by before he began painting them. That's when he'd seen these men, taken their photos. Thank goodness he always kept the photos he used and she'd found those taped to the back of the painting in the shed, because she doubted even Booger could have found a match from only an oil painting of the guy's face. But her dad had kept them and it was those photos and that painting and what he'd threatened to do with them that had gotten her father and mother killed.

Tears stung her eyes. The young Alexey Perez he'd painted

that long-ago day was still alive and well, and her parents were dead. Her father had asked these men for money for his pictures with no idea what he was getting into. If he'd discussed it with her mother, Kirra knew she'd have talked him out of it, convinced him they'd find another way, but he hadn't, and he'd signed their death warrant. And almost hers. These men had to know her uncle Leo had taken her to Australia straight out of the hospital to protect her from them. Evidently the Grissoms, father and son, and Alexey Perez must have decided they were safe when she didn't come forward, that she didn't know anything useful. She swiped her hand over her eyes.

She set her wine on the coffee table and scrolled through the three-page file from Interpol Booger had sent her. Alexey Perez was a native of San Salvador, a member of MS-13. He'd arrived in Los Angeles when he was fourteen years old. At thirty, fourteen years ago, he'd been a regional distributor for MS-13. Today it was believed he was one of the top MS-13 commanders in the world. Perez never stayed in one place for long. His family was well hidden, rumored to be currently living outside Miami under an assumed name. He was wanted in Italy and Spain for murder and drug distribution.

Kirra knew well enough identifying this third man wouldn't prove who murdered her parents. Motive and opportunity weren't nearly enough to bring any of them to trial for it after so many years, even if Perez was finally caught. At least now she finally knew who the third man was. It was the last thing her father's painting could tell her.

It was up to her now. She knew she needed more, much more. She knew in her soul Ryman was one of her parents' killers. The other? Another of Grissom's thugs?

22

Kennedy Center, Concert Hall
Rehearsals

FRIDAY MORNING

Officer First Class Joy Trader walked through the rear door into the second tier of the concert hall on her rounds. These were the most distant seats from the stage in the concert hall—the cheapest seats—though no one would think them inferior in this amazing facility. The view looking down at the whole concert hall was amazing. When her lieutenant had assigned her to assist Special Agent Sherlock to help bodyguard Emma Hunt, Joy had nearly bounded up from her seat and fist-pumped she was so excited. Imagine working with Agent Sherlock herself and helping protect a twelve-year-old prodigy at Kennedy Center. She was pleased Lieutenant Raven recognized she was thorough, usually never missed a thing, and she was fast to respond and calm in a crisis. Even though no one believed the man who'd shot Agent Sherlock in the neck with a dart would be hiding between the seats up here, Agent Sherlock had told her to look everywhere and so Joy checked out every shadowed corner, looked behind every seat in this vast hall. She was wearing her newest dark blue uniform with her badge and MPD insignia, her Glock 19 clipped to her waist. She'd wanted to look sharp, and she did.

She'd already briefly met Emma and her parents, Molly and Ramsey Hunt, when they'd arrived at the Kennedy Center. Emma was not only very pretty, she was shyly charming. Joy couldn't wait to hear her play. Her parents had offered tickets to Joy's whole family to hear Emma play, along with another young prodigy, an Italian boy from Milan. She thought for a second it might inspire her own boys to want to play, and then she wondered if they'd even want to come. If it wasn't football, they mostly played video games. At least while she worked today, she was getting to listen to this amazing girl play Chopin.

Last night, Joy's husband, David, had teased her when she'd pulled out her laptop to read about the Hunts after they'd finished the dishes, dragged the boys to bed, and cleaned up the preteen debris. He shook his head at her and laughed, kissed her. "When you figure it all out, Joy, you let me know," he said. Well, of course she'd read about them. She was curious about a lot of things, like what the Russians were saying about the latest cyberattacks on US electric companies, and learning about the Hunts was no different. Joy wondered how much more Lieutenant Raven knew about the Hunts than he'd told her, wondered what Sherlock and her husband, Special Agent Dillon Savich, knew.

There was no shortage of photos and stories about Emma Hunt's kidnapping when she was a six-year-old, and about her kidnapper who'd later died. There was mention of Emma's grandfather, Mason Lord, and how ironic was that? Even she'd heard of Mason Lord of Chicago. Federal Judge Ramsey Hunt was a powerful criminal's son-in-law, and wasn't that something? Joy studied an older photo of Mason Lord. He looked like an aristocrat in the photos, with his blade of a nose, dark arched brows, cold blue eyes, and pewter hair, perfectly presented, attending a charity ball with his then young wife, Eve. There were photos of his huge compound in a ritzy Chicago suburb, with high walls and beautiful gardens, even guards patrolling. She saw a recent photo of him taken by a paparazzo, looked like London. He didn't look much older, still striking, still imposing.

Joy had also read Emma Hunt had inherited her amazing talent from her father, metal rock star and guitarist Louey Santera who'd died in a car explosion six years ago. His genius music genes had taken a different direction in his daughter. No riffing on an electric guitar for Emma; she was a pure classical pianist. There were more links to Louey Santera than Joy could possibly read and scores of photos and clips of him performing, women screaming, trying to climb up onto the stage. He was amazing in his way, like Emma.

She studied photos of Mason Lord's very young ex-wife, Eve, taken after her husband was shot and nearly died. She looked heartbroken and heroic, but very soon after that, she'd left him. Why would a young wife be hovering over her wounded husband one day and gone the next back to her father, Rule Shaker? All Joy could find out about Shaker was he owned and operated several casinos in Las Vegas. In a picture with his daughter, he wore a bespoke suit, but oddly, he came across looking like a stereotypical Hollywood gangster.

There were more recent photos of Eve standing between her father and her groom, taken the previous year at her second wedding to a Rich Doulos. Doulos was in his midthirties, fit and looked suave enough, she supposed. He was from South Florida, his family rich and well connected, but he wasn't in the family business; no, among other things, he owned a private gambling club. In another photo, he was wearing a tux, standing beside his wife, Eve, who looked drop-dead gorgeous. He still looked suave, but there was a slight sneer marring his mouth. And what was that about?

Joy sat back and wondered what hadn't happened to this young girl and her family? When her husband came in the kitchen and asked her what was so fascinating, Joy gave him a rundown of the players. She yawned, closed down her laptop, tapped her fingers on the cover. "It amazes me that Federal Judge Ramsey Hunt, and yes, he's still known as Judge Dredd, is a powerful criminal's son-in-law. And now Mason Lord's granddaughter is in danger. Talk about a mystery."

Her sweet husband had kissed her, told her she'd help figure it out. And he believed it. She'd fallen asleep wondering how much more Lieutenant Raven knew about Emma Hunt's situation but hadn't told her.

As Joy now finished walking through the second tier, she looked down at her Apple Watch, a Christmas present from her mother-in-law. It was time to head back downstairs and make her backstage circuit, look through all the rooms and closets and wherever else someone could be hiding.

Three minutes later she stood stage left and realized she had exactly five minutes before her iWatch binged an alarm and she'd check in with Sherlock who told her she'd be seated in the back of the orchestra section near the doors, with a full view of the stage and the entrances to the concert hall orchestra seats, exactly where she'd been yesterday when Dart Man got her. Sherlock was a stickler about checking in at a precise time, so Joy was certain never to be even a second late.

At that moment, she heard Emma Hunt play a dramatic glissando, the violins coming in counterpoint, the sound incredible. She was twelve years old. It was mind-boggling. *Come on, Joy, get with it.* She took a quick look at the orchestra seats on the right side, close to the stage, where Judge Ramsey Hunt and his wife, Molly Hunt, were sitting. She thought Judge Hunt fit his billing as a federal judge and Judge Dredd, tall, dark, his expression stern, a man you'd be a fool to mess with. She'd read Emma's mother, Molly Hunt, was a photographer with a growing reputation. Joy loved her red curly hair, like Sherlock's, but a very different shade. She imagined how insanely proud the Hunts had to be of their daughter, and how scared they were for her.

She didn't know the name of the Chopin piece Emma Hunt was playing, but it was fast and furious, her eyes on her flying fingers, the passionate music pouring out of her. Joy wondered how she could stay so focused, knowing danger was so close. She'd read somewhere musicians got lost in their music, and maybe it was so.

Joy checked through each of the dressing rooms, spoke briefly with two technicians and a stagehand to be sure they hadn't seen anyone they didn't know, and paused to check a pantry filled with stage equipment. She knocked on the door of the backstage men's room and looked through it, checked each of the stalls. She looked through the women's room in the same order. When she opened the door of the final stall, she saw a figure crouching on the toilet seat, heard a light footstep, felt something sharp bite her neck. She pulled out a dart and was reaching for her Glock when something very hard struck her on the side of her head, and she collapsed without a sound against the stall door and slid to the floor.

23

FRIDAY MORNING

"You have a concussion, Officer Trader. No, don't move, it's not a good idea for you to hop up and try to walk. Just try to relax." Dr. Zugoni finished looking into her eyes with an ophthalmoscope.

"And a headache," Joy said through gritted her teeth. "A monster headache."

"That's expected, and I'm sorry to say we'll have to take it slow with the pain meds." He patted Joy's shoulder. "Once we're sure you're fully awake and have no delayed neurologic symptoms, I can give you whatever you like and sing you a lullaby. You're my second concussion in two days. Agent Sherlock was brought into my fine facility just yesterday. Like her, you'll be just fine."

David Trader rushed into the cubicle, Sherlock behind him. She saw Dr. Zugoni, gave him a little wave. He did a double take, smiled. "It's good to see you upright, Agent Sherlock, great name, impossible to forget. No aftereffects?"

"Not a one. Mr. Trader and I were outside and heard you say Joy has a concussion? I guess there's some irony in that for you.

The nurse told us we could come in."

"That's right and a scalp hematoma behind her left ear. We're going to be keeping her at least overnight. Now it's time for a pain med," and a nurse slipped a needle into Joy's arm.

Dave Trader said, "I had a couple of concussions playing football and I was pretty miserable for a while. Are you sure she'll be all right?"

Zugoni smiled at him. "We ordered a CT scan right away when the EMTs brought her in. It was normal except for the injury to her scalp. She's as awake and alert as I'd expect after being drugged and knocked unconscious. I don't believe the concussion is going to leave her with anything serious, but as I said, we'll keep her here overnight for observation, make sure the neurologist examines her and agrees to let her back into the wild. We'll take good care of your wife, Mr. Trader."

"Dave? Is that you? I'm alive, don't worry. Is Emma all right?"

"Yes, Emma's fine," she heard Sherlock say. Then Dave was at her side.

Joy whispered, "That's a huge relief." She smiled up at him; whatever the nurse had injected had nearly wiped out the pain. "I feel mellow. It's wonderful."

Dave smiled. She sounded dreamy, like she was half asleep. He leaned in close, looked into her vague eyes, kissed her nose. "You hear that, sweetheart? You're going to be fine. And you can rest up without any worries about the boys. Your sister insisted on taking them tonight."

Poor Carol, five boys under one roof and only her husband to help her. "Agent Sherlock, I'm so sorry I screwed up. Emma's all right, you promise? Did you catch the jerk who knocked me out?"

Dave Trader didn't want to move, but he let Sherlock take his place. She took Joy's hand, leaned close. "I promise Emma's fine. Security has been checking through every inch of Kennedy Center and haven't found anyone. When you didn't check in, I went backstage looking for you, found you unconscious in the women's room in your underwear. So they took your uniform, your badge, and your gun. Can you tell me what happened?"

Joy was staring up at Sherlock's beautiful hair, at the red curls dancing around her fine-boned face. Her mind seemed to wobble and dip. "Your hair's so pretty," she said. Sherlock squeezed her hand, smiled down at her. "Thank you."

"Oops, sorry, I guess I fell off the rails," Joy said. She tried to take a deep breath, but couldn't stop thinking how the ceiling paint was chipping. She whispered, "I can do this. Okay, the women's room was my last stop before I was scheduled to text you. I didn't see anyone in there, and checked the stalls. When I opened the last stall door, someone was crouching on the toilet seat with her feet up, so I wouldn't see her unless I opened the door. At least I think it was a woman. She was wearing a ball cap and sunglasses and it all happened so quickly." She frowned, tried to lift her head, felt Sherlock press her back down. "No, just lie still, Joy. Go ahead."

"She blew a dart in my neck or someone else did, I can't be sure, then someone hit me with something hard, behind my left ear. I don't remember anything else. One person or two? I'm sorry, it's just too blurry. Could you tell me what happened again?"

Sherlock knew concussions, knew Joy's brain wasn't ready to operate normally yet. She said again, "I knew how punctual you were so it wasn't more than thirty seconds after you missed your time that I headed backstage and retraced your steps. I found you unconscious, a dart on the floor beside your hand and a nasty lump on your head. I called 911, ran out into the hall and out the back door, but I didn't see anyone. I told everyone to look for a woman, maybe in a police uniform since she took yours, but she must have already run. Was it her plan all along to take your uniform or did she decide on the spur of the moment to take it that very minute after you found her? She might have believed she could blend in backstage when Emma finished her piece and offer to escort her to the bathroom. More likely she hoped you or someone else would bring Emma to the bathroom yourself, planned on disabling you and Emma both with that dart, and take her out through the back door. But you found her while Emma was still playing, spoiled her plan, whatever it was. She couldn't take the chance someone would come looking for you and had to run."

Joy said, "I'm sorry, Sherlock, I let everyone down and now she has my gun and my badge. I'm never supposed to let that happen."

"You were unconscious, Joy. It couldn't be helped. The EMTs got you to the hospital in record time. I left all our people checking around Kennedy Center for the woman. As yet she hasn't been seen so I imagine she saw me and managed to sneak past the outside guards. I called Lieutenant Raven, he called your husband, and here we are."

Joy whispered, "I'm glad I wasn't wearing a thong. They're Dave's favorites, but I could never bring myself to wear them under my uniform."

As Joy Trader's lieutenant, Ben Raven, opened the curtain to the cubicle, Dr. Zugoni said, "Come on in, Lieutenant Raven, most everyone else has." They heard a beep. Zugoni looked down at his pager. "I've got to take care of another patient. I'll be back to see you in a couple of hours, Officer Trader. I'll leave it to you and Agent Sherlock to reassure your lieutenant." He walked out of cubicle in a hurry, his white coat flapping again.

Joy looked after him. She felt all loose and vague and wondered how he got his white coat to move like that. There was
no wind, but maybe he was going near the speed of light. Her
brain flipped and whirled and wondered. Her last thought was
of the footfalls she'd heard before the lights went out. Sherlock patted Dave Trader's shoulder and reassured him his wife
would be okay. She left him staring down at Joy's still face. Was
he praying?

Sherlock wasn't surprised to see Dillon in the ER working
on MAX, sitting with the half-dozen cops who'd come to the
ER when word got out one of their own had been hurt. He
looked up, his eyebrow arched.

"She's got a concussion, ketamine in her system with the
dart, but Dr. Zugoni—yep, he was here for Officer Trader,
too—he says she'll be fine. They'll keep her overnight because
of the blow to her head, hope to send her home tomorrow."

"That's good. Tell me what happened."

She did. "I was sure it was a man yesterday, Dillon, Mr. Dart
Gun. But today it was a woman who shot Joy with one and
took her uniform. Most guys wouldn't fit in it. So are there two
people? Or was I wrong? I guess whoever shot me could have
been a woman. Kennedy Center security and Metro officers are
looking for a woman. Whatever she was planning, Joy Trader
finding her put a stop to it. I hope none of this ends up online
or in the news. That's the last thing Molly and Ramsey need."

Savich said, "Ben has asked his people and security at Kennedy Center to keep it under their hats, so all digits crossed."

"Maybe that will give them a little time, at least get them
through Emma's performance tonight. I think most kids would
just fold down, but not Emma. I have no doubt she'll insist
on performing and I don't blame her. I'd want to perform too.
She's worked too hard on her Chopin numbers to suddenly

have no payoff. She'll play."

"I agree. Ramsey told me they spoke to Emma about canceling her performance tonight and taking her to Mason Lord's compound in Chicago immediately, and she gave a flat refusal."

As they left the ER, Sherlock said, "I think Emma feels she has to perform. She made a promise and will keep it. Still, for Ramsey and Molly, this has turned into a nightmare for them. Emma was well guarded today and the people who want Emma failed, but that won't stop them from trying again. And we still don't know who they are or why they're doing this."

Savich said, "There's not much time left before Emma's on her way to Chicago. The question is if they try again here, what will they do?"

They continued to discuss the case while they walked to the parking lot and got in Savich's Porsche. As he started up the car, his cell phone belted out Joan Jett's "I Love Rock 'n' Roll."

Savich passed his cell to Sherlock. "Ben? Dillon's driving. What's happened?"

"I've got some news for you, Sherlock, about the cars in the Kennedy Center parking lot. No luck there, but my people didn't stop. They checked all the cars parked on surrounding streets. They spotted a rental car, found out it was rented by somebody out of Nevada." He paused a moment, and she could see his grin. "We got a name."

24

FRIDAY, LATE AFTERNOON

The tension headache behind Molly's left ear magically disappeared when her father, Mason Lord, appeared at their suite at three o'clock that afternoon. She'd called him yesterday to tell him what had happened at Kennedy Center, and he'd told her they should come to the compound, but he hadn't told her he'd come to Washington.

She didn't say a word, simply walked to him, put her arms around his chest, and hugged him close. He pulled her in, hugged her back. She breathed in the subtle lemon scent he wore that always reminded her of the hills covered with lemon trees in Positano on the Amalfi Coast, their subtle scent in the very air you breathed. She looked up at him and simply knew he would do everything in his power to guard Emma. "Dad, I can't tell you how glad I am to see you. We still don't know who tried to take Emma and they tried again this morning. A police officer was hurt. Ramsey and I agree the best place to keep Emma safe is with you in Oak Park."

He gently set her away from him, studied her face. "You look tired, Molly, upset and worried. That's why I'm here, so I can take you all home with me. We'll figure it out, Molly."

Mason turned then and smiled at a young woman who stood off to his side. "Molly, this is my wife, Elizabeth Beatrice. Actually, we were on our last honeymoon stop in Paris when you called." His voice sounded possessive, and something else—he sounded proud. Her misogynist father sounded proud, of a woman? She was his wife? He'd said nothing about her when she'd called him the previous night.

"My dear, this is my daughter, Molly Hunt."

For a moment, Molly couldn't take it in. She felt like she'd been tossed on a stage in the middle of a bizarre play and didn't know her lines. How had this happened? Well, why not? If his new wife could overlook her new husband being a big-time crook, she'd be marrying a dashing, wealthy, and handsome man. Evidently, Elizabeth Beatrice and her family had been willing to do just that, that is, if they even knew. "Hello," Molly said. "Ah, welcome to the family."

She stepped forward, shook Molly's hand. "Hello, Molly. I'm so pleased to meet you. Your father has talked so much about you. He showed me your magazine photographs, even gave my father and mother a copy of your book of photographs of the Amalfi Coast. He said you were doing a second book. I can't wait to see it."

Her father had bragged about her? Given her book to his new in-laws? Molly felt light-headed. She had to be in an alternate universe. It was true her father had slowly changed in the last six years but had this young woman sent him over the finish line? Her father was proud of both her and his daughter? Whatever, it was amazing and really quite wonderful.

"And, of course, Mason much admires Judge Hunt"—Elizabeth's dark eyes twinkled just a bit—"and his incredible Emma. He doesn't stop bragging about the twins. I'm sorry we're rather travel worn, but we just flew in from Paris as Mason said, and your father wanted to see you immediately. I'm so sorry there are problems, but your father is here now." She sounded like she believed utterly her new husband could solve anything thrown his way.

"Thank you." Molly couldn't help it, she blurted out, "You're English."

Elizabeth Beatrice nodded. Mason said, "Her father is Viscount Bellamy of Grace Hall in Hampshire. She just took a first in economics at Oxford." Again, the pride rang out.

Molly couldn't help staring at the young woman with her handfuls of beautiful curling black hair falling to her shoulders, framing her exquisite face. Her equally dark eyes, behind large black-framed glasses, held a good deal of intelligence, and, if Molly wasn't mistaken, humor. Naturally, she had an English peaches-and-cream complexion. Molly took Elizabeth Beatrice's smooth white hand in hers and smiled at the gorgeous young woman, at least ten years her junior, now her stepmother. She felt laughter bubble up. Would her father always surprise her? It was a good thing both she and Ramsey had learned to take things in stride whenever they involved her father. An English bride fresh from university who wore glasses. She flashed an instant back to his second wife, Eve, even more physically perfect than his third. Eve herself had remarried last year. What was his name? Rich Doulos, yes, that was it, scion of a wealthy family in South Florida. Rule Shaker had a son-in-law again, probably as shady as he was. Molly's head was still spinning. She shook her head at herself, and stepped back. "I'm sorry to keep you in the hall. Please, come in." Molly held the door open and waved them in, still absorbing the astounding fact this woman was now her father's wife. She felt laughter bubble up. As Molly watched her new stepmother walk into the suite on her husband's arm, steady on her four-inch Louboutins, she'd be willing to bet this exquisite, assured young woman with the amazing name hadn't married her father for his money. There seemed to be more to her than that, and more between them.

She wasn't surprised her father had given her no warning he was going to marry a third time. She doubted he ever told anyone much of anything unless he chose to. Molly prayed he'd had been careful this time, after his near-death experience with his second wife, Eve. Would he revert to his misogynist ways in six months or a year, show Elizabeth off as his prized possession as he had Eve? Delight in other men's envy? Maybe the envy part, but Elizabeth Beatrice, a possession? No, not possible.

Mollye remembered clearly how he'd treated her, his own daughter, namely her, with his own special blend of contempt and indifference when she was growing up, because she was a girl and of no use to him, until six years ago, when she'd saved his life and he'd had to accept she'd seen threats to him he hadn't. She'd marveled at how he'd changed since then, slowly at first, from the cold indifferent king who'd treated her like his subject to a father who kissed her cheek, smiled at her, even hugged her now and then. He'd slapped Ramsey on the back and gifted him Cuban cigars when she'd birthed the twin boys. Ever since then he'd come to San Francisco every few months, and they in turn had visited him on holidays, once even on Valentine's Day. He'd come because he loved Emma and maybe her, too. And certainly the twins.

"Mama! Who's here?"

"Trail mix? Someone brought trail mix? It's Grandpa!"

The twins were on him in an instant, lifting their arms at exactly the same time, now talking a mile a minute to each other in twin talk. Mason Lord laughed, scooped both of them up in his arms, and hugged them. "You both smell like chocolate," he said, sniffing one, then the other. "And now you want trail mix?"

As they continued to babble, incomprehensibly to all except Emma and their parents, Mason looked over their heads at Emma, who stood back smiling at him. "Hello, Emma," he said. "Come meet Elizabeth Beatrice." Again, a smile lit his very handsome austere face. He laughed, shook his head. "She's your step-grandmother."

Elizabeth Beatrice looked shocked for a moment, then she shoved up her glasses and she, too, laughed.

Cal, his arms locked around his grandfather's neck, called out, "Emmy, it's Grandpa and a strange lady. Grandpa, did you bring us a present?"

Gage reared back against his arm. "You always give us presents."

Cal said, bouncing, "What's in those big bags on the floor beside the lady?"

Gage said, "For us?"

"Presents? You expected me to bring you presents? You think what's in that bag is for you? It's not your birthdays and it's not Christmas."

The twins' eyes stayed fastened on the two big bags. "It's nearly April and that's Easter."

Mason turned to his wife. "These are the twins, Cal and Gage. Boys, pay attention now, this is my wife."

Cal and Gage gave Elizabeth Beatrice a cursory look, their attention still on the two bags at their step-grandmother's feet. "Hi, ma'am. Can we have our presents?"

Elizabeth Beatrice looked from one small face to the other. "Which one are you?"

The twins exchanged looks, grinned, and said each other's names at the same time.

Molly said, "It's the other way around. They like to twist you up, if they can get away with it. You can tell them apart because Gage fell out of a tree last year. See the small scar just above this left eyebrow? Sorry, guys, you're busted."

Elizabeth Beatrice lightly touched a fingertip to each small face. "Cal and Gage. I like your names."

"Papa named us."

"Mama was too tired to think about it."

"I can only imagine." She smiled at Emma, still hanging back. "Why do you have two names?"

She cocked her head to one side, sending her thick black curls cascading over her shoulder. "Well, my mother told me she'd never make chocolate biscuits for me again if I didn't use both names. I love biscuits so what can I do? And you're Emma. I've streamed your concerts, and marveled. I've admired you before I met your grandfather. It really is a pleasure to meet you. Goodness, now I'm related to a piano prodigy."

Emma looked from her grandfather back to her new step-grandmother and couldn't help but grin. His new wife was maybe twelve years older than she was. "Thank you. I love your accent."

Elizabeth Beatrice looked over their heads to see Ramsey walking into the suite living room. He wore slacks, a white shirt, the sleeves rolled up to his elbows. She blinked, did a double take.

Molly didn't blame her. Ramsey was a beautiful man, all tough-looking and stern like the judge he was, until he smiled, and that's what he did when he saw Elizabeth Beatrice, a dark eyebrow shooting up in question.

After Ramsey was introduced to her, Elizabeth Beatrice dropped to her knees to the twins' eye level and motioned for Mason to hand her the two wrapped boxes. "You've been very patient, Gage, and yes, I know it's you. This one is for you. And, Cal, here is your almost April, almost Easter present."

There were shouts and ripped paper, then silence for about three seconds, then more shouts as the twins lifted out wooden trains, four cars each, exquisitely rendered by a wood carver in Prague, Mason told them. "We spent a week in Prague. Elizabeth Beatrice hadn't been there since her childhood."

Molly said, "Good going, you really scored. But now you've set the bar really high. The mind boggles at what they'll expect on their birthdays much less Christmas."

Elizabeth Beatrice said, "My younger brother, Thomas, adored trains when he was their age. Actually, he still does."

Elizabeth Beatrice turned back to the twins. "See the dining car? The tables are set and there are glasses. Soon the passengers will come in for their dinner." And within five minutes of her arrival, Elizabeth Beatrice had made two little boys' her slaves.

Mason Lord walked over to Emma as their new stepgrandmother showed the boys their trains. "We brought you something, too, Emma." He handed her a flat box.

25

Emma opened the box slowly, lifted out a thick sheet of cream stationery. She read it and gasped. "Oh, Grandpa! Mama, Dad, it's a handwritten invitation from Mikhail Ivanov, you know, the world-famous pianist from St. Petersburg. He's asked me to play a duet with him when he visits San Francisco to play with the orchestra in September. He wrote the music himself." She unfolded six sheets of music. "Look, he's sent it to me." She flung her arms around Mason Lord's chest, just as her mother had done, and held on tight. She pulled back, her eyes shining. "I don't know what to say. Imagine, Mikhail Ivanov. I'd admired him forever, streamed his performances." Emma hugged her grandfather again. "It's wonderful. Thank you, thank you."

Elizabeth Beatrice left the twins with their trains and came to stand beside her husband. "We met Mr. Ivanov in Milan. He was shopping for new suits, he said, because the tailors in Milan were the best in the world. He's a lovely man, Emma. When Mason told him you were his granddaughter, he pumped Mason's hand, said he'd heard you play, he'd streamed your performances, too, just as Mason and I have. He said he particularly admired your performance of Beethoven's Piano Concerto no. 3 with the Philadelphia Orchestra. He said it brought tears to his eyes. He told us our appearance was a miracle because he'd just written the music for a duet for piano and had wondered what he'd do with it, and now he knew. He'd play it with you in San Francisco."

Mason clasped Emma's shoulders in his hands. "He said he thought you're brilliant. We traded email addresses so you can keep in touch with him."

In that moment, Molly loved her father more than she ever had, master criminal or not.

The twins shouted to their father to come and look at their trains. Ramsey, smiling, stretched out on the carpet and started explaining how the engines worked. They shouted to their grandfather to come and show them where to shovel the coal, but he demurred and sat instead in one of the large living room arm chairs, crossing his legs over the perfect crease in his pants. Elizabeth Beatrice joined Ramsey on the carpet to play trains with the twins. She seemed to enjoy the twins' boundless enthusiasm. Maybe because she had a younger brother, Thomas?

Molly looked back to her father. He looked as dapper as ever in a tailored lightweight gray wool suit, a white shirt and darker gray tie, Ferragamos on his long narrow feet. His hair was a beautiful pewter now, no dye job for him, and with his thin blade of a nose, his lean face etched with high cheekbones, he looked like a slender aristocrat among peasants. She watched his eyes go frequently to his wife even as he spoke to Emma, who'd sat down on the sofa next to him. Molly wondered if he hadn't told her about his new marriage because he feared she'd make fun of him, taking a third wife ten years his daughter's junior. No, no one's opinion would concern him. She heard him asking Emma questions about the other young performer, Vincenzo Ross—and how did he know about Vincenzo? Molly shook her head. He'd come for Emma, that was what was important, new wife or not.

Emma leaned toward him. "Grandpa, how did you find out

I was in trouble?"

He looked briefly amused at her question. "Your mother called me, Emma, and told me. I hope you're looking forward to visiting us after you play at Kennedy Center tonight."

Cal and Gage yawned at exactly the same time. Molly laughed, scooped them both up, and carted them to their bedroom for their afternoon naps, the twins whining and complaining every step. Molly knew they'd be asleep in two minutes. She doubted she'd be hauling them around much longer, they were getting too heavy. She hoped the babysitter she'd arranged to spend the evening with them tonight was endowed with fortitude and a sense of humor.

When she returned to the suite living room, Emma was telling her grandfather about what had happened to her in San Francisco. Her voice was calm, without any fear or stress. Ramsey sat close beside her.

Rather than a simple nod, as was his wont, Mason took her hand. "Well done, Emma. I'm very proud of what you did. Miles and Gunther will be pleased you kept your head, but not surprised. You were very brave." Mason Lord said to Ramsey, "I'm pleased you taught her how to take care of herself."

Gunther was Mason Lord's right-hand man, something like his bodyguard. Molly had never cared exactly what he did when he accompanied her father on his visits to San Francisco. He'd worked for her father as long as she could remember, and he was a favorite with the twins. Miles, her father's majordomo and chef, had always been kind to her, always been on her side. The whole Hunt family looked forward to seeing Gunther and Miles. Gunther gave Emma shooting lessons and Miles gave them chocolate chip cookies. Whenever they visited, Molly knew she'd find the twins in the kitchen with Miles, underfoot, but he never seemed to mind. How would her father's twenty-four-year-old wife fit into that life behind the guarded walls of his compound?

Ramsey said, "Mason, I believe Molly told you Special Agent Dillon Savich and his wife, Special Agent Lacey Sherlock, are involved?"

Mason Lord sat back, tapped his long slender fingers together. "Of course. I'm pleased they are, and that Agent Sherlock has recovered."

Emma said, "Poor Aunt Sherlock. One of the men came into the concert hall during rehearsals and shot her in the neck with a dart. She's okay, but she was really mad."

Molly said, "Lieutenant Ben Raven, Metro, the MPD is helping. He's assigned four men as guards for tonight's performance."

A touch of contempt flitted across Mason's face. He said, "I have two men here who will see to Emma's safety at Kennedy Center. I'll arrange for our flight to Oak Park in the morning." He flicked a small speck of lint from the arm of his cashmere jacket. "A pity they've made no progress."

Elizabeth Beatrice came to sit on the rolled arm of the sofa next to her husband. She lightly touched his shoulder. "You said you wondered if what's happening to Emma has something to do with you, Mason."

Mason said, "Elizabeth Beatrice and I discussed this situation on our flight here to Washington. She knows Emma was taken six years ago only because she's my granddaughter. I hope I'm not responsible again for what's happened."

Ramsey said, "We've checked into all possible relatives of Father Sonny."

"Who is he?"

Mason said to his wife, "He was the pathetic ex-priest who kidnapped Emma when she was only six years old. When he tried to take Emma in Monterey—an oceanside town in California—Molly shot him. He died in the hospital."

He didn't just pass away from his injuries, though. Molly knew her father had had him killed there. She said, "We were all very grateful it was finally over, whatever the exact cause. There's no one left in his family. But he was hired by your former partner, Dad, Rule Shaker. Do you think it could be him?"

Mason said without hesitation, "He wouldn't dare. He knows I'd come after him myself, bury him in the desert if he tried anything like this again after so many years."

If Molly wasn't mistaken, Elizabeth Beatrice's eyes glittered.

Ramsey said, "Well, he certainly knows how dangerous it would be for him, but if he is involved, it's because something must have happened in the past few months, something he believes critical to him and his interests. Can you think of anything you've done in the past few months, Mason, to make him think you broke the truce? Something that sent him over the edge?"

"What truce?" Elizabeth Beatrice asked.

Mason took Emma's hand as he said to Elizabeth Beatrice, "Molly arranged an agreement between us six years ago forcing us to stay out of each other's business. I'll tell you all about it on our flight back to Chicago." He continued to Ramsey, "I've had no contact with him for six years, no involvement with any of his business dealings. Actually, I hadn't given him a thought in a very long time. Wait, I did hear he was having his own problems, business falling off at his casinos, some of his croupiers leaving, some of his waitresses attacked on the street, even vandalism. I suppose it would be natural for him to wonder if all that was a coincidence, and maybe think of me, but he wouldn't take a risk like this unless he was confident of his facts." Mason shrugged. "But he has to know I want to keep the truce in place so there'd be nothing for him to find."

"Could it be someone else besides this Shaker, Mason?" Elizabeth Beatrice asked.

Instead of giving her a dismissive nod as he had Molly most of her life, Mason gave his wife his full attention. "I'm considering all my competitors, of which there are only a few nowadays."

Ramsey said, "No major blowups with any of them?"

"No. As I told Molly, I've been out of the country a good bit not only these past weeks with Elizabeth Beatrice, but also in England quite a lot of the time these past six months wooing this incredible woman. Still, I've got all my people working on it. I do want to speak with Savich and Sherlock." He gave a small smile, said to his bride, "The two FBI agents I've told you about. They're good, but if this has anything to do with me, they simply don't have my resources."

"Still," Elizabeth Beatrice said, closing her hand over his, "they might have fresh ideas."

Mason nodded, then said in his commander-in-chief voice, "Gunther has already collected some interesting rumors. It's too soon to know if the rumors are legitimate. Everyone's agreed, our next step will be to get Emma safe at Oak Park?"

Yet again, Molly marveled at him. Her father was concerned about what they thought? Molly, Ramsey, and Emma all nodded.

26

Porte Franklyn

LATE FRIDAY AFTERNOON

Kirra thanked the gods of justice the ridiculous plea bargain she'd been forced to offer to Marvin Bailey's defense attorney and stoically present to Judge Rupert Blankenship that morning in court had left the good judge red in the face. Judge Blankenship was disgusted and showed it. He looked from her to Bailey's attorney, while Bailey, who'd been smirking at her from the defense table, looked uncertainly back at him. The judge told them to go back to conference and come up with a more appropriate sentence for Bailey, and the wonderful man had set a date for them to reappear before him, not any other judge. Bailey, who had a sheet longer than her arm, had looked at the judge like he wanted to murder him, then her. She'd given Bailey and his attorney a big smile. It was all she could do not to shout and wave a fist.

But there'd been another case that afternoon in Judge Obermeyer's court that had made her so angry she'd pictured pulling the judge out of his chair and smacking him on his bald head and then storming into Hailstock's office, kicking his desk and calling him a slag, a bogan, a wombat, and a lot of other things, because Aussie curses were endlessly inventive. She'd had to plea-deal out DeVon Crowder, a three-time felon, to only six months in county lockup for breaking and entering, robbing a dozen houses with a gun in his pocket, ready to use it if any of the homeowners resisted him. She'd nearly gone over the edge when Obermeyer had practically congratulated Kirra on her enlightened approach, working with defense attorneys rather than against them. Obermeyer gave nothing short of a pep talk to DeVon Crowder, the wanker.

Alec Speers, her boss, said from behind her, "Are you done preparing the Delone case? Or have you been too busy cursing in Aussie about Crowder?"

"I started with calling Hailstock a wanker and Obermeyer a wombat and it went downhill from there. In the privacy of my own head, of course."

He laughed. "Wombat? I thought a wombat was a really cute little animal, right?"

"In Aussie, a wombat is also an overweight, lazy, slow idiot, the definition that fits in Obermeyer's case."

Alec gave her a big grin. "Listen up, Mandarian, you won with Judge Blankenship refusing the plea bargain. You must have really played it well. I wish I could have been there."

"One win and one Hailstock-ordered six-month deal is a good thing? That's only fifty percent, Alec. A quarterback with that pass completion percentage wouldn't be around long. There at the end the defendant was nearly laughing with glee, the defense attorney was giving me a victory smile, and it looked to me like Obermeyer was going to come down from the bench and pat me on the head."

Alec laughed again. "Nah, his knees are too bad. Obermeyer's nearly ready to retire, so there's hope. Enjoy the wins, Kirra, they're all the sweeter working with Hailstock. At least you'll get to tell him Blankenship thought his plea deal was a lame excuse for a sentence. Maybe he'll see the light, who knows?"

"Yeah, like that would ever happen. I wish I could quote him Blankenship's exact words—'Are you kidding me, Ms. Mandarian? You made a deal to put this lifelong felon with a gun in his pocket back on the street in six months?' Better yet, I wish Hailstock had been there to hear it."

"So do I," he said over his shoulder as he turned away. "You've had a long day, Kirra. So have I. Go home, enjoy your weekend."

As Kirra walked to her car in the nearly empty Justice Plaza garage, she pulled out her new cell phone to call Uncle Leo, but realized he wouldn't have coverage because he was somewhere in the wilds of the Northern Territory on an extreme adventure tour, probably the roughest terrain he could find because, he'd told her, he'd be leading a bunch of young bruisers from a climbing club in Memphis who believed they were in better shape than he was. She sighed, put her phone away. She'd wanted to hear her uncle's voice, telling her whatever he wished, about the team members and how they were doing, about their kids, all of it, or laughing with her about his latest group of sooks. He always made her feel less alone. How she wished she could confide in him, tell him she knew who was responsible for her parents' death—his sister's death. But she couldn't, not yet. If he knew what she'd done, what she was still doing, he'd be appalled, yell at her for endangering herself. Didn't she understand she was the most important one? No one else? He'd stop her cold, even if he had to fly to the States to see to it himself.

There was her best friend, Cila , but telling her was out of the question. Kirra wasn't about to make her an accessory. No, Eliot Ness would never be spoken of between them.

Kirra held her car fob close to her leg, the key out. Since she'd become Eliot Ness, she'd made it a habit. As she walked down the ramp to the second garage level, she stayed alert for any unexpected movement. She wished she wasn't leaving so late. She heard none of the usual voices, the occasional laughs, the sounds of cars starting. She was alone, with only the sound of her heels ricocheting loud as bullets off the concrete walls. She gave a nod to one of Jeter's detectives, said hi to a secretary from personnel who jumped at the sound of her voice. She walked past empty car slots. It was quiet, too quiet, the shadows becoming deeper and darker. As she walked through them, they seemed to shift, making bizarre patterns on the concrete walls. Kirra tried to talk herself out of the seed of fear growing in her belly. *Keep walking, it's all right, no one's hiding in a dark corner waiting to leave you lying on the concrete floor. Keep walking.*

She'd parked her rental RAV just to the right up ahead, next to the big concrete column at P2. She froze at a sound behind her, whirled around, brought up her key fob, and waited, not moving, listening. She heard nothing else. Kirra let out a harsh breath. She was being an idiot, making herself crazy. She was disgusted with herself and cursed. Then she laughed, her laugh returning to her as an unworldly echo.

When she slipped inside her RAV, Kirra locked the doors first thing, pressed her forehead to the steering wheel, and slowed her breathing. Everything was all right. But was it, really? Could Grissom or Oliveras know who she was? When Ryman Grissom chased her out of the woods, he could have seen her Audi, maybe even made out a couple of the letters of her license plate, enough to find out her name. She hadn't thought to muddy up her plates that first night at the Oliveras house. Maybe he'd even snapped photos with his cell phone, like Detective Foxxe had when Aldo Springer drove away from Corinne Ewing's house.

Kirra stayed watchful as she drove toward home. Her stomach growled and she pictured a pizza for dinner loaded with black olives and sausage. She looked in her rearview and spotted a white van three cars behind her. A delivery van? She couldn't see the sides, where there might be a name, some kind of designation. The van stayed back three cars, always three cars. She made a couple of turns to be sure the white van was following her. It always turned with her, keeping its distance. She tried to see how many people were in the van, but the afternoon sun was bright in her eyes and she could only make out the shape of the driver.

All right, they know who I am. It was a hard pill to swallow, but no choice. It meant she'd been careless, something Eliot Ness would never be. But now on the open road, out of that dark empty Justice Plaza garage with all its shadows, Kirra wasn't afraid. There was a good chance she could outdrive them. She was in an all-wheel drive RAV, whoever it was behind her in a clunky van. She was comfortable driving at speed while weaving and dodging because she'd had a one-semester fling while she was at university in Canberra with an off-road racing fanatic who'd taught her how. But she needed a plan to deal with whatever they'd throw at her. She could drive toward the police station rather than home, but that would take her into downtown traffic, and red lights. If they were armed, they could shoot her if she let them get too close and a bystander could be hurt.

She glanced again in her rearview, slowed. Two cars, and then the van was right behind her, but not crowding, just another commuter heading home after putting in a late day at work. The sun went behind clouds and Kirra saw the driver more clearly—a man wearing a watch cap. If there was anyone else in the van, they were in the back, out of sight.

"Let's see what you've got, then, you bloody wanker," she said aloud as she turned right onto Grapeseed Avenue, away from town. She drove sedately for three blocks toward the Ross Parkway. At the last second she veered away from the parkway on-ramp and drove instead onto what was now the frontage road, once, years before, one of the main thoroughfares through Porte Franklyn. It was in miserable shape now, not maintained for a good two decades, a remnant of the 1960s. Few people used it anymore unless they'd had too much to drink, because it was dangerous, the ancient hardtop broken and potholed, but Kirra knew it well. She'd practiced on it often because it was challenging and usually empty. The road twisted and climbed when it parted from the parkway, switchbacked over the rising hills east of town, until it flattened out some five miles from Wilmont. There were only a few old exits that gave onto narrow country roads to smaller communities, overgrown and hardly used and no guardrails to keep a car from flying free down naked cliffs covered only with brush. She speeded up when they approached the first hill.

The white van kept up, staying a good fifty yards behind her. The driver had to realize she'd noticed him. Did he wonder where she was headed on this ancient unused road? Pleased they'd soon be in the middle of nowhere where there'd be no witnesses?

The white van suddenly speeded up and honked, as if to pass her. She looked back. He was ready to make his move. The van smashed into her rear bumper at an angle, forcing her into a slide toward the edge of the road and the drop-off into a deep gulley below. Kirra steered into the slide to get back control, turned back toward the middle of the road, and floored it, pulling away from the van. She was headed downhill again toward a flat stretch she knew would veer suddenly into another curve, this one sharp, dangerous at high speed. She slowed a bit and let the van roar up behind her again. Just before the van struck her rear again, she powered away, so the RAV barely felt the blow.

She knew one of the exits to a country road was coming up, a sharp right immediately after a blind turn. She floored it, squealing a good distance away from the van. She downshifted into the blind turn and skidded the RAV off the exit onto the side road. She pulled behind a stand of maple trees and waited.

27

A few seconds later the van screeched around the turn, the driver nearly losing control before he managed to straighten the van. He didn't slow, didn't see the side road, and roared ahead down the hill.

Kirra pulled back onto the road, saw the van racing ahead of her. The driver thought she was still in front of him, but he would realize very soon she wasn't. She hit the gas. The driver saw her only the second before she slammed into the back of the van. His rear wheels went into a skid, and she saw him twist the steering wheel hard the wrong way, turning the skid into a spin, the tires squealing as the van lurched toward the edge of the road. She heard him scream as the van tilted up on two wheels and went hurtling over the edge into a narrow gulley, ripping through bushes, flipping over on its mad fall to the bottom.

Kirra pulled the RAV close to the edge of the road and jumped out. She was shaking, adrenaline flooding her. She ran to the edge of the road and looked down. The van had crashed into a gigantic old oak at the bottom of the gulley. It lay on its side, smoke billowing up from its smashed engine. The driver's-side door shoved out and a man rolled out of the van onto the rocky ground. He lay on his back, unmoving.

Kirra called 911, texted Jeter, even though she knew telling him a man had tried to kill her would make him wonder if she was Eliot Ness. There was no hope for it. Was it Ryman Grissom lying motionless on the ground beside the accordioned van? She took off her heels and slipped on the sneakers in her gym bag. She made her way slowly down, holding on to bushes to keep from skidding and falling.

He was hugging his chest, panting and groaning. It wasn't Ryman Grissom, it was a young man she didn't recognize. His chinos were ripped, showing a gash in what looked like a broken leg. No need for a tourniquet, the gash was only oozing blood. She didn't see any other obvious wounds. She went down on her knees beside him. His eyes sharpened on her face. He whispered, "How'd you do that?"

"A race car driver taught me how to take care of any clacker who tried to take me on. I've got to say, too, that only a clacker would take on a RAV on that road in a clunky van."

"What's a clacker?"

"Haven't said that in a long time. Let's say a clacker refers to your rear end, and not in a good way. I've called 911. They'll be here soon." She studied his face. "You must have come really cheap since you're not even voting age yet."

He gasped out, "I can vote! You weren't supposed to go off on this road like you did, you were supposed to go home where I could put you down fast and easy." He turned his face away from her, hugged his ribs, and moaned.

He didn't look good. His face was bone-white, his eyes blurred with pain. "Hang in there." She sat back on her heels, stared down at a man who hadn't yet reached his twenty-fifth year. He had thick tangled blond hair flecked with blood and light-colored eyes nearly blind with pain. She saw acne scars on his cheeks. She knew he was in a bad way but there was nothing she could do for him. She leaned down. "I thought the man trying to kill me was Ryman Grissom, but I got you instead. Did he hire you? Or Khan Oliveras? Elson Grissom?"

She saw he recognized the names. "He'll get you. You're dead." He tried to spit at her, but his spittle landed on his shoulder.

"I've got to say you were pretty easy. I don't understand why they sent a rookie like you. Did they pluck you out of a schoolyard?"

He was breathing faster now, harder. "I ain't no rookie! I'm twenty-three and I'm really good. You weren't supposed to go off on this stupid road. You're only a girl, you shouldn't be driving like that." He clutched his ribs. Tears seeped beneath his lashes, ran in rivulets down his cheeks.

Kirra leaned close. "Tell me your name."

He was fading fast, she saw it. He whispered, "You were just lucky, that's all. My van's totaled."

Again, she asked, "What's your name?"

He gave her a pain-filled death stare. She took his hand, squeezed it. He was shaking now uncontrollably and she was helpless. There was nothing she could do for him, nothing. Blood flecked his mouth. He whispered, "Mama," and his eyes rolled back. From one moment to the next he was gone.

Kirra sat back on her heels. He stared up at her unseeing. He was twenty-three years old, just starting life, and he was dead. "I'm sorry," she said. "I'm really sorry."

She realized she was on the edge, shocky, and fought to keep her focus. She saw a Beretta stuffed inside his belt, didn't touch it. As he'd said, he'd expected her to go home, where he would have slipped into her condo and shot her with it. She slipped her hand into his pockets. No ID, nothing but a twenty-dollar bill and some breath mints. She wondered if he'd killed before or if she was his first, wondered what his mother would say when she found out son was killed trying to commit murder, and yet, he'd thought of her when he was dying.

Kirra rose, pulled out her cell, took photos of him, the car, his path down the cliff. She emailed the photos to Jeter. She took off her suit jacket and laid it over him.

She walked around the white van. The driver's-side door was nearly ripped off its hinges. She looked inside and did a double take. On the floorboard lay a Sig Sauer pistol with a suppressor attached, a SIG 551 assault rifle beside it. It was the assault rifle that got to her. She knew it could blow a hole through you the size of a baseball. She swallowed bile. She looked back at him. He was twenty-three, and in the moment before he died she felt terribly sorry for him, she'd held his hand, tried to give him comfort. She was only three years older than he was and he'd come to kill her.

She knew she could easily be the one lying there dead. There would have been no one around. She would have died alone. Kirra gulped, felt a moment of nausea, swallowed.

It seemed like forever until she heard sirens.

After Kirra gave her statement to the responding officers, she and Jeter watched the EMTs slowly and carefully gurney up the young man who'd tried to kill her. One of them waved.

Jeter called out, "Hey, Atina."

A tall lanky woman with her signature cornrows, Atina Cooper had seen just about everything in her thirty-eight years. Jeter had known her ever since she'd passed her exams fifteen years before. She walked over, nodded at Kirra. She stared toward the cliff edge of the road, shook her head. "I haven't seen a little killer boy like him in well-nigh five years, and he wasn't loaded down with weapons like this one. You're Kirra

Mandarian, right? A prosecutor?" At Kirra's nod, Atina said, "Like you told Robbie, no wallet, no ID. I gotta say, girl, I saw what he did to your RAV's rear end, and I'm impressed it's still up here on the road. You've got to be some driver."

"He wanted to kill me with that van."

"Well, he didn't, did he? We'll see what the ME has to say, whether he had any drugs on board. I'm off. Hear you've got a new girlfriend, Jeter. You sure can pick 'em—a federal prosecutor?" Atina saluted him, climbed into the back of the ambulance, and called out, "Jeter, you take care of that pretty little girl. I don't want to be hauling her to the ME, like this one."

Jeter and Kirra watched the ambulance carefully make its way past the police tape and the two black-and-whites down the frontage road back toward town. Jeter's cell buzzed a message. He said, "Savich. He said he's loaded down with another case, can't come out, but to keep him in the loop. He's sending Special Agent Griffin Hammersmith." Jeter texted back an okay and shoved his cell back into his pants pocket.

Jeter looked at Kirra's face, not as pale as it had been; still, his voice was gentle. "You know there'll be an inquiry, of course, and what happened here will get out, to your office, around town. You'll have to answer some questions, but with all the weapons in his van and damage to your rental car, there won't be any doubt he was chasing you, out to kill you. I'm sure he'll have a record to prove it. Even if they find you ran him off the road, it was in self-defense. You're lucky he came at you here. Still, you could easily have ended up at the bottom of that gulley."

Now he had to walk on eggshells, no choice. "I thought you didn't have any enemies, Kirra, since you're always complaining you spend your time plea-bargaining people back on the streets. So tell me, why would a thug you've never seen or tried want to kill an innocent young prosecuting attorney?"

She'd nearly stopped shaking, thank goodness. She managed a shrug. "I piss off a lot of people, Jeter, but enough to kill me? Nobody I know." She was trying her best to look guileless, but she managed to look only pale and pathetic.

He'd been stupid, baiting her, being sarcastic. Of course Oliveras and Grissom must have found out who she was. He didn't want to make her lie to him and she couldn't confess to him she was Eliot Ness. He hated playing a game of "let's pretend" with her, but at least he could try to keep Oliveras or Grissom from killing her. He could surveil her again until Agent Hammersmith showed up. Chief Pershing wouldn't be happy with the overtime, but he'd justify it somehow.

Jeter pulled Kirra against him, rubbed her back, and whispered against her hair, "I'm sorry, kiddo. Really sorry you had to go through this. That's right, breathe deep. We don't have to talk now, it can wait."

Kirra burrowed in. She hadn't realized how starved she'd been for human contact, for kindness, for touch. Jeter said, "Savich has asked Chief Pershing to work with him to nail down exactly what happened to Josh Atwood and his mother. They already got a warrant and looked through Grissom's deleted emails, found one where Grissom asked about the going rate for pest control for a small house."

Kirra reared back in his arms. She wasn't trembling now and color was coming back into her cheeks. He'd said the right thing. Kirra said, "You know he's talking about Josh. Small house—" She shuddered. "Grissom's a monster."

"We looked up the IP address. It belongs to a Rodriguez Ells, native of Clinton, Delaware. He's a suspected member of MS-13."

He paused, knew she was thinking, planning, but he knew

she'd do something.

Kirra got herself together, couldn't take a chance she'd blurt out something to make Jeter suspect her. "Thank you, Jeter. Is there any word on the man who killed Corinne Ewing?"

"Aldo Springer. He's in the hospital with a guard, keeping his mouth shut for now. I'm thinking it'll be a race to see if we get him to talk before Oliveras takes him out. Pepper and I finished questioning Oliveras and Ryman Grissom yesterday. They had more lawyers with them than my daddy has coon guns, so it was a no go from the beginning, even for Pepper."

He forced himself to add, "I want to know about everyone you've sent to Red Onion who's out now and might have done this. Make a list, give it to me. Whoever it is, they either couldn't afford good help, or they thought you'd be pretty easy to take care of."

"Sure, I'll make up a list. You'll let me know, right?"

He gave her a last hug, dashed his fingers through his hair. "We don't have to stay any longer. Come on, I'll follow you home. Don't forget, Hendricks will be surveilling you until Agent Hammersmith gets here."

Kirra took one last look over the cliff at the smashed white van and wondered if she should take the first flight back to Australia and Uncle Leo. She imagined her own body being hoisted up out of that gulley, saw her Uncle Leo's face etched in grief, not understanding.

28

FRIDAY NIGHT

Molly gave her daughter a final hug, careful not to mess up the light makeup on Emma's beautiful face—a dash of pale pink lipstick, some powder because the lights were merciless, and nothing else. Her thick dark hair was a shining fall to below her shoulders, held back from her face with two gold clips. Her dress was midi length, long-sleeved, and black, as she preferred when performing. She wore only the golden locket around her neck with her family's pictures inside it.

She held her daughter's face between her palms for a moment. "Emma, when you hear the mountain of applause, you'll know your father and I will be the loudest, louder even than Aunt Sherlock and Uncle Dillon and your grandfather and Elizabeth Beatrice." Molly kissed her forehead. "We love you to pieces."

Molly turned and left without looking back, closed the dressing room quietly behind her. It was their routine, hadn't varied for the past three years. Molly took deep calming breaths as she walked down the side steps stage left and slipped in next to Ramsey. Dillon and Sherlock sat beside her, her father and

Elizabeth Beatrice beside Ramsey. Molly gave Ramsey a quick kiss, another ritual, and leaned close. "Emma's ready. She's going to be remarkable tonight." Ramsey didn't have to ask if Emma was safe, not with six guards stationed at the periphery of the stage and around the concert hall, trying to blend in with the magnificently dressed audience and doing a pretty good job of it. Four of them were Ben Raven's plainclothes police, and two were the men Mason had brought with him. The only difference was her father's men wore custom-made tuxes. Ramsey had been more worried about Emma's state of mind than he'd let on, but now Molly had put that to rest. He leaned over, whispered, "It's a pity we couldn't bring the twins."

Molly spurted out a laugh, slapped her hand over her mouth, embarrassed at herself, but no one was paying any attention over the buzz of conversation in the packed concert hall. She rolled her eyes. "Can you imagine what they'd do when Emma walked onstage?"

He gave her a mad grin. "The mind balks."

Molly turned to Sherlock sitting next to her, took her hand. "You're sure you're feeling all right?"

"Yes, of course." Sherlock lowered her voice. "You can't fault Mason's taste. Elizabeth Beatrice is very beautiful." She paused a moment, added, "He looks proud as punch, not at himself for acquiring such a prize, but proud of her, proud of them, together."

Sherlock had done a double take when she'd first set eyes on Elizabeth Beatrice in the lobby at Kennedy Center. She was wearing an off-the-shoulder pure white dress, simple and elegant, her glossy black hair framing her exquisite face, like a princess with black-framed glasses and intelligent eyes. She wore diamonds in her ears and on her wrist, and her wedding ring sparkled and gleamed in the bright lights. At first

Sherlock had been the cynic, wondering why this beautiful young woman would marry a man so much older than she. Of course there was a lot to be said for being young and newly married to a wealthy man who took you to Milan and had all your clothes designed for you. But now her cynicism had fallen away. She rather believed the obvious love between this odd couple would only grow in the upcoming years.

Molly said quietly, "I've never seen my father this content before, or so happy. It's like he's finally found the one person in this world to complete him." She still marveled. He was treating his new wife, all of them, warmly, with approval. Elizabeth Beatrice was certainly beautiful. Molly had thought she herself looked very nice in her long blue gown lightly skimming her body, her hair piled on her head and diamond earrings flashing, until she'd gotten a glimpse of Elizabeth Beatrice when she, Ramsey, and Emma had met them at her father's limo two hours before outside the Hay Adams to ferry them to Kennedy Center.

Her jealousy had gone to zero when her sweet Emma said, "Mama, you look so beautiful. I love the gorgeous shoes. Please don't trip in them."

Molly had laughed, squeezed her daughter's hand. To her surprise, Elizabeth Beatrice had said, "I agree. Your hair looks incredible, Molly. And do you know, I'm always afraid of tripping if my shoes are higher than sneakers."

Mason said then in a distant voice, "Molly's hair is her grandmother's, on her mother's side."

She grinned at her father, punched his arm. "Dad, Grandmother never liked you, and you didn't like her. I have her hair. Get over it."

Her father's face was severe as he said to his wife, "Her mother believed I wasn't good enough for her precious daughter." He paused, his voice even colder. "She was wrong."

Elizabeth Beatrice leaned up and kissed his cheek, said into his ear, "I bet she wanted you for herself."

Mason Lord had stared at her, then, incredibly, laughed. He said in a clear happy voice, "You're right, Molly, I've decided I'm now over it."

He sat now next to Savich, both drop-dead gorgeous in tuxes. Mason said quietly, "I suppose you've spotted my two guards I've posted here tonight. Mine are the ones who are well dressed although the local police officers don't look bad. They won't take their eyes off Emma."

Molly said to Sherlock, "I spotted them right away. They look like they belong in a box seat."

Mason asked Savich, "Have you found out anything helpful today?"

Savich, knowing Lord was at once distrustful and hopeful, said, "I'll let you know when we need your help." Savich had included him. He saw Mason looked pleased.

Molly saw Vincenzo Rossi move into position with Emma, stage left. Like Emma, he was dressed in black, handsome as a young Italian nobleman. Both kids looked calm, settled, relaxed. Vincenzo's parents sat on the opposite side of the concert hall, obviously afraid to even sit near them.

The lights dimmed, signaling five minutes until the performance began. The audience slowly quieted. The orchestra finished tuning their instruments, sat still in their chairs, ready. Conductor Leonard Slatkin came onstage in his bespoke tux looking like a king, his rooster tail of white hair towering high. He introduced his first violinist and beckoned to Emma.

Their beautiful girl walked onstage, head high, shoulders back. She bowed toward the darkened audience, sat on the bench, adjusted it. She took a moment to settle, took two deep breaths, as was her longtime habit.

Slatkin nodded to Emma. In the next moment the silence of the concert hall was broken by the first chords of Chopin's popular Prelude in D Flat Major. Molly closed her eyes, listened intently for any sign of nervousness or anxiety. It was perfect. No, Molly wasn't biased, not her, the mother of the Chopin goddess. Ramsey let out a breath and Molly squeezed his hand. She'd hold his hand until intermission, as always.

When the Chopin Retrospective came to an end, Slatkin called both Emma and Vincenzo to center stage. Holding hands, they bowed. Molly was on her feet, applauding wildly, along with everyone else. The applause continued until Slatkin said into his microphone, "Rather than individual encores, I'm pleased to announce Emma and Vincenzo have prepared a special surprise for you." He said nothing more as another Steinway was wheeled onto the stage. Vincenzo and Emma sat down next to each other, adjusted their benches. The lights went down. Against the back wall of the stage, a large screen slowly descended. Emma smiled at Vincenzo, lowered her head, and played the Harry Potter theme, "Hedwig's Song," as animated images of the characters from the Harry Potter movies flashed across the screen. Vincenzo segued into "Moaning Myrtle." There was laughter and oohs and aahs from the audience as the images morphed quickly, nearly blending together, but not quite. Emma continued with "The Chamber of Secrets," and Vincenzo was next with "Gilderoy Lockhart."

To close, Emma and Vincenzo played "Harry's Wondrous World" along with the orchestra. On the screen, Harry, Ron, and Hermione stood looking out over the walls of Hogwarts, until the screen went blank.

There was thunderous applause again, many bows and smiles. The applause grew even louder when Slatkin presented both Emma and Vincenzo with huge bouquets.

Knowing two twelve-year-olds wouldn't welcome the French food he favored, Mason had made reservations at Vincenti Restaurante, a popular Italian restaurant Savich recommended to him. It was rustic and softly lit, promised Italian comfort food for the children, and best of all, was only a mile and a half from Kennedy Center. The owner, Vincenti himself, directed white-coated waiters to serve their finest champagne to the adults and sparkling cider to Emma and Vincenzo. He congratulated both kids, told them he'd wished he could have heard them perform, and offered them spaghetti with his homemade meatballs.

Molly knew Vincenzo had insisted he and his parents join them, and they did, nervously, until they'd finished two glasses of champagne. Elizabeth Beatrice spoke Italian to the Rossis and they opened like roses blooming. When Emma spoke her few Italian phrases, they beamed at her.

Molly heard Sherlock's cell beep a text. Sherlock pulled out her cell, read it, and excused herself. Molly followed her to the long hallway by the bar that led to the restrooms and kitchen. Sherlock pressed in numbers, waited, then "Hello, Ben. What's up?" When she punched off, she slipped her cell back into her small evening bag. She grinned big. "That was Lieutenant Ben Raven. I already told you they'd found the rental car, a high-end Lexus. Now they know it was rented by an M. J. Pederson of Ender City, Nevada. The address was real, Pederson has lived there for twenty years, but he never left Ender City, didn't know anything about a rental car. Evidently someone had spoofed his credit card and his driver's license without his knowing it, because they were still in his pocket. The guy who has them is very likely Mr. Dart Gun.. He was sloppy leaving his car so close, but of course, he didn't expect it would be seen."

Molly's eyes danced with excitement. "Sherlock, look on my phone map—Ender City is very close to Las Vegas and Rule Shaker."

"If that's not a coincidence and Shaker is involved, he won't be happy Mr. Dart Gun pinched an ID that close to Las Vegas. We'll have video of the man from the car rental office tomorrow morning. Dillon will put him through facial recognition. If that doesn't turn up his identity, then—" She paused a moment, looked over at Dillon, who was speaking to Mason Lord. "Hmm, regardless, I think Dillon will agree it's time we took a vacation to Sin City. You'll be leaving Washington tomorrow with your father, won't you?"

29

Hay Adams Hotel
Washington, D.C.

SATURDAY MORNING

Molly had wanted desperately to sleep a little while longer, just another thirty minutes, twenty maybe, but it wasn't to be. Unlike Emma and her parents, who hadn't arrived back to the suite until well after midnight, the twins had enjoyed their regular nine hours and were rearing to go at six thirty A.M. They were already on their parents' bed talking twin talk a thousand miles an hour, hopping up and down, laughing like loons. "Mama! Papa! Waffles, can we have waffles?"

Ramsey cocked an eye open at her and managed to look pitiful, so she rolled out of bed, grabbed the twins, and hauled them out of the bedroom. She ordered a huge pot of coffee and waffles from room service and played Punk the Weasel with them until the suite doorbell rang and a bright young man with red hair in a short ponytail wheeled in a tray, a big smile on his face. "Good morning. It's a beautiful day, isn't it?" He broke off when the twins came barreling toward him, shouting, "Waffles!"

"Hey, little dudes. Yep, I brought you waffles, the cook made them himself just for you." He winked at Molly as he set the plates and silverware, lifted out two covered domes, and set them down with a flourish. "Best waffles in the Washington. I'm guessing they got you up early, right?" Molly, her hair sleep tousled, barefoot in a bathrobe, didn't know whether to punch him for his good cheer or kiss him. She decided on a smile and signed the check. She poured herself a cup of coffee, watching her sons drown the waffles in syrup.

When Ramsey and Emma walked into the living room an hour later, they saw Molly spooning the twins on the sofa, her arms around both of them to keep them from falling to the floor, all three of them asleep. When Ramsey finally woke them, it was because Mason and Elizabeth Beatrice would be due soon, and Savich had called to say he and Sherlock were on their way over to say goodbye.

Molly laughed when he woke her. "Goodness, look at the time. I haven't finished packing the twins' suitcases yet. Have you and Emma ordered your breakfasts?"

She was still dressing when Sherlock and Savich arrived, telling the twins Sean said goodbye. He was staying with his grandmother. They were drinking coffee and tea together, and thankfully Emma was playing a game with the twins in the far corner of the living room, when Molly remembered something, and groaned. "Drat, I forgot the twins' trail mix. It's a must for any trip longer than half an hour. My dad wouldn't like the twins asking him to land every five minutes for trail mix." She called downstairs to the concierge, asked for the closest convenience store.

She punched off, said, "That's a relief. There's a 7-Eleven only a block from here. Don't worry, I'll be back in plenty of time."

Emma rose. "I'll come with you, Mom."

"Emma, a favor, please. Your grandfather and Elizabeth Beatrice will be here at nine thirty. He's always on time. I'd really appreciate it if you'd stay here and keep them company. I won't be longer than ten minutes. You can tell him that."

Sherlock smiled. "I'll come with you, Molly. It's been too long since we've had some time together."

They said good morning to the two guards posted outside the suite and headed to the elevators. Molly said as she punched the down elevator button, "My dad is always on time, so be prepared to move out."

They sailed through the magnificent lobby. A doorman opened the door for them, gave them a sharp salute, and wished them a fine Saturday.

Molly said, "I figure we've still got seven and a half minutes before Dad arrives and starts agitating. He sets a time and that's it. Only death can get you a free pass." She laughed. "And it's not like we'll miss the flight. We'll limo to Dulles where his Challenger 650 is hangared at Jet Aviation, then we'll be off in luxury to Chicago. He told me he upgraded to the larger Bombardier when he decided to marry Elizabeth Beatrice, said it seats up to eleven. I bet he'll want to put the twins way in the back. Can you imagine flying all over Europe on your honeymoon in your own private jet with two bodyguards?"

Sherlock thought about this. "No," she said, "I really can't."

As they walked down H Street, Sherlock said, "Emma played wonderfully last night, despite everything. That first Chopin prelude opened every heart."

Molly weaved around a couple of teenagers who were staring at their cell phones. She drew a big breath. "Thank you. But still, though she tries to hide it, the threats these past weeks have taken a huge toll on her. She looks at people she doesn't know with suspicion and low-level fear. She's losing trust,

Sherlock, wondering if some stranger is going to come up and try to take her. Actually, it's taken a huge toll on Ramsey and me as well. Even Cal and Gage know something's not quite right in their world." Her hands fisted at her sides. "We have to end this but I have no idea how."

What could Sherlock say that didn't sound lame? She could only try. "None of you would be normal if you weren't scared, Emma especially. But you've given her valuable skills. She had no one to help her in San Francisco, but she faced down the man at Davies Hall and escaped. She has a lot of people looking out for her now—your dad, all of us, Ben Raven, and Virginia Trolley in San Francisco." She smiled. "We'll get to the bottom of this very soon. I just hope your dad doesn't have Shaker murdered in the meantime, on spec."

They wove around an older couple talking about visiting the Lincoln Monument, and a family of four, the parents valiantly trying to control their kids. Molly said, "Goodness, there are so many people out and about. It's Saturday, why aren't they sleeping in? Kill Shaker on spec? My father promised me he'd never do that, Sherlock, unless Shaker forced his hand. And he does share one thing with Shaker—he doesn't act unless he's certain."

They walked into the 7-Eleven where Molly luckily found the twins' favorite trail mix. "Plenty of M&Ms," she said, shaking the two bags. "Each twin has to have his own. Oops, we've got to hurry, four and a half minutes before Dad starts frowning and looking at his Patel Philippe."

They were swept along by pedestrians, primarily tourists, back toward the Hay Adams. Sherlock paused, looked up at the façade, at the doormen tipping their hats, ushering guests to their cabs and packing luggage into trunks. "Look at her, she's a magnificent old queen isn't she, reigning since 1928. Molly, listen a moment before we go in. You know Emma will be safe at your dad's compound, and Dillon has agreed he and I will fly to Las Vegas. Ben Raven has a BOLO out on M. J. Pederson. We will find him. There will be an end to this."

"I guess I should tell you. My dad will want to go to Las Vegas with you, no doubt in my mind."

Sherlock rolled her eyes. "Oh, joy. Well, on the plus side he'll be able to open some doors. We'll talk to Rule Shaker, maybe see your former stepmom, Eve, and her new husband."

"Be sure to give her my regards," Molly said, her voice dripping acid. "The bitch."

"Don't blame you for that shot, Eve deserves it. Try not to worry, Molly. Let us do our jobs."

A man bumped Molly, sending her into Sherlock. As Sherlock grabbed her to keep her from falling, she felt a gun muzzle dig into her back. She reached for her Glock clipped at her waist as she pivoted, brought up her knee. A man whispered in her ear, "I know what and who you are. You pull that gun and I'll kill her right here, where she stands. Get that knee down. You understand me?"

30

Sherlock saw another man was pressing a gun against Molly's back, no, not a man, a woman dressed like a man wearing a short black wig. There was nothing she could do. She let the man pull her Glock out of her waist clip. The gun muzzle pressed harder against her ribs. The man said against her ear, "Now all of us will walk nice and easy to the limo directly across the street and get in the back. Let me say it again, anything more from you, Agent Sherlock, and she's dead. We didn't expect you to be with her, but we'll make do."

As they crossed H Street, Sherlock saw the back door of a black limo being pushed open. Could she make her move now? The gun muzzle pressed hard into her back. "Don't even think about it. Move, get yourselves inside."

The woman walked around toward the driver's seat. Molly slipped in the rear, Sherlock beside her. The man followed them in, closed the back door, and locked it. His Beretta was aimed at Sherlock, center mass. She saw he was young, maybe midtwenties, his features too hard for his age, black scruff on his face he must have thought made him look sexy, but didn't. It only made him look more like a thug. And he wasn't a pro, she was certain of that because he hadn't automatically checked her for more weapons. She still had her Glock 42 in her ankle holster.

But it was the man who was already in the limo on the seat

facing them who captured Sherlock's complete attention. No doubt in her mind he was a pro. He was dressed in a sharp suit and white shirt, his face almost as white as his shirt and as smooth as Sean's, not a hint of a wrinkle anywhere. How old was he? Forty? Sixty? No way to tell. His hair was blond white. He wasn't quite albino, but it was close. His eyes were a color Sherlock had never seen before, so light a blue as to be nearly silver, his eyebrows thick blond-white slashes that nearly met, but not quite. His cold eyes looked from her to Molly, unblinking, like an alligator looking at his prey, or simply commodities he'd procured for a customer, which seemed the case. Sherlock knew it to her bones—this man was a stone-cold killer. Molly gave a small shudder beside her, so she felt it too.

The woman had quickly slid into the driver's seat without saying a word. She pulled the limo smoothly into the thick H Street traffic.

Albino sat back against the seat and folded his arms, showing them he was armed. "Zip-tie their wrists, Pope, in front of them will do."

Pope leaned toward Sherlock, his Beretta loose in his hand as he pulled zip ties out of his jacket. Sherlock jerked the Ruger out of her ankle holster, shoved it into his chest. He froze for a second, long enough for Sherlock to wrench his gun out of his hand by its barrel. She called out, "Stop the car or he gets a bullet!"

Albino laughed at her. He was pointing his Sig not at her, but at Molly. He waved a long thin white finger at Sherlock. "You didn't think this through, Agent Sherlock. Now give Pope his gun back or Mrs. Hunt dies."

"You won't kill her, you need her."

He shrugged. "It doesn't matter, one way or the other. She can be dead and fulfill her purpose. Now, Agent Sherlock, give the gun back to Pope or I'll shoot her between the eyes."

Sherlock shoved Pope back, held his Beretta and her Ruger out to him. He took them, sent a terrified look at his boss.

"Good decision, Agent Sherlock. Both of you hold your wrists together in front of you. Get the zip ties on them, Pope. I want no more misguided attempts to escape. Then take their cell phones and throw them out the window."

As Pope zip-tied them, Albino studied Sherlock then Molly with his unblinking eyes. "From a distance you look like sisters with all that red curly hair, but up close, your hair is very different." His voice was flat, detached, almost bored.

Sherlock was afraid, knew Molly was as well, but she would keep thinking, keep looking for an opening. "I have to say I didn't see this coming. You couldn't take Emma, so you came for Molly."

"I had so many choices. I could have even tried for one of those cute little boys. In fact, I still might take one of them."

Molly lost it. She lurched across the narrow space, brought her bound hands up, and scored her fingers down his face. He shoved her back, cursing, breathing hard.

Pope raised his Beretta. For an endless moment, Molly wondered if he would shoot her.

Albino said, "Pope, no. Relax. Our ladies have played their tricks. As for Mrs. Hunt, I'll punish her as I see fit." He lightly touched his fingertips to the two long scratches on his cheek. He looked at his hand. No blood. "You're lucky," he said, leaned over and slapped her so hard Molly fell to the side.

"Agent Sherlock, don't move. I will kill you if you try anything more. You're not as important to us as she is. Now straighten up, Mrs. Hunt." Molly was breathing hard, tears sheening her eyes. He leaned forward, took her chin between his fingers, and squeezed. "Be a good girl now or I'll have to hurt you. Your skin is so very fine I might already have bruised you." He stroked his fingers over the violent red mark on her cheek, pressed in hard, making her jerk with pain.

He sat back and nodded as if in approval. "When I got the call the two of you heading out on foot, I must admit to feeling lucky you were making it so easy. As for you, Agent Sherlock, I'm sure Pope would like to put a bullet in your head and dump you in the Potomac after what you just did. No man likes to look like a fool. But you're lucky. The boss asked us to bring you along."

"Who called you?"

He frowned. At himself? "None of your business, Agent Sherlock."

Sherlock said matter-of-factly, "You must know taking us is a huge mistake. You know I'm FBI, but did you know my husband is as well? There is nowhere you can take us the FBI won't find you. When they do, my husband will peel the skin off your face."

Albino laughed, showing square white teeth, but his unnerving eyes never blinked. "Such faith in a broken-down bureaucracy. I have to say, though, your husband seems rather competent."

Sherlock said, "You have no idea."

"Indeed I do. I always know all the players I face. Your husband, no matter how smart you think he is, won't find you. You will simply disappear until—until we make other arrangements."

Molly said, "Who are you? What's your name?"

He studied her a moment. Molly's chin went up. She was so scared she wanted to puke, but she wouldn't let him see it, she wouldn't.

"You may call me Nero."

Albino had a name now, ridiculous as it was. Nero? Sherlock poked the bear. "Your parents named you after an insane Roman emperor?"

If he was angry, he didn't show it. He remained motionless, no expression on his smooth white face. "It is my nom de plume, you could say. It seemed a good fit since I did a little dance while I watched my parents' house burn down with them inside it. Is that shock I see on your face, Mrs. Hunt? At murdering the two sterling citizens who spawned me?" He shrugged. "I did everyone a favor, removing those worthless losers from the planet. They were the first problem I solved."

Sherlock's studied Nero's face, saw only ferocious satisfaction. "Exactly what problem are you solving now?"

"Isn't it obvious? Pope and Domino failed to complete the mission. I was sent here to fix that problem."

Pope stiffened beside him. Nero touched his hand to Pope's sleeve. "Not really their fault. You surprised Pope at Kennedy Center and he was fast, I'll give him that, managed to shoot you in the neck with a dart and get out of there. I give you credit, Agent Sherlock, you spread an impressive net around Emma Hunt after that. Even Domino's plan to use the officer's uniform to lure Emma Hunt somewhere they'd be alone didn't work out. There you were, unexpected, right there in the women's room, seeing to your fallen police officer. Domino didn't have time to do anything. I was impressed, Agent Sherlock. It was then I judged it impossible for them to secure Emma Hunt." His eyes went to Molly. "Emma Hunt was preferable, but you, Mrs. Hunt, as I said, will do nicely."

Nero was taunting her, but it wasn't fear Molly was feeling now, it was relief. Emma was safe. Sherlock was with her only because she'd been in the wrong place. They were now in this, whatever it was, together. Molly trusted her implicitly.

She saw Ramsey's face. He'd be frantic, ready to tear the hotel down. And the twins, they'd want their mother but she wouldn't be there. No, she couldn't think about that, she had to stay focused, like Sherlock, and think. The ten minutes she'd promised was long up. Her father would be frowning by now, wondering where she was, maybe even pacing. Dillon would know they were both late. They might already have tried to call them or text. Pope, as instructed, had thrown out their cell phones. Molly wondered if their phones would be found and turned in. She said, trying to keep her voice as calm as Sherlock's, "Since you claim to know all the players, you know I'm married to Judge Ramsey Hunt, surely you've heard of Judge Dredd—and you know my father is Mason Lord. Do you have any idea what he'll do to you when he finds you? The FBI would arrest you, Agent Savich would peel your face off, my husband would kick your heart through your back, but my father?" She leaned forward, said right in his face, "My father would boil you alive. If your boss is Rule Shaker, he'd be in the same pot with you, then the two of you would be buried deep in the desert."

Nero leaned back and laughed. "Pope, just listen to her. Yes, she's Mason Lord's daughter, all right, a right chip off the old block." He lightly ran his fingertips over the scratches on his cheek. "I like women with guts, not that it matters. Neither of you understand anything, but you will."

Sherlock said, "The FBI already knows you cloned the real M. J. Pederson's driver's license and credit card Pope used to rent the pretty silver Lexus he drove to Kennedy Center. Didn't you think we'd find the rental car? Or did you simply want to be thorough? I've got to say, Nero, selecting a mark in Ender, Nevada, so close to Las Vegas, doesn't seem very smart. As for you, Pope, we saw you on camera at the car rental at Dulles. You were wearing sunglasses and that ball cap, but FBI tech is amazing, only thing they got wrong is your eye color. I have no doubt facial recognition will nail you. Big mistake. It means we'll have your boss identified in no time at all."

There was dead silence for a moment. Nero slowly turned to face Pope. He raised his Sig and shot him between the eyes. There was a huge explosion in the confined limousine, and the smell of cordite, acrid and strong. Pope didn't make a sound. He fell against the door, his eyes open, staring up at the roof of the limo. The driver, Domino, cried out, swerved the limo into an oncoming lane. Nero said sharply, "Get yourself together, Domino! He was dangerous to us, stupid!"

Molly froze, a scream clogged her throat. Nero had shot him, simply shot him. Molly had never seen anyone die in front of her. She felt bile rise in her throat. She leaned down and threw up on the floor.

Sherlock wasn't about to let him see how shocked she was. *Get it together, get it together.* She said, her voice cool, "You're insane. Nero is the perfect name for you."

He threw back his head and laughed again. "It stinks in here." He pulled a bottle of water from a side door pocket, tossed it to Sherlock. "Here, have her wash out her mouth."

He kept his Sig aimed at Sherlock's heart. "I wonder what I'll do with him. Domino, how much farther to Dulles?"

Her answer came out in a choked whisper. "Twenty minutes."

Nero buzzed down both windows. "If I knew she was going to vomit, I'd have waited. Death doesn't smell as bad, at least at first."

Molly couldn't help herself, she kept looking at Pope. He was dead, dead. Sherlock took her hand. No one said another word.

Molly couldn't believe it when the limo pulled into Jet

Aviation at Dulles and she saw a Bombardier Challenger 650 being serviced. Her father's?

Nero pulled his buzzing cell phone out of his jacket pocket, listened, glanced over at Sherlock. He said into his cell, indifference in his dead-cold voice, "Or, if you prefer, I can have Domino shoot her, wrap her in plastic, and plant her in a dumpster. Or maybe drop her out at ten thousand feet."

31

Hay Adams Hotel

SATURDAY MORNING

Mason Lord smiled when the twins came out of their room,
each with one of their small hands in their father's and the
other pulling kid-size carry-ons, both black with a large fire-
breathing dragon on the side. Ramsey walked them to the front
door, where they left their carry-ons beside Ramsey and Molly's bags. Ramsey called out, "Em, your mom will be back in a
minute. You about ready?"

There was a pause, then Emma said in a breathless voice,
"Just about, Dad. I'm saying goodbye to Vincenzo. He said to
thank you and Grandfather for the lovely meal with his parents
last night." She paused and her chin went up. "He thinks we
make a great team. He wants to play with me again. Maybe he
can come to San Francisco or I can go to Milan."

Ramsey was momentarily stopped cold by that guileless an-
nouncement, but not really surprised. The two kids were good
together. He gave the age-old parent response. "We'll see." He
said to the boys, "Come on up on the sofa with me and we'll
listen to *Surprise Dragon* until your mama gets home. We can
finish it on the plane ride with your grand—" He paused, then,

grinning at Elizabeth Beatrice, "grandparents." He pulled out his cell phone and punched up the audiobook. Cal and Gage bounded up to their father's knee, Cal always on the left, Gage always on the right.

When the narrator began, Ramsey said to Savich, "Does Sean like to listen to audiobooks?"

Savich sipped his cup of tea and stretched out his legs in the oversize chair. "Not as much as Sherlock or I reading to him. We try to get into the parts. If he's not laughing at us for trying to sound like Russian spies, he's transfixed."

Elizabeth Beatrice said with a smile, "And that way he knows he has your attention."

"Exactly."

Mason looked down at his watch, said to the room at large, "Molly's late. Her ten minutes was up five minutes ago. It's a good hour's drive to Dulles."

Elizabeth Beatrice said, "Molly knows you're a stickler for being on time, Mason, so I'll bet she's having trouble finding the trail mix the twins like. Give her another few minutes before you text her."

Mason turned on the sofa and took her hand, kissed her fingers. She leaned over and kissed his cheek. "Would you like some more coffee?"

He shook his head. "All right, I'll indulge her. We can listen to this Triston trying to ride his dragon."

"The dragon's name is Tulip," Cal said.

Savich asked Emma, "Are the Rossis leaving today?"

"Vincenzo said they're flying to New York tomorrow, to sight-see for a couple of days before they fly back to Milan. They've been invited to visit Juilliard. They're even giving a party for him." Emma paused a moment. Savich saw a blush stain her cheeks. "Maybe I'd like Juilliard better than Stanislaus."

Ramsey said, "I don't know, Em, Stanislaus is pretty famous and has an impressive campus. I could give them a call, see if they want to throw you a party."

Savich said, "Actually, I could make that happen, Emma." He wiggled his eyebrows. "I have big-time connections at Stanislaus."

Ramsey said, "Now that's something she won't forget, Savich, will you, Em?"

"That would be wonderful. Thank you, Uncle Dillon. I wonder if Vincenzo would attend Stanislaus rather than Juilliard?"

Mason said, "This isn't like Molly. She's probably wondering why I haven't texted her already." But he didn't text her, he punched in her number, frowned, punched off and tried again. "It sent me straight to voice mail. Why isn't she picking up?"

"I'll try to text her," Ramsey said and typed in a message to Molly. "That should get her attention. She usually answers right away."

Emma said, "Maybe Mama's phone is out of juice." She frowned. "But no, that never happens. She's always careful, thinking about any emergency."

Mason was staring at his iPhone. "I've tried three times."

Savich felt a punch of concern. He sat forward, pulled his cell phone out of his jacket pocket, and tapped the single key for Sherlock. "It's ringing." Her voice mail came on. He looked up, met Ramsey's eyes, tried again. He stood. "There's something wrong."

Emma's face turned white. "Do you think those horrible people couldn't get me so they took Mama and Aunt Sherlock? What will they do with them?"

"Emma."

It was her judge father's voice, the one she and the twins rarely heard, calm, deep, commanding. Emma swallowed, quieted.

Savich found Sherlock's cell phone on the location app they shared. "Sherlock's phone is close. It's only two blocks from here, west of us on H Street, but it's not moving."

Gage and Cal jumped off her father's knee, raced to their sister, and grabbed at her legs. Gage pulled on her hand. "Emmie, what's wrong?"

Savich saw the panicked look leave her face. She went down on her knees and hugged the twins close. "There's nothing wrong, guys. Mama's just a little bit late. Let's go back and listen to your book, okay?"

Savich said to her, adult to adult, "Emma, if you would please keep an eye on the twins, your dad and I will go downstairs and see where they are. No need to worry yet."

Emma started to open her mouth but her father said, "Em, we're going to have a division of labor here. Here's my phone. Please, watch Cal and Gage and listen to their book with them."

Mason and Elizabeth Beatrice both rose. "I'm going with you." He turned to his bride, whispered close to her ear, "Please, my darling, stay with Emma, keep them all calm." He saw she was ready to argue and added, "Please."

Savich said, "Emma, we'll probably meet your mom and Sherlock in the lobby," but she didn't believe him, not for a second. Their cell phones were two blocks away. Elizabeth Beatrice didn't believe him, either, but someone had to watch the twins, so they held their peace.

Just as Ramsey was leaving the suite, Cal called out, "Papa, will Mama have our trail mix?"

He turned. "I'm going to fetch her and your trail mix now, Cal. Take care of Emma and Elizabeth Beatrice, and don't let Gage tear up the furniture."

Gage shouted, "I don't want to listen to the dragons, Papa. I want to go with you to get Mama."

Elizabeth Beatrice said, "Please stay with Emma and me, Gage. We want to play with your new trains." There was a moment of silence, and then Gage said, "Okay, but I wish Sean was here. He had to go to church with his grandma."

The three men were alone on the elevator for only a few floors before two couples got in, laughing, talking, making plans for lunch. Forever passed before they finally got to the lobby. Savich knew he shouldn't jump to the worst thing possible, but he knew Sherlock well enough to know she wouldn't have let this happen, knew it all the way to his lizard brain. Something had happened beyond her control.

They left the hotel and followed Savich's location signal together, finding both cell phones two blocks away in a gutter next to the curb. Molly's phone wouldn't turn on, Sherlock's was cracked but working. There was nothing else, no sign of a struggle. The phones had been thrown away so they couldn't be tracked.

When they got back to the hotel, Savich sent Mason inside to speak to the concierge and reception. Savich and Ramsey stayed outside to speak to the two doormen. Savich showed each doorman his creds, simply folded Ramsey in. They showed them cell-phone photos of Molly and Sherlock. No luck. Neither remembered them, but they said a third doorman was on break if they wanted to ask him. They found the man in the hotel gift shop.

"Why, yes, sir, Agents," C. J. Clooney told them. "Just a little while ago, less than half an hour. Couldn't forget two pretty redheads. They were with two guys, walked with them across the street and got in the back of a limousine."

Savich felt fear hit deep. He'd hoped, prayed, when Sherlock hadn't answered, but Emma was right, both Sherlock and Molly had been taken.

Savich wondered if C. J. Clooney could hear his heart beating a mad tattoo. He said, "Could you tell us what the men looked like?"

"Well, now, that's harder," Clooney said, as they walked back into the lobby. "I remember both had dark hair, black suits, you know, the sort aides and bodyguards wear, and they were standing really close to the redheads, actually behind them, all the way across the street."

Ramsey said, "Did you see anyone inside the limo? Waiting?"

Mason came out of the Hay Adams, shook his head at Savich, and joined them. Clooney hummed a moment, scratched his ear. "I can't make any promises, I mean, it was only for a moment, but I'm pretty sure I saw a white guy in the limo, you know, on the back-facing seat. I remember thinking he looked like a ghost against all the black, but I really wasn't paying all that much attention and I could be wrong. We're always rushing around here in the mornings, with everyone leaving."

Mason said, "Do you remember anything about the limo that would help identify it?"

"It was a rental, I do know that. I've seen that small red logo before."

They asked him more questions, until Savich knew the well was dry. He thanked Mr. Clooney and Mason gave him a hundred-dollar bill wrapped around his card. "Mr. Clooney, if you think of anything else at all that could possibly be helpful, I'd appreciate it."

"Of course, sir! Thank you, sir!"

Clooney hurried off to help a portly senior and a woman hovering close by with three large pink suitcases.

Ramsey was shaken, but he kept his voice flat, repeated Savich's own thought to him. "Emma was right. They couldn't get to her, so they took Sherlock and Molly."

"It's that little shite Shaker," Mason said. "The bastard's broken the truce. I really believed he cared about his miserable hide more than getting back at me. He's just signed his death warrant."

Savich laid his hand on Mason's arm. Mason looked down at the big tough hand, calmed. He said, "I know our best chance to find them is right now, while they're still close."

Savich nodded. "We can deal with whoever is responsible later."

Ramsey felt fear swallowing him whole. His hands flexed and unflexed at his sides. All he could see was Molly—hurt maybe, scared, and he wasn't there with her. But Sherlock was. She was smart, resourceful . . . but who was he kidding? It wouldn't matter if the National Guard was with her if they had no weapons.

Savich knew he had to step back, put away his fear, and think logically, as he would with any kidnapping. It was the hardest thing he'd ever done. *Think.*

He said as he dialed, "First thing to do is call Ben Raven." When he disconnected a minute later, he said, "A BOLO's going out right now on the rented limo. We have to hope they haven't ditched it already. Ben knew the rental company with the red logos. He'll try M. J. Pederson first, the name one of the men used to rent the Lexus they spotted at Kennedy Center."

He continued, "I don't believe whoever took Sherlock and Molly are from Washington. Since it isn't their turf, I doubt they'd want to stay here and try to hide."

Mason said, "Agreed. If I were in their shoes, I'd want to get them out of here as fast as I could."

Ramsey said, "But not on a commercial flight or Amtrak. I can't see them driving the rented limo any distance. Wouldn't they realize we'd figure out Molly and Sherlock were gone pretty quickly? They'd have to know they might have been seen at the hotel, that there might be a BOLO out on the limo fast."

Mason said, "Ramsey, Savich, it seems most likely that like me, they'd fly private. And not a rental service, no, they'd have to have their own jet, their own pilot, so there'd be no one to wonder why they were holding two women prisoner."

Savich nodded. "That means a private airfield. Where would a private plane large enough to hold them all fly out from around here, Mason?"

"The main venue is the private airfield facility at Dulles. I'm hangared at Jet Aeronautics. They're the best—a helpful staff, excellent facilities if you need to wait, maintenance people you can count on. That's where I'd go."

Savich checked his Mickey Mouse watch. "I'll call Jet Aeronautics. If they're there, there might be time to stop them."

Mason said, "They won't tell you, Savich. They'll cite client confidentiality and demand a warrant. I'll call them."

Savich didn't doubt for a second Mason would get all the information he asked for. "Yes, go ahead. I'll call Ben Raven back, get his officers out there."

Mason ended a short conversation with the manager. He punched off his cell phone. "You were right, Savich, they used the name M. J. Pederson to hangar a Gulfstream 500 overnight. They took off only minutes ago. Five passengers, two men and three women, two pilots in the cockpit, their own pilots, of course. No surprise here—their flight plan shows their destination as Las Vegas."

Ramsey was shaking his head. "Las Vegas. It's hard to believe. Does Rule Shaker think we're stupid?"

Savich said, "Don't jump yet, Ramsey. Now, we'll have them met by federal agents when they land. I'll alert them to avoid a possible hostage situation. And I want to get there as soon as we can. My Porsche is too small. We'll take a taxi. Mason, can you get your jet ready for us?"

Mason said, "It already is. I'll call Elizabeth Beatrice and have them hurry down to the limo and meet us at Jet Aeronautics."

C. J. Clooney himself whistled in a taxi for them. Mason sat in the front seat next to the driver, a young Latina with a glossy ponytail. "I'll give you an extra hundred if you can get us there in forty-five minutes."

She grinned at him. "Make it one fifty and I'll get you there in thirty-five minutes. Name's Chili."

"You're on, Chili," Mason said and strapped his seat belt. He turned in his seat, one hand on the chicken stick as she scooted around a corner. "They'll have over an hour on us by the time we're airborne. Do you think you can beat their time to the airport, Chili?"

Chili said, "Hang on, fellows, we're taking a little shortcut," and she swerved onto Beltson Avenue.

Savich stared out the taxi window, wishing he could tell Sherlock he'd find her, that he loved her. He thought of Sean and called his mother, asked her to keep him for a couple of days, saying only something urgent had come up and he and Sherlock had to go out of town.

He closed his eyes, concentrated on what might come next. *I'll find you, Sherlock, I swear.*

32

KIRRA'S CONDO

SATURDAY MORNING

They know you're Eliot Ness. Do they know you're Allison Rendahl, too? Doesn't matter, they want to kill you either way, like they killed your parents.

Kirra swiped her hand through her tangled hair, forced herself out of bed and into ancient sweats. She was brushing her teeth when the voice came out of nowhere—*I see the little bitch! Let me do her.* Then the words were gone, fast as a light switched off.

She stared at the face in the bathroom mirror, too pale, her eyes too shadowed. She looked afraid and hated it. She knew they wouldn't stop trying. Jeter had told her the young killer's name was Todd Winters, with a sheet longer than her arm, but she was his first try at murder. Kirra knew in her gut if Ryman Grissom had come for her himself yesterday, she'd be dead at the bottom of that gulley. She doubted Jeter would be able to trace Winters or his weapons back to Oliveras or Grissom.

She heard the voice more often now, sounding in her head, not a voice, really, but the words, like flashes of lightning. She closed her eyes. She was in very deep trouble. She wished she could speak to Jeter, confess everything, but he was a cop and she'd broken the law. She wouldn't put him in that position. Kirra thought of her boss, Alec Speers, of other attorneys in the office, but she could no more speak to any of them than she could fly to the moon. She'd never felt so alone in her life. If Uncle Leo were here, she knew she couldn't keep Eliot Ness from him, and if she told him, he'd take her back to Australia, or put his own life at risk. There was no one else she could tell, without putting a target on their back.

She said to the woman in the mirror, "I know Ryman was one of the two men who murdered my parents. I'm going to find out who the other one was, and put them both in prison."

I see the little bitch, let me do her. The voice sounded in her mind gain, sharp, vicious, and then it disappeared like smoke in a wind. She froze. Who was that second man? Ryman Grissom seemed to be a loner now, but fourteen years ago he'd had a partner.

When Kirra's doorbell sounded, she flinched. She knew Officer Hendricks was in his car across the street, but he never came in. She didn't have a gun, but she did have her razor-sharp Benchmade AXIS lock knife she'd used for years. She slipped it out of its pouch and walked quietly to the front door. She looked through the peephole, whooshed out a breath.

She knew that FBI face, it was Special Agent Griffin Hammersmith. Kirra pushed back the dead bolt, unhooked the chain, and opened the door. She hadn't thought he'd be here this early. She gave him a big smile, actually relieved it wasn't someone there to kill her. She grabbed his hand, shook it. "You're a welcome surprise, Agent Hammersmith, even this early on a Saturday morning. Come in."

Griffin hadn't expected such an enthusiastic welcome. Kirra

stepped out onto the small porch and looked up and down the street before she pulled him in. One neighbor, Mr. Farber, was walking his prancing white poodle and looking at his petunias. She smiled up at Griffin, wanted to throw her arms around him, but instead she said, "Hey, I know it's early, but maybe you want to go to a movie?"

Griffin looked down at the wild-eyed woman in baggy gray sweats and no makeup, her feet bare, her hair a tangled mess. He watched her slide a wicked-looking knife back into its pouch and slip it into her sweatpants pocket. "The attempt at humor wasn't bad. I see you're a bit on edge, but that's okay, I'm here now. Makes me feel needed. I spoke to Officer Hendricks sitting in his gray Honda across the street, let him know I was here to take his place. I gave him a go-cup of black coffee and a donut, told him to enjoy his weekend. Yep, Agent Savich assigned me to be your second skin, to keep you safe." There was no reason to tell her why Savich wasn't here, that Sherlock and Molly Hunt had been taken. He quashed thinking about them. He was now in charge of Kirra Mandarian aka Eliot Ness, and nothing was going to happen to her, not on his watch. He said, "Did Jeter text you about your would-be killer, Todd Winters? It's a pity, but no real surprise he's dead. He was a bad seed since the age of eight, when he tried to rob a 24/7 with a water pistol."

She blinked. "A water pistol? What happened?"

"The Asian woman who owned the store punched him, took the water pistol, and squirted him in the face, but that lesson didn't set him on the straight and narrow. He escalated from there to auto theft, breaking and entering, you get the idea." When Kirra didn't answer him, he said, "Jeter told me you don't know who might have paid Winters to come after you."

"That's right. I'm preparing a list of possibles, people I've prosecuted who might want to do me in."

Griffin said, "You're pretty new at it, so the list can't be long."

"True enough," she said, "particularly since I plea-bargain so many criminals out you'd think they'd want to throw me a party, not shoot me. Forgive me, please come in. Here I am thinking I'm the center of everyone's universe."

He stepped into the small entrance hall. She again looked up and down the street before she closed the door. Griffin said, "Let me say you're now the center of my universe given what happened yesterday. Jeter said you're an excellent driver and saved yourself. He also told me he'd scour Winters's phone, his car, and his apartment. Hopefully he'll find out who paid him."

She didn't look like she believed Jeter would find out anything. She was standing in front of him, looking scared yet somehow gallant. He lightly touched her arm. "I'm going to see to it no one's going to hurt you. Try to trust me, okay? I'm so tough even army boots avoid me."

Kirra studied his face. She didn't doubt he was sincere, but he was only one man and he wasn't a killer, not like Ryman Grissom. It didn't hurt he looked tough and fit, but she'd learned from her years in the outback you never knew how tough someone was until they showed you. "All right," she said, nothing more.

Griffin flashed back on Jeter's text he'd also sent to Savich and Pepper, short and to the point: I HAVEN'T CONFRONTED HER.

As if any of them needed reminding the situation was fraught with potholes. Griffin, like Jeter, hated the ongoing charade.

"You look like you've had a tough night," he said.

"You think?" Kirra looked down at herself, began pulling on a loose thread of her tatty sweatshirt. She looked up at him. She didn't know where it came from but a laugh burst out of her.. "Sorry, I'm a mess. Give me five minutes." She happened to glance in the mirror beside the living room arch. "Make that fifteen minutes," and she dashed away, calling out over her shoulder, "Fresh coffee in the kitchen. Help yourself while I go make myself presentable."

Griffin watched Kirra race down the hall, her tangled hair flying. He walked into her kitchen. It was small, with shiny new appliances and a cozy feel. Her coffee wasn't bad, not as good as his, but only Savich's was better. Griffin walked back through a nice archway into her living room, his eyes immediately drawn to the colorful pillows she'd tossed haphazardly on her sofa, itself covered with a South Seas Island print, a bright red chair facing it. Cream painted walls drew in light from four big windows. He saw amazing canvases, at least a dozen, on the long wall framing the fireplace. Each canvas was colorful and intricately rendered, with swirls and squares and dots that seemed to mean something. He was mesmerized.

Kirra said from behind him, "What's so cool about Aboriginal art is each painting tells a story using symbols. Actually their art is the oldest unbroken tradition of art in the world. My favorites are these by Jeannie Petyarre. I met her when Uncle Leo and I were in Utopia—great name, right? It's a small town in central Australia."

Griffin tore himself away from the art to the many photographs that covered the mantel and every tabletop in the living room. He turned to her and stared. He'd seen her in her professional getup—suit and heels—and seen her only a few minutes before looking like she'd just rolled out of bed after nightmares hounded her. Now she looked going-to-meet-friends chic—in snug jeans, sandals showing a French pedicure, and a white cami covered with a boxy pale green jacket, probably cashmere. She tossed a purse the size of his two-year-old nephew on a chair.

"You look nice," he said. Now that was an understatement.

Kirra said, "I'll take nice as opposed to what you saw when I opened the door for you. Look at that one—that's my uncle Leo." Griffin looked at teenage Kirra pressed against a big man's side, both smiling widely at the camera, both dressed in jeans and T-shirts that said across the front: SURVIVE THE WORST AND APPRECIATE THE BEST. She looked tanned and strong, a pretty girl with promise of becoming a beautiful woman.

He heard pride in her voice when she said, "I designed the clothes and came up with that motto for Extreme Australian Adventures, my uncle's business. Every one of Uncle Leo's clients buys them for themselves and all their relatives. That photo is of Burleigh Headland, right on the ocean. Whenever Uncle Leo and I just wanted to be lazy, we'd go on the easy trail. If you're lucky you can see whales migrating and lots of parrots and lizards."

"It looks beautiful," he said.

Kirra pointed to another photo. "This tough-looking guy with the machete in his belt is Jawli. He's Aborigine, one of the team, with his wife, Mala. Mala taught me how to cook and use a boomerang. I swear Mala could take on a pissed-off crocodile and turn him into a delicious meal, or a pet."

"And that's you in scuba gear at the Great Barrier Reef, right?" At her nod, Griffin said, "I was there with a friend five years ago. Amazing diving and everyone looked out for everyone else. I'll never forget it."

"It's an unwritten rule what with unexpected currents out there. Uncle Leo's house is in Port Douglas, on the northern coast, as you probably know. When we were home and not on expeditions with clients, I'd drink coffee at sunrise and stare out over the reef." She sighed. "I haven't been home in three months, and it's time. It's like half my heart is there."

He paused in front of a group photo. Kirra said, "I had my seventeenth birthday party on that outing. We were leading three couples to the Blue Mountains. They made me a cake using the camp stove. It was awful, and the best birthday ever."

Griffin looked up and around the living room. "This is a good space, a comfortable space. I like the high ceilings. They're maybe a bit higher than mine." He nodded toward a big easy chair in front of a huge TV, much like his own. "And you're such a guy."

She grinned. "Even though I'm something of a dag, I love American football and basketball."

"Dag?"

"Sorry, Aussie for a nerd. You know, Griffin, it's nice having someone here with me to talk to, after all that's happened."

"I can imagine it can't be a good time for you to be alone. As I said when I got here, it looked like you'd had a rough night. Makes sense; after all, someone just tried to kill you. I bet it brought back some frightening memories."

Kirra looked up at him, saw understanding and real concern, and it broke her. Her voice shook. "I can't seem to let go of what happened to my parents. I keep remembering hearing what one of the men who killed my parents shouted when he was trying to kill me. It comes back to me, even during the day. I can't see what he looked like. I don't even remember what he sounded like. It's always just out of reach, and it doesn't leave me alone. It's like I'm always trying to remember, and I can't."

She must have been struggling with that all by herself for so long she finally had to tell someone. Griffin wanted to give her comfort, to hold her and reassure her, but of course he couldn't. He was a professional. She was an assignment. She was looking at him with haunted eyes. To hell with it. He pulled her against him, rubbed her back, up and down, slowly, lightly. She was stiff, then slowly, she eased, leaned into him. He said against her hair, "You want to remember what happened that night, don't you? It's been weighing on you a long time. I know we've just met, Kirra, and I wouldn't suggest this unless I was sure. I know just the person to help you. His name is Dr. Emanuel Hicks. He's a psychiatrist who works for the FBI and is one of the foremost hypnotists in the country. He's great at helping people we've worked with remember traumatic events, even after many years. He's a magician, eases you right into it."

Kirra stiffened, obviously wary, and drew a deep breath. "My mom believed hypnosis was dangerous. Why would you let someone monkey around with your brain, and who knows what could come of that? So I refused hypnosis years ago, even though Jeter thought it might help me remember more of what happened that night." She pulled away from Griffin and paced back and forth. She paused a moment, straightened a picture. Finally, she turned back to him. "You promise it's safe?"

"I promise. Dr. Hicks will be able to help you go back to that night your parents were murdered. He'll help you remember details you believe you've forgotten. It's very possible you'll find things out to help find your parents' killers. If you choose to go forward with hypnosis, I'll give him a call."

An hour later, Kirra walked out the door in front of Griffin. When he was out and he'd looked up and down the street, he nodded to her, and she locked it.

"Let's go in my Range Rover, she's nearly brand-new, still has that just-bought leather smell."

"Fine by me. My rental RAV put in a hard afternoon yesterday, not to mention a dent in the back fender. And to be honest, the last thing I want to do today is drive."

When Kirra fastened her seat belt, she breathed in. "Yep, love that new smell."

Once Griffin was on the highway, and she'd checked to make sure no one was following them, she said, "I hope you brought your Glock even though it's a Saturday."

"I sleep with my Glock," he said, "so, as you say, no worries, right? You know, I didn't expect Dr. Hicks to agree to see you right away, particularly on a Saturday, but he said it sounded like you needed to put this behind you, no need for you to worry about it all weekend."

She swallowed, hugged her purse closer, and didn't say a word.

Griffin was aware Kirra Mandarian was checking for anyone following them until they reached Quantico. He didn't blame her. He thought again of Sherlock and prayed.

33

Dr. Emanuel Hicks' Office
Jefferson Dormitory
Quantico

SATURDAY

Kirra stared around Dr. Hicks' office with its pale green walls
and three colorful throw rugs on the wooden floor. There were
two framed photos on a small antique desk in the corner. In one
he was dressed like Elvis and he was hugging two young women
who had something of the look of him, probably his daughters,
all of them smiling wildly. In the second he was smiling down
at a petite blond woman. His wife? There were three chairs in
the room, and a large green nubby lounger. *Probably for me*, she
thought. A tall thin man with glasses and a head full of dark
hair with dashes of white at his temples came forward.

Dr. Hicks smiled at the lovely young woman who looked
like she wanted to bolt. Agent Hammersmith had told him
Kirra Mandarian was wary of hypnosis—no surprise since her
mother had been adamantly against it—but now she wanted to
remember, had to remember what she'd obviously suppressed
from that night. He held out his hand. "I'm Dr. Hicks and I
swear on the head of my always-hungry beagle hypnosis is
harmless. Griffin told me you realized you had to remember

more of the night your parents were killed. I believe hypnosis will help you do that." He saw a mix of dread and hope in her eyes, an unusual shade of green. She wore highlights in her dark brown hair, like his daughter Ellie did, pulled back from her fine-boned face with a clip at the back of her neck.

"I'm Kirra Mandarian."

"It's a pleasure to meet you. Please be seated, Kirra—may I call you Kirra?" At her nod, Dr. Hicks motioned her to the big lounger. "Griffin, did you tell Kirra about me on your way here?"

"I told her you'd been on the FBI payroll for more than a dozen years and you were really bad at baseball—"

"Fifteen, actually, and how did you know about the baseball?" Then he laughed, shook his fist at Griffin.

"I told her you're one of the foremost hypnotists in the country, but I believe she was more impressed with your Elvis persona."

Kirra saw a beam of sunlight coming in through one of the three windows. Odd, but it lightened her heart, calmed her. She could do this. She wanted to do this. She said, "I am indeed impressed. I see from your photo with your daughters that you must wear a pillow strapped around your middle when you perform."

"That I do, selected by my wife after trying a dozen different kinds, from soft pillows to those hard as a rock." He took her hand again, smiled at her, nonthreatening, like a parent trying to reassure a child. She heard her mother's voice in her head, warning her away, but for only an instant did she want to slowly back out of this office with its soothing pale green walls and its big comfortable lounger where she knew she'd be expected to sit and close her eyes and waft away to never-never land. She simply didn't understand how this man she'd only just met could make her remember anything from fourteen years ago. Kirra swallowed, drew a deep breath. But if she remembered anything to help her identify those men, it would be a miracle and worth any dire consequences her mother believed were possible. She ignored the clammy sweat making her silk cami stick to her skin, the greasy ball rolling around in her stomach. It was time to suck it up, time to act. "As Agent Griffin probably told you, this is very important to me, so I'll try, I'll really try. I'm ready. And thank you for seeing me on a Saturday with no notice."

"Griffin assured me it would be my pleasure." Dr. Hicks patted her hand. "You sound like you're in a tumbrel on your way to the guillotine. But here's the thing, Kirra, you don't have to try. You don't have to do anything at all. All you have to do is trust I know what I'm doing. Please sit down. You, too, Griffin."

When she was settled into the chair, her heart beating too fast, she eyed the beautiful watch Dr. Hicks slipped out of his breast pocket. A watch? A friggin' gold watch? How clichéd was that?

Dr. Hicks laughed at the appalled look on her face. "I know, I know, but the watch belonged to my grandfather, a grand old man. I've always had an affinity for it, I suppose you could say. For our purposes the watch is merely a tool, Kirra, merely something for you to focus on to help that active brain of yours quiet down. All you have to do is look at the watch—that's right, focus on it, follow as it swings back and forth. Sit back and close your eyes, picture the watch. That's good. Now, do some square breathing. Deep breath, slowly release it, that's good. Think about your breathing as you count to four, in and out. That's right." He waited, listening to her breathing smooth out. "Kirra, I want you to tell me about one of your happiest childhood memories with your parents."

A happy memory? She remembered Uncle Leo had once asked her to tell him about her best birthday with her parents. She'd known he wanted to hear a good memory she had of her mother, his sister. She also knew he felt guilty he hadn't visited more often although he hadn't known about his sister's illness and just how dire their financial problems had become.

"It was my sixth birthday party. Mom made me my favorite red velvet cake, with lots of buttercream frosting so thick you could swipe your finger through it and no one could tell. Dad tied balloons all over the dining room, even on the backs of chairs. A dozen kids came and several parents so there'd be some control with all the kids on sugar highs. Everyone was laughing, talking, excited. All of us kids wanted that cake and ice cream.

"I remember blowing out the six candles and everyone singing happy birthday, the kids yelling it really. My mom and dad were laughing, and they looked so happy. I knew they loved me—" Kirra's voice caught and she swallowed tears.

"A lovely memory. Tell me more about it."

"Their present was the best, a big stuffed white unicorn with a red bow around his neck. I named him Jared after my seven-year-old boyfriend. He burned up in the house fire."

Dr. Hicks said, "Let's talk about Jared a moment. I want you to concentrate on him. Can you see him?"

"Oh yes."

"Did you talk to that unicorn?"

She nodded. "He was my best friend."

"Let Jared fill your mind, Kirra. Now open your eyes and look at the watch, follow its movement. That's it, relax and remember that beautiful perfect birthday and Jared the unicorn."

The day was crystal clear, that fantastically happy day six-year-old Kirra hoped would never end. She remembered how she carried Jared around by his horn. She felt her child's excitement as she opened the small presents from the other kids. It was a lovely time then, bittersweet now.

Her eyes followed the swinging watch. She hugged Jared. She licked frosting off the cake. The kids jumped around and yelled with delight when they won a game. Slowly the birthday party, all the kids' voices began to fade. She kept her eyes on the watch, listened to Dr. Hicks's quiet voice talk about red velvet cake, his daughter Pat's favorite. She felt herself relaxing, felt herself sinking into the chair, feeling it enfold her, comforting her. Everything began to move more slowly, one small moment flowing into the next, blending almost together, moving outside of time, outside of herself. Gently, easily, the world faded away.

Dr. Hicks took Griffin's hand, laid it on Kirra's. He said, "Kirra, can you feel Agent Hammersmith touching your hand?"

She nodded. "Griffin—he told me to call him Griffin—he has big hands. He's warm and solid. I think he's a nice man, but I don't know yet if he's as tough as I am."

"Griffin's as tough as my beagle's old chew rope. Do you feel relaxed? Safe?"

She felt Griffin's fingers lightly stroke the back of her hand. "Yes." Her voice was slow and easy.

Dr. Hicks leaned close. "I want you to remember that night, Kirra, I want you to relive what happened. No, don't stiffen up. Never forget, everything you remember happened a long time ago. Those men can't hurt you. We'll keep you safe. Do you understand?"

"Yes, I understand."

Dr. Hicks nodded to Griffin. Griffin said, "Kirra, I want you to go back. It's July, and you're twelve years old. It was a hot day, a hot night. Tell me about that day, start at the beginning."

Her voice began to subtly change, lighten. Stranger yet, her voice was younger. "I was wearing my gym shorts and a tee. Mom braided my hair so it wouldn't be hot on my neck. I was watching TV, when Dad told me to put on my sneakers. He wanted to show me something outside." Her breathing hitched.

He gently squeezed her hand, let her settle. "What did you do then?"

"I went outside, but I didn't see my dad. I went back into the house to look for him. I heard him and Mom talking in the kitchen. They were talking real quiet, like they were sharing secrets, and I moved closer. I heard Dad tell Mom not to worry, to trust him. He said he knew what he was doing, that he'd have the money they needed so she could have her operation and be just fine. But I heard Mom's worry voice. I sneaked a peek around the door. Mom was standing by the stove wringing her hands and there were lines between her eyes, worry lines." Kirra raised her fingers and touched the skin between her eyebrows. "I didn't understand. Mom needed an operation? What operation did my mother need? But they didn't say."

"Did your dad tell your mother where he was getting the money?"

She shook her head. "I heard Mom coming so I ran back outside. Later, I—I was afraid to ask my dad what it was all about, he'd know I was eavesdropping."

Her parents were murdered on the very same day she'd overheard them talking? She hadn't told Griffin that. Is that why the men had tried to kill her, too, because of what she might have known?

"It's late now. You're in your bed."

"Yes, it's really hot so I'd opened the window. I'm wearing my favorite my pink sleep shorts and top mom bought me at Target."

Griffin kept his voice low and calm. "You wake up. Why?"

"I have to go to the bathroom."

"You come back to bed. You're nearly asleep when you hear something?"

She began to twist in the chair, shaking her head, looked ready to leap out of it and hide. Griffin again squeezed her hand. "Kirra, this happened a long time ago, fourteen years ago. You're here with me now and with Dr. Hicks. You're safe. These are only memories. Don't be afraid."

She swallowed. A child's voice said, "I hear footsteps on the stairs, coming up, not going down, so I know it's not my parents. I can tell they're trying to be quiet but some of the stairs creak."

"You know it's more than one person on the stairs?"

"Yes. There's one creak then a second later there's another creak on the same stair." She moaned, shook her head. Griffin stroked her hand, spoke low to her. "You're safe, I promise you're safe. What do you do?"

She became still again. The girl whispered, "I get up. My heart's pounding and I want to puke. My door's open and I ease it wider, I don't want to, but I have to—and I see them, two large shadows. They're holding their arms out in front of them and I see the guns, the guns are leading them. I see them go toward my parents' bedroom. I turn back into my bedroom, grab my cell phone and dial 911, and then I hear two popping sounds and I know what they are, what it means. I want to yell and I nearly scream. I slap my hand over my mouth to keep it in. I want to run to my parents' bedroom, but I know there's nothing I can do. I tell the 911 man what's happened and he tells me to get out of the house and run and hide. The world's crazy-spinning, it's exploding. I climb out my bedroom window and down the big oak tree. I hear a man's voice from above me. He's leaning out the window. There's a popping sound and I feel a sharp pain in my head that nearly knocks me off the limb, but I know I can't stop or I'll be dead like my mom and dad. I'm crying and nearly fall, but I don't. I hurt my arm, I don't know how. All I know is my head and my arm are bleeding. I jump to the ground and run toward the woods.

"I know my parents are dead, deep down, I know. It's hot, but I'm shivering, my teeth are chattering." Kirra began to rub her head where she'd been shot, keening now, a helpless, wounded young girl, in shock.

"You were very brave, Kirra," Griffin said. "Jeter found you in your cave?"

Her young voice sounded infinitely weary, pain leaching through it. "I'm so afraid when this strange man crawls into the cave. I think he's there to kill me, but he didn't, he saved me. Jeter saved me. I owe him my life."

He very probably had saved her life. Griffin said, "Go back a moment. When you're climbing down the oak tree, do you hear another voice?"

"Yes, a horrible, vicious voice. I still hear it sometimes, but then it fades away. *I see the little bitch. Let me do her.*"

"When this man says those words, does he sound old, young, foreign?"

"It's not a man."

Griffin reared back, shot a look at Dr. Hicks who nodded slowly. Griffin said carefully, "It's not a man?"

"No, it's a woman. She sounds younger than my mom, lots younger. And crazy."

"Does she have an accent?"

"She has a light southern accent, maybe from somewhere around here. I remember a man's voice, but I couldn't hear what he said. I don't know which of them shot me in the head.

But it was a man and a woman, they were a team. They killed my parents together." There were tears in the girl's voice.

Griffin nodded to Dr. Hicks. He said, "Kirra, we're going to come back now. I'm going to count to three and you'll wake up. You'll remember everything you told us about what happened fourteen years ago, but you'll leave your fear, your pain, behind you. You'll remember the woman's voice. It will be very clear in your mind and stay clear. When you wake up, you'll feel calm. You'll feel well rested and alert."

On the count of three, Kirra blinked, straightened in the chair. She felt relaxed, her mind sharp. Best of all, she wasn't afraid. She looked from Dr. Hicks to Griffin. "I remember all of it. A woman shot at me but her aim was off because I was shimmying down the tree like a monkey. She was young, in her early twenties, no older. Her voice was manic. She was crazy excited, laughing, scary happy. She was having fun and she wanted to kill me like she and the man had killed my parents. As I said, I couldn't hear the man's voice clearly. But who was she?"

The woman was young, her accent light southern. She was manic, crazy. Griffin remembered Melissa Kay Grissom in her father's hospital room, her hands fisted at her sides, her face twisted in rage simmering just below the surface, waiting for a trigger to erupt. Not hard to see she was a psychopath. *A man and a woman.* There were only two people who fit the bill, and it made sense. The Grissom siblings. He knew Ryman Grissom was about forty. Fourteen years ago, he was in his midtwenties, Melissa Kay about twenty. Had they killed together or separately even before they'd killed the Rendahls? Had Melissa Kay murdered anyone since? And Kirra, was she pretending not to know for sure the man was Ryman Grissom? She'd never met Melissa Kay Grissom, but she knew Ryman had a sister. If she didn't already know everything there was to know about

Melissa Kay Grissom, Griffin had no doubt Kirra would find out everything about her before the day was out. What would she do with what she knew? Given what Eliot Ness had done, it scared Griffin to his toes. Well, he was with her now, to keep her from doing anything crazy. Griffin said, "Do you think you've heard this woman's voice before?"

Kirra stilled, seemed to gaze into herself again, into the past. Then she said, shaking her head, "No, I've never heard her voice before, except for that night."

Dr. Hicks took her hand, helped her to rise.

"Thank you, Dr. Hicks, thank you. I don't think you gave me a brain tumor. But who can tell, it's early."

"If you don't have symptoms right away, you're in the clear."

"Good to know. You know there's one excellent memory I'd forgotten. My sixth birthday party. It was a fine thing to remember. I was so happy that day. Thank you for taking me there again. You are a very kind man. I bet I would have liked your grandfather, too."

"That's about the nicest thing anyone's said to me in a long time. Griffin, take good care of her."

Griffin said, "Dr. Hicks likes the Boardroom pizza as much as I do. What do you say we stop there for lunch?"

Kirra managed a half smile. "Do you like anchovies?"

"Who on earth does?"

They were eating pizza in the Boardroom, Kirra's loaded with anchovies, when she said, "Bet you didn't know Jeter is seeing Pepper Jersik. She seems really nice. I hope it works out."

Griffin paused in midbite. Hard-nosed, kick-your-butt Pepper Jersik, falling for a cop in Porte Franklyn? He didn't doubt Kirra knew the scoop. He marveled how life never ceased to offer up unexpected twists and turns.

"Thank you, Griffin, for convincing me to come, for everything you've done for me today. I can't wait to see Dr. Hicks do his Elvis impersonation. You can drop me off at home now, maybe go on that date I'm sure you must have canceled."

Griffin sat back in his chair, gave her a slow smile. "No dropping you off. No date for me. We're going back to your condo together. Consider me your second skin, Mandarian. I told you—Savich's orders."

34

In the Air

SATURDAY

"Emmie, where's Mama? Why isn't she here with us on Grand-pa's airplane?" Emma touched her fingers to Gage's little face. She wanted to cry, but knew she couldn't. Her voice was steady and calm. "She went on ahead, Gage. She didn't want to, but she didn't have a choice. She told me to give you and Cal big kisses. You'll see her soon." She was surprised the lie didn't stick in her throat. It was so hard to keep her voice matter-of-fact, to stay steady for her little brothers. When they'd boarded, she'd seen her father's set face, seen the unspoken fear in his eyes, and told him she'd settle the twins on the plane herself. At first Cal and Gage were fascinated, touching every plush light-gray seat, climbing on the two padded benches, staring at the galley with its high-tech appliances, opening the small wine cooler. Cal saw juice boxes and Emma gave one to each of them. They marveled at the bathroom to each other in twin talk. Gage had to flush the toilet, and both twins laughed when the water got sucked down with a big whoosh. The bathroom amazed Emma, too. It was special order, nearly as large as her own bathroom at home. She tucked the boys in together on one of the large plush seats, smoothed a soft blanket over them. Emma looked up to see her dad was sitting alone, stiff and silent, staring out the window of Grandpa's plane, his hands fisted in his lap. Uncle Dillon was on his cell phone. Grandpa and Elizabeth Beatrice—Emma wasn't ready to call the gorgeous woman her grandma—sat close together, her hand in his resting on his leg.

A small hand clutched hers. She smiled down at Cal. "Emmie, sing the song Mama always sings."

She sang "Soft Kitty" from *The Big Bang Theory*, watched both little faces go lax, saw both sets of beautiful blue eyes slowly close. She sang it three times. It soothed her as much as it did the twins.

Finally, they were out for the count. Emma leaned down and kissed their little faces. She whispered, "I promise we'll find Mom. She'll be with us again soon." She felt overwhelmed with guilt, just couldn't help it, even though she knew it wasn't logical. But it didn't seem to matter. They'd wanted to take her, not Aunt Sherlock, not her mother.

She looked over at her grandfather's two bodyguards, Linc from Omaha and Toulouse from Haiti. He'd assigned them to stay in the rear of the plane and keep an eye on the little boys. They'd first eyed the twins with some alarm, obviously not used to children. Emma said to them now, "I think they'll sleep until we land in Las Vegas. If they wake up, call me. They'll want a snack." She dredged up a smile. "Then maybe you and Toulouse can play Punk the Weasel with them. There's only one page of rules, tucked in the seat pocket. It's pretty simple." She looked over to see Cal sucking his fingers. He hadn't done that in a long time and she knew why.

Emma made her way along the wide aisle and sat next to her father, took his tense hand, smoothed out his fingers. His hand was cold. Ramsey squeezed hers, leaned over and kissed her cheek, and tried his best to smile at her. "Thank you for seeing to the twins."

"They know something's wrong," Emma said.

He said nothing, there were simply no words. Emma leaned into him and he hugged her close. "Linc and Toulouse are grateful the twins are asleep."

Ramsey nodded. He'd worried about taking the twins and Emma to Las Vegas with them, but Mason was right, this was an emergency and when they landed, both Linc and Toulouse would stay on the plane with the twins and Emma. He knew they'd be fine. He glanced over at Savich who was looking at nothing in particular. He said, "Savich, I never told you I met Rule Shaker only once, the time when Molly and I went to Las Vegas to show him copies of the evidence Molly had collected against him and his daughter, Eve, that put an end to the war between the Shakers and Mason. I have to say Shaker in person surprised me. I expected someone like Mason, I guess, not a small dark man who looked like a Hollywood gangster." Ramsey was aware he had his father-in-law's attention, too, and he continued louder, "His world was all about unspoken power and control, he wore them like a mantle, like you do, Mason. I found him highly intelligent. I remember watching him silently calculate the odds when Molly showed him what she had. I saw the moment he realized he had no choice but to do what Molly wanted from him. He nodded to his daughter, Eve. She studied his face a moment, nodded back, and both of them agreed. Molly had an audiotape of Eve, essentially confessing she'd killed Molly's ex-husband, Louey, and she'd written out everything she knew about how they'd kidnapped Emma and tried to kill Mason. Molly told them she'd sent the originals to her lawyers to be sure the war would really be over. I remember how Eve looked at Molly and me when it was done. She looked fierce, that's what I thought. She didn't look at us, didn't say anything at all to us, simply turned and walked out of the room. It was like we no longer existed."

Savich said, "Since I've never met Shaker, your impressions will help when we meet with him."

Elizabeth Beatrice said, "Ah, the infamous truce."

Mason said, "How on earth do you know about that?"

"While Emma and I were waiting for you in the suite, I asked her to tell me about this Rule Shaker, the man you believe is behind Molly and Sherlock's kidnapping. I believe I understand what happened now."

Mason said, "But, Emma, how did you know? You were a little kid. Neither your mother nor I said a word around you."

Emma shrugged. "I'm a first-class eavesdropper, Grandpa. I knew about the war between you and Rule Shaker." She paused. "I was one of the casualties, wasn't I?"

"I've told you how very sorry I am about that, Emma," Mason said. "Believe me, when I found out what happened to you, I was ready to bomb his casinos in Las Vegas for what he did to you."

Elizabeth Beatrice said, "What Emma didn't know was exactly what her mother used as a threat to get you and Shaker to make peace."

Mason said matter-of-factly, "She threatened Eve Shaker with prison for murder, and for attempted murder, namely of me. And Molly's threat to me? That I'd never be allowed to see Emma again. I guess you could say she had both Shaker and me in her hands. We both had to trust she'd keep what she knew hidden."

Savich marveled at Mason's new wife. He wondered if she'd get an honest accounting out of her husband about everything

that had happened six years ago, if she'd ever find out that most
of what he called his business interests were against state and
federal law. If he had to bet, he'd say, yes, she'd find out whatever she wanted to know.

Emma said slowly to her grandfather, never letting go of her
father's hand, "I remember before that awful time, you looked
right through me. I wondered what I was doing wrong. Then
after, you changed. You smiled at me, hugged me. You gave me
great gifts. You flew out to see me. I started to think you liked
me."

"Of course I liked you, Emma," he said, his voice austere.
"It's just that I had no idea what to do with you, a little girl.
I didn't learn that with your mother, but I did with you. I've
always loved you. I hope you believe me."

"Yes, Grandpa, I do."

"And I love your mother. Maybe she came to believe that
too."

Emma smiled. "I love you, too. I always have." She squeezed
her father's hand. "Mama thinks you're a powerhouse, that's
what I heard her call you. I think she knows you love her now,
but you should ask her." She turned in her chair. "Dad, Mama
and Aunt Sherlock will figure out how to get away, you'll see.
They're very brave."

"You're right, Em," Ramsey said, "and if they can't, we'll be
there soon to help them." But deep inside where despair hun-
kered down, he saw shadows, only shadows.

Savich looked out the window into thick clouds, their
shapes fantastic. He started to tell Sherlock he saw a bearded
lion and a leaping goat, caught himself. He'd never expected
he'd ever be on the family's side of a kidnapping. He felt their
fear now, their feeling of helplessness, their tug of guilt, even
if that didn't make any sense. Their only lifeline had been to

pray, and to hope the people in charge knew what they were doing. Now he was both the family and the one in charge of finding them. Savich closed his eyes. *I'm sorry, Sean, I failed her. Your mother isn't coming home.* He got hold of himself. He had to keep everything he felt at a distance, he had to stay objective, hard as that was. It was the only way he'd find Sherlock, and he couldn't deal with the alternative. And it was Sherlock they were dealing with. She was smart and strong, devious and endlessly inventive. She wasn't a helpless victim. His cell phone belted out "Smoke on the Water" by Deep Purple. It was Agent Ollie Hamish from the CAU, checking back with him. Savich had called him earlier to tell him they hadn't seen the limo at the airport. "Savich, Metro officers spotted the limo two blocks from the private jet facilities. There was some blood on the back-facing seat. Not much, and it looked like they tried to wipe it off. And someone vomited."

"It's not Sherlock's or Molly's blood, Ollie. They were both seen boarding a plane so it means the blood belongs to one of the kidnappers." What had happened? Had Sherlock managed to get to her ankle pistol and shoot one of them?

Ollie said, "I was scared out of my mind until I remembered that. We'll start DNA testing, see if there's a match in the database. I'll get back to you on that as soon as I can.

"I've got some answers on the Gulfstream, Savich. It's owned by an LLC incorporated in Maryland, nominally owned by an offshore investment firm. The owners don't want to be found. And we can't track the Gulfstream's location by its tail number—they've turned off the automatic tracking signal. All we can do is estimate when they'll land."

Savich said, "Keep working on who owns it, Ollie. That's key."

Savich punched off, sat back in the plush leather seat. There was only a faint hum from the plane's engines. It was like flying in a private mansion with no noise from the neighbors. He looked at Mason, seated diagonally from him. He was toying with Elizabeth Beatrice's wedding ring, focused on it really. What was he thinking?

He said, "Mason, do you know if Shaker owns any other properties close to Las Vegas? Maybe with a private airstrip?"

"I should have thought of that. They might not land at the airport. No, I don't know if he does. I'll call Gunther and find out." He pulled out his cell phone and made the call. "Gunther, I need to know as soon as possible if Rule Shaker had access to any property with a private landing strip anywhere near Las Vegas." He listened a moment, then, "We're still in the air. They should be landing at the airport soon. If they don't, we'll need to figure out where they landed. Get me the information as quickly as you can."

Mason pressed the cockpit button. "Ellis, how far are we from Las Vegas?"

"About thirty minutes, give or take. We pushed to maximum air speed, as you asked, and we got some unexpected tailwinds."

Mason said, "Gunther should get back to me by then. No telling if he can help."

Ramsey said, "Has the FBI field office in Las Vegas made it to the airport?"

Savich was forced to smile. "It's a resident office, only one agent. Don't laugh—his name is Agent Poker. I always wondered if that was why he was assigned to Las Vegas, but no, he requested the assignment. He's got the local cops involved, and they'll be at Jet Aeronautics when the plane lands. He won't approach if there's a chance that it would turn it into a hostage situation. He'll wait for us. No one on board knows they're waiting for them."

Ramsey excused himself, checked in with Mason's two bodyguards, who were sandwiching the sleeping twins, both of them reading magazines. He poured cups of coffee and a soda for Emma, grabbed sandwiches and chips to pass around.

Fifteen minutes later, Mason's cell rang. He listened, frowned. "Thank you, Gunther. I'll call you back in five minutes."

He raised his voice, "Rule Shaker owns a Bombardier he keeps hangared in Las Vegas and a number of properties nearby, rents others. None of them near Las Vegas has a private airstrip."

With luck it would be over soon after they landed in Las Vegas. Sherlock and Molly would be safe. Yet at the back of his mind Savich wondered if it had all been too easy. The kidnappers had to know that eventually they'd be tracked to Las Vegas, though not so quickly. Mason hadn't waited long to call Molly's phone, and they'd been lucky enough to draw all the right conclusions. Had they planned to have the jet take off again, and see to it they couldn't be followed from the airport?

Savich heard Mason say to Elizabeth Beatrice, "I'll wager this isn't what you expected."

She lightly rubbed her hand over his thigh. "What I expected, Mason, was that being your wife would mean never being bored. It seems I was right. We're going to nail this miserable person, you'll see."

Savich's cell phone rang out "Smoke on the Water" again. "Savich, it's Poker. I'm at airport flight control. The Gulfstream hasn't even begun an approach yet. It's not on their radar. They radioed the flight crew to ask if they've got any problems, got no answer. They're saying it means they're not going to be landing here at all."

35

Kirra's Condo

SATURDAY

Kirra opened the Chinese take-out cartons, spooned hot and sour soup into two bowls on her kitchen table. "There is really no need for you to stay here with me, Griffin."

"You want me to sleep in my Range Rover?"

"Well, no, but you could come back in the morning."

"Sorry, Mandarian, I have my orders. Anything happens to you I'm busted to resident agent on the Mars colony."

"Sure you are," she said, but she did grin. "Sit down, you bloody moron, and eat the soup. Feng Nian makes the best hot and sour soup in Porte Franklyn."

"I've always thought moron was enough, but bloody moron?"

"Well, sure. Fact is there's a truckload of other things Aussies call each other, but I held back; I mean, you're a federal agent and all, it wouldn't be good to be crude."

Griffin took a sip of the soup. "Not bad." He studied Kirra. She was trying hard to stay natural, to hide the fear that had to have been eating at her since a hired assassin had come close to killing her yesterday. He saw the strain in her eyes, how she seemed to fold in on herself when she wasn't engaging him.

He'd bet she knew in her gut it had to be Melissa Kay Grissom's crazy psycho voice she'd heard shouting at her the night her parents were killed, even if Kirra had never met her. She was pointed right at Ryman Grissom, so why not both of them? Was she planning to prove to herself it was Melissa Kay Grissom she'd heard, to get close enough to her to hear her voice?

Kirra got up and fetched a couple more napkins from a drawer. She was still wearing her snug cigarette jeans and white sleeveless cami that showed her arms, winter pale, smooth with muscle. He looked at her hands, capable hands, her fingers long and slender. She wore an unusual ring on her left pinkie finger, with symbols that looked like the Aboriginal art in her living room. She was lean, coltish, he supposed, except for her butt. She had an excellent butt. He did a fast slam on his mental brakes, but out of his mouth came, "You smell good."

Her head jerked up. "What? I smell good? You mean like the soy sauce in the soup?"

"Well, maybe a touch, but no, you smell mainly like roses, faded roses, just about ready to droop."

"That sounds like an awesome insult."

"I like faded roses. Their smell is sort of vague, with a whiff of sweetness, not as much in-your-face."

"You just made that up. What if I told you it was jasmine, not roses?"

"You're lying, it's roses."

"Yes, all right. My uncle Leo bought me a bottle for my sixteenth birthday. He said it was his favorite. He got this sort of sweet faraway look on his face and I knew even then he must have been fond of a girl who wore it." She shrugged. "I've worn it ever since. And no, Uncle Leo never mentioned her name to me. You're really not planning on going anywhere, are you?"

Griffin smeared peanut butter sauce on his green onion

pancakes, breathed in as it melted over the pancakes. "Nope. How's your sofa? Springs nearly ready to break through the fabric? Is it long enough for me?"

She sighed. "It's long enough and really quite comfortable. Uncle Leo always insists on sleeping on that sofa. It's good to know I smell vague."

"With a whiff of sweetness. I'll get my duffel from the Range Rover later." Time to stick a toe in the water. "Do you have any idea who that woman was you heard?"

There was no doubt who he was talking about. "No, but I'm going to find her."

He took another bit of soup. "What you said about her voice—she sounded crazy, wild, scary?"

"That's right. If I had to put on a label, I'd say she was a card-carrying psychopath. She didn't sound sorry she'd helped murder my parents, she sounded excited."

"I just might know who she could be."

Kirra reared back in her chair. "How could you possibly know? You live in Washington."

"Last Tuesday, before we came to speak to you, Savich, Pepper, and I went to see Elson Grissom in the hospital. His daughter, Melissa Kay, was there. She was like a bomb, ready to explode. If she'd had a gun, she might have shot the lot of us. Only her father could rein her in. Do you know anything about her?"

Kirra fiddled with her chopsticks. "Like you, I read everything Eliot Ness sent to Dillon and Jeter about Elson Grissom. I did some research on his family online, including Melissa Kay. She's been out of control on and off since she was very young. There were DUIs, bar fights, and car wrecks, but none of them turned out to be her fault. Daddy always bailed her out of trouble. If I could hear her voice, I might know for sure."

He said, "Say it was Melissa Kay, she would have been very young, right?"

Kirra nodded. "Early twenties."

"Who do you think her partner was?"

Go ahead, spit it out, it's pretty obvious. "If it was Melissa Kay, it might have been her older brother, Ryman."

"Okay. I agree. What do you suggest we do?"

Kirra thought a moment. "Well, you could arrange to plant a bug on her car. I could hear her voice then, and we could see where she goes, who she talks to."

He met her eyes, smiled. Quite pretty eyes, actually, green as moss. He watched a thick hank of dark brown hair laced with soft blond fall over her shoulder. He slammed on the brakes again and took another bite of the green onion pancake. "Maybe we should be more proactive. Let me think on it awhile, we'll talk about later. Tell me what you thought of Quantico."

She wanted to throw her moo shu pork at him. "Well, all the trainees I saw seemed focused, driven."

"If they weren't, they wouldn't last long. It's four months of grind, both physical and mental. But there's always some crazy fun."

"They weren't kids. Most of those I saw were older than me."

"The average age of an FBI trainee is thirty-one now. It was a smart decision because right out of college or law school, you don't have much experience of the world under your belt. And it's in your twenties you learn a lot about what you really want."

"Tell me the craziest thing you did."

"Sorry, state secret. Well, maybe if you give me a soft pillow."

Kirra spooned some Szechuan beef on her plate, careful to push the hot red peppers to the side. "If you're married, I bet your wife would rather have your hide home on a Saturday night than bodyguarding me."

"Not married."

"Ever?"

"Close to it once, but it didn't work out."

"Do you snore that loud? Do you belch after meals?"

He raised a hand. "No. It was about—something else entirely." Griffin shut his mouth, shrugged.

Kirra sat forward. "What do you mean it was about something else? Good grief, you cheated on her, didn't you, and she found you out?"

"No, she was my fiancée. I'd made a commitment. I would never have cheated on her." He shut his mouth again, wondered why he'd opened it in the first place, and studied his soup.

She nailed him with her prosecutor's eye. "So then what did you do? Criticize her mother's meatloaf? Kick her dog? Decide you're gay?"

Griffin spurted out a laugh. "No, none of the above."

Kirra tapped her chopsticks on the back of his hand. "Tell you what I'm willing to do. I'll give you my softest pillow if you tell me what happened."

He thought about this, tapped his fingers on the tabletop. "All right, but my head better sink right down into that pillow."

"It's amazing." She crossed her finger over her heart.

"It was—well, hell—the fact was Anna was always jealous."

She cocked her head. "She was jealous? Of you? Why was she jealous?"

"I couldn't look at another woman without her believing I'd slept with her." He stopped cold. "And that's too much, no more, gate's closed."

Kirra sat back in her chair, studied him a moment. "Hard to believe, but hey, Griffin, don't get me wrong. You're not ugly, I mean, you're okay looking, and your big draw is you're an FBI agent, right? Is that it? Or didn't Anna approve?"

"She was DEA, looked at FBI agents with mild contempt."

"Could she outshoot you?"

"Sometimes. Look, that's enough, Kirra."

"No, wait. I want to understand. Like I said, you're not ugly and you do look like you could take down a biker gang. Was that too macho for her?"

Griffin said slowly, eyes on her face, "You don't think I'm ugly?"

"No, really, you're fine in the looks department. Don't be insecure just because you're no Daniel Craig, well, when he was younger." She cocked her head. "She really was jealous over you because of your looks? You did something, didn't you?"

He shook his head, amused. She wasn't messing with him. Anna, and most women, saw him as a chick magnet, something he'd had to put up with since he was thirteen and found love notes in his locker, had messages passed to him in class, answered giggling calls on his cell phone. His father had patted his shoulder, told him to get used to it. But Kirra was treating him like nothing special, just a regular guy. He'd take it. "No," he said smiling big, "I'm no Daniel Craig."

She cocked her head to the side, gave him a tentative smile. "Okay, you get the soft pillow."

They tossed the empty take-out cartons and plastic chopsticks, cleaned off the small table, and covered it again with a bright yellow tablecloth. Kirra said as they walked to the living room, "I want you to tell me what you think we should do about Melissa Kay Grissom."

We— She'd included him. It was a start.

"You've looked at her police record. Let's see what she's got on social media. I'll bet you Melissa Kay has a Facebook page."

Kirra grabbed her iPad, typed in Melissa Kay's name, looked

at Griffin, and gave a fist pump. "Melissa Kay does have a Facebook page, and she's on it a lot, nearly every day. Here, look, there are photos of her, alone and with friends, and with her brother and father." He looked over her shoulder, and they scanned her posts together. "She posts about her clothes, her hairdresser, her makeup, her vacations. She comes across as perfectly normal. I guess her family doesn't mind, so long as she keeps their business completely out of it. Look, Griffin, the post she wrote just yesterday—*I'm going to Green Briar but I won't be alone. Jared is flying into Washington and he'll meet me there. Three days of heaven!*"

Kirra added, "Green Briar is a fancy resort some two hours from here nestled in the Appalachians. I've never been there, but I've heard they're usually booked up. Skiing in winter and swimming and hiking in summer. Great spa and food to die for. What do you think? Do you think I should follow her there, see if I can hear her speak? Maybe identify her?"

Griffin was a cop to the souls of his feet, a born cop, his mother said. He was also a cop who obeyed the rules. Well, he'd had to bend them some on occasion, but what Kirra was asking of him now, helping a vigilante, was off the charts. He saw Savich beating the crap out of him at the gym and assigning him to clean the Washington Field Office bathrooms for a month. He saw Pepper Jersik shaking her head at him, telling him he was a moron and a judge might just toss his butt in jail. He looked again at Kirra's face and saw what he thought he'd have felt in her place—hope and determination, and out of his mouth came, "Why don't we go together to Green Briar? You'll hear Melissa Kay's voice and we'll go from there. What do you think?"

She gaped at him, opened her mouth and closed it, continued to stare at him as if he'd suggested they walk naked together in Justice Plaza at noon. He wanted to smile, but didn't. "Give it some thought," he said and walked away. Griffin could feel her eyes on his back, but he didn't turn. He walked over to her big lounger, eased back as his legs came up. . He picked up the remote, handy in a side pocket, and turned on a Washington Wizards basketball game. Kirra curled up on the South Seas sofa and opened her iPad again. She didn't look up at him. "If you really mean that, Griffin, I'll make reservations."

Griffin said, "I meant what I said."

He heard her let out a breath. "Okay, thank you. It's pricey. I don't think the FBI is going to spring for it, not just for the chance I might recognize the voice of the woman who killed my parents fourteen years ago." She looked up at him. "It'd never fly in court. Even a mediocre defense attorney would shred me—just a kid, terrified, in shock, trying to escape being murdered. Even if it turns out I'm sure it was Melissa, we'll have to find more, but how is that possible? Melissa Kay's going there to be with her friggin' lover, not planning anyone's murder. They'll probably spend all their time in their room." Her voice trailed off. She looked defeated.

Griffin said patiently, "One step at a time, Kirra. First we find out if you do recognize her voice, that's what's important to you right now." He paused a moment. "We'll figure out where to go from there. Trust me."

She met his eyes. "It's hard, Griffin. I've been on my own for so long, ever since I left Australia."

"I understand. Take a deep breath. You've got a partner now."

She gave him a blazing smile; she looked like the weight of the world had been magically lifted off her head.

At a time-out in the Washington Wizards game, Griffin turned to see she was still working on her iPad. "Kirra, we know what we're going to do, so why ignore a Wizards game?

The Celtics have a three-point lead."

She didn't look up. "I'm a Warriors fan, actually."

"Makes no sense, they're on the wrong coast for you."

"You forget the West Coast is the closest to Australia, so I went with the Warriors. And I'll admit I fell in love with Steph Curry and his three-pointers. ... Okay, I got us reservations. The Green Briar had only one of their two honeymoon suites left. I booked it." Kirra stretched. "Hey, I'll bring you blankets and that soft pillow for the sofa."

Griffin tapped his fingertips on the chair arm. "Melissa Kay has seen me, knows what I look like. I bet she knows what you look like, too, since you were the one who took charge of those Eliot Ness documents. And don't forget, the Grissoms were probably the ones to hire out your murder yesterday so of course they both know what you look like. So we'll try to stay out of her sight as much as possible and disguise ourselves." He eyed her. "So who do you want to look like?"

Kirra laughed. "I want to be Lady GaGa."

"All right, that means a blond wig for you."

"Okay, but it's got to be long and curly. I want to look like a hit babe. A dark wig for you, maybe? A fake beard, maybe a mustache?"

"You can wear glasses, maybe change up your makeup. And we'll have to act like newlyweds since we'll be in a honeymoon suite, at least in front of hotel staff."

"Don't worry, I'll put away your sofa bedding every morning."

"How long is Melissa Kay staying?"

"Tomorrow through Tuesday, which—hallelujah—isn't a problem for me. When my boss, Alec, found out I was almost killed yesterday, he asked me to work from home until he thinks it's safe for me to come back into the office."

When the game was over, Griffin rose. Kirra rose too. "Go brush your teeth, Griffin, and I'll get you blankets and the softest pillow in the universe."

He stepped in front of her, took her hands. "Good night, Kirra. Please remember, you're no longer alone. That means no haring off somewhere by yourself. You promise?"

"A partner. Yes, I promise." She sounded as if she still couldn't believe it.

When Kirra's bedroom light went off, Griffin was lying on the surprisingly comfortable sofa, his arms cradling his soft pillow, his mind still going at warp speed. He knew he'd have to walk a very fine line between helping Kirra the commonwealth attorney and Eliot Ness the vigilante. He realized she knew the Grissoms were involved in the murder of her parents, but how did she know? Did she have some kind of proof already, besides her memory of a woman's voice?

He had to be patient. Trust was a fragile thing, easy to lose and a bitch to regain.

36

Captivity

SATURDAY AFTERNOON

Bile rose in Sherlock's throat as nausea ripped through her. She lay perfectly still, her head pounding, and pressed her hands to her stomach. She took light square breaths until a wave of nausea passed. She hadn't felt this miserable since she'd had food poisoning last year. She'd never forget hugging the toilet for what seemed like hours. She would not throw up. She would not.

Molly lay on her side against the wall, still drugged and unconscious, one hand fisted. Her curly red hair covered half her face. One of her black ankle boots was halfway off her foot. Sherlock pressed her fingertips to Molly's neck. Nice steady beat. She started to shake Molly awake, drew her hand back. No, she'd her come out of it on her own.

Their wrists were free of the zip ties. Nero had strapped them to their seats with zip ties on the jet, but now he had left them off. He had to believe they were helpless here. It was hard, but Sherlock knew she had to tamp down on the fear. Fear froze you, paralyzed your brain. The good news was she and Molly were together and alive. And no zip ties. She knew

Dillon was moving heaven and earth to find her and Molly. She also knew he was counting on her to assess her situation and try her best to get both her and Molly out of it. Slowly, the headache and nausea receded. She drew several deep breaths.

Sherlock looked around the room, surprised at what she saw. They were in a finished basement that looked like an old-fashioned game room from a 1940s movie set. There were thick cobwebs everywhere, like Halloween had come early. An antique mahogany pool table stood in the center of the room with ornate legs and beautifully carved sideboards. An exquisite old Tiffany lamp hung over the middle of the table, crisscrossing web loops hanging off its curved metal arms. Some of the balls sat together on the faded green baize, stuck to it with spiderwebs and dust so thick only a cue stick could move them. A fancy antique mahogany cabinet filled with a display of standing cue sticks behind its cobwebbed glass stood against one of the far walls. They looked protected and pristine, ready for play. There was a seating area with four oversize chairs, much of their stuffing pulled out and examined by rodents. A small cathode-ray tube television stood in splendid isolation in front of the chairs. Beside it was a liquor cabinet, so dusted over she couldn't see if there were bottles of hooch inside. Piles of boxes and trunks and old furniture were stacked against the far wall. It was a game room for men, expensive and very old, built long before she'd been born, outdated now and forgotten.

She drew several deep breaths, turned toward Molly again. At least they could see each other. They'd left a single light on, one measly overhead that gave off no more than twenty watts.

Sherlock leaned back against the wall beside Molly and closed her eyes. She queried her body and knew that soon she'd be good to go. Her headache spiked only now and then in short, sharp pulses. She'd stopped swallowing convulsively to fight the blasted nausea. But where? She had no idea where they were. It didn't matter—wherever they were, she'd have to get herself and Molly out of there. She knew they shouldn't have taken a drink of anything offered to them after the jet took off, but when it came down to it, it hadn't mattered. Nero would have made sure to put them out some other way so they'd have no idea where they were going.

Sherlock remembered sitting zip-tied next to Molly in the large private jet after it taxied down the long runway and climbed to thirty thousand feet. Molly had been pale and silent. .Sherlock guessed she was reliving Nero shooting Pope between the eyes a foot in front of her. Sherlock had been horrified at the naked violence. She knew Molly would relive that moment for years to come, no way to stop it. Then Domino had brought sandwiches and orange juice over, sat down in a seat opposite them, bit into her own sandwich, drank orange juice from a juice box, and nodded toward theirs. She and Molly had followed suit. Sherlock had said, "You look much better as a woman."

Domino shrugged, chewed on her sandwich. "I like playing parts." Still, Sherlock saw her hand shake as she looked sideways to where Nero was sitting. He was typing on a tablet on the tray in front of him. Was he emailing Shaker, telling him he had Molly? That they were bringing both of them to him?

Sherlock said to Domino, "I don't blame you for being afraid of him. Nero shot Pope for no other reason than he'd made a mistake? Or was there more to it?"

Domino kept her head down; she didn't say anything and chewed faster.

Sherlock took a drink of her OJ, said, "I hope you don't make any mistakes, Domino, like Pope did. Or that Nero ever decides he's better off without you. We could help you out of all this, you know."

It was the last thing she remembered.

Sherlock reached over now with her free hand and clasped Molly's. For a second, there was no reaction, then Molly squeezed her hand like a lifeline. They stayed hands together for a long time.

Sherlock had no idea how long she and Molly had been unconscious, if a day had passed or merely hours. But it was time to get it together, to figure out where they were and how to escape. She reached for the empty holster of her Ruger LCP pistol still strapped to her ankle. Nero had the Ruger now, Dillon's birthday present to her, only thirteen ounces fully loaded. She remembered she'd weighed it on her palm and laughed, told him it couldn't be more than a couple of ounces lighter than her current small pistol. He'd kissed her, said every once counted if you were running after a bad guy. She'd get it back, she had to believe that, but right now, it meant they had no weapons.

She eyed the two high-set skinny windows that gave no clue if it was night or day because they were nailed shut with plywood planks. She wondered if she and Molly would be able to squeeze through them, if need be. There was the main door, and it would be locked tight. A smaller door was on the opposite wall. A bathroom? She hoped so.

Molly moaned. Sherlock leaned in close, laid her palm against her cheek, and rubbed. "Molly, lie still and take light shallow breaths. You'll feel nauseated and like your head is going to split open, but it will go away. Lie still, it'll help. Don't rush it, okay?"

Molly whispered, "Okay." She didn't move. Sherlock saw her hands clench and unclench, heard her breathing light and even.

She said aloud, to distract her, "We're in a finished basement,

Molly, an old-fashioned elegant game room. Now it's a storage room. There are piles of stacked boxes and trunks along the far walls, and generations of decaying furniture piled high next to them. I think we're in a large old house, and given the Tiffany lamp that looks quite authentic, and the pool table that had to cost thousands even way back when, it was probably a very elegant rich house once.

"Molly, I don't think we're in Las Vegas. From everything I've learned about Rule Shaker I can't imagine his owning a huge house with an outdated man cave in the basement, not anywhere near where he lives, in Las Vegas."

Molly said, "He lives in a huge suite at the top of his largest and most profitable casino, Sovereign. The suite is at least four thousand square feet and over-the-top opulent. He refurnishes it every year."

"Could this large house be a vacation home?"

"I don't know. From all I can gather, he loves where he lives. I can see him standing on his penthouse balcony, enclosed in glass, of course, since it gets so hot there, looking out over the city, knowing he owns a good chunk of it. If anyone tried to move in on what he has, he wouldn't hesitate to kill. To him and his kind, it's only the cost of doing business." Molly, her eyes open now, gave Sherlock a crooked smile. "Sound familiar?"

"Yep, your daddy."

Molly paused and lightly ran her fingertips over her forehead. She pointed. "Look at those two ancient trunks, Sherlock. Those suckers are so huge they could hold bodies. And that television, I don't think I've ever seen one that old." She stopped cold and moaned, closed her eyes.

Sherlock waited a moment until Molly opened her eyes again, tried for a slight smile. "Okay, it's better."

"Good. Here's the truth, Molly. Neither Nero nor Domino ever wore a mask. Nero knows we'd identify him, find him, that I'd never stop looking for him. Whatever Shaker wants, once he gets it, they're going to kill us, which means"—she pointed to the two windows—"we're going to have to get through those windows or take down whoever comes through that door. Nero took my ankle gun so we need to go through the boxes to find anything we can use as weapons, discarded silverware, cutting knives or forks." She paused a moment, eyed Molly. "I'm telling you the whole truth because I know you can handle it. You've been through fear like this before, when Ramsey was shot and when Emma was kidnapped six years ago. You're tough, Molly, and we're going to have to work together. So here's the rest of it. I have no idea if Dillon even knows we left Washington on a private jet, if they've even found the limo or Pope's body. We don't know how long we were out and how far we came. We won't even know if it's night or day unless I can pull that plywood off those windows. Bottom line, we have to assume we won't have anyone to help us but ourselves. We're on our own."

Molly looked Sherlock square in the eye. "I'm so scared I don't have any spit in my mouth, but I'll try not to let you down. Just tell me what to do."

"I'm scared too. The trick is to not let the fear paralyze you, freeze your brain. We can do this."

"Okay. At least we know whoever is behind our kidnapping, Rule Shaker or not, doesn't want us dead yet. We're leverage, though for what I don't know. They'll need us for some sort of ransom demand." Molly pressed her palm against her temple, cursed. "Why won't the headache stop?"

"It will, keep breathing lightly and don't move. You're right about the ransom. They know Ramsey will demand proof of life. Nero's a stone-cold killer, but they'll have to keep us alive until then."

"He's evil. He killed Pope without hesitation, shot him like he was nothing to him at all, like he was flicking away a fly. Even Domino was terrified. She realized he could do the same to her."

Sherlock said thoughtfully, "I do wonder if Pope's mistake was the only reason Nero shot him. I mean, it seemed so unnecessary, killing him right then."

Molly said, "Maybe so, but Pope is dead."

Suddenly, unbidden, Sherlock saw Nero shooting Pope between his eyes, heard again the sharp loud explosion of sound, smelled the acrid cordite in the air. Molly had screamed, unable to accept what had happened in front of her. Sherlock swallowed. She wouldn't accept it either. She put the thought away.

Molly said now, "We don't know how long we have before Nero and Domino come back to fetch us."

Sherlock rose, felt a moment of dizziness. "You're right, I need to hurry. I'm going to check those windows, see if it's still daylight, maybe get a clue where we are."

She took a step forward and nearly fell, braced herself against a paneled wall.

Molly moved to get up.

"No, no, stay there."

"Are you all right?"

"Yes. Don't worry." Sherlock walked to the side door and opened it, saw it was an old-fashioned bathroom with a pedestal sink, a toilet, and a small shower. She called out, "We have a bathroom." When she came out, she walked to the main door and turned the handle. It was locked, no surprise there. She hadn't noticed before, but now she saw their captors had left them bottled water near the door. Had Nero and Domino left the house for some reason? She looked back at Molly, still sitting against the wall, her eyes closed.

"I need a couple more minutes," Molly said, "then I'll visit the bathroom. Sherlock, if you had to guess, where would you say we are?"

"Somewhere in the US, maybe even in the Caribbean, like St. Thomas or one of the smaller islands. They would have stayed clear of customs. Time for me to check those windows."

Sherlock pulled over a discarded chair from the fifties, swiped away the spiderwebs and checked to see it would hold her weight. She climbed up and reached, but it wasn't enough. She spotted a coffee table, pulled it off a jumbled pile of furniture, moved it under the window. She set the chair on top of it and carefully climbed up on top of the chair. It wobbled a bit, but thankfully it held her weight. She pulled at the rotting plywood nailed to window frame, but she couldn't loosen it by hand. She climbed down, looked for some kind of tool she could use as a lever. She saw a bridge stick with a metal head in the mahogany cabinet, hefted it in her hand, and climbed back up to the basement window. She managed to force the metal head of the bridge stick under an edge of the damp plywood and lever it partly away from the frame. She called out, "It's daylight, but it's hard to tell how late because of the thick oak and maple trees. But this isn't the Caribbean or the Nevada desert. We may be able to get through this window, but it's going to be very tight. We might have to break out the frame. When you're up to moving around, we'll give it a try."

To be careful, Sherlock pushed the plywood back in place and put the chair and coffee table back with the discarded furniture. She saw Molly still had her eyes closed. She crouched down beside her. Molly whispered, her voice shaking, "I feel like I'm a complete drag on you, Sherlock. Maybe you should get out of here and leave me. I'm the one they want."

"Yeah, like that's going to happen. Don't forget, we're a team, together we have genius IQs, off the charts. And we've got grit and guts. In addition we've got our cavalry looking for us. They'll find us if we can't get away." She picked up a bottle of water, twisted it open. "The water isn't drugged, the seal's still on it. Drink this down, then we need to move."

Molly drank. "First he sent his thugs after Emma, but she was too well guarded and he had to settle for me. I'm sorry, Sherlock, you shouldn't have been with me."

"Don't make me hurt you, Molly. How do you feel?"

"Better, the headache's easing."

"And the nausea?"

"It wasn't as bad for me as it was for you."

Sherlock got to her feet, grabbed another couple of water bottles. "You go ahead to the bathroom. I'll wrap up the water in the blanket and when you're ready, we'll start trying that window, go through it if we can."

Sherlock waited until Molly came back out and checked her over. She looked stronger and she was standing tall, her back straight.

"Ready to do this?"

Molly gave her a fierce smile. "Our team can do anything, right?"

Sherlock wished she could sound as full of bravado, but she knew in her gut it was a desperate plan, the odds stacked against them. And how could Dillon find out where they were? Nero wouldn't have filed a flight plan Savich could follow. Maybe he could track the jet, unless Nero had thought of that, too, which she'd bet he had.

Before Sherlock could reposition the coffee table and chair, she and Molly froze at the sound of voices coming toward the basement door.

37

The door opened and Nero walked into the basement, his weapon held loosely at his side. Behind him came Domino carrying a tray.

Nero raised his Sig, pointed it at Sherlock as Domino walked past him. She set the tray on the floor three feet in front of them, backed away.

"I see you're awake, ladies. Glad to see you're both alive. Getting the narcotics dosage right is tricky and sometimes people die." He pointed to the tray Domino had left them. There were two plastic bottles of water, still sealed, two wrapped sandwiches, and two unopened bags of potato chips. "You'll be here a while, so you might as well eat. You want to keep body and soul together, don't you?"

"Where are we?"

He cocked a dark eyebrow at Sherlock, pulled a chair from a pile of discarded furniture in the corner, tested it, and sat down. "As you can see, you're in a lovely long-ago man cave." He stretched his legs out in front of him and crossed his arms, like a man in control of his world and he knew it, basking in the knowledge. He held his Sig in his right hand, resting on his thigh. In the limousine, he'd been dressed to the nines in a black suit, white shirt, and dark tie. He'd shed the suit coat and tie now, his white shirt rolled to his elbows. His forearms were hairless, smooth and pale as his face. In the dim light he looked so winter-white he could have played a murderous zombie in a Halloween horror film. He said, "Domino, stay by the door and keep your Glock on our two ladies, particularly Agent Sherlock." He paused, his cold eyes roaming over her, making her skin crawl. He added, a half smile on his thin lips, "I've read about your exploits, Agent Sherlock—stopping that bombing at JFK, bringing down that Algerian terrorist at the Lincoln Monument. It was quite a performance. You gave the tourists a big show, a story to tell back home about lawless America. But alas, Agent Sherlock, there will be no more daring deeds for you. I have you now and trust me, I never suffer defeat." He raised his Sig, aimed it at her face, held it steady. "Never."

Sherlock didn't look away from his cold emotionless face as he spoke. Her face showed only indifference, a hint of boredom. No way would she let him see her shock of fear, not only at his words and the gun, but at his face as he spoke. There was no doubt in her mind he planned to kill them both. Dillon's and Sean's faces flashed through her mind. She looked at Nero again and shook her head, no expression on her face. "Big words are easy to say when you have the weapon," she said and turned away from him. Could he smell her fear?

Nero laughed, a hollow sound, and slowly lowered his Sig. "Brave words, but I made your heart race, didn't I, Agent Sherlock? No answer?" He said to Molly, "Believe me, Mrs. Hunt, you want to do what you're told or she's dead." He smiled. "You see, I also came to convince you not to try to escape." He pointed his Sig toward the boarded windows. "If you did manage to squeeze through one of those windows, which you couldn't, given Mrs. Hunt's very nice curves, I have men outside, patrolling the grounds. My orders to them are to shoot you both. Much better for us if you're both dead than if you escape. My advice to you is not to try."

Molly said, "What do you want with us?"

"What I want doesn't concern you, Mrs. Hunt, until I choose to tell you. Just know that if you choose not to cooperate, I will shoot Agent Sherlock in the head in front of you, like poor stupid Pope."

Sherlock waved at the food and gave him a sneer. "Do you think we'd eat the sandwiches?"

Nero shrugged. "They're quite good actually. Tuna salad. They're not drugged, but then again, why should you believe me?" He turned to Domino. "Did you slip in some ketamine into them while I wasn't looking, my dear?"

Domino only shook her head, didn't move or speak. Sherlock didn't blame her.

Molly said, "So you haven't yet made a ransom demand yet from my husband and father? How many millions are you planning to ask for our release?"

The half smile was still in place when he said to Molly, "Let me just say you can consider it a ransom of sorts. I suggest you not worry about it, Mrs. Hunt, just do what I tell you if you hope to be released."

Molly ripped open a bag of potato chips, took a chip, and crunched down. Her chewing was loud in the basement. When she'd swallowed, she said, "Now there's a lie that won't travel far."

Nero gave a full-bodied laugh, showing big square teeth and a gold incisor. "Ah, no terrified little housewife, are you? You're the famous judge's wife who saved her daughter. I doubt your bravado will last now I've got you." He studied Molly as he had Sherlock. "I saw your young prodigy in the flesh last night performing at Kennedy Center, and you as well, Agent Sherlock. She's a lovely girl, an amazing talent. And no, no one paid me any mind. I had lovely orchestra seats." He paused, looked thoughtful. "Wait, it was your first husband, Louey Santera, who gave her that talent, wasn't it? Not you. When it comes down to it, like most women, all you were good for was birthing her."

Sherlock gave him a full-blown sneer. "You think you know so much about us, but you don't." She laughed. "If you didn't have that gun, she'd eat you for breakfast."

She'd startled him, but only for a moment. He gave her his cold smile that promised payback.

Sherlock pulled one of Molly's potato chips out of her bag, chewed on it. "So you've been instructed to wait, Nero, is that right? Until when? Until Mason Lord and Ramsey Hunt and Agent Savich visit Rule Shaker in Las Vegas? Will it be Shaker who tells you what to do then?"

He stared at her and then said in a dead-calm voice, "We all have our parts to play in this little chessboard drama. You'll be silent and accept your situation. It's important all the pieces are played in the proper order."

Molly said, "In other words, it's too soon for a ransom demand. Why is that? What has to happen in your proper order?"

"Shut up, you stupid woman."

Molly ate another potato chip, chewed slowly. "Trying to take Emma—a spectacular failure—and then you managed to grab Agent Sherlock. It's obvious your boss needs us for leverage of some kind. All your talk about the chess pieces played in the proper order. I'll bet you have no idea what's involved, do you, Nero? You're only his worker bee, after all."

He sat back in the chair, let his gun dangle from his fingers. He studied her for a moment. "And I suppose you know?"

Molly laughed. "Yes, I do now. I should have figured it out much sooner." She didn't say another word, only smiled at him, ate another potato chip as he waited.

"Do tell me what you think, Mrs. Hunt."

"I'll just say it all started six years ago."

Nero blinked his nearly colorless eyes. "And what about six years ago? Your daughter was taken and your husband managed to recover her. So?"

Molly shook her head, said nothing. Sherlock laid her hand over Molly's, gave it a squeeze.

Violence stirred in Nero's eyes. "You just made that up, didn't you? You have no idea, do you, you stupid bitch. Don't you agree, Domino?"

Domino said without hesitation, "Yes." Smart girl.

The words were out of Sherlock's mouth before she could stop herself. "It makes sense you don't know anything, Nero. You're only the hired help, like Mrs. Hunt said, a bit player, nothing more. Why would Molly tell you anything?"

He leaped to his feet. "Shut up or I'll shoot you both here and now." He towered over them, moving his gun from one to the other. Sherlock held her breath. She saw his rage. She'd pushed him too hard. *A little late to realize you should have kept your mouth shut.* Sherlock prayed.

Slowly, very slowly, Nero calmed. He said in a dead voice, "I will delight in killing you, Agent Sherlock, but not today." He motioned to Domino, and together they left the basement room without another word.

Molly and Sherlock heard the key turn in the lock.

Molly grabbed Sherlock. "I was afraid he was going to kill you!"

"Believe me, Molly, I realized fast I should have kept quiet. I've got to be more careful with him. Now let's eat the potato chips and have a look at that window. We can't stay here."

"I am hungry. Do you really think the sandwiches could be

drugged?"

"I'd bet my lucky two-headed quarter on it." She grinned at Molly. "I use it with Dillon. He's never guessed even though I beat him every time. Or maybe he knows and he's just letting me get away with it. Let's stick with the potato chips. Do you really think you know why we were taken? Or were you trying to get Nero to tell us?"

"I'm not sure, but it's the only thing I can think of that makes sense. I think it could all be about the confessions I forced my father and the Shakers to sign six years ago to put an end to the war between them. The original documents are in our lawyer's safe in San Francisco. Maybe Rule Shaker wants them back. The question is why? And why now?"

"You're thinking he wants to start up another war with your father?"

"I'm afraid that might be it. Sherlock, if that's what this is about, we can't let it happen."

"You're right. We can't, so let's see if your butt is too curvy to get through the window."

"If I can squeeze through, what about Nero's men?"

"It can't be long now before it gets dark. We'll get the window open and wait."

38

Sovereign Casino
Las Vegas

SATURDAY AFTERNOON

The monolithic tower of the Sovereign speared eight stories above the two casinos flanking it, a paean to Las Vegas extravagance. Its windows glittered in the late-afternoon sun, its fountains flashed high in the air and cascaded down into wide koi pools. Half a dozen doormen dressed in black with gold bow ties ushered taxis and rental cars toward the entrance, helped arriving guests out of their cars, and passed off their luggage to bellmen.

When their limo driver had let them off at the curb in front of the Sovereign to avoid the crowd, Elizabeth Beatrice's eyes nearly popped out of her head. She stared. "Goodness me," she said.

They walked toward the entrance on a sidewalk beside the curving driveway. They knew Shaker was in residence, as the concierge put it to Mason when he'd called, on the top floor, in his huge apartment with its view of the Strip and the endless miles of desert and rugged barren hills beyond.

Mason stopped beside a gorgeous blooming wisteria, took

Elizabeth Beatrice's hand in his. She'd insisted on coming along and meeting Rule Shaker herself and, she'd pointed out, she'd never seen Las Vegas. He'd resisted at first. "What is it, Mason? You're afraid a crazy gambler is going to throw dice at me?" and she leaned up and nipped his earlobe. He'd looked over at Ramsey and Savich. Both men wore stone faces. She added, "Stop your worrying. Nothing's going to happen to me. Who knows, maybe I'll be able to help." Mason thought about that. Maybe she was right. At the very least she'd help him control himself when he met with the Shakers. He would have killed Rule Shaker and his daughter, Eve, six years ago if Molly herself hadn't stopped him. Just maybe he'd need her to stop him again. It was still clear as day in his mind when Eve had betrayed him, nearly killed him. Talk about being a fool. She had killed Emma's father, Louey. He remembered his rage. Only Molly had put a stop to everything. She'd saved his life and Eve's and her father's lives as well. From him.

He lightly rubbed his knuckles over his wife's smooth cheek. "All right, but stick close to me."

Elizabeth Beatrice looked now out over the huge fountains and the beautifully manicured flower beds that surrounded them, and said again, "Goodness me," then added, "I have to admit to feeling speechless when the limousine turned into the Strip as you call it, Mason." She grinned. "I had only a snooty Brit's view of Las Vegas—a degenerate wasteland designed to take money from people who can't afford it. That may be true, but to me it looks like an adult Disneyland, and, yes, I did visit Orlando when I was a teenager."

Savich hadn't been to Las Vegas in a couple of years and wondered if he and Sherlock would ever want to come back here. The sidewalks swarmed with tourists, many dressed in exquisite bad taste, women in tight short-shorts and potbellied men in Bermuda shorts, tight T-shirts, and sandals with white socks. A few came to see the shows, but most of them came here to gamble, and most would lose; a precious few would win big bucks and spend them on a Prada bag for the missus or a strapless Givenchy gown for the mistress. The women who won would buy the Prada bags for themselves.

He thought of Sherlock again, swallowed. He would do whatever he had to do to find her and Molly. He'd beat the truth out of Shaker, kill him if he needed to. The thought stilled him, made him wonder whether he was in control of himself, if his rage was too close to the surface. It didn't matter. Savich knew in his gut if he didn't get Sherlock back safe and unharmed, Shaker would die here in this make-believe city, his fiefdom. He simply couldn't imagine telling Sean his mother wasn't coming home. No, it wouldn't happen, he wouldn't let it happen.

Ramsey hated Las Vegas, hated this man who'd made a fortune here off people's endless optimism and greed. He was so afraid for Molly, so afraid of what might happen to her, he knew he'd have to hold back when he saw the little bastard, or he'd kick Shaker's kidneys through his back. He looked over at Savich. He looked calm, controlled, but Ramsey knew Savich would race him to get to Shaker. He remembered being with Molly the last time they were here six years ago, never once since. But Molly wasn't here with him, Molly was gone. He thought of Cal, Gage, and Emma. Mason's jet was flying them to Chicago, then flying back. They'd soon be safe at Mason's compound with Gunther and Miles. If something happened to their mother, what would he tell them? How would any of them go on?

As tourists flowed around them, Mason said, "If Shaker is behind this, his thugs will contact you, Ramsey, and demand the evidence against them that Molly has kept safe with her lawyers in San Francisco for six years. If it has nothing to do with Shaker, if this is about something else entirely, killing Molly would send Eve and Shaker to prison regardless because Molly's lawyers have been instructed to release all of it to the police if something happens to her."

"What evidence, exactly, Mason?" Elizabeth Beatrice asked.

Mason said, "Six years ago Molly put together enough evidence against us all—the Shakers and me both—to end what had turned into a war between us. The Shakers started it, by arranging to kidnap Emma." He paused. "Someone in both our families was killed after that—Emma's father, Louey Santera, and Shaker's younger daughter. They tried to kill me, too. Molly put an end to it by putting everything that had already happened in writing and forcing us to attest to it." Mason shook his head, squeezed Elizabeth Beatrice's hand. "I was enraged when Molly told me exactly what I was going to do, that she would give me orders. My own daughter was threatening to go to the police with everything she knew about me if I refused. Her biggest threat, the one that stopped me in my tracks, was I'd never see her or Emma again. I signed, and so did Rule and Eve. For six years there's been no trouble." He shook his head at himself, laughed. "That was when I finally realized how smart and strong Molly was, and well, how manipulative she could be when necessary." He smiled. "I saw her in a new light from that day on. I realized I was proud of her. She's impressive, my daughter. I want to tell her that when we find her and Agent Sherlock."

Ramsey could only stare at his father-in-law. He said, "She would like for you to tell her that, Mason."

Savich said, "Obviously something has changed. Do you know what it could be, Mason?"

Mason shook his head. "I've thought but I just can't pin-point anything. I mentioned Rule has had some problems in his casinos, croupiers leaving, money missing, cocktail waitresses quitting for no apparent reason. But I don't see that those pis-sant problems would make him want to restart the war." He shrugged. "But it is possible Rule has decided he's waited long enough to get his revenge on me. As long as we get Molly and Sherlock back, believe me, I'll be happy to let him try."

A doorman spotted them and rushed to open a shining glass door for them. Mason slipped him a five.

They stepped out of the sun-exploding heat into the im-mense lobby with air-conditioning blasting out cold air. The reception area was immense, glittering chandeliers hanging from fourteen feet above, yards of green-and-gold-veined mar-ble floors polished to a high shine. The walls were covered with three-dimensional floral glass sculptures, so exquisitely done you recognized each flower and wanted to see what the petals felt like. Trails of new arrivals slowly walked from one sculp-ture to the next, talking and pointing.

There were at least thirty beautiful young people manning the long exquisitely carved mahogany reception desk, but Ma-son didn't go there, he walked to the discreet VIP concierge desk in a private corner. In a few minutes he was back, a key card in his hand. "This way." He led them through one of the casinos toward a private elevator.

Elizabeth Beatrice had played baccarat in Monte Carlo's in-credible casinos among the glitterati, but they were nothing like the Sovereign casino floor. Here the men weren't in tuxedos, or the women in strapless evening gowns, dripping with dia-monds. People were dressed informally like those strolling on the streets, mostly in shorts and T-shirts. The noise level on the floor astounded her, with the hum of underlying conversation, the beep and whistles and jingles from the slot machines, and the occasional cheer when someone won. It was a different world. She realized it could be midnight or high noon but it wouldn't matter, not in here where it was endless daytime.

Mason slid in a key card and the elevator doors opened. They soared silently upward, so fast Elizabeth Beatrice had to clear her ears. They stepped out into a wide hallway, not onto carpeting, but highly polished oak floors. They walked to the end of the hall. Mason nodded to a set of rosewood double doors in front of them. "Only the best for Rule," Mason said, and he rang the doorbell.

The door was opened at once by Eve Shaker, now Eve Doulos, Mason's former wife, and Rule Shaker's elder daughter. For six years Eve had been Rule's only child. Mason hadn't seen her in person in six years, though he'd seen some photos of her when he'd glanced at the big spread in the *Las Vegas Review-Journal* about the Shaker/Doulos over-the-top wedding Miles had printed out for him and slipped under his coffee cup. She was thirty now, as gorgeous as ever, her thick blond hair falling free around her face, down past her shoulders. She was wearing a tight-cropped white top showing lots of smooth tan skin, and tight white jeans. She was barefoot, her toenails showing a perfect French pedicure. She was still built like a showgirl only more beautiful. Mason said, "Eve. You're looking well."

She wasn't surprised, of course. Mason knew the minute he'd spoken to the concierge, the man had called up to Rule's apartment. Eve looked him up and down. "For an old man, you don't look bad either, Mason."

"Thank you."

Eve eyed the young woman beside him, gave a small laugh. "You're such a cliché, Mason. Like most rich men you like to go younger every year. But you've never brought a toy to meetings."

Elizabeth Beatrice smiled at the woman gorgeous enough to be a Victoria's Secret angel. "I would say rather we're each other's favorite toys. I'm his wife. My name is Elizabeth Beatrice," and she stuck out her hand.

Eve took her hand without thinking. She hated the feel of the smooth young flesh. She saw the wedding ring, nodded at it, and a perfect eyebrow arched. "I see you held out for a wedding ring. Good for you. Mason gave me a seven-carat marquise diamond, but who's counting carats? You're a Brit. Where did Mason find you? Not in some little out-of-the-way village, but maybe playing a bit part in a show on Shaftsbury?"

Mason said, "Elizabeth Beatrice's father is Viscount Bellamy of Grace Hall in Hampshire."

Eve didn't change expressions. "I don't suppose you gave her daddy a load of bearer bonds to overlook how you make your living?"

Ramsey said, "Enough cattiness, Eve. We're here to speak to your father."

Eve didn't move from the doorway. "Ah, Ramsey, how lovely to see you. I trust Molly and your children are well? I heard Emma played at Kennedy Center last night. Did it go well?"

"You know it did," Ramsey said. "Your father, Eve. Now."

She smiled at Savich. "And certainly I remember you, Agent Savich, Mr. Tough FBI. You and your wife have a little boy, I believe. What do you three gentlemen want with my father?"

Ramsey said, "We want to know where he's stashed Molly and Sherlock."

Eve cocked her head to one side, studied each of their faces. "Your wives are missing? That makes no sense unless they decided to do a runner on you two fine gentlemen. All right, I see from your faces you're dead serious. You can speak to my father, but I know he didn't have anything to do with their, what?—disappearance?"

"Move, Eve." Ramsey walked directly at her and she stepped out of his way before he plowed into her.

They walked down a short hallway and stepped into an Italian Renaissance palazzo. It looked like a museum setting, replete with tapestries, old faded carpets, and paintings grouped around the gold-veined marble fireplace. Elizabeth Beatrice would wager one of them to be an original Caravaggio, cast into relief with special lighting.

Savich glanced around the huge space, out the far windows to the vast desert beyond. He imagined Sean flying his drone from one end of the long main room to the other. He'd never met Rule Shaker, only seen pictures. He had to admit to surprise seeing the man in the flesh. Like Mason, Savich knew he was ruthless, a hard-nosed powerhouse, a man who ruled his world just as Mason ruled his. It was strange to see such a man top out at five foot eight, tops. He was sleek, that was the word, in better shape than Savich imagined most men were at sixty years of age, and his dark hair, surprisingly, was white flecked only at his temples. His face was hard and his eyes dark, five-o'clock beard scruff on his cheeks. He was wearing black shorts and a tight black sleeveless T-shirt, wiping his face with a monogrammed white towel. He'd obviously just finished a workout.

When Shaker spoke, his voice was a deep rich baritone. "Carlo was concerned when he saw you, Mason. He called me right away. I can't say this is a pleasure, but it's certainly a surprise. You'll have to explain why you think you're welcome here. Ramsey, you're looking well. And Agent Savich, isn't it? I recognize you though we've never met. And who is this lovely young lady?"

Mason said, his voice calm, "Rule, this is my wife, Elizabeth

Beatrice."

Rule Shaker smiled at her, a smile full of charm and appreciation. "The one thing I've always admired about Mason is his taste in women."

"Thank you, Mr. Shaker. I'm told my taste in men is superb as well. Your home is spectacular. I feel like I've walked into an old Tuscany villa. Is that an original Titian beside the Caravaggio?"

Shaker gave a brief look toward the fireplace, gave her a closer look, nodded. "It's time for you to tell me why you're here, Mason."

Ramsey took a step toward Shaker, towering over him. "You know why we're here. What have you done with Molly and Agent Sherlock?"

39

"What? What in the world are you talking about, Ramsey?"

Ramsey didn't shout, repeated in his calm judge's voice, "I'll ask you again, Shaker, where did you take Molly and Agent Sherlock?"

Rule Shaker took a step back, stared at Ramsey. He frowned, cocked his head to the side. He said slowly, "You're saying Molly and Agent Sherlock are missing? And you're here because you think I took them? Are the lot of you completely nuts? Kidnap Molly and Agent Sherlock? Where are your brains? I'd have absolutely nothing to gain and everything to lose." He turned and strode across an antique carpet to what looked like a dark green velvet sofa that belonged in a palazzo in Florence. He knotted his white towel around his neck, sat down and stared at them, his face hard with anger. He made quite a picture, a man in gym shorts sweating up his muscle shirt on a piece of priceless antique furniture.

Mason said, "Nothing to gain? Come on, Rule, don't play the injured party."

Shaker continued to dry sweat off his arms after he sat. "Wait a minute. I can understand Molly being taken because she's your daughter, Mason. Revenge, money for ransom, something along those lines, but why Agent Sherlock?"

"She happened to be with Molly, as you know," Mason said.

"You had them taken together right in front of the Hay Adams Hotel in Washington."

"For heaven's sake, don't stand there looking at me like you want to rip my head off. Sit down and tell me what happened."

Eve sat down in a high-back chair with beautifully sculpted arms beside her father. She said, sarcasm combing through her voice, "Sit down, the lot of you. So you actually think my dad had Molly and Agent Sherlock kidnapped and taken somewhere? What kind of proof do you have he had anything at all to do with it?"

Mason sat on a love seat next to his bride. "A Gulfstream 500 left Jet Aeronautics with two women, both with red hair, in the close company of two men. Both Molly and Agent Sherlock have red hair. They filed a flight plan for Las Vegas."

Shaker spread his muscled arms along the back of the sofa. "Obviously the flight plan was a fiction. Even so, you decided to barge in on me?"

Savich's cell vibrated. He slipped it out of his jacket, looked down, and rose from a high-back burgundy velvet chair fit for a cardinal. "Excuse me." He walked toward the dining end of the huge room. When he returned a couple of minutes later, Ramsey was on his feet, shouting, "You took Emma six years ago and you've hated Molly ever since because she outwitted you, she beat you. She won."

Shaker nodded. "Yes, she did. And yes, I'd just as soon see her at the North Pole, but still I had to admire her for risking everything to protect Emma and her family. Whatever has happened to her, I know nothing about it."

"Cut the crap, Rule." Ramsey's voice was hoarse now. "You tried to take Emma first in San Francisco, but my girl is well trained and she kicked the crap out of the man you sent and she ran. Agent Sherlock saw to Emma's protection at Kennedy

Center, so you failed there as well. Then you decided to go after Molly. You thought it wouldn't matter, either Emma or Molly would do."

Ramsey looked like he might run at Shaker. Savich walked between them. He said, "There's more than the flight plan connecting you, Mr. Shaker. We found the limo the kidnappers used a couple of blocks from Jet Aeronautics at Dulles. There was blood on the rear-facing back seat, not Sherlock's or Molly's since they were seen boarding the Gulfstream uninjured. Our agents got a warrant to jimmy the trunk and found a man's body in it, a bullet through his forehead. They just called to let me know they've identified him in our facial recognition database. He was the same man who tried to take Emma at Kennedy Center, the same man who rented a car and a limousine in Washington using the stolen identity of an M. J. Pederson of Elder City, Nevada. His name was James Pope, aged thirty-four, Mr. Shaker, and his criminal record shows you as his employer. Perhaps you'd like to reconsider what you've said?"

As he spoke, Savich moved past Ramsey and stood over Shaker, staring down at him, rage banked in his eyes. He said softly, fists clenched at his sides, "They took my wife. It's time to tell us the truth before I take you apart."

Eve roared to her feet. "Don't you dare threaten him, or I'll have you thrown out one of those windows! Dad fired Pope months ago, caught him taking protection money from working girls at the casino. We haven't heard from him since. It sounds obvious to me someone wants you to believe my father is the mastermind here. You've been played for fools. My father had nothing to do with this. And believe me, I would know."

Mason said, "I'd easily believe you were a partner with him in this, Eve."

Eve took a step toward him. Shaker said, his voice sounding

tired, "Evie, sit down. What would you expect Mason to say? Believe you're magically now a saint? Now, they're not about to touch me. Savich is FBI, basically toothless without his bloody warrants and so many bureaucratic hoops to jump through I'd die of old age before he could haul me to a police station."

Savich laughed. "And you think I care about the rules? Convince me you didn't take my wife, or I'll lay you out."

Shaker shrugged. "How can I do that, since I have no idea who took her? Listen to Eve, you idiots. Like she said, I fired Pope months ago and I haven't seen him since. I don't know where he went or who he works for now. If he was involved in taking Molly and Agent Sherlock, that's not on me. Both ties to Elder City and Pope—sounds to me like someone's setting me up."

He slowly rose. "You can take this to the bank, all of you. I have no idea where Molly or Agent Sherlock are, no idea who took them. Get out now, all of you."

Mason got up, and Elizabeth Beatrice rose to stand beside him. He sounded quite calm. "You've always been a convincing liar, Rule, but you forget I know you well. What I don't understand is why take them and not tell us what you want? Is it as simple as you want another war with me?"

Shaker was so angry he shook with it, but his hard voice was calm, controlled. "I don't want anything you've touched, Mason, especially your daughter. As for this bit of skirt you've married, you've despoiled her just as you tried to despoil my Eve. But you failed with Eve. It's a pity she didn't shoot you dead years ago. You killed Melissa, my daughter. Of course I hate you, and you hate me. What else is new?" He paused, eyed Mason. "You talk about starting a war again. I've wondered if that's what you want, not me. Someone has been disrupting business at my casinos, as you doubtless know. Is it you? Is this all a ruse, Mason, an excuse you've arranged so you can attack me?"

"That's absurd. I haven't given you a single bloody thought for at least the past year, too many important things on my mind. You are nothing to me. About the penny-ante crap happening in your casinos, Rule, sounds to me like what every casino owner has to put up with now and then, one of the costs of doing business that's built into your overhead."

"Penny-ante?" Shaker said. "Someone set a fire in Caliph, my newest casino. No one was hurt thanks to the Las Vegas firefighters I pay privately. They were there in three minutes, herding out the screaming patrons without anyone getting trampled. The inspector said the fire started in the high-stakes poker room and spread from there, but luckily not far into the casino itself. They got the fire out quickly, but the water damage was extensive. The Caliph will be closed for two months." He looked directly at Mason. "I'm told it was arson. You're the first man I thought of, but I had no proof. And neither do you about Molly's kidnapping."

Mason said, "Sounds like you have an enemy, Rule, but you know I'd come right at you, not nibble at you and hide in the shadows, so I don't give a crap if you want to think I'm behind it. It's quite true I haven't given you a single thought in months. I've been in England with Elizabeth Beatrice." He glanced at his wife. "If you fell off the face of the earth, Rule, I'd drink a glass of champagne, and move on. I wouldn't give you a further thought. Talk about an enemy attacking you, sounds like you have a list." He paused. "Tell us where they are, Rule, and stop this show of innocence. You've never been innocent of anything in your life."

Shaker raised a blunt-fingered hand with manicured fingernails toward Mason's face. He said in his smooth powerful voice, "Are you getting senile? We both know your precious Molly saw to it six years ago that if I touched a hair on her head, or Emma's, the cops would come down on me like a freight train. Molly's lawyers in San Francisco would release the recording she made of Eve admitting to killing Louey, and that thick pile of everything else Molly wrote down about us. I'd be the first on their list of suspects." He sneered. "Or is that all a lie, too? Do you already have the documents?"

Ramsey said, "You know what I think? You want all that evidence back, you don't want it hanging over you anymore, and you took Molly to get it." Ramsey strode to Shaker, grabbed the white towel around his neck and jerked him close. "I'm going to kill you if anything happens to her. Do you understand me?"

Eve raised a 9 mm pistol, pointed it at Ramsey. She said, anger thick in her voice, "Back up, Ramsey, get away from him. Dad told you he had nothing to do with their kidnapping and it's true. Like he said, it could only have ended with me going to prison for killing Louey. Dad would never want that. I've really had enough of all of you. We don't know who took Molly and Agent Sherlock, which means, Judge Dredd, you need to check your own enemies list. Just think of all the criminals you've sentenced over the years. Now, get out of here, all of you."

Savich looked at Ramsey, gave him a shake of his head. He said, "Mr. Shaker, your daughter has a point as far as it goes. It's possible the kidnappers will prove to be someone else. Your life here seems very pleasant and financially rewarding, except, I suppose, for your competitors here in Las Vegas who appear to mean you harm. But you know, if it isn't about getting the truce documents and going to war again, what is it about?"

"Like Eve said, a criminal the judge here sent to prison. Revenge is always a powerful motive."

Savich looked at Eve. "You hate Mason for murdering your

sister six years ago, after you killed Louey. You hate Molly because she found you out and closed you down. Was it you who arranged to take Molly, to get revenge for your sister?"

Eve's pistol wavered a moment, then she straightened. "We've told you, neither my father nor I know anything about this kidnapping. We're going around in circles. It's enough." She paused, sent a vicious smile toward Elizabeth Beatrice. "I'll bet you had no idea what sort of man you married, did you? He's a ruthless, murdering bastard. Probably for the first time in your young life, you got first prize."

Elizabeth Beatrice said in a clipped, very upper-class Brit voice as she took Mason's arm, "I've found you and your father vastly entertaining. I'm very glad Molly—my stepdaughter—found you out and drew your teeth, and left Mason for me. Oh, and congratulations on your own marriage last year. And where is he? Did your second husband leave you as well?"

Eve looked her up and down, smiled. "A pity the kidnappers didn't take you."

40

Captivity

SATURDAY AFTERNOON

Molly held the table steady with one hand and the chair balanced on top of it with other as Sherlock pried the plywood off the window again with the bridge cue. This time the wood broke apart, and she handed the pieces down to Molly. She stared at the filthy window caked with grime and spiderwebs and dead spiders. "Well, this is disgusting."

"What do you see outside?"

"It's still daylight. I can't see much more, the window's too grimy, but I can make out lots of trees. Toss me one of those blankets."

Sherlock rolled up the blanket Molly passed her and rubbed it over the windowpane. "That's better. Still I don't see anything but trees everywhere. I don't see any guards. It's a hinged window with a handle. I'm going to give it a try." She pulled on the rusted handle, but it didn't budge. No surprise. She rolled an edge of the blanket tight and wrapped it around the handle, pulled down on it with all her weight. The window creaked and groaned and finally started to give. She cranked the window open as far as it would go.

She said over her shoulder, "Molly, it's time to give it a go. Hold the chair steady." Sherlock hoisted herself up into the window frame, stuck her head through, and worked her shoulders until they were free. Her hips were harder, but she fit, barely. She pushed herself back in and stepped carefully down from the chair and off the table. "Now you, Molly. Give it a try."

Molly climbed up on the table and then the chair as Sherlock held them steady for her, eyed the narrow window opening. Sherlock gave her a boost as she pulled herself up and pushed her shoulders up against the frame. She got stuck and pulled back, twisted into a swimming motion and pushed again, one shoulder first. She pushed and twisted and groaned as the window casing cut into her and finally got her shoulders through, but it was obvious she couldn't get her hips through no matter how hard she tried. Finally, Molly pulled herself back. She was nearly in tears when she stepped off the table. "It's a no go, Sherlock," she said. "Nero was right. I can get my shoulders through but my butt's too big."

"It's all right," Sherlock said, patting her shoulder. "We'll figure out something else." She looked down at the broken pieces of plywood on the floor. "There's no way to put that plywood back in place."

Molly grabbed her hand. "Sherlock, listen. You can squeeze through. I think you should go—"

Sherlock squeezed her hand, said matter-of-factly, "I've thought about going out alone if you couldn't fit, at least to look around, maybe try to find out where we are. But here's the problem, Molly. There's no telling what Nero would do in retaliation if I'm caught or can't get back. I think this house was built a long time ago by people with money. It looks like it's surrounded by lots of acreage, mainly forest. We could be a long way from the nearest town, and I wouldn't have a cell phone or a weapon or any kind of transportation. It's worth the risk together, but not alone. We're not splitting up, I mean it. We're going to find some other way out."

Molly sighed. "Maybe you're right, Sherlock, but what scares me is you're not the one they wanted. I'm terrified Nero sees you as expendable and will shoot you any time he wants."

Sherlock was well aware of her situation. "Don't go there, Molly. It does no good to scare ourselves senseless. Dillon and Ramsey and your father are scouring the earth for us, probably facing down Shaker in Las Vegas already. But right now there's no one but us who can get us out of here. We're going to do it."

Molly said, "I feel like a failure for not getting my butt out of that blasted window." She paused, drew a deep breath. "Do you know my first thought when I couldn't get through the window? 'I wonder if Ramsey really likes my butt or he thinks it's too big too.'" She snorted a laugh, shook her head. "I'm losing my mind. All right, what are we going to do?"

"You have a very fine butt, Molly. The way Ramsey looks at you tells me he fully agrees." She pointed to the piles of boxes. "What we're going to do is look through all those boxes for something useful, something that might help us."

Molly looked over at the mountains of piled boxes, nodded. "A loaded old Colt .45 would be nice."

They worked quickly, and five minutes later, they were halfway through the third box. All they'd found were piles clothes in the styles of the 1940s and 1950s, even a bright blue poodle skirt.

They hit a jackpot in the fourth box. Molly said, "Look at those ancient photo albums. Maybe they'll tell us where we are." She pulled out the one that looked the oldest, wiped the dust off it with one of the skirts. Black-and-white photos from the 1920s and 1930s were carefully pasted to each page, mainly of two women posing in front of the house, alone and together, vamping for the camera.

"Look at the plants in front of the house. They look like they were just planted, so maybe that means the house was just finished. And look at their clothes." Molly pointed to the woman wearing what looked to be a satin dress with a band around the hips, and a beaded headband in her waved hair. She said, "They both look so happy, like they're headed out on the town, maybe to a speakeasy. I bet they never thought one day in the future there'd be prisoners kept in their basement." She choked back a sob, looked at Sherlock. "They're dead now, however their lives turned out. I wonder if people will look at pictures we've taken and shake their heads at how old-fashioned we all look. Maybe wonder when we died."

Sherlock grabbed Molly's hand. "Stop it! I know you're thinking about Emma and Ramsey and the twins. I'm as scared as you are. The thought of never seeing Sean or Dillon again makes me want to curl up in the corner and give up. But we're not going to give up. We have a problem to solve and that's what we're going to do. Look at this photo. The house is a huge square, three stories and the basement. Light gray stone, wide wraparound porch. I'm thinking a house this spectacular might even have a name attached to it. Maybe we can find it, or even an address."

Molly got herself together. "That garage, it's got to hold six cars. And what is that gorgeous old car in the driveway?"

"That hood ornament—a big 'B' with wings; it's a Bentley, probably late twenties or early thirties."

Molly looked closely at the photo. "The tires are barely wider than a bicycle's. Can't see a license plate."

They rifled quickly through the more recent photos albums. There were children, grandchildren, and the same two women they'd seen earlier, older now, styles and hair changed with the times. By the 1970s, only one was left and she looked old and tired, but still had a hint of that wonderful smile she'd had in the 1920s.

Sherlock said, "Here's a color photo, probably from the seventies or eighties. The front yard is huge, must be at least fifty yards from the driveway to the road. Look at the oaks and pines and maples pressing in. It doesn't suggest any particular part of the US to me, only places we're not. What do you think, Molly?"

Molly studied the photo. "It's obviously early spring in the photo, like it is now. I'm thinking we're still on the East Coast, more north than south, I really can't say why, but it's something about those trees, and the style of the house. We're talking old money, Sherlock, very old money."

"Agreed."

Molly sighed, pointed to the stacks of old dust-covered photo albums. "I hope the family looked at all these photos now and then, at their mothers and grandmothers, before they were tossed into boxes and forgotten. At least they didn't throw them away."

Sherlock opened another box. "Look, Molly, a pile of letters." She untied the ribbon holding them together, looked through the ones on top. "They're dated back in the twenties, and they're all written to a Roselyn, probably one of the women in the photos. Maybe they'll tell us who these people were, or mention where we are."

Molly pulled out a box of stationery, sat back on her heels, and opened it. "Expensive stationery, never used. It's engraved with the name Williard House. That's got to be where we are, Williard House. I wonder if the same family still owns it."

Sherlock shuffled through the letters, muttered under her

breath. "They don't have any envelopes, so we don't have an address. But there's got to be one somewhere in this pile."

But no luck. Molly sighed. "Finding an address would have given us the moon, Sherlock. I wish we could pull out our cell phones and type in Williard House."

Sherlock swallowed her disappointment. "Let's keep looking, Molly; there's still a good chance we'll find the address, but really what we need more is weapons, something sharp or heavy—silverware, knives."

They found silverware in three heavy burgundy leather boxes, each box etched with a "W." There were enough place settings for twenty, all elaborate heavy silver pieces, tarnished to near black. And several big carving knives.

Sherlock hefted one of the knives, balanced it in her hand, then another. "They're perfect and heavy enough, but not very sharp. Too bad they won't stop a man with a gun."

Molly hefted another one, testing its balance just like Sherlock. "I don't know why I'm doing this. I have no idea how to throw a knife. But, hey, I can sure wield it if push comes to shove." They heard footsteps outside and quickly closed the box of silverware, sealed it, and slid it neatly against the other boxes. They raced back to the blankets, sat down, and shoved the knives under their legs.

When Nero and Domino walked into the basement, they saw Molly and Sherlock sitting side by side on the blanket, their backs against the wall, both looking depressed. Molly said, "I don't suppose you brought us some dinner?"

Nero looked toward the table with the chair sitting on top, the open window, and the pieces of plywood on the floor. He gave a rictus of a smile. "Mrs. Hunt couldn't make it through, I see. And you could hardly hope to cover all that up, could you? I do wish I could have seen your faces when you realized you'd failed. Actually, you're lucky you didn't make it through because like I told you my men would have shot you, or at least you, Agent Sherlock. So, ladies, better you failed." He sounded very pleased with himself. Sherlock thought of bringing up the heavy carving knife and throwing it at him, but he was too far away. She doubted she'd have the time before he shot her in the head. She hadn't thrown a knife in too long a time. She had to get him up close and personal.

Domino carried a tray to where they sat and laid it on a blanket. She picked up the old tray with the uneaten sandwiches, rose, and backed away.

Nero said, "A pity you wouldn't eat the tuna sandwiches. My men will enjoy them. But now you have something better, meatball subs."

Molly pointed to the plastic-wrapped subs. "Are these drugged, too?"

Nero shook his head. "No reason to drug you tonight. I want you to have one last night worrying about what's going to happen to you."

Domino shot a glance at Nero. "No, they're not drugged. There's no reason for you to go hungry."

Nero said in a flat voice, "Domino isn't lying. Enjoy them, they're tasty. You'll want to keep your strength up. For what, you wonder? I'll give you this much—we're having a photo shoot tomorrow." He glanced toward the window, smiled. "No, you two little birds won't be flying off anywhere."

Sherlock said, "You know Agent Savich and Judge Hunt will demand proof we're alive so that's why you want to shoot a video."

He rested his cold, nearly colorless eyes on Sherlock. "It's rather obvious, don't you think, Agent Sherlock? And do give thought to what's going to happen to you if you don't cooperate."

He fanned his Sig up and down over her. "It seems very cliché, doesn't it, but that's what is required. Enjoy your meal, ladies." He motioned to Domino and she walked out of the basement in front of him. Nero gave Sherlock a last look and a sneer. "You're not such a hotshot agent, are you, Agent Sherlock? I was expecting so much more given all your heroics at JFK and the shootout at the Lincoln Monument. But it seems like you've met your match." He smiled wide at her, his big square teeth on display.

He waited but Sherlock didn't say anything.

He pointed his Sig at her face. "Say it, bitch, or I'll kill you this instant."

Sherlock smiled up at him. "Sure, Nero. I've met my match, no doubt in my mind."

He nodded, pleased. "Get your beauty sleep." He looked toward the window. "No, you two little birds have roosted. Do get lots of sleep, you want to look your best tomorrow." He walked out and closed the door . They heard the key turn in the lock.

Sherlock looked at the meatball subs sitting on the tray. "Do you want to take a chance or not?"

Molly said, "I'm hungry. While you were thinking about logistics, I was thinking about food."

"Trust me, I'm as hungry as you are," Sherlock said. "I don't see why he'd drug us overnight." She picked up a sub and bit into it. "Molly?"

Molly picked up the other one and chewed on it.

Sherlock took her own bite, chewed. "I wonder what Dillon will do to Nero after I'm done with him."

For a moment, Molly felt optimistic. She grinned at Sherlock. "Will there be anything left of him for Ramsey?"

Sherlock licked the tomato sauce off her fingers. She took Molly's hand and squeezed it.

41

Gully Hollow, Virginia

SUNDAY

Kirra and Griffin stopped about ten miles from the Green Briar Resort at a gas station in Gully Hollow, a picturesque little town nestled in a valley in the Blue Ridge Mountains, not because they needed gas, but to change into the disguises Griffin had ordered delivered to them at Kirra's condo in the morning. Griffin came out of the men's room in a black wig, on the long side, sporting a small mustache and wearing aviator glasses. Kirra appeared a few minutes later, her wig light blond curling wildly around her face. She wore tight skinny jeans, a white blouse with too many buttons open, and a white fur jacket since the new Mrs. Hammersmith would have dressed for the mountains, where the temperature was at least ten degrees cooler than in Porte Franklyn. She wore big-framed sunglasses that darkened in sunlight and lightened indoors. The glasses and the wig really changed her look.

They looked each other up and down. Griffin had changed from a sweatshirt, jeans, and sneakers to black slacks, white shirt, black leather jacket, and black boots. Kirra whistled. "Wow, your eyes look really blue with all that black hair. The mustache is good, too, not over the top, but it really does change your face. The aviators are cool, make you look sexy."

"And you, Ms. Mandarian, look like a fluffy confection with all that thick curling blond hair and the open buttons on your blouse. The hint of cleavage will have the guys looking down and not so much at your face. If I'm not close by, count on every guy in the vicinity hitting on you. Oh yes, the black frames on your sunglasses—talk about sending mixed messages."

She laughed, buttoned up one button. "Who says a rich matron won't give you the eye?" She turned serious the next moment. "You think we'll pass muster, Griffin? Melissa Kay won't recognize us?"

"I doubt if she even sees us she'll take any notice. After all, she's there with a lover she hasn't seen for a while. Don't forget, the place is booked full so there'll be lots of people roaming around, good cover for us. By the way, I know who her lover is."

"What? How do you know that?"

"While you were changing, I got a text from the CAU, that's the Criminal Investigation Unit. Agent Savich is the chief. I had them run facial recognition on the man Melissa posed with on her Facebook page. His name is Jared Talix, the grandson of Finley Talix, a fine fellow trafficking in human beings and importing and distributing drugs, mostly cocaine and fentanyl, from China and out of Mexico and all the way up the West Coast to Seattle. After Jared's parents, both in business with Finley, were shot by a rival cartel, it was left to the old man to raise Jared himself. Finley Talix is still around, but he's getting up there, near ninety now. Jared is all set to take over."

Kirra digested this. "I can't say I'm surprised. Do you know how he met Melissa Kay?"

"Seems likely old man Finley and Grissom did some business together and he sent Jared out here to seal the deal. He met Melissa Kay and they must have taken quite a liking to each other. Melissa Kay's photos with him go back over a year. Oh, he's married, has three kids."

"That's excellent, Griffin. Here I thought we were going to have to sneak around the reception desk and try to find his name in the computer. But you, you used your brain, found out everything about him. Show him to me again on Melissa Key's Facebook page when we get up to our room."

"I'll also show you the files Ollie Hamish—he's second-in-command in the CAU—emailed me on Talix and his grandfather."

"It sounds like he's as dangerous as Ryman and Melissa Kay." She grinned at him. "But they're not in our league."

Without thinking, Griffin raised his hand to touch her, dropped it. "I have no doubt they're all like matching gloves, but no, not in our league. Still, we're going to be very careful."

Kirra nodded, then she shuddered. Was she remembering how she'd almost died on the frontage road only two days ago? Griffin didn't shudder, but thinking about her driving on that frontage road, Winters behind her, trying to make her fly over the cliff, made his blood run cold. But Winters had been the one to go over the cliff, and Kirra had watched him die, and that had to hit hard as well. Not to mention Eliot Ness going back for her frigging cell phone.

"Do you think maybe they're here on business, too, like cooking up some other way to kill me?"

"Nah, you're not in on their radar. They're here to have nonstop sex."

"So you think sex outweighs the killer instinct?"

"I imagine it always does."

"But they'll have to come out of their room to eat, right? Maybe walk around in the resort?" She eyed him, decided it was time to come clean. She bestowed a bright winsome smile on him and words bulleted out of her mouth. "Ah, Griffin, you should know I brought some really small high-tech bugs a friend of mine gave me. He showed me how they work, how to plant them in their room or on their luggage or whatever. I didn't want to worry you, because, strictly speaking, that would be sort of breaking and entering, and after all, you're an FBI agent." She took a breath, gave him a bright winsome smile. "So, if I'm the one who actually breaks in and plants the bugs, will you arrest me?"

Bugs? She'd brought frickin' bugs to plant in their room? Griffin was without words. He was amazed. She'd nearly gotten herself killed two days before, but it didn't matter. She was fired up, not about to stop. He had to laugh. "No, I won't arrest you. In addition, you've got some handy friends to keep your butt out of jail." He could have mouthed the words that as a commonwealth attorney she knew planting a bug on someone without a warrant isn't exactly legal. But since the Grissoms were trying to kill her, he wasn't going to say a thing. The name Eliot Ness threatened to fly out of his mouth, but he knew he had to keep quiet. "Tell me about the bugs."

"They're really good, Griffin. Booger, my friend, is something of a genius."

That didn't surprise him. "And just how do you plan on getting into their room to plant the bugs?"

"Well, I asked Booger if he could get me past the key card access system they use in the hotel rooms at Green Briar. He hacked in to their management system, broke the encryption." She sounded like a proud mama. "He sent me over a key card this morning he says has the master access code on it. You were, ah, in the shower at the time. I thought it might be better to tell you when we were nearly to curtain time."

Griffin stared at her. While he'd been doing facial recognition to find out Jared Talix's identity, she'd already been planning her attack. He wondered what Savich would say, but it really didn't matter. He said slowly, "You're fighting for your life, Kirra. And I'm here to protect you. As to the ethics of what you've done, what you're planning to do, I don't think they're pertinent. Don't worry, we'll figure out when to plant the bugs in their room."

They climbed back into Griffin's Range Rover and started an uphill climb with half a dozen other cars on the winding road that ran the final three miles up to the Green Briar Resort. He buzzed down the window and breathed in the fresh air, noticeably cooler as they climbed. It actually tasted crisp on his tongue. The higher they climbed, the more spectacular the vistas became; distant hills and mountains seemed to roll on forever. They were thick with maples, spruce, and red oaks and what he thought were hemlocks. There were lookout points along the way, visitors lining up to look through the three telescopes.

Kirra said, "Green Briar even has a small observatory, looks sort of like a silo fastened to the side of the main building. If we're not busy hiding in Melissa Kay's closet, we could stargaze. You know, Griffin, the way you're dressed and with your black hair and mustache, I swear you're better looking. The aviators help."

Where was she going with this? He smiled, couldn't help it, and waited.

"Not that you were a dog before, but the disguise really boosts your chick rating. Don't get me wrong, you've got a ways to go to get to Colin Firth in his heyday but it's a definite improvement." She laughed, punched his arm.

Music to his ears. She was the first woman he'd met who

hadn't ranked his damned face number one of her list, who only cared he looked like some idiot sex god. Griffin beamed at her, saw she was surprised by his reaction. He couldn't very well tell her he was relieved she didn't think he was anything out of the ordinary. He said, "Moving right along. Too bad it's not winter, we could stay and ski. Or maybe you'd like to hike? Stupid question, you've probably hiked every inch of the out-back."

"Ain't that the truth. Well, not every inch. There are lots of rocks and boulders. Now, our Green Briar brochure says the hiking here is great. Maybe when this is all over, we can come back and roam the trails, maybe fish for trout, though I never seem to catch anything, so forget that. But go camping with me and you'll be awed. I can set up a tent, make dinner and coffee while you're brushing your teeth. Just like that," and she snapped her fingers.

He didn't want to be charmed by her, but he was. Here she was, a woman who didn't run from danger, a woman who was now racing toward another cliff, this one with Melissa Kay standing on top, undoubtedly a psychopath who'd find plea-sure in shoving her over with no hesitation at all, a smile on her face.

Griffin turned his full attention back to sawing safely back and forth on the switchbacks. He had to slow when he came around a curve to see a bright red Chevy in front of them, the driver driving really slow, being careful with his load of kids in-side. Griffin eased back, gave the Chevy lots of room. He said, "Kirra, let's say you recognize Melissa Kay's voice, that you're sure it was her. There's still Ryman Grissom. It's likely he was the one with her that night, but you can't be sure, can you? But we're sure he's a hired killer—Eliot Ness texted Jeter who texted Savich and me that Oliveras hired Ryman to kill Misha

Misel and the young woman who was with him, then reported back to Oliveras that it was done. It's a shame we have no proof because Eliot Ness dropped his cell phone and it broke."

It burned her to the bone Oliveras and Ryman Grissom might both already be in jail if she hadn't been such a klutz. When Kirra answered, her voice was dead serious. "I could drug Ryman, fly him in a private jet to Australia, haul his butt deep into the outback, and threaten to leave him there unless he confesses all his sins. Think that would work?"

"You can fly a jet?"

"No, only props. Well, truth is, it's been a while. I was sixteen and I practiced only twice with Uncle Leo sitting next to me."

"A prop wouldn't make it, anyway. Do you know anyone with a private jet who'd fly you and Ryman to Australia? And what drug would you use on him?"

"All right, so there are a few challenges, but I know it would work. Sure Ryman's a psychopath, but he's also a coward. It would scare the crap out of him to wake up in the blistering sun thinking about all the snakes and crawling critters eyeing him like a four-star restaurant. Maybe I could find a creek that's home to a couple of crocs. Hmm, should I leave him any water?"

Griffin liked how the touch of Aussie in Kirra's voice grew stronger when she talked about Australia. He said, not looking away from the road, "Let him drink out of the creek with the crocodiles."

42

Green Briar Resort

SUNDAY

The Green Briar lobby was a vast single room with gigantic beams high overhead, dozens of lights beaming down. Huge light gray pavers covered the floors, with occasional accent rugs in bright colors, made by local artisans, according to the online blurb. Seating arrangements were set around two huge fireplaces made of local stone, and beyond them large hallways stretched out on both sides. The Chalet, the resort's four-star restaurant, was straight ahead, and on the far left, reception agents were busy with check-ins at a long counter made of distressed oak. The concierge, activities desks, and luggage handlers lined the right. Griffin and Kirra reached a smiling young woman dressed head to toe in the required black, wearing the name tag *Holly*. She didn't wait for them to give her their names. She said immediately when she saw them, looking only at Griffin, "You must be our newlyweds, Mr. and Mrs. Hammersmith. Congratulations and welcome to Green Briar."

Kirra wasn't paying attention or behaving like a newlywed. She was looking for Melissa Kay. Griffin squeezed her hand and she jumped. He kissed her cheek and Kirra remembered she should be hanging all over him. She grabbed his arm, gave the woman a brilliant smile. "Thank you. Yes, we're Mr. and Mrs. Hammersmith. I'm his wife now. Isn't that an amazing thing to say?" She put emphasis on the "Mr." and gave Griffin a possessive smile. "Isn't he the handsomest husband you've ever seen? Look at those gorgeous eyes."

Holly gave her a wide grin. "Yes, I was just thinking that." It was a professional compliment, but the look she gave Griffin wasn't designed to please the bride.

"And he's all mine." Kirra pressed her breast against his arm, smiled adoringly up at him. "I hope your honeymoon suite is as incredible as advertised."

Holly's eyes were still on Griffin. "It's amazing, I promise. There are so many activities for you here—hiking and swimming in our heated pool, looking at the stars in our observatory, touring the grounds, or just relaxing here in the lobby."

Kirra gave Griffin an adoring look. "Doesn't that sound wonderful, darling?"

"Yeah, say on a visit in about ten years."

Holly's expression never changed, but her eyes heated. "Shall I take you up?"

Griffin said, "No need, just point us to the elevators." He leaned down and planted a quick kiss on Kirra's mouth. He saw she'd unbuttoned the two blouse buttons again, showing enough white flesh to make any man drool, including him. "You ready, sweetheart?"

"Yes, of course." She gave a knowing smile at Holly, added a wink to rub her nose in it, just a little. She and Griffin walked together holding hands along the side of the lobby toward the elevators, pulling their carry-ons.

Griffin leaned close to her ear. "Button up those buttons, and stop cooing, you sound ridiculous."

"Be careful what you say, new husband, or your new bride might kick you out of the bridal bed."

The elevator let them off on the fourth floor. They pulled their bags down a thick gray carpet with woven pine cones and greenery to the end of the corridor, past large color photographs of the Blue Ridge Mountains in all four seasons. Griffin inserted his key card into the slot beside the double doors. They walked into a large room dominated by a king-size bed covered with a bright blue quilt, two bathrobes, and a basket filled with the requisite chocolates, body oils, and a loofah. A bottle of champagne on ice was set on the bedside table. Four large windows gave out onto the swimming pool and the mountains beyond it. The living area had a large TV on the wall next to stylized nineteenth-century pre-Raphaelite romantic paintings, meant, Griffin supposed, to inspire the groom on his wedding night. Kirra walked straight into the bathroom.

She came out a moment later, grinning. "Hey, Griffin, there's a Jacuzzi in here the size of a small pool. We could go skinny jacuzzying. No need to leave the room."

He pictured the two of them all too clearly in his mind, forced a laugh. "Come look at this incredible view."

She stood beside him, sighed. "Too bad they allow criminals here. It messes with the juju."

He smiled. "At least there's no mirror above the bed."

"Well, that shows some class on their part."

Griffin looked down at his watch. "Why don't we unpack and go trolling for our prey?"

Kirra said, "I'm thinking they'll have lots of sex first, then a late dinner at the fancy restaurant downstairs, the Chalet. I bet they've got a reservation. I wonder if we can find out for sure."

"Not easily. We can't ask because the maître d' might mention it to Talix. Let's have an early dinner. Maybe I'll have a chance to get a look at the reservations book. We'll see. Otherwise, after we have our foie gras, we can sit in the lobby and wait for them to show."

"Talix. You said you'd show me his file, his picture."

Griffin unpacked his iPad and logged into an encrypted CAU database. "Here he is," he said, handing her the iPad. Kirra looked at the mug shot of a forty-year-old man with the brutally handsome face of a fire-and-brimstone preacher or a small-time politician. His complexion was swarthy, maybe a Mediterranean lineage? His eyes were dark and ancient with violence, his hair long and ink black, curling at his neck. His lips were seamed together. He gave off an air of malevolent power. She said, "Jared Talix has Ryman Grissom eyes—cold and flat. They both look at you as someone they can use, or as no more important than a cockroach. What did he do to get arrested?"

"A drug bust eight months ago in Seattle when one of the gang members ratted him out. He was arrested, but the charges were dropped, insufficient evidence. Nor surprising, the gang member who'd informed on him thought twice about testifying, and Talix had the best lawyers money could buy."

"I'll bet you if he'd been arrested in Porte Franklyn, Hailstock might have let him out with a stern warning. I'm thinking once we're sure they're having their dinner, we could find their suite. I don't suppose you know their suite number?"

"Oh ye of little faith. I have my ways. I asked Holly at the front desk." Griffin had hoped she'd cooperate even though it was against policy. "They're in the suite below ours on the third floor, 325, and yes, it's the second honeymoon suite."

After a fairly spectacular spaghetti alfredo at the Chalet, Griffin and Kirra strolled to the seating area in the lobby, careful to hold hands, sit close to each other, and talk, while waiters came by to offer the guests who gathered around the immense fireplaces trays of coffee, cheeses, and liqueurs.

At nine o'clock sharp, Kirra saw Melissa Kay and Jared Talix strolling toward the restaurant, Melissa Kay laughing at something he'd said, leaning into him, her hand stroking his arm. Kirra's heart started pounding. She nodded at Griffin, stood up fast, and raced to intercept them. Would she finally know if this was the woman who'd murdered her parents, who'd wanted to kill her? Would she recognize her voice, know it for sure? She slowed to a fast walk, lowered her head, and began rummaging through her purse. She ran right into Melissa Kay, hard, and jerked to a flustered stop.

"Hey! Watch it!" Melissa Kay looked at the sexy little blond number who'd crashed into her, well aware Jared was looking at her as well, probably guessing her bra size.

"Oh, goodness! I'm sorry, I wasn't paying attention! Are you all right?"

Melissa snapped, "Of course I'm all right. You need to watch where you're going."

Kirra froze. This was the voice she heard as a twelve-year-old girl escaping down the oak tree. Now she felt the same helpless terror the girl had felt years ago, the girl who thought she was going to die. She knew she'd recognize that voice when she was ninety.

I see the little bitch. Let me do her!

Talix leaned toward Kirra, smiling, managing to move his eyes upward to her face. "What were you looking for?"

Kirra gave a fast nod, too embarrassed to look either of them in the face. She managed to say, her voice still apologetic, "I'm really sorry, I was trying to find my cell phone. I'm supposed to call my mother."

He held out a strong square hand, touched her shoulder. "Can I help?"

Melissa Kay said sharply, "She doesn't need your help, Jared. Come on, I don't want to be late for our reservation." She gave Kirra a venomous look.

Kirra couldn't help it, her words came out as a near whisper. "Again, I'm sorry. I'm so clumsy," and she hurried away. She didn't walk back to Griffin, who was standing not twelve feet away; she ran to the women's bathroom into a stall and fell to her knees. The terror flooded her, and she vomited. A woman said from outside the stall, "Are you all right? Can I get someone for you?"

Kirra had to get hold of herself. Here she'd fallen apart, not exactly brave of her. She took a breath, slowly rose, and came out. An older woman gave her a worried look. "I'm fine now," Kirra said. "Cramps from something I ate that didn't agree with me. Thank you, really. I'm okay."

Kirra washed out her mouth, used some mouthwash, one of the many amenities on the long counter, and tried to repair her makeup. Griffin was waiting for her when she came out of the bathroom. She walked straight to him, clasped her arms around his back, and pressed her face against his shoulder. "It's her, Griffin, it's her." She wanted to weep and scream at the same time. She swallowed, leaned back, and looked up at him. "I guess it hit me hard, hearing her voice. I threw up, Griffin, I threw up."

He pulled her close again, his hand on the back of her head. He hadn't thought through how she'd react to hearing Melissa Kay's voice. Of course it had to hurl her back fourteen years to that night. He said against her hair, "It's over. And now you know. And now we can act."

Griffin led her back to a seating area in front of one of the fireplaces, people streaming past them, not paying them any particular attention. He pulled her down on his lap because that's what a groom would do and called to a waiter for some tea.

Kirra saw an older couple smiling at them and whispering to each other. She'd forgotten she was a newlywed. She drew in a deep breath, hugged him close, and whispered in his ear, "Sorry for being such a mess. And I am sure, Griffin, completely sure."

The waiter brought them tea. Griffin saw her hand was steady as she dumped sugar and milk into the Green Briar tea-cup. Kirra took a drink, felt the warmth all the way to her raw stomach. They were quiet as she sipped the tea. Finally, she said, "Jared Talix is dog. He came on to me, didn't even try to hide looking at my cleavage. Melissa Kay was standing right there, and it burned her. We know he cheats on his wife, but I'll bet you if he were married to Melissa Kay, he wouldn't dare cheat on her. She'd rip his guts out." She paused, drank more tea. "But you know, I don't think she blamed him. I was the one at fault, the slut, and she turned all her anger squarely on me."

Griffin put his arms around her and squeezed. He lightly kissed her hair. "You feel better now? Don't lie to me."

Kirra's eyes narrowed. "Yes, yes, I'm good. I feel like planting some bugs."

43

Green Briar Resort

SUNDAY

When Kirra and Griffin stepped off the elevators on the third floor, they'd already tested and tweaked the four bugs Kirra had brought with her and set the receiver in their room upstairs to forward the transmissions to their cell phones. They saw no one. The maids had already finished their evening service. They walked to the door at the end of the hall directly beneath their own. Griffin said, "Where's that master key card Booger sent you? I assume you've checked to see it works?"

"Yes. Of course it works. I tried it on our door upstairs." She slid in the card, pressed down on the handle, and the door opened smoothly. Melissa Kay and Jared Talix's honeymoon suite was an exact copy of their suite one floor above, down to the pre-Raphaelite paintings on the walls, same romantic themes but different painting, and a pale green bedspread on the king-size bed, not blue.

Griffin wasted no time. "The suite is about seven hundred square feet. I think three will do it." They fastened one of the bugs, not much bigger than his watch battery, to the base of a living room lamp, one behind the nightstand by the bed, and one under the sink in the bathroom. "Now let's check to see they're all working." He punched in the receive function on his cell phone. "They're voice activated. Walk over to each of them and talk in a normal voice so we can be sure we're transmitting properly. Why don't you tell me about your dad's paintings."

Kirra said as she walked back into the bathroom, "Daddy loved boats, all sizes, from old fishing boats to fancy yachts, it didn't matter and he always took photos before he started to paint them because to him the details were vital, and the lighting could change so quickly. He liked to paint right on the shore of the Potomac, particularly at a curve near Cantor Point and that's when—" Her voice fell off a cliff. She'd nearly spit out that her father had seen the *Valadia*. Would Grissom's name have popped out of her mouth too? "Well, are we recording?"

"Loud and clear. Now let's get out of here." Griffin's hand was outstretched to open the door when they heard voices in the hallway, a man's low voice and a woman's flirty laugh, coming closer. It was Melissa Kay.

Griffin grabbed Kirra's hand and ran to the balcony door, unlocked, and slid it open. They eased onto the balcony, quietly slid the glass door closed, and pressed against the building at the far end of the balcony, out of sight.

Jared Talix said clearly, "We didn't need dessert. You're my dessert, babe. Come here."

Melissa Kay laughed. "You wouldn't even let me finish my clams. I'm still hungry."

"Consider me your next course. We can order up room service later. Much later."

Griffin looked over at Kirra standing beside him. She seemed more excited than afraid. He squeezed her hand. He knew Talix and Melissa Kay would soon be having wild sex on the bed, focused on each other, but even so, they couldn't take the chance of trying to slip back into the living room and sneak out the door without being spotted. He would bet his mom's apple strudel Melissa Kay had a gun with her and that she could shoot an acorn out of a squirrel's mouth.

Kirra leaned up, whispered in his ear, "I have an idea, Griffin. I'll stand on the balcony railing with you holding me steady, then I'll pull myself up to our balcony. I can twist a sheet and throw it down to you and you can climb up after me."

He wished he could think of something else to try, but there was nothing else, except to stay where they were and hope they wouldn't be seen until Melissa and Talix were asleep. That seemed even more dangerous. Would she be tall enough to get a good grip on the railings, and strong enough to pull herself up?

Melissa Kay called out, "Take off those clothes, Jared, I'll be back in a minute."

They heard her moving around in the bathroom. "Just a moment," Griffin whispered, and pulled out his phone again. He heard the sound of running water in the bathroom, a woman humming an Adele song in the background.

Kirra said, "I think you'll have to push me up a couple of feet so I can grab the bottom rails." She was nearly bouncing in place, as excited as when she raced down the hundred-foot sand dunes on Lizard Island, Uncle Leo yelling at her to slow down.

Griffin said, "You don't have to look like you're having the time of your life."

She whispered, "It's my honeymoon, Griffin, of course I am."

They both quickly realized they had a problem. He said, "I'll go first. I'll knot the sheet and toss it down to you and pull you up."

She paused briefly, whispered, disappointed, "I think you

may be right, the railing isn't wide enough for you to balance on
it and push me up at the same time." She muttered something
under her breath. "Fine, you go up first."

He touched his hand to her shoulder. "I'll send down a
twisted sheet. Don't move and don't make a sound."

Griffin climbed up on the railing next to the building wall,
pressing his hand against the wall for balance. He stretched up
and jumped, grabbed the rails of the balcony above them, took
a firm grip. He pulled himself up high enough to swing his leg
and hook his foot on the ledge. He climbed upward on the rails
hand over hand until he was high enough for his leg to take his
weight. He climbed up and over the top of the railing, opened
the balcony door, and raced to the bed. He pulled off the bedspread, then the sheet. He twisted the sheet round and round
and ran back to the balcony.

Kirra stood on top of the railing, her back against the building to keep her steady, waiting for the sheet to come down to
her from the railing above. She heard Jared Talix call out, "Let
me see if it's warm enough to have our tequila on the balcony."

There was no more time, no time, only one choice. She
looked down at the swimming pool below her and jumped.

44

In Captivity
Williard House

SUNDAY

Sherlock was coaching Molly on how best to use her knife as a weapon when they heard steps on the tile floor outside the basement door.

"Molly, back to the blankets! Remember, lean against me, play dead."

They managed to slide onto the blankets as the key turned in the lock and the door opened.

Nero walked into the basement with his Sig in one hand and a cell phone in the other. "Time to prove you're alive, ladies." He stopped cold when he saw they were sitting with their backs pressed against the wall, leaning into each other, their eyes closed. They looked dead.

He yelled, "Open your eyes!"

They didn't answer him, didn't move.

"Open your eyes or I'll hurt both of you!"

They didn't move.

Nero cursed, pushed his Sig into his belt, walked over and dropped to his haunches, pressed up against Sherlock's face.

"You little bitch! Stop this, now!"

Sherlock head-butted him, jabbed her knuckles hard into his Adam's apple and twisted. He grabbed for his neck and gurgled, because suddenly he couldn't breathe. She smashed the butt of her knife up into his groin, and he fell on his side, trying to breathe again, cupping himself. Sherlock jumped on him, grabbed his Sig, and dug it into the back of his head. He tried to crawl away, until she hit on the head with the gun. "Hold still, Nero, or I'll finish it."

He froze for a second, then pulled out his cell phone from underneath him and smashed it hard against the floor, once, twice.

"Stop it!" Sherlock slammed the gun against the back of his head, harder. He groaned, fell onto his face.

Domino shouted, "Back away from him or I'll have to shoot!"

Sherlock's heart skipped a beat—a gunshot would bring the other guards down on them, trap them in the basement. She said, "Domino, his head will explode if I pull this trigger. It wouldn't be neat like the bullet hole he shot in Pope's forehead, there'd be a splash zone. If you shoot me, some of us will die, maybe you as well. Is he worth it? Do you think he cares at all about you? Think, Domino. Do you think he'd hesitate to shoot you dead in a second like he shot Pope? Throw your gun on the floor, kick it over to Mrs. Hunt, and no one has to die." She dug the muzzle into the back of Nero's head. He wheezed, gasped out, "Do it, Domino. She'll shoot me."

Domino shook her head at him. "You've really screwed it all up, haven't you, Nero? You were going to fix all our problems, all we had to do was listen to you, because you know everything. You murdered James—that's James Pope in case you didn't even know his name—you murdered him without a thought because he made a mistake. I guess that means we should shoot you now? Go ahead, Agent Sherlock, kill the bastard. I'd applaud you, but I'd also have to shoot you."

There was nothing to do but pray Domino was bluffing. "I'm not going to shoot him, Domino, and you're not going to shoot me. Why don't we both lower our guns so no one gets hurt and talk? See, I'm putting his gun down."

Domino looked at her, confused for a second, then nodded and lowered the muzzle of her Beretta. Sherlock rolled off Nero's back and hurled the knife that was still in her hand at Domino. Domino raised her gun again, but the knife went into her upper arm and stuck. Domino yelled, and the gun fell from her hand as she grabbed her arm. It skidded across the floor, fetched up against the blanket. Molly slid over to it, snatched it up.

Sherlock said, "Come here, Domino, sit down on the blanket."

Domino staggered over and sank down, clutching her arm below the knife. With no warning or hesitation, Sherlock pulled the knife out of her arm. Domino groaned as her blood gushed out of the wound. Sherlock pressed her hand tight around her arm. Molly picked the napkins off the dinner tray, pushed them under Sherlock's fingers. "Now you do it. Press as hard as you can, Domino. The bleeding will stop, I know. I have three kids."

Sherlock looked over at Nero, still on his side, his smashed cell phone beside him. "Molly's right," she said to Domino. "The bleeding's not arterial. Keep the pressure on it and you'll be fine. I rarely get to say this—but it's just a flesh wound." She picked up Nero's smashed cell phone, pushed on the power button, tried the screen. No go, it was dead. Still, she slipped it in her pants pocket. It still had its SIM card, and Dillon could track the calls he'd made, and maybe the owner. Sherlock said, "Nero managed to break his cell so I'm going to need yours.

Where is it?"

Domino said between gritted teeth, "I don't have it. Nero took all our cell phones and hid them."

She had to be lying. "Don't give me that crap. Tell me or I'll hurt you more." As she said it, Sherlock patted down her blouse, her jeans. No phone.

Tears fell from Domino's eyes, trailed down her cheeks. "No, please, I'm not lying. Nero told me he was on an assignment a while back and one of his men called his girlfriend and she told someone else, and he got ratted out. He barely escaped with his life. So no cell phones, only him." She sucked in her breath, closed her eyes again, and cursed. "It hurts."

"Well, you were going to shoot me," Sherlock said matter-of-factly." She rose to stand over Nero, who was still on his side, cupping himself. "Molly, search his pockets for zip ties."

Molly dug into his pants pockets and pulled out two sets of zip ties, meant, she knew, for her and for Sherlock.

Sherlock shoved Nero onto his stomach, straddled him, and pulled one of his arms behind his back. He moaned and thrashed, until she dug her knees into his back. "Hold still or I'll whack you again. One more good hit and it just might scramble your brains." He froze. She jerked his other arm behind his back and zip-tied his wrists together. "Let's see if you have anything helpful in your pockets. The name of your boss would be nice." She searched his pants, his shirts, his jacket. She pulled out the basement key. "Look what I found, Molly."

"There's nothing else, no ID?"

"No, he's a professional, he wouldn't carry any ID. Molly, move our girl so we can restrain her."

Molly said, "Domino, get up and walk with me to the radiator by the window. Keep pressure on your arm." Molly zip-tied Domino's uninjured arm to the radiator. She rose, dusted her hands, and walked over to Nero. "Now for this monster." She gave him a kick in the ribs, hard enough to make him hurt.

"You bitch!"

"You bet, and don't forget it."

"You'll never get out of here."

"Quiet, Nero, or I'll kick you too," Sherlock said. "The zip ties aren't enough to hold him, Molly."

Molly said, "The boxes, Sherlock—there were sashes, ties, belts." She walked over and rummaged through them, picked out anything that would hold a knot. She tied them together, pulled them tight, jerked on them. They held. She looked up at Sherlock. "We can pull him to the pool table and tie him to one of the legs."

When they finished tying him, Domino said, "He'll kill me once he's free."

Molly said, "Sherlock, maybe we—"

Sherlock shook her head, said to Domino, "You chose your path." She paused. "I'll make you a deal. I'll solve your problem if you tell us how many guards there are and where they are."

"How will you help me?"

"I'll give you the knife I threw through your arm. You can kill him first, if you like. Talk to me. And don't lie to me or the deal's off."

"Not a word, Domino, if you want to live," Nero said.

Domino looked at him, paused, swallowed, and slowly shook her head at him. "There are two guards in the kitchen, both of them foreign, Serbian. Ilic and Stankovic. They've been with Nero for years, their loyalty is to him. They barely tolerated Pope or me. And there's a guard patrolling outside. He was here when we arrived. His name's Caruso."

"Where are we?"

"Miles from nowhere, that's all Nero would tell me. He

keeps everything close to his vest, especially with me. Ilic and Stankovic know, they picked us up at a private airstrip maybe ten miles from here. It was too dark to see much of anything. And their cars have Pennsylvania license plates."

"Who hired you?"

"Not Nero, that's for sure. My service, and, no, I'll never give them up or I'd get a shiv in my gut. Nero didn't tell Pope or me who hired him. He just looked at us like we were the lowest of the low, said we'd failed, so he was brought in." She laughed. "He likes to call himself the Fixer, like he told you. And just look at him. You really did a number on him. That's all I know. You promised. Please."

Sherlock set the bloody knife down three feet from her. "By the time you get yourself free, we'll be out of here. Maybe you'll use it on Nero, maybe you'll escape, maybe let him go, throw in with him, and the guys upstairs again. Up to you, but if you yell out, try to warn them, or you let Nero do that, we'll all end up trapped down here in the basement, and neither of you will survive, I promise you."

"If I were you, Domino," Molly said, "I'd stick the knife through his heart."

"You ready, Molly?"

Molly was terrified and excited, a roller-coaster combo flooding her with adrenaline. She gave Sherlock a manic grin. Now they had a chance. "I'm more than ready."

Sherlock and Molly went through the basement door, closed and locked it. They were at one end of a long, well-lighted hallway. Sherlock looked for steps leading up to the outside, but there weren't any. They walked down the hallway on the tiled floor, opened a closed door along the way that held only the furnace. They walked past a laundry room with appliances that looked to have been there since the moon landing, the smell of mildew thick in the air. There was a closed door at the end of the hallway. Sherlock quietly opened it. Basement stairs, wooden, narrow, and bare. Slowly, Sherlock in the lead, they walked up as quietly as they could, listening for any sound. As they climbed higher they saw the door at the top was partially open. They heard a man's voice. "You pathetic bleater, you keep talking, and then all you do is lose and whine."

Another man's voice. "Yeah, yeah, bet you have a couple of deuces. You should fold, Ilic, no way you'll beat what I'm holding."

Two of the three men were in the kitchen, as Domino had said. Caruso had to be outside, and that could be really danger-ous. Sherlock looked back at Molly. "Ready?"

Molly held up Domino's Beretta, nodded.

Sherlock slowly opened the door onto a dogleg passage to-ward the kitchen. She didn't see any way out except straight ahead. The two men were sitting at the kitchen table, Ilic skinny and bald, with a shiny face, and Stankovic built like a linebacker, big and beefy, his face pockmarked. She stepped into their view and said very precisely, "Ilic, Stankovic, both of you pull out your guns, drop them to the floor. Kick them over to me. If you do not, I will put bullets in your knees and work my way up. You know I'm FBI—so believe me, I can do it."

Ilic slowly stood and reached for the gun in its shoulder hol-ster, his eyes on Sherlock. Stankovic reached under the table, upended it, and threw it at Sherlock. Sherlock jumped away as Ilic pulled his gun. She shot him in the knee. He groaned, fired wildly as he fell to the kitchen floor. Stankovic jerked his gun from his shoulder holster, rolled to the floor behind the table, and fired, but Sherlock had already grabbed Molly and pulled her down. His bullet hit the wall where she'd been standing. They ran for the door followed by a barrage of bullets. The gunshots stopped. He was out of bullets. Did he have another magazine?

"Now, Molly!" They raced toward the back door and out into a large yard, firing back at Stankovic to keep him pinned. Oaks and maples pressed in, the grass and weeds growing tall. They ran around the side of the house toward the front, not knowing if one of them had hit Stankovic. "Keep an out for Caruso, Molly."

Two SUVS were parked in the driveway. Sherlock opened the door of one of them, found no key. There was a pile of overcoats in the passenger seat. She grabbed two of them and shouted out, "No key!"

Molly shouted back, "No key in this one, either."

Sherlock threw one of the coats to Molly as Stankovic came running around the side of the house, firing. "Molly, drop, roll behind the SUV." Molly fired back at him and he dove for cover. She fired several times, until her gun was empty. He laughed at her. "Got you, bitch. Now where's the FBI agent?"

"Right here." Sherlock rose from behind the other SUV, took two fast steps before he saw her and she fired. The bullet struck his shoulder. He groaned and bent forward, but he managed to raise his gun toward her. She shot him again, center mass. He fell to his knees, trying to suck in air, stared at her a moment, disbelieving, and fell onto his back.

They froze at the sound of a man's voice. "Stankovic, what's going on? I heard gunshots. Where are you?" It had to be Caruso, and where had he been? They heard him curse when he saw Stankovic, and then he saw them and fired.

Sherlock grabbed Molly's arm. They ran across the overgrown driveway, juking left to right, Caruso firing after them, his bullets cutting into the tall grass beside them. Finally, he stopped. He was out of ammunition, running back into the house for more.

"Okay, there's only Caruso left and he'll have to hunt up Nero and Domino, so we've got some time. But they'll be after us again soon."

Molly blew on the muzzle of her Beretta like a gunslinger, gave her a manic grin. "Not that soon. I shot out a tire on both of the SUVS."

Sherlock hadn't heard any tires blow. She grinned at Molly. "I love you. That was great. You've given us more time. We can run along the road for a while, hope a car comes by. But when they've changed the tires, they'll be patrolling the road so we'll have to be watchful. I have no idea which way to go."

"Let's go right. The hero always goes right."

Sherlock didn't know where it came from but a laugh burst out. They broke into a fast trot down the asphalt two-laner toward the right.

Sherlock raised her hand for Molly to stop several minutes later. They both bent over, breathing hard, slowing their heart rates. Sherlock said, "No sign of any vehicles yet coming out way. They've got the tires changed by now, so let's walk along the side of the road. We can duck into the woods when we hear them coming." She looked down at her watch. "It'll be dark soon. Crap, Molly, we don't have a car and we don't have a cell phone."

"We still have these coats, so we won't freeze to death, and you've still got some bullets left, right? We left four of them in sorry shape, and we're free, Sherlock. I call that a big win."

But for how long? Whoever Nero's boss was—Rule Shaker or someone else—Nero would call him for help, and others would come. They'd been lucky neither of them had been shot already. "You're right, Molly, we'll count our blessings. I figure if we keep moving we shouldn't get hypothermic."

Molly looked up at the darkening sky. "Well, drat. I sure hope it doesn't rain."

Sherlock looked up at the darkening sky. She imagined the temperature would turn freezing once the sun set, and rain would mean real trouble. They'd have no choice but to stop and look for shelter. But she wouldn't think about that now. Now, they had to run.

She said, "Let's go find ourselves a nice warm house."

They broke back into a fast trot.

45

Bellagio
Las Vegas

SUNDAY

Ramsey held the phone against his ear, drew a deep breath. Emma was asking him questions he had no answers for. He knew she was scared, and she deserved to know whatever he could tell her. He kept his voice matter-of-fact. "Yes, we met with Rule Shaker and Eve, but no sign of her husband. He seemed surprised, denied everything, seemed astounded we'd suspect him because the last thing he wanted, he said, was another war with your grandfather and that's what it would mean if he was stupid enough to take Molly. He reminded us if anything happened to her the cops would be all over him and Eve once they had the confessions in their hands. We had no way to force him to say anything else, and Savich couldn't arrest him, so we had to back off." Ramsey imagined her frowning the way she did when she didn't agree with him.

"But, Dad, there's no one else, unless it's Eve and she wants revenge against Mom. Eve hates her, you know that. But why would she wait six years? I mean she got married only last year, she should be over it. It's got to be Rule Shaker, Dad."

"But she doesn't hate you, Emma, and you were their first target."

Emma chewed this over. "Okay, but what about Eve's husband?"

"His name's Rich Doulos. I don't know if he's a criminal."

Emma said, "I'll bet he is and he fits right into the family and Eve into his. Why wasn't he there with Eve? I mean they're married, right? You and Mom have been married forever and you don't ever like to be apart."

Ramsey swallowed. "That's a good point, Emma. We'll have to check on that, but it could be as simple as Doulos having obligations in Palm Beach and Eve has casinos to run here. Your uncle Dillon has been working on MAX, his FBI data mining program. He's looking for the jet that took your mom and Sherlock out of Washington and the company that owns it. He's looking at the records of a man called Pope, who was with them. And of course he's looking at Eve's husband, Rich Doulos, and if he's left Palm Beach." Such a paltry number of facts they had to work with so far, and time was running out, he knew it in his gut. And what would happen to Molly and Sherlock? No choice, he had to keep it together. "Now tell me what's going on there, Em. How are you doing, sweetheart?"

A pause, then, "I'm okay, Dad."

He said nothing, waited her out.

Then, the words spilled out in a rush. "I'm scared, Dad, I'm scared all the time, wondering what's going to happen to Mama and Aunt Sherlock."

"I am too, Em," Ramsey said simply. "But we have to keep faith. A whole lot of people are working to find them."

"I'll try."

"All right, now tell me about the twins."

"They love Granddad's gym. They wrestle with each other

until they're exhausted, with Gunther supervising, of course, showing them moves and holds. They sort of understand, but not really, then they jump all over Gunther, and I swear to you he has as much fun as they do. I've never heard Gunther laugh before, Dad, until he started playing with the twins. He has a really big laugh. The twins love it.

"Mr. Miles made too many chocolate chip cookies for them, which they stuffed down until he cut them off. I put them to bed a while ago and read them their favorite story, you know, *The Last Train to Beaverville*. I'm trying really hard with them, Dad, but they want you and Mom."

Ramsey could hear Molly's voice miming the beaver characters. He always chimed in with the mean voice of the beaver villain, Mr. Mogul. "What have you told them?"

"I told them Aunt Sherlock needed Mama to help solve a case about stolen trail mix, and Mama was the perfect one to help her because she knew all about the trail mix and the suspects. Cal laughed, but Gage didn't; he gave me that look of his. He's starting to worry, Dad, he knows something's wrong." Her voice wobbled. "I don't know how much longer we'll be okay here. I nearly cried tonight when I tucked them in and kissed them good night. It was close. The twins don't need that."

He closed his eyes a moment. "I'm proud of you, Em. I swear we'll find your mom. Will you believe that?"

"Yes, Dad."

Emma's voice sounded mechanical, but what else could he say? "I love you, Em, try to sleep, okay? I'll call again in the morning." He paused, said again, "Have faith, sweetheart." Ramsey punched off his cell, looked up to see Mason's eyes on him.

Mason said, "Emma's an amazing kid, Ramsey. She's got your guts and Molly's positive outlook. She'll hold up."

But that was the point, Ramsey thought. Emma was a kid, she shouldn't have to hold up, and he should be there with her. "Miles fed the twins and Gunther wrestled with them. From the sound of it he really got a kick out of is so I imagine on future visits it'll be the gym for Gunther and the twins."

Mason nodded. "Gunther is one of a kind."

They had all settled into the living room of the large three-bedroom suite at the Bellagio in the early evening. Elizabeth Beatrice's head rested on Mason's shoulder, but she wasn't asleep, Mason could tell, she was listening to them, thinking. He said, "While you were speaking to Emma, Ramsey, my man Linc called to report Shaker and Eve haven't left the Sovereign. They're still in the penthouse apartment. They'll contact me if either of them makes a move."

Savich said, "I got a text just now from Agent Brenda Lawless from the Miami Field Office—yes, I know, she puts up with a lot with that last name. As far as she knows Doulos is at home, but she hasn't got eyes on him yet. His house sprawls over a huge property with lots of trees and lots of ways in and out, including beach access and a dock with mooring for a fifty-foot yacht. She'll call me when she knows for sure. The Miami SAC says he'll keep up surveillance for as long as we need it."

Mason heard Elizabeth Beatrice's breathing even out. She was falling asleep against his shoulder. He looked down at her hand, and at her engagement ring, elegant and simple and not what he would have chosen for her. But it was what she'd wanted. He had to admit the plain wedding band she'd picked out to go with it looked perfect on her long slender finger. They were young fingers, so very young. What would happen to her when he died? What sort of life would she live? Mason shook his head. He hated thinking about all the years that separated them, knew he'd only worry more about that as the years passed by.

Savich said, "MAX found quite a bit about Doulos, Shaker's son-in-law. The Doulos family is second-generation wealth. They own a multinational security firm, Doulos International. Timothy Doulos, Rich's older brother, is following in his parents' footsteps, second-in-command to the CEO, Vitoriana Doulos, the matriarch. His father is long dead. Unlike his upstanding older brother, Rich Doulos got himself a rap sheet when he was still a teenager—theft, shoplifting, burglary, but nothing more recent. He's paid as a consultant by his mother's company, but most of his income is from an import/export business, primarily artwork he buys in Europe whenever he's there, maybe four times a year. He likes to gamble in Monte Carlo. As you already know, Doulos owns his own popular private gambling club called Exotica. Believe me, MAX will look deeper into his club and his import/export business. Doulos is thirty-three, and he's been married only once, to Eve Lord Shaker a year ago."

Mason said, "I've actually met his mother, Vitoriana, and her heir apparent, her son Timmy. She's one of the grande dames in Palm Beach society so you can hardly avoid meeting her. Perhaps that's how Eve and Doulos met, through his mother. I wonder why they don't live together?"

Savich said, "Eve flies often to Miami, but strangely, Doulos is rarely in Las Vegas, so she does all the heavy travel lifting. Eve runs two of the casinos and Rule runs the jewel of the crown, the Sovereign. It sounds like a strange marriage to me."

Ramsey said, "Molly and I weren't even in different cities the first year of our marriage." A smile kicked up. "If I hadn't had to work, we'd have been together 24/7 the first year."

Savich said, "Agree, but who can say? Oh yes, Ollie texted me too. Our quarry paid for the hangar at Jet Aeronautics with a wire from a holding company registered in Nevada."

Ramsey crossed his arms. "And yet another arrow pointing straight at Rule Shaker."

Savich rose. "And it's as obvious an arrow as James Pope, Shaker's employee, stuffed into the trunk of the limousine with a bullet in his forehead. They've been looking into Pope at the CAU—his phone records, credit cards. The M. J. Pederson identity he stole hadn't been used here in Las Vegas, only in Washington, which may or may not be significant."

"My people haven't had any luck finding the Gulfstream yet. The people who took Sherlock and Molly turned off the tracker, so all we know so far is they haven't landed at any airfield with air traffic control. I think it's safe to say the jet is stashed at a private airfield somewhere in the boondocks with a long-enough runway to accommodate the Gulfstream."

Ramsey said, "Maybe having a long-enough runway near their destination was what decided where they'd take Molly and Sherlock. I wonder if the pilots were part of it. Otherwise, they'd have to have been coerced."

Savich said, "More likely they were paid off." He covered his mouth, yawned. "Sorry, I'm still on East Coast time. Maybe we should get some rest. Everyone at the CAU is working on this. Maybe they'll find a new direction for us tomorrow." Savich knew he wouldn't get much sleep himself. He had more work to do on MAX. He thought of Sherlock, knew she'd do whatever it took to protect herself and Molly, to try to keep them alive. He had to trust in Sherlock's judgment and her skills or he'd go insane. Still, he knew Sherlock. If she had to, she'd take chances and it scared him to his boots. He knew he had to keep the faith, just like Ramsey had said to Emma. He looked over to see Mason gently stroking Elizabeth Beatrice's hair as she slept. Life, Dillon knew, was made up of small moments, precious moments that made precious memories.

46

Somewhere

SUNDAY

Sherlock stopped, breathing hard, a stitch in her side. Molly leaned over next to her, said between panting breaths, "I haven't run this hard in far too long."

"It's been about fifteen minutes. I'd say we've covered well over a mile. We're good, Molly." She drew in a deep breath and straightened, looked back down the two-lane country road with oaks and maples pressing in on it, and too many potholes. They hadn't seen a break in the thick forest since they'd left Williard House, no crossroads, no driveways, not a flicker of a light. "I thought we'd see a car by now, but there hasn't even been a road sign." She shook her head. "Not even a horse and buggy."

Molly's breath was finally evening out. "Well, it is Sunday night. I guess most folk are at home resting up for the work-week. Hey, maybe you're right about a horse and buggy and we're in Pennsylvania, in Amish country."

"Oh yeah, that'd be great—no cell phones, no landlines, no cars, the ultimate sad situation for us."

Molly laughed. "Okay, forget Pennsylvania." She felt the cold standing still, and shivered, despite the large men's warm coat that smelled of lemons. "Listen, Sherlock, I've felt this cold in April visiting Boston so maybe we could be somewhere up in the Northeast. If so, we're lucky it's not snowing."

Sherlock hugged her own heavy oversized men's woolen coat around her. "Could be. We have to keep moving, Molly. You ready?"

They broke into a fast walk. Sherlock said, "I wonder if Domino was smart enough to kill Nero, or at least not release him, and get away."

Molly said, "Who knows? Say she just left him in the basement. Caruso would have freed him by now. Do you think she'd take off?"

"Domino's a soldier, hired only for this one job. Her neck isn't on the line, not like Nero's. If she did kill him then she'd head out, leave Caruso and Ilic to fend for themselves." Sherlock shrugged. "It's only a guess, Molly."

Molly said, "I do know this, Sherlock. If Nero's alive, he won't give up." She paused a moment, exhaled a deep breath, and watched it condense in front of her. She dug her hands deep into her coat pockets. "Nero will want more than anything to kill you. You humiliated him. You'll be his focus now, even more than I am. I'm only a means to an end, you're the enemy."

Sherlock said, "I think assignments like this one have always been a kind of game to him. Every move he makes he's thought out and weighed before he makes it. Like every self-respecting psychopath I've come across, he thinks he's invulnerable and he's smarter than any opponent. He can't envision or deal with failing. You're right, Molly, if he's alive, he'll be coming after us." She heard an owl, heard a small animal moving around among the trees. Overhead, dark clouds floated past a quarter moon leaving them very little light, barely enough to see the road. She saw Molly was shivering again. "Time to move out again, Molly," she said and broke into a trot, Molly beside her.

A minute later they heard a car in the distance. They veered off the road and into the trees, hidden from view.

Molly chanted, "Maybe let it be Mr. and Mrs. Smith with their cell phones with them."

They peered back down the road, ready to jump back out on the apron and wave down the driver if it wasn't Nero in his SUV.

An SUV did come into view, driving slowly, blinking its headlights. A woman had her head out the driver's window and she was yelling. "Agent Sherlock! Mrs. Hunt! It's me, Domino. I left Nero tied up, and I got away. You'll freeze to death out here. I can help you!"

Molly jumped out before Sherlock could stop her, the *Wait, Molly!* dead in her mouth. She stepped out, too, no choice, and trained her weapon on Domino's face.

"Great, I've found you. Hurry, I know Nero will be coming! Get in!"

But something wasn't right, something—Sherlock realized too late the back window was down. Suddenly Nero's head appeared in the window and he had a Walther in his hand, trained on Molly. "Hello, ladies. No, don't shoot me, Agent Sherlock, or Mrs. Hunt is dead where she sta—"

Sherlock fired, hit the door an inch from his face. "Molly, run!"

Sherlock sprayed the SUV with gunfire as she ran back toward the forest. Nero fired back at them, and then there was a second gun, the shots loud in the still night. It was Domino's gun.

Molly yelled out in pain. Sherlock grabbed her and they stumbled into the forest. She heard Nero and Domino slamming the car doors. Sherlock knew they couldn't outrun them, not with Molly hurt. When Nero fired again, she went down on her stomach, pulling Molly down beside her. She didn't move.

Nero laughed, ran to where Sherlock lay facedown in the mess of leaves. Molly lay beside her on her back, pressing on the wound in her side, her eyes closed.

He leaned over Sherlock. "Too bad you're dead, bitch. I wanted to put some bullets in you before I shot you in the face."

Sherlock rolled, jerked up her gun, and shot him in the neck. Nero dropped his gun, grabbed at his neck, and stared down at her, blood spurting out between his fingers. His voice gurgled with blood. "You can't be alive—" He fell to his knees and toppled over.

"That was well done, Sherlock. I personally won't miss him. But now it's all over."

Sherlock stared up at the gun trained on her chest, looked up into Domino's eyes.

"I'm not who you think I am. I am sorry, but I will kill you, you know, if I have to. Now, I really don't want to splash your brains all over your beautiful hair, so throw the gun down and we'll take Mrs. Hunt back to Williard House. Neither of us want her to die."

Sherlock threw the gun on Nero's body beside her.

"Good choice. Now, you get Mrs. Hunt. We'll leave Nero here. I'll send Caruso to fetch him. You shot Ilic in the knee so he's not much good. Caruso can bury Nero alongside Stankovic and maybe then he and Ilic will stop their whining and be thankful they're not dead. Get up."

Sherlock rolled up onto her knees. "Molly, I'll help you. You keep pressure on your side and don't let up." Sherlock didn't know how bad the wound was. If Molly died, it would be her fault they'd escaped in the first place. There'd have been another way, surely there'd have been another way. She flashed on the pain she'd felt when she'd been shot in the side, remembered the pain was bad. Molly was pale, grimacing, but she was holding it together. Sherlock helped her to her feet, whispered against her cheek, "Don't give up, you hear me? And keep the pressure on."

"I hear you," Molly said. But her voice was thin, barely above a whisper. Still Sherlock heard the grit, the determination. Together they slowly made their way back to the SUV, Domino behind them.

47

Green Briar

SUNDAY NIGHT

Time stopped. Griffin could do nothing but watch, paralyzed, when Kirra jumped off the balcony railing and cannonballed toward the deep end of the pool. The instant before she hit the water, she stretched her arms and legs out away from her body and broke the surface with a huge splash. He worried she'd slammed into the bottom of the pool and couldn't believe it when she surfaced sputtering and spitting out water, her blond wig beside her. His breath whooshed out. She was alive and she appeared all right. How's she know to spread out like that? Griffin watched her grab her wig to keep it from floating away, swim to the side of the pool, and pull herself against the apron. *She was alive.* Heart pounding, Griffin ran out of the suite and down the resort stairs.

Kirra felt like she'd been body-slammed, slapped hard all over, which she had, but she'd survived. Nothing was broken and she wasn't really hurt. She pulled herself out of the pool and slipped through a side door near the bell captain's desk. Only one employee was there, a young man who stood there, gaping at her. He stepped toward her, his hand out. "Are you all right? Ah, did you fall into the pool? I mean, there's no swimming at night, no lifeguard, and the water's really cold."

She shook out her blond wig, gave the young man a big smile. "Sorry if I scared you. I had to jump into the pool because I lost a bet. That'll teach me to bet when I've drunk too much champagne. It won't happen again, I promise. Wow, you're right about the water being cold, it kicked the alcohol right out of me. Now I'm sober as a judge."

Griffin came running around the corner. He stopped short when he saw her speaking to the bellboy. She looked all right, standing straight. Nothing appeared broken and she didn't look like she was in pain. She was holding her blond wig, and her hair was plastered around her head. He let out a slow breath. Kirra looked up, saw him, and called out, shaking her finger at him. "Here he is, the wicked man who poured champagne down my throat and bet me knowing I'd lose. He should have known better than to dare me. I jumped right in." She smiled as two more bellhops crowded around, all of them staring at her. If any of them wondered why she was carrying a wet blond wig in her hand they didn't mention it. Kirra walked to Griffin, gave him a mad grin, went on her tiptoes, and bit his earlobe. "Take me to bed, Agent Hammersmith."

Griffin stared down at her. "I heard your boots sloshing water on your walk over to me."

She looked down at her feet. "It's a pity, these boots cost me a mint."

"Kirra, what you did—"

She shot a look at the bellhops, turned, and nodded toward the elevator. They were at the edge of the huge lobby, so few people noticed them. When the elevator doors opened, two couples came out, both of the women dressed to kill. They gaped at her. Kirra merely smiled and kept smiling until the doors closed on her and Griffin.

They rode to the fourth floor in silence. Kirra's boots squished on the thick carpet on their way to their suite at the end of the hall. Griffin slid in the key card, pushed the door open. He paused a moment, gave a prayer of thanks, and locked the door. Kirra was on him in an instant. "Did you listen to what they're saying? Did Talix hear me jump? See me?"

He marveled at her. He wanted to strangle her and at the same time hug her until she squeaked. He tried to keep his voice calm. "Let's get our priorities straight here. Get out of those wet clothes and into the shower before you catch pneumonia. We can listen later."

A minute later Kirra's clothes were in a pile on the bathroom floor and she was in the shower, her face raised to the hot spray. She flashed back to Kiwi, the team member who'd taught her how to dive into shallow water without killing herself. She said a prayer of thanks to him. Kiwi loved to haul his ancient snowboard to Mount Cook in New Zealand. She'd ask Uncle Leo to get him a new board.

When she came out of the bathroom wearing a hotel robe, her hair turbaned in a towel, Griffin was pacing the length of the sitting area. He stopped when he saw her. He stared at her a moment, cleared his throat. "Are you thawed out?"

Kirra nodded. "What's even better, I don't smell like chlorine anymore."

He said slowly, his voice raw, "I've only been that scared twice in my life. The first was when I thought my sister, Delsey, was going to die and the second was when I saw you jump from that balcony into the pool thirty feet down—as in three stories. What you did—flatten out before you hit the water—how'd you know to do that?"

"Kiwi, a member of my uncle Leo's team, is a cliff diver. He showed me how to spread out over the surface if I wasn't sure the water was deep enough to slow down as fast as possible in the water. Believe me, I prayed, Griffin. Kiwi saved my life."

He closed his eyes against what could have happened if she hadn't had it together enough to remember what to do. "I hadn't realized what it would mean to me if you died. When I saw you make it back to the surface, I knew." He slowly walked to her, pulled her against him, and took her throat in his hands and stared down at her. Without her makeup and her tousled blond wig, she looked like a scrubbed teenager.

She tried for a smile, but she couldn't dredge one up. "Please don't strangle me, Griffin." What he'd said, it touched her deeply. She kissed him, light, playful kisses, then deep, and deeper yet. She jumped up and hooked her legs around his waist, pulled his black wig off and stroked her fingers through his hair, kissed his mouth, his forehead. It was as if a door had been kicked open and she'd rushed through it. Kirra knew in an unimportant part of her brain she'd lost control, but it didn't matter. She didn't care. She tightened her legs around Griffin's waist, wrapped her arms tight around his neck, and her blood surged and pounded at the feel of his hands all over her. She wanted more, she wanted all of him, and she wanted it now. She said his name over and over as she tried to pull his shirt off. He jerked open the belt of her robe, pushed it open. When his hands touched her bare flesh, he nearly lost it.

Griffin pulled the towel off her head and slicked his fingers through the tangles of her wet hair. He said into her mouth as he kissed her, "Speak up now because if you stop me later, I'll have to jump off the balcony into the pool."

She bit his earlobe, her wet hair curtaining his face. "Take me to bed. Now. Right this second."

Griffin was fast. He ran to the bed, dropped her onto her

back. She lay there like a pagan goddess, stretched out, staring up at him, her robe open, her white flesh a feast. Griffin knew he'd die if he didn't have her, now. Immense ungoverned feelings tangled up inside him, prodding him, and suddenly it all became simple. He pulled back from her and stripped, never looking away from her. Nothing mattered except Kirra Mandarian and consuming her, becoming part of her. He helped her shrug out of her robe and eased down on top of her, felt her full length against him, and moved down over her body, kissing a path until he rested his head a moment against her belly, nuzzling her. She pulled on his hair, said his name again and again like a chant, then "Hurry, hurry."

Griffin nearly forgot protection. Leaving her even for a second was the hardest thing he could remember, but he pulled away, panting like he'd run a marathon and grabbed his wallet out of his pants. Then he was over her again, kissing and nuzzling all of her, and then he was a part of her, and when he felt her muscles clench heave against him, felt her fingers digging into his back, heard her cry out, he let go.

He lay flat on top of her, breathing hard against the pillow beside her face. Kirra didn't want him to move, not for a long time. She tightened her arms around him, aware only now how hard his muscles felt under her palms, how solid he was. She leaned up, toyed with his earlobe. She felt well and truly alive.

Griffin managed to raise his head and look down into her vague eyes, an incredible green. She looked satisfied sprawled out beneath him. He balanced himself on his elbows, leaned down and kissed her slack mouth, pressed his forehead to hers.

When her breathing slowed, Kirra lightly bit the tip of his nose. "So you're not going to strangle me?"

"No, not this minute. Maybe not in the next, either, but I do feel like I could bring down a woolly mammoth all by myself and drag him back to our cave."

"Well, we'd need a lot of barbecue sauce."

He kissed her again. Her brain never disappointed, her brain and her fast mouth. He slid off her onto his side and Kirra turned to face him, pressing close. She kissed his chin. "Sorry, Griffin, even if you're a manly man, I really can't see myself carving steaks off your mammoth. You'll have to make do with some plastic-covered steaks from the grocery store."

His lips on hers, Kirra felt him smile against her mouth. He touched his fingers to her hair. "Your hair's nearly dry."

Kirra said, "After what we've been doing, I'm not surprised. Fact is, you nearly loved the hair right off my head."

Griffin couldn't help himself, he laughed, kissed her again. He didn't want to stop. He loved her mouth. He looked into her eyes, not quite as vague now as they were a minute ago. He said, "You're beautiful, Kirra, and you're stupidly brave and smart. When I saw you were alive and okay, I wanted to kill you and kiss you silly and make love to you right on the lobby floor."

"You really think I'm beautiful?"

"That's all you got from what I said?"

"I got the *stupid* part. Brave all by itself would have been perfect. Smart was good, too." She whispered against his mouth, "If you think I'm beautiful, then I'll admit you're not an eyesore. I have wondered, though, why women stare at you in that wig like they want to gobble you right up. I guess the wig does dash you up a bit, you know, covers your boring blond hair."

"Yeah, yeah, I know I'm homely," and he gave her a huge smile.

"I never said homely, not exactly."

He kissed her mouth. "I can't keep my hands off you. I love the feel of you. You're like silk with muscles." At her laugh, he stopped, said slowly, "I hadn't intended this to happen, Kirra."

"Well, no, who did? I mean, I hadn't really intended to fall all over you, either."

"You mean you thought about it?"

"Well, no. Everything just happened, and it was perfect, Griffin."

He had his brain back together enough to say, "I'm an FBI agent, and you're in danger. I'm supposed to be protecting you, not making love to you." He paused, frowned. "I'd apologize but the fact is I don't like to lie." He pulled her in even tighter and buried his face in her hair. "What's important is you're alive, Kirra. The world simply stopped when I saw you jump into that pool. But you're here with me, smart mouth and all."

Kirra ran her hand up and down his back, and thought *silk with muscles*, just like him. She kissed his shoulder, his chin. "It sort of stopped for me, too, but it didn't, Griffin, and yes, now I'm here with you and like I said, it's all perfect." She fully realized he was no longer just an FBI agent to keep her alive, he'd become much more. And she owed him honesty. No matter the cost.

Griffin's cell phone buzzed a message. Griffin didn't want to, but he pulled away from her, read the message, and thumbed his reply. "That was Savich, checking in. I haven't told him about the bugs yet." He stared at her, shook his head, and laughed. "I guess we forgot all about Jared Talix and Melissa Kay."

She blinked at him. It was a reprieve. "Let's see what they've been saying. I really do wonder if Talix heard me jump from his balcony and land in the water."

48

"Let's see." Griffin pressed the recorder on his cell phone, hit play.

The first voice they heard was Melissa Kay's, languid and soft. "It's so much nicer inside. It's too cold out there. What were you saying about someone jumping into the pool?"

Talix said, "I heard the splash before I got out there, looked down, and saw it was a girl. Looked to me like she splatted. I couldn't believe she jumped in with all her clothes on."

"She was probably drunk and having fun, like we are." She giggled. "Are you ready? Again? Let's get to the bed this time."

There were moans and sounds of sex, Talix was panting.. When he had his breath back, he said, "You just keep getting better and better, M. K. I miss you all the time, babe, but you know I can't get away from Seattle except when I can come up with a good reason for a business trip."

"I miss you, too. Seeing you only every couple of months is torture. Hey, I was thinking. What if I come out and kill your wife for you, make it look like an accident? I could, you know. We'd make sure you have an excellent alibi so even if the cops suspected you, they couldn't touch you."

He slowly shook his head. "It's a good idea, but sorry, babe, I can't allow it. There are my three kids. They'd miss their mother. I have to admit Tara takes good care of them. And you know divorce is out of the question. Tara's father would have me buried deep before I made it home from my lawyer's office."

"How about I knock off both her and daddy? Make them both look like accidents, so no blowback on you? We could raise your kids, how hard is that? What do you say?"

"My kids are hellions, particularly my girl. I think she'd love you, you're practically alike. She's much more like you than her own mother." He laughed, there were more sex sounds, then his husky whisper. "My naughty, naughty girl, when did you ever kill someone and make it look like an accident? You like the spotlight too much, you like to brag to Daddy and Ryman to just look at what you did, all out in the open and you were so good the stupid cops wouldn't ever nail you."

Melissa Kay said, regretfully, "I guess you have a point. It is fun knowing the cops won't ever figure it out. It's Ryman who prefers his hits to look like accidents. He keeps score, you know, it's a point of pride."

Talix said, "I thought so. It was Ryman who sent that accountant's car over a cliff. That didn't work out for him though."

"Still, the cops can't prove he did it. It makes me so angry. I still can't believe my father might be going to jail for the rest of his life because of that bitch who's been spying on us. I wanted to kill her myself but Ryman said it could be dangerous, what with what's happening to Daddy, so I hired a young guy to take care of her, Winters was his name."

"Was? Wait, was he the guy who got himself killed trying to kill some prosecutor? Tried to run her off a cliff?"

"Yeah, was, the incompetent fool. He couldn't manage to take her out." She shook her head. "And here I let him talk me into giving him a chance. He was certain he could handle it, swore it'd be a piece of cake for him. Ryman laughed, made me promise not to do anything to her, to let him handle it."

"I bet that's the last time you hire someone still learning the business."

"You're right, he was young, but how was I to know he wouldn't just lie in wait and shoot her? I know, I know, he should have been able to knock her car off a cliff, but she was better. But, you know, I don't want Ryman to off that wretched woman. I want to do it. And yes, I'll make it look like an accident, however I decide to off her. Fact is, I'm better than Ryman. He knows how to kill someone, sure, but I'm a better thinker, something he'll never admit. So I made a mistake with Winters, but I was the one who handled that nosy kid."

"My money's on you, Babe."

It sounded like Melissa Kay was purring, nuzzling against him. Talix said, "I'm starved. You pulled me out of my chair in the dining room with only a taste of the clam appetizer."

She laughed. "You liar! Come on, let's look at the menu."

Griffin pressed his recorder off. "That just happened. It's all we've got so far."

"It's more than I hoped for, Griffin. She all but spit out Josh Atwood's name when she said she'd killed a nosy kid." *Eliot Ness could send the tape to Jeter.* No need to mention an FBI agent was also there. It meant Eliot Ness still had work to do. She said, "Do you think Melissa really would fly to Seattle and kill Talix's wife and father?"

"She made a joke out of it, but I think she would in a New York minute if Talix gave her the go-ahead."

Kirra turned on her back and stared up at the ceiling. She'd been lucky Melissa Kay hadn't spit her name out when she talked about her father. But she would, of course she would, it was just a matter of time. She couldn't wait any longer. She'd been ready to tell Griffin when Savich had texted him. No, she had to tell him now even though she wouldn't be able to send the recording to Jeter. There was no way she could start a relationship with Griffin based on a lie, a huge honker lie. Griffin had to hear it from her, no choice. She swallowed, spit it out. "I'm Eliot Ness."

Dead silence. His hand lightly squeezed her arm. "I know."

Shock shot her straight up in bed. She felt as if he'd slapped her. She jerked the sheet up to cover herself and twisted around to stare down at him. She managed to keep her voice even at first, but anger bubbled up and her voice climbed. "What do you mean 'you know'? I only met you last Tuesday. That's only three breakfasts ago! How could you possibly know?"

Griffin faced her. He reached out to take her hand but she jerked it away. He backed away in his mind and said matter-of-factly in his professional voice, "Actually, Savich, Pepper, and Jeter all know. It was pretty obvious, Kirra, but none of us wanted to confront you since there were a few illegalities along the way. We were waiting to see how it would play out. Then everything changed on Friday when Melissa Kay hired Winters to kill you. You had to save yourself on Friday just as you did tonight." He saw no bending on her set face and plowed on. "That's when Savich assigned me to guard you from the Grissoms. To be honest it's been hard not to bring it all out in the open with you. I know Jeter has had a very hard time playing around it, pretending, asking you for a list of suspects."

Kirra looked beyond him toward the front door of the suite. She was utterly still. "I see." She wanted to laugh at herself, at her hubris, at what she'd thought was her amazing acting. She'd been obvious after all. She said in an emotionless voice, "So you figured maybe if you slept with me I'd roll the truth right out? Please the little lady and she'll spill her guts? It wasn't even a contest, was it? I'm really pathetic, aren't I?"

Griffin said, "Kirra, I didn't sleep with you to get you to confess you're Eliot Ness to me. I wanted you desperately. You wanted me. Believe me, Eliot Ness had nothing to do with it. It was you, Kirra. Only you."

Only her? He sounded so cool, so calm. Could she believe him? She covered her anger and hurt with a sneer. "Well, Agent Hammersmith, you have a confession now from the dangerous vigilante who's sending Grissom senior to jail for life, something the cops didn't manage for two decades!"

Griffin felt the earth sliding beneath his feet. Well, what could he expect? "That's why I called you stupidly brave. You took incredible chances, Kirra, you even went back after your dropped cell phone. What you did took guts. All of us were equal parts proud of you and afraid for you, particularly after Friday."

She looked away from him, toward one of the paintings on the far wall. "I still don't see how Melissa Kay and Ryman found out."

He shrugged. "I imagine they figured you wouldn't drive the Audi again and probably traced your rental car. You rented the RAV under your own name, right?"

She hadn't made that obvious leap. She felt like an idiot. She wanted to scream at herself, wanted to scream at him for pointing it out. She continued to stare at the painting, silent.

He said, "It's a pity that young man who tried to run you off the road Friday was killed. He more than likely would have rolled on Melissa Kay." He wanted to take her hand, to pull her against him, tell her he understood and it didn't matter, but she turned back to stare him and it was like he was a stranger, a stranger she'd like to punch out. She slowly pulled away, jerking the sheet with her, and rose to stand beside the bed. "What are you going to do now I've confessed to being Eliot Ness?"

49

Palm Beach, Florida

SUNDAY EVENING

Rich Doulos shrieked into the phone, "What do you mean it was an accident? How the hell did they escape?"

"It was no one's fault," Nero said and Rich heard it in his voice, a sort of contempt, as if explaining to the man paying him bored him to tears. "Yeah? So just how did this *accident* happen?"

"Domino gave up her gun. And then she told them where our men were to save her own skin."

Nero's cold, calculating voice enraged Doulos more. He knew his life would be over if the two women led anyone to Williard House. Rich tried to calm his voice, but it was hard. He gritted his teeth. "When I hired you, you assured me I had nothing to worry about, that you'd take care of everything. The women were locked in the freaking basement at Williard House and they couldn't get out. So tell me exactly how this could have happened. And just where were you, Nero?"

Again, there was no deference, no apology in Nero's voice, only the voice of a reasonable man to an unreasonable boss. "Look, Mr. Doulos, none of what happened matters now. The

FBI agent got hold of a gun and trained it on Domino, threatened to kill her if she didn't give hers up. Would you prefer the bitch shot Domino?"

Rich started to tell him that's not what he asked him, when Nero added, "That's not all. The agent shot Ilic in the knee when she and the Hunt woman were escaping, and when Stankovic tried to stop them, the agent killed him. Only Caruso can walk." A slight pause, the whiff of contempt. "And Domino, of course, but she proved she's next to useless."

If Nero were here, Doulos would shoot him without a moment's hesitation. "That's rich. What planet do you live on? Domino's worth both of your men, worth more than you unless you can get those women back. Get after them, Nero. I expect to see them locked once again in the basement game room when I get there. You will call me back in an hour and it had better be good news."

Rich Doulos contacted his pilot, gave him orders. He was pacing in his study, back and forth over the rich Aubusson carpet, wondered if he'd walk a hole in the damned thing. It would serve his bitch of a mother right. She'd given his brother, Timothy, the family house when Timmy married the woman his mother had picked out for him, and she'd moved this moth-eaten old rug to his house. He wanted to burn it, but of course he couldn't because she'd notice. He laughed again to himself. He couldn't wait to tell her what he thought about the fricking carpet, tell her what he thought about a lot of things, when this was all over and he didn't need either the rug or her any longer. Rich stopped pacing to stare again at his cell phone sitting on a pile of papers atop his desk. He sat down at his desk, tried to calm himself. His knee started to bounce. His knee bounced

whenever he was nervous, ever since high school when a jock
and his buddy had beaten him bloody because he'd flirted with
his girlfriend. It was the last time the jocks had laid a hand on
him, and the first time he'd realized what having real money
meant. He'd paid to have both of them mugged in Slater Park
near Lake Ragoon, a dangerous enough place after dark. They
stole their wallets and broke the jock's legs, so he couldn't play
football anymore. He'd survived and so had Rich. So his leg
still bounced now and then, up and down, a reminder of that
beating he took. The jock sure couldn't do anything with either
of his legs for a very long time. It was a good memory. Then he
saw Eve lightly press her palm against his leg when it started
to bounce.

He closed his eyes. He hadn't planned any of this before it
was forced on him by his debts. It had been sheer bad luck because he was an expert on the odds, he'd learned them on his
grandfather's knee, and he was good at gambling. Who could
have planned on sheer bad luck? And his precious mother,
who'd never forgiven him for paying off one of his debts with
company money, wouldn't even give him a chance to prove
himself to her again though she knew he had her clients eating
out of his hand, unlike his stolid colossal bore of a brother.

Rich saw Eve again in his mind's eye, remembered the moment she'd laughed up at him at the roulette wheel, asked him
to give her the odds of rolling a red twenty-one. He had, and
she'd won. She'd kissed him in front of everyone, told him how
much fun his little gambling club was. His *little* gambling club?

They'd been apart for two weeks now. It was her turn to fly
here on Wednesday. He'd never forget he'd taken one look at
Eve in Exotica and decided he wanted her. When he'd found
out who she was, who her father was, he gave up the idea of
making her his lover. He courted her and married her in a lovely

ceremony on the beach, with the famous Rule Shaker of Las Vegas giving her away. He knew Shaker had done a deep dive on him, from his first-grade report card to his import/export business and his finances at Exotica, but Rich's prime hacker had hidden any traces that might make Shaker's eyebrow go up and so the king had approved. His mother was aloof and cold to Eve, the witch even bad-mouthed her to Rich again the morning of their wedding. "She's a tramp, Richard. It doesn't matter she's got a degree in economics and pretends she's cultured. She's still the daughter of a mobster who runs casinos in Las Vegas. Her sister was murdered by another mobster. She will ruin you, Richard, can't you see that?"

He'd wanted to shove her to the floor, but of course, he couldn't, the witch would disown him. He told her calmly Eve was everything he wanted, and she'd misjudged her just because Eve was beautiful.

"You're a fool, Richard, just like your father was," she'd said, shaking her head at him. "Thank goodness I have Timmy. He's worth ten of you."

He wanted to tell her Timmy was her puppet, common with no imagination, but Rich only stared at her, his hands flexing. He thought again she might disown him, he felt the threat beating in the air, but he realized she couldn't, it would hurt her company's reputation.

He remembered how hopeful he'd been when he married Rule Shaker's only living child. It was his chance to get out from under his bitch of a mother, away from his pious brother. Eve was beautiful and smart, sure, but she still wasn't in his league; she couldn't be, she was still only a woman. He knew the gambling business better than she ever could. Didn't he run his own private club? Best of all, he was now a member of Rule Shaker's own family. Shaker would recognize his gifts, his talents. He'd use Rich, promote him, and eventually give him the kind of power he'd always wanted.

A year had passed and none of that had happened. He finally had to admit Eve was the only help Shaker needed, or wanted.

He'd never forget telling Eve while on their honeymoon to Cypress how well he would fit into her father's empire, how he couldn't wait to prove himself. She'd kissed him, patted his hand, and told him not to worry about the casinos in Las Vegas, she and her father had all the help they needed. He'd thought about killing the old man until he found out just how dangerous the Shakers were. Eve had confided in him about the long-standing bloodshed between her father and Mason Lord, escalating to Emma Hunt's abduction, Eve's dead sister, Mason Lord's dead son-in-law, and Mason Lord himself almost killed. Eve had also told him how Lord's daughter, Molly Hunt, had stopped the violence in its tracks.

Eve had no idea she'd given Rich enough to start crafting his plan. He saw breaking the Shaker/Lord truce as his chance, maybe his only chance, to cut the Shakers' reins of power in Las Vegas. It would be a coup, and Mason Lord would do it for him. Rich would be safe from any retaliation. Maybe it was a long shot, but he was a gambler, and he rarely lost. He didn't plan on losing this game, either. If Eve survived, she would need him, welcome him in. And he'd take control, of her and the casinos. He, Rich Doulos, would depose the king. It was then he'd set his plan into motion. He wondered what Eve would do when she found out he'd betrayed her.

When his cell phone finally did ring, Rich lunged to grab it. "Domino? Why didn't Nero call? Do you have the women?"

Domino said, shock clear in her voice, "He's dead."

"Who's dead? What happened?"

"I have the women, but Nero's dead. We chased them down in the SUV after they escaped. Nero thought he'd killed the FBI agent, but when he walked up to her she flipped over and shot him in the neck. He was a fool. But I got them both, Rich, and took them back to Williard House."

As much as he despised the man, it was still hard to believe Nero could get suckered like that. He was so rational, cold, and calculating enough to freeze blood. Domino had told him Nero had shot Pope without a second thought. How could that soulless killer have let himself get fooled? He remembered he himself had told Nero not to kill the FBI agent in Washington for the simple reason Rich thought it would bring too much attention, too much publicity, not to mention the force of the FBI. All right, so that had been a mistake, a big one. He should have told Nero to shoot her in the head along with Pope, leave her with him in the trunk of the limo.

But it was over. Nero was dead. Rich wasn't going to let things spiral out of control again. He hadn't wanted to go up to Williard House, but he'd realized he'd have to see to things himself, make sure everything was done right. And then it would be over. He steadied himself. "Lock them up, Domino, but this time keep your distance and make sure the FBI agent is secured, so she doesn't get the drop on you again."

"Is that what the bastard told you? She never got the drop on me, Rich, it was Nero. She threatened to shoot him if I didn't drop my gun. I wish I'd let her. He treated us all like his lackeys, even me. He was so bloody convinced he was better than anyone else, only what he said counted. And look what all his conceit got him, a bullet in the neck by someone smarter. But he'll never be able to tell you the agent took him down twice. The first time in the basement, he wanted to get in her face,

threaten her. She put him down and the two women escaped."
Domino drew a breath, slowed down. "And then he underesti-
mated her again, and she killed him."

So Nero had lied to him. Was he surprised? He supposed he
was because the man's reputation had been sterling.

When she spoke again, Domino's voice was urgent. "Rich,
you are coming up here now, aren't you? I have only Caruso
really because the agent shot Ilic in the knee. Nero told you she
killed Stankovic, right?"

"Yes, he told me. Don't worry, Domino, I'm on my way." He
should have hired the frigging FBI agent to kidnap Molly Hunt,
talk about getting the job done. He said, "I've already arranged
getting us two more of Nero's men. If they're pissed off about
their boss being dead, we'll point them at the agent. Domino,
keep sharp. I'll be heading to the airport as soon as they've
gotten here."

Domino sucked in a breath, spit the rest of it out. "Molly
Hunt was shot, too, in the side. It doesn't look that bad, I don't
think she'll die, but maybe we should send Caruso to get a doctor and bring him out here."

"What? No, that's the last thing you'll do. Talk about very
likely bad complications. No, stay completely clear of the locals, don't draw their attention. Tell Ilic we'll take him to a
hospital when I'm there with two more men. We'll take him
far enough away they won't be able to connect him to us. Molly
Hunt will have to make it on her own."

Rich hung up, placed his fingertips together, and admitted to
himself he'd have to kill the women when he no longer needed
them. He'd counted on Nero handling it, but everything was
different now. It was all up to him. If Domino hadn't realized
what had to happen, she'd know it soon enough. He hired two
more of Nero's men, ordered them to meet him at his Learjet.

When he hung up, he immediately left his house, and drove to Miami International where his jet was hangared. He could still pull this off. He'd had to think quickly more than once already, and he'd made the right choices. When his people failed to take Emma, he'd sent Nero to take Molly Hunt instead. He couldn't have predicted she'd have an FBI agent with her, or that the agent would kill Nero. He couldn't control everything, he wasn't a god. There was always an element of luck. But the dice seemed to have rolled his way again. He knew what he had to do now.

Rich patted his long-favorite Ontario MK3 Navy Knife with its sawback six-inch blade clipped to his belt, the knife used by the SEALs. It was a gift from his grandfather when he'd graduated from high school. He'd clapped him on the back and told him he was giving Rich his own knife, a knife he'd used many times in his life. On what, Rich had wondered. Just maybe he'd have to use it on Eve.

Rich's knee started bouncing again when he was seated on his jet waiting for takeoff. He popped a Xanax, washed it down with scotch. He pictured the FBI agent firing up at Nero, and blood gushing from his neck. He saw Eve lying on her back and she was smiling up at him as she jammed his Ontario knife into his own neck. He jerked, spilled his scotch with the shock of the image. Where had that come from? He could deal with Eve. He would deal with her. His fingers closed around his knife. He could still make it work. He had to.

50

SUNDAY NIGHT

Savich's cell phone sang out David Bowie's "Heroes." He listened, then hit the off button. "That was Agent Lawless in Miami. Rich Doulos and two men took off on the family Learjet a few minutes ago. They're headed to Camden, Maine."

Mason punched off his own cell phone and said with satisfaction, "Now, isn't that interesting? Shaker's Bombardier was just towed out of the hangar at McCarran. Their flight plan is to Palm Beach."

But why were Shaker and Eve headed to Palm Beach, and Rich Doulos to Maine? Were all three involved? What was happening? Nothing made sense. "My money's on Maine," Savich said at last. "Let me tell Ramsey."

Ramsey walked into the living room with a young man pushing a room service cart. "He says these ribs are the best thing at the Bellagio." Ramsey looked from Savich to his father-in-law, didn't say anything more until he'd given the young man a generous tip and showed him out.

"What's happened?" Ramsey was standing stiff, as if waiting

for a blow to fall.

Savich said, "We might know where they are, Ramsey."

Mason punched in a number on his cell phone. "Chuck? We're leaving for Camden, Maine, in an hour."

51

In the Air

Eve Shaker picked up her cell phone and dialed her home in
Palm Beach. She'd tried to reach Rich on his cell, but it had
gone to voice mail. Now Dorothea was her last hope. Eve herself had hired her housekeeper, Dorothea, the previous year
and installed her and her three children in one of the guest
cottages on the estate. Eve prayed Dorothea would know why
Rich wasn't picking up his cell phone, why he hadn't contacted
her or called her back. Her father was sure he knew why, but
she still hoped he was wrong. He had to be wrong, otherwise .
. . No, there had to be another reason.

Dorothea answered the phone in her soft musical voice.
"Doulos residence."

"Dorothea, it's Mrs. Doulos. I've tried calling my husband
but I keep getting voice mail. Is he there?"

"No, ma'am, he left well over an hour ago. He didn't say
where he was going only that he had to leave. Days, I think,
from the way he spoke. I think he was upset."

Eve felt her heart beat faster, felt a knot of nausea in her
belly. "He didn't say where he was going?"

"No, ma'am, he didn't tell me."

"Dorothea, something's happened and I'm worried for him.
Would you please go into his office and look around his desk,

see if you can find out where he went? I must find him, it's an emergency."

Eve looked up to see her father studying his casino accounting reports, but she knew he was listening, listening and planning out what he would do next. She really believed he'd been wrong, but now it seemed he wasn't. He'd been so gentle when he told her he'd had a serious talk with his pit boss, Pope's old drinking buddy, who told him that Pope bragged about leaving Las Vegas to go to a much better job with Shaker's son-in-law, Rich Doulos, in Miami. Now Pope was dead, shot dead during Agent Sherlock and Molly's kidnapping. Her father didn't have to tell her what that meant, but she still wasn't ready to accept that her husband of only thirteen months had betrayed them both. Surely there had to be a reason he'd hired Pope, there had to be. Maybe it was all a mistake and he hadn't answered his cell phone because he was up to his nose dealing with his family's business. He was a prized consultant for his mother, and his hours could be erratic.

While Eve waited for Dorothea to get back to her, she drummed her fingernails on the plush arm of her seat, listening to the low smooth drone of the engines. She knew if Dorothea found anything, she'd tell her. Dorothea's loyalty was to her, no one else. But what could she find? Maybe there'd be nothing to find, and Rich would call her, tell her he'd closed a deal, or dealt with a client, and ask her if she wanted to jet off to Aruba with him for the weekend.

"Mrs. Doulos?"

"Yes, Dorothea."

"I'm not sure if this is a destination, but I found a sheet of paper he'd shoved into his desk. It said only *Williard House*, and under that Mr. Doulos wrote *3 hours*. He didn't ask me to pack for him so I don't know what he took or how many changes of clothes. Does that help you, ma'am?"

Eve felt hope die in that moment. Had he ever loved her? Or had she simply been his entrée into hers and her father's world? A world he himself wanted to run, to own? She firmed her voice. "Yes, Dorothea. Thank you. I'll keep in touch." She tapped her cell's off button and closed her eyes against the enormity of his betrayal. She wanted to close out the pain, the growing rage in her belly, but it wasn't going anywhere.

Rule Shaker raised his head from the reports he really hadn't been reading. "Tell me, Eve."

She said in a dull voice, "You were right. He's left Palm Beach without even telling Dorothea, and needless to say, without telling me." She laughed, a harsh angry laugh. "But I know where he went. I visited Williard House with him once, maybe six months ago when he bought it. It's near Camden, Maine. It's isolated, off an old country road, nearly buried in trees. The house itself is surrounded by a thick forest of oaks and pines and sweet gum. It's huge and it's really old, built back at the beginning of the twentieth century by a wealthy local family who wanted to get as far away from the riffraff as they could. Rich told me he was going to update it, he said it would make a great vacation spot to take our kids, when we had them." Her voice fell off a cliff. She wasn't going to cry, she'd be a fool if she did. She was going to figure out how to hurt him, hurt him bad. She was going to get even. "It's a perfect place to take Molly and Agent Sherlock."

Rule knew all about betrayal, knew what it felt like when a supposed friend was really an enemy scheming to destroy him. But Rich Doulos had targeted his daughter. He'd courted Eve, married her, all because he wanted to take the brass ring. Rule wondered what he'd planned, exactly. Was he behind all the assaults on his casinos? Had he ordered the arson of Eve's casino? He couldn't bear seeing Eve in such pain. What he felt for Rich

Doulos was beyond anger. It was ice-cold rage. He pressed the intercom to his pilot. "We're going to change course for Camden, Maine, Fin. Tell me when you have an arrival time."

A pause, then, "Yes, sir." Not two minutes later, Fin came back on the line. "If the winds continue as they are, we should land in about three hours, give or take ten minutes."

"Thank you, Fin." Rule rose and walked over to his daughter. He sat beside her, took her in his arms. "I'm sorry, Eve. It's my fault. I should have had the man investigated more carefully."

She was stiff, her hands fisted. "No, this isn't your fault. Why would you think you needed even more information about him? He's not from a crime family. His family is two generations in construction and real estate, all aboveboard. There was nothing to find. He didn't get along with his mother, but I never blamed him. She's a snob and he stood up for me. But I should have seen it. It's all so clear now. He took one look at me when I visited Exotica and of course he found out soon enough who I was, and he wanted it. I was only his ticket in, the pretty girl who was the apple of her father's eye, the tool he used to try to take as much of it as he could. All the problems at the casino, the things we've never seen before, he paid to have them happen, didn't he??"

"It makes sense. He was escalating. Did he believe we'd think it was Mason Lord?"

"Probably. Dad, I'm the one to blame, not you. I believed he loved me, believed I could trust him, so it didn't even occur to me not to tell him our history with Mason Lord and his daughter."

"Of course you told your husband. It was a natural thing to do. I don't blame you for that."

"I want to kill him."

"I do, too, Eve. I do, too. We have proof enough of what he did, what he wanted, no matter what he says. But he's failed."

He pulled away, pulled out his cell phone, and began texting;

when he finished, he sat back in his seat.

"Who did you text?"

"Mason Lord."

She reared back. "Why?"

"He needs to know, Eve. It's his daughter. And Savich and Ramsey are with him."

"He gave you his email?"

"Oh no, I still have it from six years ago."

"Wouldn't he have changed it?"

Rule shook his head. "It wouldn't occur to him, any more than he'd change to jockey shorts. I told him he could probably find Molly and Agent Sherlock at Williard House, outside of Camden in the middle of nowhere. They'll find it. They might even get there first, unless they're still in Las Vegas. I do wonder why Rich took off for there at the last minute. He couldn't have known we were coming, and of course he'd want to keep his hands clean, keep his distance from Molly and Agent Sherlock. And that means something happened, something big enough for him to fly there now."

Eve said, "Dorothea said he was upset, so you're right. Something happened he wasn't expecting. It wouldn't surprise me if Agent Sherlock is giving the people he hired trouble." She reached out, squeezed his hand, and her voice trembled. "Daddy, you're the only man in the world I can trust now."

He wanted to tell her she'd find someone, tell her all men weren't like Doulos, but he didn't say anything, her pain was too raw, her sense of guilt too deep. His poor girl. No one was immune from being sucked in, even Eve. He would put an end to Rich Doulos, he could do that much for her, and it was a start. He sat back, closed his eyes, and thought about how he could make that happen.

He never let go of Eve's hand.

52

Williard House
Near Camden, Maine

SUNDAY NIGHT

Sherlock looked over at Domino standing against the closed bedroom door, her gun at her side, her face pale. She hadn't planned for any of this to happen. Sherlock knew she'd called her boss. Was it Rule Shaker? Whoever he was, he was probably on his way, she knew that much. With Nero and Stankovic both dead and Ilic wounded, he wouldn't leave Domino in charge with only Caruso to help her.

She looked over at Ilic sitting on a chair with his back against the bedroom wall, holding his freshly bandaged knee. He'd bitched and complained until Domino gave him some oxycodone out of her stash, told him all he had to do was stay awake enough to keep his Beretta pointed at Sherlock. She'd promised him Caruso would take him to a hospital to get the knee looked after, so stop his whining. As for Caruso, he was out fetching Nero's body. Would Caruso bury Nero and Stankovic together in the woods?

Sherlock examined Molly's side and felt immense relief. She said quietly, "The bleeding's stopped. The bullet went through, and the entry and the exit sites are close together, and that's good. You can stop pressing. The bullet couldn't have hit your bowel, or you'd be much sicker by now. You're going to be all right. Are you still in pain? Has the oxycodone kicked in?"

"It sure has. I feel like I could fly up to the ceiling and hover there awhile."

Sherlock patted her hand. "You go ahead and hover." She leaned close, smoothed a curl back from Molly's cheek. She whispered, "We're going to get out of this, Molly. I swear it."

Molly closed her eyes. Sherlock felt her let go into a drugged sleep.

Sherlock said to Domino, "At least we're moving up in the world. An actual bedroom."

Domino looked around her, her distaste clear. "This old dump, I hate it. It's a piece of crap, but he loves it, talks on and on about its good bones." She gave an ugly laugh. "Well, this pile of bricks sure outlasted Nero. We're all going to stay together from now on, right here." She eyed Sherlock. "I still can't believe how you fooled him into thinking he'd killed you, but you won't do anything like that to me. I have no reason not to kill you if you try."

Sherlock said, "I know your boss is coming, since you called him. I heard some of what you said on your cell in the hall. So you lied to me, Nero didn't hide your cell. That was well done."

"Thank you."

"You told your boss everything was falling apart, didn't you? If he's coming from Las Vegas, he won't be here until the middle of the night." She paused a moment. "You have to know, Domino, he's going to kill us."

Domino's lips seamed. She shook her head.

Sherlock said, "You told me in the limo you like playing roles. You were very good playing Nero's underling, pretending to be terrified of him. But I saw it—you really were shocked when he shot Pope between the eyes."

"Sure, it was a shock. I liked Pope. I asked him if he did it to scare you both into submission. If that was his reason, he was sure wrong. You never give up, do you, Sherlock?"

Sherlock smiled at her.

"Nero finally told me shooting Pope was the plan from the beginning. Not telling me was his idea, to make it seem more real. I think he got a kick out of it when I nearly fell apart. Now he's dead."

"And you trust your boss not to do the same to you? To shoot you dead like Pope? Domino, you're smart, you have to know your boss never intended for either Molly or me to live. Look at her, Domino. Her only sin is trying her best to protect her daughter from being kidnapped again. Did Shaker tell you he kidnapped Emma when she was only six years old? Did he tell you Molly and Ramsey had to save her daughter from a pedophile? And that pedophile never gave up getting her back until he was killed? And Shaker sent you to kidnap her again? Were you supposed to kill her, Domino? A twelve-year-old girl?"

"No!"

"But you think it's all right if he kills Molly and me because we're not children, we're adults? Will what he pays you be worth watching him kill us?"

"That's not the plan. Now shut up, I don't want to listen to you." She raised her Beretta and pointed it at Sherlock's forehead. "I mean it. Lie down beside her and keep quiet."

She turned when Caruso knocked on the bedroom door. She opened it. "Is it done?"

Caruso nodded. "Nero's in the SUV. Even waiting for the boss to bring two more men, it'll still be a bitch burying him and Stankovic. The ground's still frozen."

Domino nodded. "Ilic and the Hunt woman are practically out from the oxycodone. You might as well take Ilic out of here, put him in a bed. Then come back. We're not going to leave these women alone again. You'll take Ilic to the hospital when help arrives."

Caruso helped Ilic up, shoved his shoulder under his armpit, and walked him out. He gave Sherlock a long last look. "You're not going to walk away from this, lady. There's no way."

Sherlock looked down at the scratches on her hands, scabbed with dried blood. She didn't have her man's coat any longer. Ilic had taken one look at her and nearly ripped it off her. At least he hadn't tried to shoot her for putting a bullet in his knee.

Domino said, "Just to let you know, there aren't any trees outside the window for you to climb down, and it's a long drop. Why not take a nap with Mrs. Hunt?"

She gave Sherlock a last look, closed the bedroom door behind her. Sherlock heard the bolt slide in.

She felt a wave of fatigue. Domino was right, there was nothing to do now but wait to see who came.

Molly whispered , "I wonder if Eve will come with him? If she's in it with him, she will. She always despised me, believed I was a frump. Do you know she put the moves on Ramsey?"

"No, I didn't know," but Molly was asleep and didn't respond, pulled under by the drugs. Sherlock stretched out beside her and closed her eyes. She pictured Dillon throwing Sean in the air, their son laughing his head off. She had to believe he'd find her. But how? She swallowed.

Sherlock hated it, but she was afraid.

53

Kirra waited. Would Griffin tell her it was out of his hands, that she, Eliot Ness, would be arrested?

Griffin searched her set face, her fierce eyes, her seamed lips. She was angry, and she was afraid. He would be, too, in her place. He'd known she might tell him the truth, suspected Savich knew it, too. At least his brain was functioning again. He said matter-of-factly, "You've done the world a great service, Kirra. You thought it through and made the decision to hunt down a criminal who'd been free for far too long. Because of you Grissom should go to jail for the rest of his life." He gave her a lopsided grin. "What's even better, Hailstock's no longer involved."

Her voice was stony. "You didn't answer my question."

He looked her straight in the eye. "I know Savich and Pepper well enough to know that short of perjuring themselves they won't tell anyone you're Eliot Ness—especially not that lame boss of yours, Hailstock, although given his philosophy, he would probably only give you a slap on the hand. Literally. The same goes for Jeter, and you know that better than I do. You're safe, Kirra. My only proviso is Eliot Ness has to toss her shotgun, hang up her spurs, and ride off into the sunset. No, not even go after Oliveras. When we leave here, Eliot Ness has to retire. Forever."

Kirra said slowly, "Of course the four of you discussed this?"

Of course. He said only, "I'm asking you to trust us, to trust all of us."

"So Jeter knew all along?"

"Yes. He told me after you nearly died on Friday that he only just managed to play along with you, nearly blurted out he knew. He wondered if he should have." He paused a moment, reached out his hand.

She didn't move. "You wanted me to be the one to tell you."

"Yes."

"Melissa Kay could easily have mentioned my name. And if she had, you'd believe I told you because she outed me."

"The truth? Either way, it wouldn't have mattered to me. I would even have lied to the others about it if you asked me to. I need to know why you put Grissom first on Eliot Ness's list? You didn't know about Melissa Kay and Ryman then."

Kirra wrapped the sheet around her, tucked it tight over her breasts, and paced from the bed to the bedroom door and back again, the tail of the sheet dragging behind her like a wedding train. Her fists clenched and unclenched. She seemed to be arguing with herself. Arguments for him and against him? Let her work it out. He kept quiet and watched her.

Finally, she stopped, and hung her hair, her hair curtaining her face. When she looked up, she said slowly, "I've been keeping it all to myself for so long, thinking I had to—but I want you to know all of it now." She drew a deep breath, spit it out. "I went after Elson Grissom first because fourteen years ago, my father painted a yacht named *Valadia* from the shore of the Potomac. He always took photos of the scenes of the people and boats he was going to paint in case he couldn't finish them in one session or the light changed. That day he snapped photos of the *Valadia* with Grissom, Ryman, and another man in full sight on deck. I'm assuming when looked closely at the photos later, he saw a tattoo on the man's arm, an MS-13 tattoo. Even my unworldly father knew the man was in a drug cartel. You know my mother was ill and there was no insurance and no money to get her the treatment she needed. I believe my father tried to sell the photos and the painting to Grissom, and that's why he and my mother were murdered, why they tried to murder me. They were looking for the painting and the photos, but they couldn't find them, so they burned down the house."

"How did you know about the painting?"

"Because I found it myself, only a few weeks ago, in an old shed behind the house, bubble wrapped. They probably didn't even notice the shed when they came back to burn the house down. And there the painting was, photos fastened to the back of the *Valadia* he'd done, showing the three men on the deck. When I realized what those photos meant, I spent hours researching everything I could find on Grissom's activities over the years, which led nowhere. He was really good at covering his tracks and his lawyers were top-notch."

"And there was Josh Atwood. You knew Grissom ordered his murder too."

"Yes. Josh's murder was the trigger, I guess you could call it. After he and his mother were both dead, both murdered, I believed, I knew I had to do something other than wasting time researching Grissom or I couldn't live with myself. I decided it was up to me, up to Eliot Ness. I spied on Grissom, recorded him whenever I could from outside his house. My goal was to put him in prison for the rest of his miserable life. I figured the chief of police in Bellison was on Grissom's payroll and he destroyed the email Josh was writing to Agent Savich. So I made plans and figured out how to nail Grissom so even Hailstock couldn't sit on it." Kirra paused, sighed. "I only wish I could have proved he ordered my parents murdered."

"But you knew one of the two people sent by Grissom to kill your parents had to be Ryman Grissom. It only makes sense. But the other killer? You remembered what the other killer said."

"Yes, but that was all. Thank you, Griffin, for getting me to Dr. Hicks. And now I know it was Melissa Kay's voice I heard that night. Of course she and Ryman did it together. Will you help me, Griffin? Even if I am Eliot Ness?"

He paused a moment, smiled. "I imagine I'll help you do most anything you want from now on."

She turned to stare at him and cocked her head to one side, sending her hair to cascade over her shoulder. He wanted his hands and his mouth in her hair, but he only smiled at her, patted the side of the bed. "You must be wiped. Come over here and let's get some sleep. If Melissa Kay says anything else, we can hear it in the morning."

Kirra eyed him, eyed the bed. She pulled pajamas out of her travel bag and went into the bathroom. When she came out, he had to grin. Her pj's were red with grinning pink cats. She turned off the light and eased in beside him, leaving a good two feet between them.

He turned on his side to face her. "You want me to sing you a lullaby?" What he really wanted to do was make love to her again, but he knew it wasn't the time.

"A lullaby would be nice, but I'd rather listen to Melissa Kay right now. She might already have said something important to Talix. I want to hear it, even if a jury can't."

He picked up his cell phone, tapped the app. It came alive

when he pressed the recorder.

It was Talix's voice. "You can't mean that. Why would Ryman want you to leave early?"

"Because Ryman can't find her."

"So maybe you scared the woman and she ran. Why is he in such a hurry?"

They heard her toss her cell phone on the table. "Because she won't stop. Ryman found out Mandarian is Allison Rendahl, and believe me, she's out for revenge."

"Who's that?"

"She was like twelve the last time I saw her. Ryman and I had to take her parents out a long time ago because her dad was a lame-ass painter who tried to blackmail Daddy. She's all grown up now, a prosecutor, and she's out for blood."

"She changed her name?"

"I shot her, injured her, and someone stole her out of the hospital before we could finish it. It turns out it was her uncle. He took her to Australia and adopted her. That's where she grew up. I hadn't thought about her since. She should be married and raising kids in the outback. Instead she's back here, and Daddy is going to prison because of her. I'm not going to let the bitch do the same to me. Do you know, I think I have an idea how to take care of her. Is there any more vodka?"

They heard the sound of glasses filling and clinking together, and the recording ended.

Griffin pulled Kirra against him. She was stiff as a board at first, and then, slowly, she began to cry, deep, wrenching sobs. When the storm was over, she said, "She thinks she's going to kill me, Griffin, but she's wrong. She's going to spend her life in a cell, like Ryman and her father."

He held her close to him until she fell asleep.

Near dawn, he woke up to Kirra's mouth and hands on him.

He didn't slow her down, didn't think he could, and honestly didn't want to.

And afterward, Griffin held her again as she wept.

54

Williard House

SUNDAY NIGHT

Molly was in no pain, because Domino had given her two more oxycodone. "Weirdest thing, Sherlock, when I was shot, it was like a movie. I felt the bullet, sort of a sharp jab that almost knocked me off my feet, and then a strange numbing cold. It didn't hurt right away. I heard more shots, saw you fall on your face and I thought you were hit, and then Nero was standing over you, gloating. But you weren't shot at all, he was. I couldn't believe it. And then you were helping me. There weren't any closing credits, only the pain started up, bad enough I wanted to yell. Which one of them shot me, Domino or Nero?"

Sherlock said, "I don't think even they knew which of them fired the bullet. The numbing cold, it's not uncommon, and then the pain seems to come out of nowhere. It's lucky Domino brought a supply of oxycodone along. Well, not luck at all, I suppose, given her profession."

Molly was staring up at the ceiling. "There's a dark spot up there. I wonder if the roof is leaking. I bet Emma and the twins are at Dad's compound with Miles and Gunther. I'm sorry, things make sense then they don't. The kids, Sherlock—Sean and Emma and the twins—"

Fear had burst through the oxy and Sherlock said quickly, her hand rubbing Molly's shoulder, her voice soothing, "Yes, you know your father sent them to Chicago to keep them safe. You know they're all fine, so don't worry about them. You don't have to make sense, Molly, just rest—" She broke off when she heard a man's voice outside the bedroom door. "Is that Rule Shaker's voice, Molly?"

Molly tried to concentrate. "No, that isn't Rule Shaker, that voice is young. I wonder who he is. Do you think maybe Shaker sent someone in his place?"

Or had they been wrong all along? Sherlock heard a man say clearly from the hallway, "Caruso, load Ilic into the SUV and take him to the hospital in Mount Jewel. It'll take you about an hour to get there. If he has any trouble with the hospital not believing he shot himself by accident, make sure you get out before the cops come. Go now. The two men I brought with me have us covered here."

Domino said, "I'm so glad you're here, Rich. Mrs. Hunt's okay, loaded up with oxycodone. It was Agent Sherlock who killed Stankovic and Nero. She's dangerous, Rich."

He lowered his voice, but not enough. "You did well, babe; even with Nero and Stankovic dead you got everything back under control. Now we can take care of business."

"I just don't know if Mrs. Hunt will cooperate, Rich, even drugged up."

"Of course she will. You watch."

Sherlock whispered, "Rich? Whoever that is, we're about to meet him." She rose to stand beside the bed as the bedroom door was unlocked and opened. Domino came in first, and Sherlock noticed she'd put on lipstick and brushed her hair. Her gun was on a clip at her waist.

The man who walked in behind her was tall and looked fit. He was wearing a black bomber jacket, jeans, and black boots. His dark eyes met Sherlock's and iced over. He looked her up and down, studied her, and a sneer marred his mouth. "So you're the girl who's caused all this trouble, brought down Stankovic and Nero. I can't say you look like much."

"Ouch, that really hurts my feelings. I can't say you look much like Rule Shaker. Who are you, Rich? Is Shaker your boss?"

He ignored her. "Domino, why aren't they zip-tied?"

"I left them alone only for a minute. Molly Hunt's in no condition to do anything. I loaded her up with oxycodone like I told you, so she's out of it. Agent Sherlock wouldn't leave her, and there's nothing she can do, anyway, except jump out a window. As you saw, Caruso was sitting outside, just in case."

Molly said in a singsong voice, "Ah, finally, I know who you are. You're Rich Doulos. I recognize you from the photos at your wedding to Eve Shaker. That was quite a bash. Palm Beach, right? What are you doing here?" She stared at him, eyes vague, but her voice was hopeful, like a child's. "Did you come to save us?"

"That's right. That's my goal in life, Mrs. Hunt, to save you."

Eve's husband? Sherlock knew what his showing himself meant. He could never let them go. Sherlock said to Domino, "You know he's going to kill us, probably his plan all along even if he didn't spell it out to you. Is this what you signed on for, Domino? Murdering us in cold blood?"

Domino wouldn't look at her. "All you have to do is cooperate. Now be quiet. Do what he says."

"Come on, Domino, Nero shot Pope. He's dead. Do you expect anything less for us?"

"Shut up, Agent." Doulos pulled his knife out of his waist

sheath. "Now we're going to get this done, Agent Sherlock. Mrs. Hunt is going to make a nice clear recording, recite the words I tell her to. If she doesn't, Agent, I'm going to have to start cutting her, beginning with her little finger. You can watch me do that or you can tell Mrs. Hunt to make a simple recording."

Sherlock knew he meant it. Would Doulos kill them as soon as he had the tape, or would he think they were still of use to him? She didn't think so. Sherlock wondered if she could take him down before he knifed her or Domino shot her. Odds weren't good. She said, "A little late to be sending a proof-of-life tape, isn't it?"

He blinked, looked surprised, then laughed. "Not very bright, are you, Agent? Shall we get this done?"

Molly gave Doulos a dopey smile, started humming. "I remember in the article about you and Eve, it said you imported art, said you were charming and cultured. Now you're acting like Nero." She gave him a big silly grin. "You said you want me to make a recording? You mean you want me to sing? Do you have a favorite? Maybe I know it."

"How much of that narcotic did you give her?"

"Sorry, Rich, I gave her more oxy just before you came and she's loopy. I didn't want to listen to her cry and whine."

"Sherlock, did I cry or whine?"

"Not even for a minute."

Molly said to Doulos, "Do you know Eve was married to my father for a while? She was my stepmama and I'm older than she is." She giggled. "Then she tried to kill him. I'm glad she failed. Maybe you should be careful of her, not make her angry at you. I know, I love Adele. Can I sing Adele?"

"Shut up, you idiot!" He turned to Domino. "No way will she make a sensible recording. How long before the drug's out of her system?"

"It was a hefty dose. Maybe a couple of hours."

His hands clenched, primed for violence, but when Rich spoke to Domino again, his voice was calm. "It's a pity you had to dope up the bitch." Molly started singing Adele's "Remedy," slurring the words, her voice soft and dreamy. "'When the pain cuts you deep, when the night keeps you from sleeping, just look and you will see that I will be your remedy.'"

"I told you to shut up."

Molly's face crumbled, like a child being scolded. "Ramsey says I have a nice voice. You don't like that song?"

He slipped the knife back into his sheath. "We'll be back." He motioned for Domino to go ahead of him, gave them one more look, and stalked out. Sherlock heard the lock snick, heard Doulos speaking to someone. A man answered, "Blick is outside the window, Mr. Doulos, and I'll be staying inside and keeping a watch on them. We'll trade off in an hour or so."

Doulos said, "Sounds good, Billy. We'll be back in a couple of hours. But pay attention. Domino, let's have some coffee and talk. I can't believe it's damned near the middle of the night."

Their footsteps faded down the hall.

Sherlock leaned close, whispered against Molly's cheek, "Well done."

Molly gave her a lopsided grin. Her eyes were still vague, but she was mostly there. She ran her tongue over her lips. "I didn't know what else to do. It just came to me. Emma loves Adele, that's her favorite song, she's always singing it around the house."

"You bought us time, Molly. When he comes back, I've got to try to take him, so you'll have to distract him, all right?"

Molly nodded. "I'll try."

"Let me check out your side." Sherlock pulled down the bed-covers, checked the bandage she'd placed over Molly's wound.

It was dry, no blood. She said, "Looks as good as I hoped, Molly."

Molly pressed her palm against her head, whispered, "I wish I could think clearly. I know he's planning to kill us, Sherlock. If he'd come in wearing a mask there was a chance, but not now." She closed her eyes. A tear slipped down her cheek.

Sherlock's voice was a promise. "We're not going to die, Molly, don't even consider it. The more I think about it, the more I doubt Rule Shaker or Eve are involved in this. Did you notice how he spoke to Domino, how she looked at him? I think they're lovers."

55

Knox County Regional Airport
Near Rockland, Maine

SUNDAY NIGHT

Savich looked down at Williard House on Google Maps. It was isolated, the nearest neighbor five miles away, with a single country road cutting by it through a thick forest. Savich looked at Mason. "Do you believe Shaker and Eve really aren't involved in this?"

"I hate to say it, but it wouldn't make sense for him to tell us where Molly and Sherlock are being held if he was behind the whole thing."

Ramsey said, "To draw you out there? Lie in wait?"

Mason would have consigned Shaker directly to hell long ago, but he knew his enemy well. "No, the Rule Shaker I've known for longer than I care to remember wouldn't lie in wait if I was his target. He'd be in my face, that's how he'd do it. So no, he's not involved in this and probably not Eve, either. I think his son-in-law has betrayed them both, plotted all this to start up a war between Rule Shaker and me. He wants control of Rule's casinos, with Eve or without her." Mason shook his head. "Poor fool. Rule will crush him now, maybe even before we get there. You asked him to wait for us in your last text to him,

Savich, but he didn't even answer you. Rule's a lot of things but rarely does he make decisions without thinking them through. And that means he's got a plan."

Ramsey said, "You mean shoot his son-in-law in the head before we can arrest him?"

Mason shook his head. "I doubt it. He knows we're coming. He can't very well kill Doulos, he'd have to deal with Savich. I don't know what he's planning, but he won't want to take any chances he or Eve would be arrested for murder."

Elizabeth Beatrice said, "Why aren't we calling the Camden chief of police or the FBI in Maine, Dillon?"

Savich said, "The closest field office is in Bangor. I don't want to involve them until I need them. Too many people, too many explanations, too much chance of things going sideways, maybe a hostage situation. I want to keep control." He eyed Mason. "Whatever Shaker's planning, I have a gut feeling he's going to be a cowboy and there's nothing we can do about it."

Mason walked to a safe in the galley, brought out two hand-guns and ammunition, gave one to Ramsey and kept the other. Savich didn't stop him. Elizabeth Beatrice held out her hand.

Mason shook his head. "No, you're not coming. You're going to stay here on the plane."

She opened her mouth, ready to argue, and Savich said quickly, "Please, Elizabeth Beatrice, there's enough danger without adding you to the mix. Let me do my job. Let me add, both Ramsey and Mason are trained. Your being there would divide our attention."

Mason lightly touched his fingertips to her cheek. "Please, stay on the plane. Will you do that for me?" He was used to people jumping to do what he asked, but knew Elizabeth Beatrice wouldn't ever be one of them. He said, "The truth is I won't take the chance of your getting hurt. If you insist on coming, then I'll stay here with you."

Elizabeth Beatrice frowned at him. "That was well done. Oh, all right, I'll stay on the plane and guard Chuck. You promise you'll be careful?"

"As careful as I can be. It's time I ordered a car."

When the plane landed smoothly at the empty airport, Mason was silent. For the first time he could remember, he was terrified, about what might happen to Molly. There was nothing more he could do to save her life but trust Savich and Ramsey, and even Rule Shaker.

A young man with a white-blond mullet was waiting for them at the edge of the runway. He handed Savich the fob to an SUV, looked back at the big private jet, and said, "Nice wheels."

Savich drove out of the airport onto Airport Road and onto Owls Head. He floored it. "No traffic. GPS is working fine. Fifteen minutes to Williard House. Our first priority is getting to Sherlock and Molly. The rest isn't important, except for whoever tries to stop us. They'll have men patrolling, but they can't know we're coming, unless Shaker gives us away."

Mason's cell buzzed. He listened, punched off. "Chuck, our pilot, wanted to let me know Rule's plane landed about twenty minutes ago."

Ramsey said, "Why don't you text Shaker this time, Mason, tell him we're close and try to get him to wait for us."

When he finished, Mason read his text aloud. TEN MINUTES, KNOW WILLIARD LAYOUT. WAIT FOR US, A HUNDRED YARDS FROM DRIVEWAY. "I don't expect he'll answer, and he won't wait, not Rule. I keep wondering why hasn't Doulos contacted me, sent a proof-of-life, made any demands? Maybe even forced Molly to implicate Shaker?"

Savich said in an emotionless voice, "Because Sherlock did something that prevented it." And it scared him spitless.

56

Williard House

SUNDAY NIGHT

Sherlock jumped to her feet at the sound of Doulos's voice in the hallway. "Stay around the windows, Billy. You see a shadow, kill it."

They heard Domino's voice, low and upset, bulleting out words they couldn't understand.

"Not now, babe," Doulos said. "Trust me, okay?"

The lock snicked open and Doulos walked in, a SIG in his right hand, his knife in a sheath at his waist. Domino was behind him, her weapon at her side. He pointed his SIG at Sherlock. "Sit down and don't move or I'll shoot you. I don't need you that much, so believe me."

Sherlock believed him. She sat down beside Molly.

Doulos said low to Domino, "I promise we'll talk later, Domino. Right now, I need you to watch the agent while I conduct our business with Mrs. Hunt."

Sherlock said, "Talk later about what, Domino? About how important you are to him? That he might even marry you once Eve is out of the way? Don't hold your breath. Doulos thinks you're only hired help and you'll do whatever he says, including sleeping with him."

Domino said, "I'm not hired help, I'm—"

Doulos pointed his SIG at Sherlock's head. "Ignore her, Domino," he said. "She's just trying to cause trouble. Mrs. Hunt, you've had enough time to get your wits back together. Now you're going to do something for me."

Molly felt the oxycodone still humming happily along in her brain. She didn't feel much pain but her head was more clear than not. She'd bought them a couple of hours but he wouldn't believe her act again. She propped herself up on pillows, nearly sitting, because she couldn't stand to be flat on her back looking up at this man. She thought of Emma and the twins. And Ramsey. Her hand fisted. She wanted to kill this man. Sherlock gently smoothed out her fingers, gave her hand a squeeze. Molly said, "So you want me to record a message to my father to prove we're still alive. Maybe go ahead and demand Ramsey and my father give you the evidence against your wife and your father-in-law I left with my lawyers in San Francisco? And then Sherlock and I will be home by morning, is that correct?"

"You've got a smart mouth on you, but yes, that's exactly right. I've written out a script for you."

"And you'll release us?"

Doulos smiled at her. "After they give it to me, yes, of course."

Sherlock said, "You don't lie very well, Mr. Doulos."

Domino said quickly, "No one will die, Agent Sherlock, as long as Mrs. Hunt does as she's told."

Sherlock said, "Domino, for heaven's sake, I thought you were smart. How can he let us go? We know who he is now. Would he think we won't tell? I forgot—you have no say in any of this, do you?"

Doulos turned his SIG back toward Sherlock's face. "Neither

Domino nor I give a crap what you think, Agent. It's only Mrs. Hunt who's keeping you alive. Now we're going to get this done. Here's my cell phone, Mrs. Hunt. Start the recorder and read the script."

Molly accepted his cell phone and a sheet of paper from him. "I want to read it first." She read aloud, "Dad, it's me, Molly. It's Sunday, in the middle of the night. I don't know who these people are but we've been told we'll be released if the audiotape incriminating Eve Shaker and the papers I left with my lawyers in San Francisco are delivered to them. Ramsey can get them. They'll send more instructions later. Please, Dad, Sherlock and I want to come home."

Molly looked over at Rich Doulos and slowly shook her head. "So Eve told you about everything that happened between my father and Rule Shaker six years ago and you dreamed up this ridiculous plan? Both you and Eve? No, wait a minute. Rule Shaker and Eve know very well what would happen. You're not working with the Shakers at all, are you?"

"Shut up and read it."

Molly laughed at him. "Have you lost your mind? Do you honestly think you can manipulate my father and Rule Shaker into restarting the war? Into killing each other? And then you'd swoop in and take over? That isn't going to happen. I guess you didn't know my father just got married. He isn't interested in any war. If one was threatened, he'd put an end to it with one phone call. You've got to stop this, Richie, hang it up before you get yourself killed."

"Don't call me Richie! As I said, Mrs. Hunt, it doesn't matter what you think. I don't mind a gamble, and I like my odds. Maybe I'll shoot your daddy's new wife, that'll be enough to get him riled up enough to go after Shaker."

Molly shook her head at him. "You're dealing with Rule

Shaker and Mason Lord. They've both stayed on top this long because they're smart. You, Richie, you're nothing compared to either of them. You're a joke, a little man of no account at all. Trust me, they'll see right through this."

Doulos was breathing hard. "Shut up, you stupid bitch! Read that damned script!"

Sherlock said, "Does your wife of one year know what you're trying to do?"

He shrugged that off, calmed. He said, his voice perfectly serious and confident. "Whatever happens, Eve's my wife. She loves me, she'll stick with me. And she's his heir."

Sherlock managed a full-bodied sneer. "Are we talking about the same Eve? Do what you tell her to do? You honestly think she'll let you take her father's place? If you believe that, you're pretty stupid. When Eve finds out what you're planning, be afraid. She'll gut you. If she lets you live, nothing would save you from Rule Shaker." She wanted to bait him more, but she saw ungoverned rage building in his eyes.

To her surprise, he hesitated, she saw it. Sherlock said slowly, "You plan to kill Eve, too, and blame her murder on Mason Lord. She'd be another casualty of the war you're going to try to start."

"Murder is nothing to either of those two old men. It's easy for them, a snap of the fingers, and it's done, by them or by their thugs. Both Shaker and Lord warred on each other for years, unlimited murder and mayhem until Mrs. Hunt stopped them six years ago. They'll do it again. They'll explode each other's worlds and when they've destroyed each other, I'll come in and take over. I married Eve, I'm Shaker's son-in-law. I'm his natural heir like I said. Eve's a knockout, sure, but she's still just a girl. If I have to, I'll make her my partner. She's tired of taking daddy's orders. She wants the power. I'll make her believe I'll share it with her."

Sherlock said, "Eve told you this? She wants to take her father's place now? Sorry, there's no way that's true. She will see through you, Richie, see to your rotten core."

He was so furious his hand was shaking.

"And what about Domino? Will she survive? Or will she be another casualty of your war?"

"Rich? Is she right?"

He got hold of himself. "Domino, don't listen to her. Now, Agent, I've had enough. Turn on the recorder, Mrs. Hunt, and read."

57

Williard House

MONDAY, 3 A.M.

Eve and Rule Shaker crept through the woods to the back of the property. It was near freezing, the wind whipping through the trees. The coats they wore weren't warm enough, but Eve discovered rage was more bitter than the wind. Her father's face was set, his eyes hard. She knew he wanted to kill Rich. She did, too. Under cover of the thick copse of oak and gum trees they watched a single guard patrolling, bundled up to his ears in a black coat, black watch cap, and black gloves, an AR-15 held at his side.

Eve whispered. "I doubt Rich has thugs on his Rolodex and whatever happened here, he had to move fast. He's got to be the only guard outside. I can't imagine he's got an army of guards inside, either."

It was nearly three in the morning, only a sliver of moon. Rule felt a vibration in his pants pocket, dug out his cell phone. "A text from Mason. They're twenty minutes behind us, he wants us to wait." Rule quickly texted back, slipped his cell back into his pocket.

"Are we waiting?"

"No."

"Good. Follow me, Dad, we're going through an emergency exit out of the basement. It's hidden on the inside behind a pool cue cabinet. On the outside, it's covered with a huge bush."

He nodded. "First we take down the guard."

Four minutes later, Eve slipped her derringer back into her jacket pocket and held the guard's AR-15 at her side. "Now, I'm ready."

58

Savich pulled the SUV to the side of the country road, a quarter mile from Williard House. The three men ran into the forest, came out again at the back of the house. Mason held up his hand, pointed his Beretta. They saw a man lying on the ground, his wrists zip-tied behind his back. He looked dead.

Savich fell to his knees, pressed his fingers to the pulse in his throat. "He's alive." He rose. "Shaker took his gun. He's not going anywhere. We'll go in through the kitchen."

Ramsey said, "I'll bet the last thing the guard was expecting was anyone to come here in the middle of the night."

Ramsey and Mason ran bent over after Savich toward the house, their weapons at the ready. It looked like every light in the house was on to help the guard see the grounds. Savich crept up to the back of the house and looked through a window into the empty kitchen and felt his heart seize. Blood smeared the tile floor. A table was overturned, two chairs on their sides. Violence had happened here. He gently tried the door. It was unlocked.

The three of them walked as quietly as they could, alert to any sound, through the kitchen, past a dining room with two crystal chandeliers high above a long table, and into a huge entrance hall with a floor of massive black-and-white stone squares. A wide central staircase went upward.

They heard voices. Savich motioned them quietly up the stairs.

Where were the other guards?

59

They aloud voices. Sav the other guards.

Where were the other guards."

Slowly, quietly, Rule Shaker eased the bedroom door open, but Doulos didn't hear him, he had his back turned and he was holding a gun on Molly. Domino gasped. Rich whipped around. Eve's gun was raised to his chest. "Hello, Rich. Fancy meeting you here. No, don't even consider firing at me or my father will shoot you between your eyes."

Doulos couldn't believe what he saw, just couldn't. It made no sense she was here. Eve here at Williard House, in fricking Maine? He stared at his wife, frozen. He couldn't seem to breathe or think.

"You usually have lots to say, Rich. Nothing this time?" Her gun never wavered. Rich slowly lowered his weapon, thinking furiously. "Eve? Mr. Shaker? What are you doing here? I don't understand."

Rule Shaker said, his voice hanging-judge cold, "Rich, drop your weapon now"—he moved his gun toward Domino standing silent and disbelieving, her back against the wall—"and you drop yours. I'd rather not shoot you."

Doulos felt light-headed. He slowly sucked in air. He still couldn't believe all his dreams, his plans, his world, all exploding.

He saw death in Rule Shaker's eyes. He dropped the gun as Domino leaned down and laid her SIG on the floor.

Sherlock scooped both guns up, kept one pointed at Doulos, stepped back to the bed, and gave the other to Molly.

Molly knew these two were here to help them, but she couldn't begin to understand how or why. She said slowly, "I hadn't expected to see you, Mr. Shaker, and you, Eve, but thank you for coming. As you can see, Sherlock and I have been held prisoner here." She winced, pressed her hand against her side.

Rule said, "What happened to you, Mrs. Hunt? Did this moron shoot you?"

Molly almost smiled. "No, it was another moron named Nero. Well, either him or Domino, it was wild out there in the woods for a while. I'll be all right. Where's Ramsey?"

Shaker said, "Savich, Ramsey, and Mason are just a bit behind us. They flew out from Las Vegas after we did. I sent your father a text so they knew where to come. Are you sure you're all right?"

Molly couldn't believe it. Everything seemed sideways and backward, but who cared? Both Rule Shaker and Eve had come to save her and Sherlock. Molly shot a big smile to the man she'd considered an enemy for many years, jerked her head toward Doulos. "Yes, no thanks to this clown. I'm wounded in my side, but I'll survive. Thank you both for coming. How did you find us?"

Eve sent a frigid smile to her husband. "Easy, really. My dear husband was supposedly at our home in Palm Beach. When he didn't answer his phone, I called my housekeeper. She told us where he was headed."

Rich couldn't believe it. Words spurted out of his mouth. "No, that's impossible. Dorothea didn't know, I didn't tell her."

Eve laughed at him. "You're so smart, you left Williard House written on a piece of paper in your desk. You should know Dorothea is loyal to me, not you. She would have looked

in your underwear drawer if she'd had to." She turned away
from him or she might shoot him. "We heard the recording
he wanted you to read, Molly. I have to say it shows thought
on his part, threatening and vague at the same time, but still
clear enough to point squarely at my father." She turned back
to Doulos. "Do you think it would really work, Rich? *With my
father?*"

Shaker's voice was emotionless. "She's right, Rich. It amazes
me you could think for even a minute Mason Lord and I would
believe that drivel. Then again, you don't know either of us.
Not very bright, are you, Rich? A man shouldn't act before
he has all the necessary intel and what did you have? Nothing
but a six-year-old story Eve told you. Did you really believe we
were stuck in the past?"

Rich took a tentative step toward his wife, his hand out, his
voice earnest. "Eve, listen to me, please. You have to believe
me. I did this for you, for us. I didn't want you living under the
threat of all that evidence against you. You know Mrs. Hunt
could release it at any time and send you to prison. All I wanted
to do was get it back and I would have. Sure, it was dangerous,
but it was nearly done when you came in. Let me continue. We
can continue. You can be free of her and the threat."

Eve could only laugh at this man she'd believed she loved.
She looked him up and down. "What a fool I was. You seemed
so charming, Rich, and fun. You seemed to admire me, then
to love me. And you were ambitious; I saw that and I in turn
admired you for it. I actually came to trust you. What a shock
to discover I was your mark, nothing more. Imagine, Dad, this
worm says he did it all for me. And Rich, this girl, she's your
mistress, isn't she?"

He shook his head, his voice frantic. "No, she's my employee,
she means nothing to me."

"Rich!"

Sherlock said, "Sorry, Richie, you're not even a decent liar."

He whirled around to Sherlock. If he'd had a gun, he would have shot her. "Shut up, you bitch! You don't know anything!"

Eve said to Domino, who looked white and scared and was staring dumbly at Doulos. "I recognize you. I remember you were at Rich's club. I wonder what he promised you. Didn't you realize he was a born liar after he married me?"

Domino shot a look at Rich, slowly shook her head. "No, I believed him. If I'd been rich like you, he would have married me."

"Possible. He played both of us for fools."

Molly said, "Eve, you heard what he wanted me to record to send to your father. And then—you won't believe this—he swore he'd let Sherlock and me go free. As if we didn't have a brain. If you and your dad hadn't come, I'm certain he would have killed us."

Doulos was shaking his head, his voice frantic. "Sure, I had to threaten them, Eve, but I'm not a murderer, you have to believe me. I love you, sweetheart. Please, I would have explained everything to you. We can run the casinos together, you and I, partners in business and in life. Your dad's going to retire soon, right? To his villa in Sicily. You and I can visit him there, we can—"

Eve walked over to her husband, smashed her fist into his jaw, and brought her knee up hard into his groin. He groaned, cupped himself, and slid to the floor in the fetal position. She kicked him in the ribs. "Are we going to kill him, Dad?"

"The little shite isn't worth it, Eve. And there'd be too many complications." He looked down at his watch. "We'll leave them both to Savich. He, Ramsey, and Mason should be very soon now."

Semiautomatic rifle fire sounded fast and obscenely loud from inside the house. On and on it went, as if the shooter was spraying a wide area. Dillon and the others were in the house. Sherlock ran toward the bedroom door.

Rich Doulos saw Rule look away from him. He pulled his knife out of his belt sheath aimed it at Eve, but Rule was fast, he fired first. Doulos yelled, grabbed his arm, and the knife clattered across the floor.

60

Sherlock shouted over her shoulder, "It's the other guard. He's trying to kill them! Molly, don't move. Mr. Shaker, that was a fine shot. Please stay here with Eve, guard the door and this idiot." She was through the door in the next instant. The rifle fire in the closed confines of the stairwell was deafening and it was constant. She felt spit dry in her mouth. Any one of those bullets could kill Dillon, could kill any of them. She crept toward a turn in the hallway, heard Dillon's sharp voice. "No, keep back, Mason!"

He was all right, he was all right. Sherlock dropped to her knees and crawled around the corner to see all three men crouched near the top of the stairs, guns in their hands. But they weren't semiautomatics. The continuous rifle fire sent shards of ceiling plaster raining down on them. Suddenly the gunfire stopped. Was the shooter out of bullets? Did he have another gun, another magazine ready to slam into place? A single second and he'd be firing again. She nearly cried out when she saw Dillon step out and stand at the top of the stairs. He calmly fired one shot. She heard a man groan, heard him fall.

Sherlock nearly threw up when her fear changed so fast to relief. She shouted, "Dillon, there was only one guard outside. This one's the only guard in the house. You got him. It's safe now. But please make sure he's down."

At the sound of her voice, Savich felt a boulder fall off his chest. "I'll be right there!" He ran down the stairs to check on the man who lay at the bottom, on his side, an AR-15 still clutched in his hands, breathing hard. Savich dropped to his knees, studied the man's face. He was young, his dark eyes glazed with pain and his face as pale as the plaster. "I shot you in the shoulder. Apply pressure or you'll bleed to death, and don't move." Savich picked up the AR-15, quickly turned to see Sherlock racing down the stairs, a gun in her hand. "You got him! I knew he'd be no match for you!" and she leaped at him. He laughed, caught her, hugged her close. He kissed her over and over, his hands on her face and in her tangled hair. He hugged her again so hard she squeaked. He buried his face in her hair.

Ramsey and Mason ran to the open bedroom door to see Rule Shaker standing over a moaning Doulos on the floor, and Eve holding a gun on another woman. Molly was sitting on the edge of the bed, holding her side, a gun in her hand. She saw him and tried to rise. "Ramsey."

"Don't move!" He was at her side in a second. "You're hurt, where?"

"It's my side, the bullet went through. Really, Ramsey, I'm more than okay now you're here." She stopped, swallowed. It was over, really over. It was hard to take in. She'd prayed so hard and Sherlock had kept promising her all would be well, but still she'd felt such fear, then—Ramsey was here. Molly heaved out a deep breath, ran her fingers over his face. "When we heard the gunfire, I was never so scared in my life. You could have been shot, killed. But then Sherlock ran out and I knew she'd take care of things, right?"

Ramsey smiled, kissed her pale mouth, pressed his forehead against hers, and took deep breaths. He gently removed the gun and laid it on the bed beside her. "I'm sure Sherlock would have saved the day but Savich took care of things before she had a chance. It's over, Molly." He looked at Doulas on his side on the floor holding his arm and moaning. "That's Rich Doulos?"

Molly nodded. "Yes, not much, is he? He had big plans, Ramsey, and he was going to kill us." She smiled, called out, "Thank you for shooting him, Mr. Shaker."

"Believe me, it was my pleasure."

Molly looked up to see her father standing in the doorway. He and Rule Shaker were staring at each other. Mason said, his voice stiff, "I see you've got everything under control, Rule. Thank you for texting me where to find Molly."

Shaker shrugged. "She's your daughter, Mason. I thought you should know."

Domino ran out the door before anyone could stop her. Ramsey said, "She won't get far. Savich and Sherlock are out there."

They heard Savich shout, heard the sounds of a struggle. Sherlock's voice called out, "Domino, stop fighting me. It's over."

Molly burrowed into Ramsey's chest. He rocked her, careful of her side, whispered against her ear, "Emma and the twins are fine, in Chicago, wrestling with Gunther and eating Miles's chocolate chip cookies."

"Sherlock and I nearly escaped. That's when I got shot. Sherlock took care of me, promised me I'd be fine. Bless Domino, she gave me oxycodone. The pain's still only a low throb." Ramsey kissed her again, and kissed her three more times, careful to keep his weight off her.

Mason stood beside the bed, looking down at his daughter, cradled in her husband's arms. She was pale, too pale. He hoped she wasn't in pain. He said, "Your new stepmother and I are going to get you out of here, Molly. She's back on my jet." His stern face broke into a smile. "She's guarding the pilot."

61

MONDAY MORNING

Kirra sat with Griffin near the doorway of the large elegant
dining room careful not to be seen when Melissa Kay and Jared
Talix walked in, spoke to the maître d', and went directly to the
breakfast buffet line. They were having a good time, talking,
laughing, touching each other. Kirra waited until they walked
over to an empty booth and started eating their breakfasts.

She got up, her eyes meeting Griffin's only for a second, gave
the maître d' a little wave, and walked purposefully toward the
breakfast buffet line. She picked up a tray, got in line behind
a family whose children were arguing over pancakes or scram-
bled eggs, looked over at their booth and gasped out loud. She
waved and called out, "Jared! Jared Talix." She set down her
tray and hurried toward the booth.

"It is you, isn't it, Jared?"

Jared froze in his seat, his fork midway to his mouth. He
stared up at the young blond woman. He recognized her. She'd
bumped into Melissa in the lobby the night before. She was
grinning happily at him, looking ever so pleased. He slowly
nodded.

"I knew it," she said, straightening her glasses. "When we met last night in the lobby, I thought I knew you but I wasn't sure. Susan posted you were coming back east on business. We've never met, I couldn't be at your wedding and she couldn't come to mine." Kirra waved a wedding ring in front of him. "Yes, I'm here on my honeymoon." She stuck out her hand. "I'm Allison Hammersmith, a mouthful, right? Isn't it amazing I'd meet you, Susan's husband, and here of all places? It's been ages since Susan and I have visited in person. We were best friends at Washington State and—" Her voice fell off a cliff as she became aware of Melissa Kay staring holes through her, her face cold and set. Allison Hammersmith wasn't blind to the fury building in her eyes. She took a quick step back. "Oh dear. I remember, I bumped into you yesterday outside the women's room. I was clumsy. She—you—ah, excuse me, sorry for the interruption." She nearly ran back past the breakfast line and out of the dining room, motioned with her eyes for Griffin to follow her.

Talix watched her for a moment. He shook his head, his voice disbelieving. "We're at a resort in the wilds of Virginia and a friend of Susan's is here? She actually recognized me?" His hand was tight around his fork. "Susan is always posting photos of us and the kids on Facebook, but this woman, I've never heard of her. She's really pretty, so I can't imagine her being a friend of Susan's, she hates competition."

Melissa Kay leaned toward him, covered his hand with hers. "Will she tell Susan?"

"Of course she will. You heard the bitch—talk, talk, talk. I'm a dead man."

"She said her name is Allison Hammersmith. She's on her honeymoon. And you've never seen her before?"

Talix said, "I don't care who she is." He cursed. "Maybe I've got a chance if I leave right now, get back to Seattle, and do damage control."

An eyebrow went up. "How do you propose to do that?"

"I'll tell Susan I happened to meet two friends at Green Briar where I was on business. I was having breakfast with one, namely you, when a friend of hers waltzed up and introduced herself and came to the wrong conclusion. She didn't even give me a chance to make introductions."

"Yeah, like that'll fly. You've told me Susan's her father's daughter. She'll sniff out that lie in a nanosecond. This Allison is a newlywed and a nonstop talker; she's probably telling her fresh-baked husband right now, 'Should I tell Susan her husband's screwing around on her, honey?' He might even be against his bride telling your wife anything at all, but that won't stop her for long. She'll be all too happy to share the amazing news with her best friend, Susan. I don't know when, but she will tell Susan, no doubt in my mind."

Kirra pulled Griffin with her through the lobby and outside the Green Briar, gave him a fist bump, and sat him down beside her on a double porch swing with a magnificent view of the mountains.

"I don't believe what I just saw, Kirra. What did you say to them?"

"I'll tell you later. Turn on your cell phone. We can both hear what they're saying."

He opened the recorder app on his phone and hit play.

They heard the sound of a knife tapping on a table, and Talix cursing under his breath. "Then as I said, if you're right and she talks, I'm a dead man. Susan doesn't keep secrets from her father. He raised her himself after her mother died of cancer when she was a little kid. They still speak to each other every day. He knows more about our children's lives than I do.

Something exciting happens, she calls him first, not me. You might think he'll hold back since I'm his grandchildren's father, but the thing is, he already gave me an ultimatum a couple of years ago, warned me to always be discreet and never to get caught again. Or— He didn't have to finish."

Melissa Kay said very precisely, a smile on her mouth, "Then why don't we kill her before she decides to contact Susan? An unfortunate accident on her honeymoon. So tragic, the poor little bitch a newlywed. Boo hoo."

Jared Talix stared at her, not exactly surprised since he knew who and what she was. He just hadn't gotten there yet. He hadn't realized it before, but Melissa Kay's and Susan's fathers were bookends. "We are in the boondocks," he said slowly. "There's nothing but forests and lakes around this place. But as you said, they're fricking newlyweds. Do you think she's ever out of his sight? They're probably in bed twenty-two out of twenty-four hours."

"Like us." She sighed. "So if we can't get her alone, we'll just have to kill both of them. I imagine Green Briar management have experienced their share of guests taking off and disappearing over the years. If we make them disappear for long enough, how can anyone connect us? With any luck, they've got a hick sheriff who'll offer up platitudes, how sad, and that'll be that."

Griffin and Kirra heard coffee cups clicking, then Melissa Kay's voice. "Do you know what? She looks familiar to me but I can't place her. Isn't it strange she ran into me yesterday, all apologies, and she only recognized you today?"

Talix said, "Well, she didn't really look at me. Talk about bad luck, her spotting me here in the dining room and recognizing me at all."

"Bad luck or a stupid coincidence, sometimes crap just happens, Jared. Now we're going to make it her bad luck. I'm going to give Ryman a call. He wanted me to come back and help with Mandarian, but your Allison problem comes first. Better if there are three of us here for this." There was a pause. "Trust me, we'll fix this. Let's get out of here, we've got things to do, plans to make."

Griffin closed down the recorder app. "That's it, they've left the restaurant. Getting a bug into their booth was clever, Kirra, but it was dangerous. One of them might have noticed."

"No one did. That was the weirdest feeling, Griffin, listening to them deciding to kill me."

"I hope they make their plans up in their suite where we can hear them and not while they're out scouting murder spots."

"I wonder if they'll decide to throw me off a mountain or slam me over the head and bury me in the forest, maybe drown me in one of the lakes. This place is vast. They've got lots of choices."

"You heard them, they're going to try to kill us both, not just you. I wish you wouldn't smile like a loon."

She shook his hand, squeezed it. "Griffin, don't you see, we had to do something. What else was there? If we'd gone back to Porte Franklyn, Melissa Kay and Ryman would have come at me, anyway—and picked their time and place. Can you imagine living like that? Or I guess I could run and hide, maybe go into witness protection. But now we can get them. You heard her, she's going to call Ryman, get him up here. Then they'll act. Fast."

"The first thing they'll do is try to look you up online. They don't know your maiden name, so you're probably safe, but I'm not. What if they figure out I'm Griffin Hammersmith, FBI agent? Melissa might recognize me if she gets a better look, disguise or not. I told you I saw her a few days ago with her father in the hospital."

Kirra said, "You're right, Griffin. I've been giving that some thought. You know what? Even if they find out who you are, I don't think that would stop Melissa Kay. I don't think it'll even slow her down. She's bat-crap crazy, Griffin."

"I don't suppose Eliot Ness would consider leaving here?"

"Stop giving me that brooding look of yours. Look, Eliot Ness is a mensch. He faces every threat head-on. You know I'm right about this, Griffin. This is our chance. It could be my only chance."

"Yes, I know. We'll stay out of sight for now. They've got to plan so we can listen to them up at our suite. We'll need backup. Savich is still in Maine, but I can call Jeter, get him and a few of his detectives up here. But, Kirra, listen to me. I'm going to be the one who decides what happens here from now on. Not Eliot Ness, not Allison Hammersmith. If this thing threatens to go south, I'm going to tie you up and haul you out of here if I have to."

She gave him a fat smile. "Understood. You're the boss. I know the last thing you want is for something terrible to happen to the newlyweds."

Griffin arched an eyebrow at Kirra. He knew her, this fearless woman he'd been with for such a short time. So much had happened between them. She'd opened something deep inside him and burrowed right in. He wasn't about to leave with her. He knew it had to end here or her life wouldn't be worth spit. He knew he'd do anything to stop Melissa Kay and Ryman Grissom today and stop them for good. Justice for Kirra's parents? Or revenge for what they'd done to her? He chose to believe it was both.

62

Green Briar Resort

MONDAY AFTERNOON

There were no guests outside today. The drizzle hadn't cleared up as hoped, and it had turned cold, a plus for Griffin and Kirra. They were alone, but within view of the large hotel front windows, where Melissa Kay and Jared Talix could easily see them. Kirra was walking beside him, her long legs easily keeping up with him on the expanse of rough grass bordering the golf course. Both of them were alert, constantly scanning the golf course and the copses of thick trees alongside it, and trying to be discreet about it.

Griffin said, "You can bet they now know I'm an FBI agent. Will it stop them? I doubt it, but it'll make them more careful. They might even hope to get to you when you're alone."

"I don't think they'll care one way or the other, Griffin. Actually, Melissa Kay might like to add an FBI notch to her belt. I doubt they'll think you'd bring your Glock on your honeymoon, either, so they'll believe you're as helpless as I am, right?"

He said as he looked off into the copse of maple trees beside the green, "I don't go anywhere without my Glock. Ingrained habit. I'd really hoped they'd go back to their suite and make plans, but that didn't happen. And there wasn't any way to get close enough to them to record what they're planning. At least we know they want us to disappear, not shoot us in plain sight at the hotel. We can keep our newlywed stroll going for a while longer, but we shouldn't get much farther away from the hotel." He tapped his ear comm. "Besides my Glock, I have Jeter in my ear. He and his men are in place."

"Yes, I know. It'll work, Griffin." She was holding his gloved hand and now she leaned into him, stepped up on tiptoes, and kissed his neck, whispered, "Cold doesn't matter to honey-mooners."

He laughed and felt lighter, but soon enough his worry broke through. "It's a good plan, Kirra, but the fact is you can never plan for every possibility with any op; something unexpected always happens, something always goes sideways." He didn't say it was different this time, too, because she was with him and it scared him to his bones.

She said quietly, "I know you're worried, Griffin, so am I, but this is the right thing to do. No way could they foresee this. I know, too, Melissa Kay might be crazy enough to step out of the trees and just shoot us, not caring if it's in clear sight of the hotel workers and guests, but I'm counting on Talix not allow-ing her to do that. Of course Melissa Kay has a gun or, if not, Ryman brought her one. At least it's unlikely Jared Talix has a weapon since he flew commercial. You know they'll probably try to get us at gunpoint and haul us away. Not smart to shoot us anywhere near hotel grounds. It'll be all right, you'll see."

Griffin looked down at her serious face. Who knew her se-rious face would become so vital to him in less than a week? He kissed her, lightly stroked his fingers over her eyebrows. "Do you know, it makes perfect sense they'd want to kill you to keep Jared safe. You're the one with the big mouth who'd rat

Jared out to his wife. But me? I'm an innocent bystander. It's not right what they're planning for me."

She burst out laughing but it dried up fast. She knew he was trying for humor to keep them both on track. She poked him in the arm. "They want you out of the way, too, because they're obviously scared of you, the big tough FBI agent. Must be that dark hair, it roughs you up, makes you look even more dangerous."

Griffin grinned, patted his black wig, adjusted his aviator glasses. Reality hit again, fast. He lowered his voice. "We can't let our guard down for even a second, okay?"

Kirra nodded, felt immense gratitude, and something more she'd think about later. He knew as well as she did bringing down Melissa Kay and Ryman was the only way she could return to Porte Franklyn. She swallowed. Yes, she owed him everything. And Jeter, of course. She reached out and took Griffin's hand, squeezed it. They had a plan, a good plan. But still—she prayed they wouldn't die here today at this fancy resort. *Please, don't let Melissa Kay put together who we are. Let her think we're a couple of lame civilians who don't know a gun from chewing gum, who aren't paying attention to anyone except each other.*

She said, "You said things usually go sideways. Well, we know Melissa Kay believes she has the upper hand. She believes she's going to surprise us. She won't be ready for Jeter, much less for us—two people more dangerous than she is. And, Griffin, even if I don't have a gun, I'm still dangerous. I'm a vicious fighter and in a pinch, I do have this." She pulled a knife an inch out of her sleeve, quickly shoved it back. Griffin stared at her. "I will not ask you where you got the knife."

"I didn't buy it in the gift shop. It's my favorite knife from Australia. Uncle Leo gave it to me for my fourteenth birthday."

Was that her voice? Sounding all together, calm, focused? Like Griffin?

The same woman who'd murdered her parents, the same woman who'd tried to murder her, she was close now and soon Kirra would have her. She wouldn't run away this time like the child all those years before. She'd face down the monster. She felt cold hard anger. This woman had murdered the two people she'd loved most in the world. This time she'd make her pay.

Griffin pulled her to a stop in the shade of an enormous oak tree. He touched his ear com, said quietly, "Jeter, I saw movement on the north side of the second fairway, maybe four feet or so into the woods."

He leaned down, kissed her, whispered into her ear, "Let's turn around and keep walking, sort of meander. Kiss me again, maybe laugh or moan, whatever you think. Be ready. And do exactly what I say."

She moved closer, brushed Griffin's mouth. He whispered, "Get into it, Mandarian; that wouldn't fool Sean, Sherlock and Savich's five-year-old."

Kirra got into it. When he released her, he whispered against her ear, "Hold my hand, laugh. I saw more movement, a little closer." He raised his hand, said into his ear comm , "I'm sure, behind the verge at the second hole."

He listened, smiled down at her. "Swing on my arm and try for a giggle at the lewd comment I just made. Keep your knife palmed and ready."

They came at them out of a copse of thick gum and oak trees, silent and fast, Melissa Kay's pistol pointed at Griffin, Talix beside her, a knife in his hand.

"Well, if we don't have the newlyweds out strolling around in the crappy cold weather. How sweet. Jared figured you'd get out sooner or later. Getting some exercise to whet your appetite for more sex?"

Kirra gaped at her. "I know you're Jared Talix, and she's, well, she's your companion. Why are you here? Why is she pointing a gun at us? What is this all about?" She ended with her voice shaking.

Melissa Kay smiled at her. "You stupid little bitch, we can't have you telling Susan you saw Jared with another woman, can we?"

Kirra stuttered out, "B-but who cares?"

"All the wrong people would care, and you would tell her. As for you, handsome, I'm sorry about this, but you're going to eternity with her. I'll shoot you both if you try anything. Yes, of course, we know you're FBI. I know you're trained and dangerous. I promise I'll shoot your little bride in an instant if you try anything."

Kirra started to cry. Griffin took a step toward Melissa Kay, but she skipped back, pointed her gun at him. "I told you, pretty boy. Give it up. Ironic, isn't it? Because of this little loudmouth you've got to die too. We're going to take a lovely walk into the forest. Move, both of you. Now!"

Kirra said on a sob, "Jared, how can you let her do this? I swear to you I won't tell Susan, I won't tell anyone. And my husband, he's done nothing, he's innocent—"

"Shut up!" Melissa Kay shouted, turned her gun back toward Kirra, fired, the bullet kicked up the grass not a foot from Kirra's boot. Kirra jumped and shrieked. It sounded loud, but not loud enough to be heard inside the resort.

Griffin took a fast step to the left, turned quickly to kick the gun out of Melissa Kay's hand. Talix stepped toward them with his knife. "If you don't get back, Hammersmith, this knife will be in your gut. Then I'll get her."

Kirra yelled, "But this isn't right. You can't murder us, you can't—"

This time Melissa Kay whipped around and slapped Kirra as hard as she could. Kirra cried out, fell back against Griffin. He held her, fury in his eyes. He stared at Melissa Kay and Talix. "You won't get away with this. They'll find us. They'll connect you. And they'll never stop looking."

Talix said, "By the time anyone gets around to missing either of you, Melissa Kay and I will be long gone. Besides, who will find you? Now let's take a little walk, just the four of us." Jared raised his knife at them.

Melissa Kay said, "He's FBI, Jared. Check him for a weapon."

Talix patted Griffin down, but didn't check Griffin's arms, a good thing because his Glock was inside his leather jacket sleeve. Jared said, "Of course he's not carrying, he's on his fricking honeymoon."

She turned back to Kirra. "I can't imagine you've called Susan Talix yet, Allison; no, first you'd talk it over with your new husband."

Kirra looked petrified, licked her lips. "Ye-yes, I did speak to her, but I promise, I didn't tell her I saw you, Mr. Talix, I swear! I'll never tell her, Scout's honor." Her fingers curled around her knife, but she had to wait, Melissa Kay's pistol was aimed at her chest.

Melissa Kay laughed. "You really are pathetic, Mrs. Hammersmith, so common. I'll never understand how a man like this could marry a silly little slut like you. I'll admit, you're pretty in a boring sort of way—"

"Enough of that, Melissa Kay, let's get this done. Both of you, walk in front of us. If you try to run, Melissa Kay will shoot you in the head. Do you understand me?"

"Yes," Griffin said, "I understand you just fine. My wife lied. She already told Susan you were here with your mistress. I encouraged her to do it, so it's too late."

"I'm not his mistress! We're lovers!"

Jared laughed. "Good try. This pretty little thing hasn't called Susan. I know her type—talk, talk, talk until your head's ready to explode. I hope she was good in bed. By this time next year you'd want to shoot her, anyway, just to shut her up, so maybe we're doing you a favor."

They walked into the thick copse of trees, Griffin in front of Talix, Melissa Kay's pistol pointed at Kirra's back.

Griffin leaned down close to Kirra, whispered, "Jeter's close. Be ready."

Ryman Grissom stepped out from behind a gum tree, stared at them. He said slowly, "I really don't believe this. It's you, Ms. Prosecuting Attorney, Kirra Mandarian. The blond wig and the glasses, they change you, but not enough. I'd recognize you anywhere." Ryman stepped up to her and jerked the wig off her head and stepped back again. "You didn't recognize her, Melissa Kay? You said you looked her up online."

Kirra heard Melissa Kay gasp behind her. "This pathetic little slut? No, I thought she looked familiar, but I couldn't place her. You're the little bitch who's been coming after us, trying to put Daddy away for the rest of his life? And you followed me up here to Green Briar?" She stepped up and sent her fist into Kirra's jaw, knocking her to the ground.

She stood over her, legs spread. "Shooting you in the head won't keep Daddy from dying in prison, but it will make him feel better when I tell him I shot you dead."

Talix said, "No, don't, M. K., wait a minute, we're too close to the hotel and you don't have a suppressor on your gun." He looked back at Kirra. "That was quite some act you pulled off, pretending to be a friend of my wife's. Were you and Mr. FBI here setting up some sort of lame-ass trap, Ms. Mandarian? But why?"

Kirra saw Melissa Kay thinking, growing fury in her crazy eyes.

Ryman said to Griffin, "She knows if she goes back to Porte Franklyn, she could be shot any minute of the day and never know what hit her. But your act didn't work out, did it?" He laughed, said to Griffin, "You're here to protect her, right? Didn't do a very good job of it, did you?"

"No, I guess I didn't." Griffin knew he could disarm Melissa Kay, but not Ryman. He was standing too far back. And Talix had his knife.

"I think he did a fine job, Mr. Grissom." Lieutenant Jeter Thorpe and three state police officers stepped out of the trees, their weapons aimed at Ryman, Talix, and Melissa Kay. "Sorry we're a little late, Griffin, but Ryman Grissom was staying back as their rear guard, and we had to be careful he didn't see or hear us. Both of you drop your weapons. You, too, Mr. Talix, drop—"

Jared Talix brought up his knife and threw it at Kirra. It struck her in the chest. She gasped, fell onto her side.

Griffin brought up his Glock and shot Talix center mass. Melissa Kay and Ryman fired nonstop as they ran back into the woods, Jeter and his officers firing after them. They heard a yell.

Jeter yelled, "Stay with her, Griffin. We'll get them."

Griffin was already on his knees beside her, dialing 911. The knife had fallen out when she fell. Blood was gushing out. He slapped his hand over the wound. She looked up at him as he gave the dispatcher instructions. He dropped his cell phone, pressed both his hands onto the wound.

She whispered, "I'm glad Talix picked me to kill and not you." She gasped, closed her eyes. "It sort of hurts, Griffin, hurts kind of bad." He kept pressing. "Keep breathing, Kirra, that's all you have to do. Help is on the way." She groaned, deep in her throat. "Hang on, sweetheart. You can do that. You've got more guts than Sherlock and that's saying a lot." He leaned down, kissed her forehead, her nose, said again, "Breathe, Kirra. The bleeding's nearly stopped. The dispatcher said ten minutes. Just ten minutes." It sounded like an eternity to Griffin. He was more scared than he'd ever been in his life. His hands were covered with her blood, but the blood had stopped spreading. He leaned close. "Listen to me, Kirra. You won. You hunted down your parents' killers, Josh Atwood's killers. You have nothing more to think about, just hold on, that's all you have to do. Jeter will handle them now."

He heard more gunfire from the forest, heard Jeter shout. "Down! Now!"

There were more shots, and the sound of voices. Jeter came running back, clipping his gun back onto his belt. He dropped to his knees beside Kirra, took in her pale face, her clammy skin, the blood covering her white shirt and Griffin's hands. Kirra opened her eyes. "Jeter, you're okay. What happened?"

Jeter took her hand, leaned close. "Ryman Grissom kept firing, wouldn't give it up. Melissa Kay starting weeping hysterically when he was hit, made my two men chasing her ease up just a bit. She shot one of them in the shoulder and ran into the woods. They chased her, had to shoot her when she wouldn't stand down. She's dead. Talix is in custody. The dispatcher said you'd already called, Griffin. The ambulance will be here soon, just hang on, you hear me?"

She smiled up at him. "I will, Jeter. You did good. I'm sorry I couldn't tell you earlier."

Her breathing hitched.

EPILOGUE

Molly smiled up at Ramsey as he handed her a cup of tea with a dash of milk, as she liked it. "Stop looking like you expect me to keel over. I'm fine. I didn't even need surgery, only sutures to sew me up. They released me, Ramsey. Really, I'm okay. I've got my antibiotics and I'll rest for a couple of weeks. Now come and sit down between Emma and me. I don't even see how you're moving around, I'm so stuffed. The prime rib was awesome."

She's all right. Ramsey kept repeating it to himself over and over. He knew Emma was hovering around Molly because she was thinking the same thing. Of course, the twins didn't have a clue about what had happened or that their mother had been hurt. Their father told them she had a bad cold and they had to keep their distance. So far it was working. Emma leaned close, touched her fingers to her mother's cheek. "Mama, would you like me to hold your cup to your mouth so you don't have to lift it?"

Molly didn't laugh. She said simply, "Thank you, Emma. That would be lovely." She hoped Emma didn't dribble some of her tea down her very pretty cashmere sweater, a gift her father gave her along with her black leggings to wear when she left the hospital, no doubt picked out by Elizabeth Beatrice. But her daughter looked so pleased to offer to do it for her, so who cared? She hugged Emma to her as best she could, careful of her side, and looked over at the boys, who were in a corner of the suite playing a new game with Sean, their instructor. Her father looked nearly as worried as Ramsey, bless him. She knew he'd have preferred for all of them to fly back to his compound in Chicago, but the doctor had quashed that idea, told her she should stay on the ground for a couple more days. And she didn't mind. The Hay Adams was a nice place to recuperate and besides, the twins loved the waffles. And Mason had stood down.

Molly said, "Thanks, Dad, for flying Emma and the boys here so quickly."

"It's my pleasure, Molly." He was sitting close to Elizabeth Beatrice, but he was looking at Molly. Was that pleasure she saw in his eyes?

Sherlock was tucked close against Savich's side. He'd pulled her there, as if he was afraid to let her move an inch away. She said, "Molly, I think you'll appreciate this. Our field office agents caught up with Caruso after he dumped Ilic at the hospital in Mount Jewel and ran. And Domino asked to cut a deal with the federal prosecutor. Doulos's mother will probably disown him, but he'll be going to federal prison for life whether she hires expensive lawyers for him or not. And he's broke now—we've frozen all his assets."

Molly knew Emma was listening to every word, but she wasn't going to send her off to oversee the children. Emma deserved to know exactly what had happened. Molly said, "What sort of deal will Domino get?"

Savich said, "Agent Davis Sullivan is in charge of that. It depends on what she'll have to offer."

Emma looked toward her grandfather and Elizabeth Beatrice. She said, "I know Mr. Doulos tried to get you and Mr. Shaker to start fighting each other, Grandfather, but you worked together with them to find Mama and Aunt Sherlock." She locked eyes with Mason, beamed at him. "Do you think we could invite Mr. Shaker and Eve to visit us in Chicago?"

You could hear a pin drop. The adults looked at one another, and then at Molly.

Molly said, her voice gentle, "My sweet girl, I'm afraid that won't be possible. I don't think Mr. Shaker or Eve would come, and what they did to you, to us, six years ago is hard to forgive. But I have been thinking about something else." She turned to her father. "If you agree, Daddy, I'd like to try to put the Shakers behind us. I'd like to give the tape and the evidence I've held back to them. Keeping it seems more of a risk to us than a benefit now. We could finally be free of each other."

Mason slowly nodded. "You're right. It's time."

Molly walked over to her father, careful of her side, and hugged him. "I love you. Elizabeth Beatrice, you're a very lucky woman."

EPILOGUE

Port Douglas
Queensland, Australia

THREE WEEKS LATER

Griffin and Kirra stood atop Flagstaff Hill looking out at the incredible crescent of Trinity Bay with its four miles of white sand beach and water so clear you could see the white sand bottom. Kirra said in a sigh of pleasure, "Nothing is as beautiful as this spot. I came up here a lot when I was going through teen angst, you know, when the boy I loved with all my heart dumped me and life was over. Breathing in this sweet air, watching the blue water slick up onto the white sand, it always put things in perspective for a time, even in my fifteen-year-old mind. I couldn't wait to show it to you, Griffin. And there's so much more incredible beauty I want you to see."

He smiled at her, wished he could see her eyes through her dark sunglasses. "What was his name, this louse of a teenage boy?"

"You know, I don't remember." Kirra laughed. "This exact spot, this is where I stood." Like him, Kirra wore khaki shorts and sneakers. Her well-worn hiking boots would have to stay in her closet for another week or so. She had a light stretchy pale blue T-shirt on with EAA—EXTREME AUSTRALIAN ADVENTURES—emblazoned boldly across the chest and on the back, and below it, Uncle Leo in profile holding a canteen in his hand. Griffin wore a similar one she'd given him with a koala munching eucalyptus leaves on the front, only his was black, more manly she'd said, and nibbled his earlobe. They stood quietly, the warm air like velvet on their skin, the light wind stirring their hair.

Griffin slipped off Kirra's sunglasses. He could always tell when she was tiring and he saw fatigue clearly in her eyes. He wondered if her chest ached, but he didn't ask, knew she hated it. In the grand scheme of things it didn't matter, because she'd survived and she was mending. He looked out at the water and said his prayer of thanks for the day. It was a habit now.

The trip from Dulles to Sydney, then a different plane to Port Douglas had been hard on her, but after only two days, she looked healthier, occasionally vibrant, and if he did ask, admitted only to soreness in her chest.

Leo had eaten his breakfast early that morning because he was off to lead a day trek with two couples from Atlanta to Mount Bartle Frere's Summit near Cairns. Leo had kissed Kirra, smoothed her hair back from her face. "In a couple of weeks, maybe a month, you'll be ready to lead that hike yourself. You've got to be patient." He drew her against him, a ritual with them since they'd returned to Australia. She rested her head on his shoulder and he held her carefully, as he would a wounded child. Then Leo looked over her head at Griffin, smiled, and said what he said every morning before Kirra and Griffin left for a gentle walk, "Take care of the pretty boy, don't let him hurt himself." She always grinned over at Griffin, then back at her uncle's deeply tanned face. "That one, pretty? He isn't bad, and once I get him toughened up, he'll be passable. He has a long way to go to be as pretty as you are. We're going only two miles on the Flagstaff Hill walk. You know how flat it is. No, don't worry, I'll rest every few steps, Griffin will see to it."

The truth was, she was impatient with her weakness, always wanted to push, and Griffin knew it. He planned to make sure they spent the afternoon lounging on the beach or by the pool, doing nothing more than drinking Queensland's XXXX Gold beer and munching on Cheezels and Tim Tams, chocolate cookies that could put pounds on you if you weren't careful. And mangoes, amazing mangoes, always in every bowl at Leo's house.

Standing here on Flagstaff Hill, Griffin knew Kirra was relaxed and at ease. It was time to tell her the excellent news. "I got an email from Jeter. He sends his best. And Pepper's best, too, of course. He wanted me to tell you Aldo Springer—you remember, the man who murdered the accountant and tried to kill Corinne Ewing? He rolled on Kahn Oliveras. Oliveras is going down, Kirra, as hard as it gets. Jeter says he can't believe it, but Hailstock wants to take Oliveras to court and try the case himself. He plans to ask for life in prison. All the prosecuting attorneys are bug-eyed as you can imagine. Your boss, Alec, said Hailstock now appeared like a man on a mission.

"So, Eliot Ness, you got all three Grissoms and Oliveras."

Kirra's eyes blazed. It was almost too much to take in, particularly Hailstock turning into a real D.A. She'd do anything to get him to make her second chair. She drew in a deep breath of the sweet air, said slowly, "It's so hard to believe it's over." She poked him in the ribs. "You know what else? It's weird, but it feels like a letdown. Poor Eliot Ness has nothing more to do,

but wait, there are always more criminals who've escaped the
law, maybe—"

"Don't even go there."

She laughed up at him, leaned her head on his shoulder. "I
was kidding, really. Griffin, thank you. You really were a brick
through all of it." She paused, gave him a glowing smile. "You
want me to teach you how to dive into a swimming pool from
three stories up and not splat and die?"

There was no one like her. Griffin ran his knuckles over
her cheek, kissed her hair. He was drawn back to the terror
he'd felt when Talix's knife had struck Kirra in her chest, when
for that single horrible moment, he believed she'd died. Then
her breath had whooshed out and she'd gasped with the pain.
They'd medevaced her to Washington General to emergency
surgery, and then they'd waited interminably. So many of her
friends had come and held vigil, Savich and Sherlock, Jeter and
Pepper, her best friend Cila McCayne, his parents, and lawyers
in the Homicide Unit. It seemed forever before the surgeon had
finally walked into the waiting room to tell them she'd live.
Leo Mandarian had arrived the next morning, pale and terrified. Between cups of coffee, Griffin had talked him through
everything that had happened and how his sister and brother-
in-law's murderers had at last met justice because of Kirra.
When Kirra woke up and saw them together, she'd looked from
Griffin's face to her uncle's. "When I get out of here, let's all go
home, Uncle Leo." And so they had.

He remembered how quiet she'd been when they'd finally
arrived in Port Douglas. He knew she was in some pain, but she
refused any pain meds, said it wasn't what she needed. When
she'd walked into Leo's house in Port Douglas, she went immediately to the large windows to look out at the Great Barrier Reef. Griffin knew despite the lingering pain she had to

feel from the surgery that had kept her in the hospital for a week and a half, she would heal, both body and spirit. Soon she would be whole again.

Griffin had met the whole team, including Jawli and his wife, Mala. Mala had stroked Kirra's hair, told her she was going to make her special meals to get meat on her bones. She'd turned to Griffin, eyed him up and down. "Goodness me, would you look at this incredible golden god with sky-blue eyes come to our little slice of heaven." She'd shaken his hand. "I've never seen a prettier boy than this one. You going to put a ring on his finger, little girl?"

But Kirra had only laughed. She said to him now, "You're grinning. What are you thinking?"

She was snuggled against him now, her hair in a ponytail, only a small swatch of bandage showing under her T-shirt. Griffin said, "I was remembering what Mala said to me when we met."

"She called you a pretty boy. Ha. She needs glasses, well-known fact."

A thick light brow went up. "Golden god with sky-blue eyes to be accurate about it. You still don't agree with her?"

Kirra outlined the koala on his T-shirt with her finger. "Really, Griffin, be serious. It's rare Mala sees a young guy built like you, certainly not one with blond hair and blue eyes. Because you're different to her she thinks you're pretty." She took off her sunglasses again, then his, and slipped both pairs into her shorts' pocket. She touched her fingers to his face. "You could look like a troll—not that you do, really, not exactly—and it wouldn't matter to me." She paused, then said slowly, her eyes clear, steady on his face, "When Talix sent that knife into my chest I thought I was going to die. I looked up at you and knew I didn't want to leave you, no matter how homely you are. Bottom line, I love you. It's a forever thing. Will you marry me, Griffin?"

Forever sounded right to him. Griffin thought of the diamond engagement ring he'd left in its box in his underwear drawer back at Uncle Leo's magnificent house, waiting for the right moment. Maybe after some of Leo's excellent champagne in the early fall sunset. He rubbed his thumb over her cheek. "I love you, Kirra. However before I agree, I do have a condition."

"Oh? And it is?"

"Two kids. A dog for each kid."

"That's two conditions. Sorry, Griffin, that's a deal breaker."

He felt his heart stop.

She poked him in the stomach. "I want four kids, not two."

He gave her a big smile. "I can do four."

"I have a condition, too."

His eyebrow went up.

"We spend all our vacations here in Australia with Uncle Leo, unless he wants to go off with us to Majorca or Oslo or somewhere."

"The kids and I can do that. We'll have a good neighbor who'll keep the dogs."

"Excellent. Now, I know Uncle Leo likes you, but enough to have you for a nephew-in-law? I'll have to talk to him. Oh, Griffin, there's so much we'll do, so much fun we'll have. When we're here, I'll teach you things, like how to wrap a bullwhip around a scrub python without hurting him, or how to play with joeys without their mother killing you."

"Bullwhip?"

"Yes, Jawli taught me. Are we agreed?"

He pressed his forehead against hers. "About Leo. After I tucked you in last night, we had a talk. He wanted to know my intentions. I told him I loved you and wanted to marry you. He thought it was a fine idea and we toasted with his Talisker. But, Kirra, our kids—what if they look like me? You know, homely, but kind and loyal?"

"No worries, I have dominant genes. Our kids will look like me, and Uncle Leo calls me his beauty. You can bask in our glory."

How could he not adore her? Griffin held her loosely against him, felt the wind pick up, blow her hair against his face. "After two shots of Talisker, Leo told me even if I wanted to run for the hills sometimes, with you as my wife I'd never be bored."

Her laughter rang out over Trinity Bay.

Life could never be sweeter than it was at that moment.

Savich House
Four weeks later

TUESDAY NIGHT

Sean was tottering on the edge of sleep when his father sang the third verse to him in his smooth baritone about a racehorse named King Hank who ran so fast he wore out his shoes every single week. Savich looked down at his precious son, asleep now, and wondered how fast he'd have to run to wear out his sneakers.

When Savich finally slipped into bed, he pulled Sherlock into his arms, breathed in the faint rose scent of her hair. *She was safe, she was home, she was with him.* It had become a mantra. Even after a month, he'd think of the two endless days he'd searched for her and his heart would still race. The fear was still there, burrowed down deep. He squeezed her tighter. He still worried whenever she was out of his sight. Even though he never said anything, he knew she guessed. He kissed her hair, felt the bouncing curls tickle his nose.

"Dillon?"

He kissed her nose. "Sean's finally asleep. I had to sing all three verses of the ballad of King Hank, the racehorse of a thousand shoes. I don't think he realizes a horse's shoes aren't quite the same as his."

She kissed his neck. "I have something to tell you."

He was stroking his hands up and down her back. He kissed her ear. "And what's that?"

She leaned up over him, touched her fingertips to his cheek, and kissed his mouth. "Take a deep breath."

He was immediately alarmed. "What is it? Is something wrong?"

She kissed him again. "No, no, nothing's wrong. Something's wonderful. You're going to be a father again. I'm pregnant."